RISE OF THE TEMPLE GODS
HEIR to KALE

RISE OF THE TEMPLE GODS

HEIR to KALE

K.L. BONE

Welcome to the land of Kale!

Best Wishes,

K L Bone

2015

Heir to Kale Copyright © 2013 by Kristin L. Bone
ALL RIGHTS RESERVED.

Cover Art © 2013 by Skyla Dawn Cameron

Second Edition: March 2015

All rights reserved under the International and Pan-American Copyright Conventions. No part of this book may be reproduced or transmitted in any form or by any means, electronic or mechanical including photocopying, recording, or by any information storage and retrieval system, without permission in writing from the author.

This book is a work of fiction. Names, characters, places and incidents are either the product of the author's imagination or are used fictitiously, and any resemblance to any actual persons, living or dead, events, or locales is entirely coincidental.

DEDICATION

This novel is dedicated to my brother, Sam, who played in the land of Kale long before it was ever committed to paper—Thanks for all the memories.

Prologue

IN THE HEART OF THE Rainbow Mountains lay a canopy shrouded in mist. A place of shadow where not even the brightest stars ventured, lest they be swallowed by everlasting darkness. There, he waited. His eyes were closed, yet he could see. He sensed his brother's approach long before he heard the footsteps so soft a sound they made.

"The time draws near."

"Yes."

His brother's footsteps ceased as he settled into the undergrowth.

"Who will you take this time, brother?"

"As always," he replied "The choice is yours."

"Then I shall take the one with hair as black as the raven."

"And I the one with hair of spun gold."

He nodded, and slowly opened his eyes. "I shall see you again, when they come of age. The story shall begin anew."

"For the last time."

Both brothers knew it was a lie.

Chapter I

~~~~~~~~~~~

Mary heard the guards call that they were approaching the gates to the palace, but her thoughts remained on the argument with Master Leo the day before. It was not a new argument, but one that had occurred frequently over the past few years.

"The Temple of Kale must be reunited with the crown." Master Leo's stern voice echoed through Mary's memories.

"But Leo," she'd pleaded. "Is it not enough that I wish to someday take your place here at the temple? To lead this temple as you have done?"

The temple master's jade green eyes held a hint of sadness. "You know I would be proud to see you in my position someday. But you are a princess and have a duty to reunite the temples with your crown. The king has summoned you. You must leave immediately."

Her thoughts were interrupted when the carriage finally stopped and a crimson-robed guard stepped forward and opened the large doors. Princess Mariana Dektra reluctantly accepted the guard's hand and stepped down onto the first of the wide marble steps. Garbed in long, golden robes, the princess ascended the white steps, her long black hair blowing behind her in the cool afternoon breeze. When she reached the large golden doors at the top of the steps, Mary found herself facing a tall, pale skinned man wearing a crimson council robe. He had dark brown hair, brown eyes, and a carefully trimmed mustache. Mary had never seen him before.

"Greetings, Princess Mariana," the man said before offering a low bow of respect. "I am Lord Francis, a member of your uncle's Royal Council. You had a pleasant trip, I hope?" Mary nodded toward the thin man as he continued. "The prince, your father, is expecting you."

"Good, you may take me to him," she replied, moving past the man to the large golden doors.

The councilman's gaze trailed up and down Mary's tall form. "Surely you would like to put on something more... appropriate."

Mary turned her head slowly back to the councilman. Her emerald eyes blazed and she had to fight to control her voice from leaking with sudden venom. "Tell me, councilman," she spoke slowly. "What am I wearing?" She motioned to the golden robes draped loosely around her tall frame, her pale hand lying on the hilt of her Kalian blade.

"My lady..."

"Princess," she hissed.

The man drew a deep breath, struggling to regroup his thoughts. "My princess," he tried again, "you are wearing your golden temple robes."

"That's right. I am the golden student of Kale and am wearing the robes which mark my status as such. What, pray tell, is *inappropriate*?"

"Forgive me, princess," he stuttered. "I will lead you to your parents' chambers immediately."

The councilman led Mary down a series of hallways until she finally entered a large, spacious chamber. The walls were painted deep crimson. A large open fire roared along the front wall casting warm shadows across the room. Mary's parents were seated in elegantly carved black wooden chairs. A third chair sat between them which, Mary knew, was waiting for her. Her mother sat as regal as ever, wearing a gown of black velvet. A single thread of silver traced along the edge of the black dress and a long string of diamonds ending with a deep red ruby encircled her pale throat. A silver crown graced her long black hair, marking her as the Royal Princess of Kale

Mary walked forward. Her gaze moved from her mother's still form to her father, who sat on the opposite side of the fire. He wore a long sleeve black shirt which buttoned up the front with silver buttons and matching cufflinks. His light brown hair and pale blue eyes stood in contrast to Mary's own black locks and dark eyes. "Greetings, Mariana," her mother's voice rang out with a cold touch.

Mary knelt into a low bow, kneeling on one knee, placing both arms out straight to either side of her. The edge of her long hair touched the floor as she lowered her head, baring her neck in the traditional bow of the Kalian temples. As she held the position, she heard footsteps approaching behind her as someone else entered the room. A deep, masculine voice said, "No need for your temple bows here, Mary. A simple curtsy will do." She continued to hold the position until the voice finally said, "Rise, princess." She rose in a fluid motion, her golden robes swishing as she stood. The carpet silenced her heels as she turned to face her uncle for the first time in almost twelve years.

"Greetings, Princess Mariana."

"Greetings, Your Majesty," she replied softly. The man who had once towered over her now stood only a few inches taller. The king's pale skin and green eyes were a perfect match to her own. His hair had turned gray over the years as had his short, well-trimmed beard. He wore black slacks and a white shirt with silver buttons and matching cufflinks. A rather simplistic circle of gold graced his brow, an ever present symbol of his royal status.

"My, you have grown," the king's eyes seemed to roam over Mary's still form. "I have heard of your success in the temples, Mary, but word of your beauty has been greatly understated."

A slight blush rose to Mary's cheeks. "Thank you, Your Majesty."

"I am your uncle, Mariana. You may address me as such."

Mary smiled. "Thank you, uncle."

"You are welcome, niece. I would assume that you would like to visit with your parents for a while, and then it would give me great pleasure to have you join me for dinner tonight." He eyed her for a moment before adding, "Make sure to wear something more appropriate. You are a princess here; you should appear as such."

"Yes, my kin ... uncle."

The king turned and slowly walked from the room, leaving Mary alone with her parents. "Come, daughter." Princess Annabelle motioned to the empty chair. Mary stepped forward as Prince Eadmund rose to embrace her.

"It is good to see you, daughter. Your success in the Kalian tournaments has brought much pride, both to your temple lineage and the bloodline of Kale."

"Thank you, Father," Mary said softly. "Has my sister been sent for as well?"

"Yes," Princess Annabelle replied. "She will arrive later tonight. You will see her at dinner." Her mother paused before asking, "When did you last see her?"

"Not for at least six months," Mary replied. "We compete in different tournaments, as I am sure you know."

Her mother nodded. "Yes, but you will, of course, face her in the thirteenth tournament. Will you not?"

"Yes, of course, Mother. I fully intend to see her there."

"I am not sure if I like the idea of the two of you fighting for the title," Prince Eadmund said. "However, I suppose since you have both qualified, it must be so."

"Don't worry, Father. For all we know, it will be my partner and me in the final round instead of my sister."

"Your sister," Princess Annabelle said, "is the gold student of Koloso and has an undefeated record to match your own."

An awkward silence slipped into the room. Mary stared into the fire for several moments before attempting to change the subject. "I don't remember all the red in this room," she said, allowing her gaze to travel over the red carpets and walls. "It's nice."

"We changed it a few years ago," Princess Annabelle replied. "I would have thought you would have seen it since..." Her voice trailed off and she shook her head. "No, I guess you wouldn't have seen it. You haven't been here since...when were you here last, daughter?"

"Twelve years ago. I was five."

Her mother turned towards Mary, a look of surprise crossing her face. "By the Gods, has it been that long?"

The two strangers stared at each other for several moments before Prince Eadmund said, "Why don't I show Mary to her room and we can all get ready for dinner with the king."

"Yes," her mother replied, rising from her chair, her long velvet gown silently flowing around her thin body. "I will see you later tonight, princess." She turned and walked from the room with long, graceful steps.

"You'll have to forgive her, Mary. She loves you, it's just that, well..."

He seemed to search for the words.

"Your mother spent so many years competing against students from your temple, and has such a rivalry with Leo that it's...you are the greatest threat to her temple and that makes it hard for her."

"Forgive her?" Mary's voice was cross. "She has not seen me in nine years, Father."

"Mary, I... I don't know what to say."

"Just take me to my room, please."

Mary's father led her back through the long corridors. The halls felt foreign and cold. When they finally reached the room, her father opened a mahogany door and motioned Mary inside. The room was much larger than her small temple quarters. The carpets and walls were a rich red, and red curtains framed the four-post bed, held back with a thick golden ribbon. The coverlet was black, edged with red lace along both the blanket and matching pillows.

Lying on top of the bed was a crimson gown. It was strapless, floor-length and had a full, thick skirt. Tiny crystals adorned the satin material, sparkling in the bright light of the room, the sunlight creeping in from the two large windows on the left side. "A gift from your uncle," her father motioned towards the gown, "to wear to dinner tonight with your crown." He pointed toward the dresser at the far end of the room on which lay a thin circlet of gold lined with sparkling diamond spirals on either side. In the center of the crown, the spirals met, each topped by a small jeweled flower of crimson stones.

"I'm sorry, Father, but...I don't understand." Her father looked at her questioningly. "It's red," Mary continued.

"It is fine, Mary. This is not a temple event, you can wear red."

Mary looked at him uncomprehendingly. "But I am gold," she said. "It is the symbol of my status. I cannot wear red."

The prince sighed. "Mary, it doesn't matter here. Red is your uncle's choice for the night."

"I brought a dress," Mary replied. "It is very pretty. It was a gift from the Lord of Turbamentum."

"Mary!" Her father took a step closer to the princess, his voice sharp. "The king wants you to wear this dress and you will wear it. Do you understand?"

Mary met her father's gaze head on. "Will my sister be required to wear red as well?"

"I will make sure that she does." Mary continued to stare for several moments, then lowered her gaze. Prince Eadmund's voice softened. "Look Mary, I know this isn't easy. Just...get through the next few days. Then you can go back to the temple."

He started walking towards the door when Mary called, "Father." He stopped and turned around. "Is the king going to name me his heir?"

Her father parted his lips as though to speak, then closed them. He then gave the slightest of nods, turned and left the room.

Mary walked to the bed and ran her hand gently down the satin red gown. "I don't want to be queen," she whispered to the silence of the room.

Chapter II

A FEW HOURS LATER, MARY was ready for dinner. A maid had curled her black hair and piled it high, allowing ringlets to frame her face. The deep crimson gown made her green eyes stand out more than in her usual attire. Her lips and cheeks had been painted deep rouge. The diamond tiara graced her brow. She hardly recognized herself in the golden framed mirror.

Her chocolate colored puppy, Coco, his hair groomed and a black bowtie around his neck, came to escort her to dinner. "Red looks good on you, Mary," the puppy said with a mischievous sparkle in his eye. "Perhaps you should consider losing a few fights, then you could wear it all the time!"

"Shut up," Mary said curtly. Coco laughed and Mary couldn't help but smile as they rounded the corner and entered the grand banquet room. The room, like most of the palace, was decorated in rich red carpets with a touch of black throughout. A long mahogany table stood in the center of the room, covered with a black tablecloth. Several people were already seated, including her mother and twin sister who was also wearing a gown of crimson. The deep color made her sister's blond hair seem even lighter than usual. Her sister, Ameria, gave a slight wave in Mary's direction and flashed a smile.

"Mariana," the king said, suddenly appearing beside her.

"Uncle," she replied with a slight bow of her head.

"My, you do look beautiful." Her uncle surprised her by offering a brief embrace. "Come, Mariana, say hello to your aunt."

Mary turned to her left to face the queen who, much to her surprise, wore a gown of solid gold silk. Aside from jewelry, it was forbidden for anyone outside of the temples to wear the esteemed color. Was this the reason the princesses had been forbidden to wear gold? Mary fought to hide her surprise as she hid her face in a low curtsy.

"Greetings, Aunt Katerin."

"Greetings, Mariana." Her voice was cold. "I trust you like the gown? I had it made especially for you."

"It's beautiful," Mary replied, carefully hiding the anger in her voice. "I thank you, Your Majesty."

"You are most welcome. Red really does suit you. Perhaps I should have more clothes fitted for you?"

"I thank you for your kindness, Aunt Katerin, but that will not be necessary. I would not be permitted to wear them at the temple."

For one moment, a slight scowl disrupted the queen's normally perfect smile. Her uncle did not seem to notice though, as he took Mary's arm. Acting as her escort, the king began a rapid round of introductions, presenting his long lost niece to the various lords and ladies who had gathered to welcome the princesses home. She walked through a sea of unrecognizable faces, shaking hands and exchanging polite greetings until the king was finally engaged in a political debate with the lord of a neighboring kingdom and Mary was able to quietly slip away.

She walked quickly towards the table where her sister was seated. "Ameria!" She exclaimed as she reached the table and leaned down to offer his sister a light embrace. "It's good to see you."

"It's nice to see you as well," Ameria replied. "It has been too long."

Mary nodded in agreement then embraced her sister again, burying her face in Ameria's golden curls. "Have I done something to offend the queen?" she asked. "And why is she wearing gold?"

"The queen wears gold more and more now, though I must admit, this is the first time I have ever seen her do so at a function with temple leaders present. The king and queen have no respect for temple traditions, you have always known this."

"Yes, but..."

"And as to her anger," Ameria interrupted, "she bore no children and our parents did. People say that their marriage was cursed because our uncle married outside of the temples."

Mary nodded. "I have heard those claims."

"Well, it would seem that the queen has taken these rumors to mean that the temples literally cursed her. She blames the temple masters for her barrenness, particularly yours and mine."

"She blames Leo?" Mary asked in utter disbelief. "Master Leo has no such power. Nor does Master Jiro."

"I know," Ameria said, "but the queen will heed no one, not even the king. He was never a lover of the temples in the first place, but now she poisons his ear even further. The temple leaders are here only at the insistence of our father."

"What? How do you know all of this?"

"Mother keeps me up to date on all the palace politics. Does she not send you the letters as well?"

"Everyone please be seated," one of the servants interrupted their conversation. "Dinner is served." Mary's father directed her to the seat between himself and Ameria, just one seat to the right of the king, who sat at the head of the table with the queen on his left. Seated across from Mary was one of the various young lords who held a claim to the Kalian bloodline.

"Hello, princess," the young man said.

"Hello, Lord...forgive me, I do not know your name."

"It's Lord Davith Sethrick," he informed her. "From the region of Proelium."

Mary nodded in acknowledgment. "How do you do, Lord Sethrick?"

"Very well, princess. Please, call me Davith."

"I have traveled to Proelim before, to visit the temple. Do you train there?"

"No, my lady."

"Oh, I take it you train elsewhere then?"

"No, my lady. I am not a member of the temples."

Mary looked confused. "But the High Lord of Proelim trained at the Temple of Koloso, did he not?" The young man nodded. "Then it was your birthright to attend one of the two temples."

Davith shrugged. "My parents felt that there were more important issues to deal with than to spend days in meditation at the temples."

"And you agree?" Mary asked, hardly believing her ears.

"I'm not a fighter." Davith shrugged. "I never really saw the value in studying old fairytales."

"Fairytales?" Anger seeped into her voice. "They are not fairytales; they are the history of our people. I've met the High Lord of Proelium. He would be ashamed to hear you mock his traditions so."

The young man just shrugged again. "He has his beliefs. I have mine."

"Beware mocking the Gods, Lord Sethrick. They might just hear you."

Mary was grateful when the meal was finally served and she could focus on the food instead of the insolent lord across from her. It would seem that Leo's warnings were finally coming to pass: the separation between the elite of the temples and those of the crown were growing ever stronger. Glancing down the table, she caught her master's eye. *When I am queen, this will be the first thing to change*, she thought.

She then turned and spoke with her father through the rest of dinner, describing some of the last tournaments in which she had participated and excitedly reporting her latest victories. Then, shortly after the last course was served, Mary's uncle rose and cleared his throat. "May I have everyone's attention, please." The chatter died quickly as the king continued.

"I would like to take a moment to thank everyone for gathering here tonight. It is nice to see so many of us gathered today to celebrate a joyous occasion. I would also like everyone to join me in welcoming home Kale's princesses, Mariana and Ameria." He paused for a light round of applause. "As most of you are aware, Princess Mariana and Princess Ameria are the daughters of my younger and only brother, Crown Prince Eadmund. I would like to propose a toast to them now." The King raised his glass, "Welcome home, Princesses of Kale!"

"Welcome home!" the crowd said as one.

"Thank you," the twins replied.

"You are most welcome." The king gave a seemingly warm smile. "It is also known that as I approach the latter part of my life, I have no children of my own, and that my brother, being only two years younger than I, would most likely not live long after my death. We have, therefore, agreed that the crown shall be passed to a younger heir, after my passing."

The room filled with an outburst of chatter before the king raised his hand, motioning for silence. "It is my pleasure tonight to announce two things. The first is that my niece, Mariana, princess of the pure bloodline of Kale and golden member of the Kalian temple will be crowned as heir to the throne upon the celebration of her twentieth birthday." The king's words faded as the table once again raised their voices in a collective array.

"Congratulations, Mary!" her father said, wrapping her in a tight embrace.

"Yes! I knew it!" came the words of an unidentifiable voice among the sea of faces suddenly surrounding her. "I knew it would be you!"

Master Leo fought his way through the crowd from his placement near the other end of the room to also embrace the newly declared heir. "Glory to you, and the Temple of Kale!" His voice managed to rise above much of the crowd. "All hail the future queen!"

Ameria sat still for several moments, before offering a slight nod.

"Attention!" the king shouted over the crowd. "Please everyone if I can have your attention, please."

The group moved to retake their seats as the king continued.

"There is one more announcement to make." He offered the princess another smile. "It also gives me great pleasure to introduce Lord Davith Sethrick of Proelium, a pure blooded Kalian whose grandfather served as a Defendant of Kale. I am pleased to announce that after much negotiation, it has been decided that Princess Mariana shall marry Lord Sethrick, shortly before being officially crowned heir to the throne." The King raised his glass. "To the future King and Queen of Kale!"

No one moved. Mariana sat as though frozen. The air in her chest seemed tight. Her eyes traveled the room, focusing on nothing until she finally met those of her mother. Their gaze held for several moments and it was her mother's voice that rang clearly down the hall. "Forgive me, Your Majesty. Why was I not made aware of this?"

"What is to tell?" the king asked. "It is a good match. The Sethricks are among the most respected families in the line of Kale, not to mention one of the wealthiest. They will be a fine addition to the royal line."

"The boy is not of the temples." Master Leo seemed to appear from nowhere in his golden robes to stand by the side of Mary's table. "Surely you must realize that she can only marry a defendant."

"Superstitious nonsense!" the queen said sternly from her husband's side.

"You dare to openly defy temple law!" Leo said back.

"Mariana went to the Temple of Kale so we would not have to deal with these issues," the king replied. "You will have a member of your precious temple represented on the throne; therefore the king can be from anywhere."

"It does not matter that she will be queen," came a voice from the back of the room.

Onlookers stepped aside as Master Jiro, the temple master of Koloso, stepped forward to stand by Master Leo's side. His full-length silver robe hid much of his pale skin and his shoulder-length blond hair was tied back with a thin silver band. "The heir to the throne must marry another who was trained within the temples."

"It is our most ancient law," added Master Phillip from the Temple of Dektra.

"Silence," the king shouted. "Your traditions are nothing but ancient superstition, an old legend you tell to the commoners in order to maintain your place of power. I am the king, and I refuse to be ruled by fairytales! Any who continues this argument, shall be removed by the Royal Guard."

Mary stood from her chair, her mind still in a daze. She turned to find all thirteen of the temple masters standing behind her. Guards spilled into the room, but froze when they found themselves facing the masters they once served.

Mary turned to Leo and caught her master's emerald gaze. He gave a single nod. Mary turned back to the king and did what was expected of her. "Blood and Arms!" she spoke the ancient vow.

It took several moments for all eyes to turn to the young princess, and she allowed even more time to pass before speaking. "Where is the high priest, Louis?"

"I am here, princess," came the familiar voice. A white dog two feet tall on all fours stepped forward from among the crowd to reach Mary's side, his fur covered by silks of rainbow, marking his status as the High Priest of the Kalian Temples. Around his neck hung a golden chain with a twelve point star, each point a different color.

"High Priest of Kalian Temples, whose sovereign authority surpasses that of defendants, masters, and kings." For the second time that evening, Mary lowered herself into the traditional bow of the temples, kneeling on one knee, arms out straight on either side of her body, fingertips touching the ground. She lowered her head, baring her neck and allowing her hair to touch the floor beneath her. "I kneel before you, Lord of Kale, to swear the most sacred of our oaths."

The high priest nodded solemnly as Mary continued. "As Crown Princess of the Kalian bloodline and the golden student of Kale, I take the oath of Blood and Arms to unite my blood of Kale, with the arms earned by the Champion of Kale, on the eve of the thirteenth Kalian tournament. This I swear, to the Gods of Kale and Koloso, before the Master of the Temples and the King and Queen of Kale."

The room seemed to hold its breath as the high priest leaned closer to the kneeling form of the princess. He leaned forward, softly touching her rouged cheek. "The oath of Blood and Arms has been invoked!" He pronounced to the room. "Princess Mariana, Crown Princess of Kale, will marry the highest ranking male champion of the thirteenth tournament at the Temple of Ziazan. May any who oppose suffer the wrath of the Kalian defendants and the temple Gods!"

"Guards!" the king yelled. "Remove the masters from my palace."

"Forgive me, Your Majesty," the captain of the king's guard stated, "but we, as you know, are defendants and answer to the high priest above all others. We therefore, cannot do as you ask."

"You are the captain of the king's guard." The queen rose from her seat in anger. "You will follow your orders."

"No, my Lady, we cannot. We are the successors of those chosen by the temple Gods. The high priest speaks for those Gods, and must be obeyed as surely as the oath of the young princess must be defended. She has sworn to uphold the law of the Gods and I, along with my defendants, will protect that oath with our lives, as will the Masters of the Kalian Temples. Master Leo," he addressed the Kalian leader, "I await your wisdom on this matter."

Master Leo stepped closer to the king, his loose-fitting golden robe trailing silently behind him. He was a tall man with brown hair and matching eyes. His skin was pale, a mark of the Kalian bloodline. The robe he wore was buttoned just below the neck and then split to reveal a loose gold shirt tucked into a pair of black pants. As the Master of the Temple of Kale, and a former winner of the thirteenth tournament, Master Leo was the most distinguished fighter of the land and the highest ranking master among the thirteen temples.

"We shall leave, Your Majesty, of our own accord. There is no need to fight." He turned his gaze to the Princess. "Come, Princess Mariana. We shall depart for the temple immediately and send for your things later. He shifted his eyes from Mariana to her sister. "Return to your temple as well, Princess Ameria."

The twins stepped forward together and began to leave the room in silence. As they reached the doors, both turned in the direction of the king and offered matching bows before turning in perfect unison and stepping into the hallway.

"How did this happen?" Mary asked her sister, neither slowing their pace as they walked quickly towards the palace door.

"You knew the King would do something like this eventually," Ameria replied. "It can't possibility surprise you that he would attach strings to your crown." She paused to draw breath as they reached the outer doors.

"Call the royal carriage," Mary ordered the escorts standing outside the palace doors. "We are to leave for the temples immediately." She turned back to her sister. "Our uncle's hatred of the temples has crossed the line. Is it not enough that the Gods cursed his queen for not following their laws? Does he intend to leave the throne barren for me as well?"

"Calm, sister. I shall ride with you to Kale, and then continue from there to Koloso." Ameria paused, then asked, "If you will allow me to do so."

"Why would I not?"

"Well, you are the Crown Princess now. It seemed proper to ask."

Mary turned to look at her sister more intently, searching her Ameria's face, though for what, she was not sure. "Ameria," she said softly, "you are my sister. My succession to the throne does not change this. Of course you may ride with me. I have missed you over these past months..."

"Excuse me, Your Highnesses," a member of the guard interrupted. "The carriage is ready to escort you back to the temple."

"Thank you," Mary replied. "Where's..." she started to ask, but was interrupted again, this time from a voice behind her.

"Wait!" Coco's voice rang out. "I take it back, you look better in gold than red! Just don't leave me here! These people are crazy!"

The carriage was large, a black circular shape with plush, black interior. The guards assisted the princesses into the carriage and Coco jumped in behind them. "We are going straight to the Temple of Kale," Mary told the doorman as she struggled to find a comfortable position inside the layers of stiff and suddenly itchy petticoats.

"So," Ameria offered a small smile, "you will be queen someday."

"Perhaps," Mary replied. "You never know. After that, he is just as likely to disown me as to make me queen."

"I doubt it. There's no doubt that he will be..." Ameria searched for the word, "unhappy, but to retract the announcement would be much worse for the king than it would be for you. You are beloved by the people, while the king, on the other hand, is..."

"Not," Mary finished for her.

Ameria tilted her head slightly, considering her sister, and then broke into a genuine smile. "It is nice, to have someone I can speak honestly with on these matters. At the temple, even with teammates, I always have to be so careful about what I say."

"I know," Mary replied with a smile of her own. "It's like when Father comes to watch my temple training. Finally, someone I can speak with concerning various lords and defendants, who is ranked high enough not to get his head chopped off for doing so."

"Our father watches your training?" Ameria said, unable to hide the surprise in her voice.

Mary shifted uncomfortably in her seat. "Sometimes," she said slowly. "Though, not often. Not in a long time, come to think of it."

"In all the years of my training, Father has only watched me three times, and two of the three were when the Temple of Koloso was hosting its annual tournament."

"Well, that is more than I've had from our mother," Mary told her sister. "She hasn't seen me in years! She doesn't even write." Mary sighed. "She is a complete stranger."

"Well," Ameria said, "at least you will be able to spend more time with her here at the palace, once you are queen."

"Gods forbid," Mary told her sister. "I hope the king lives fifty more years. I have so much I..." She looked at her sister. "I want to be a defendant. It's all I have ever wanted."

Her sister shrugged. "You could always renounce your birthright."

Tension filled the small interior of the carriage. "You know I cannot do that, Ameria. I am the Kalian heir by blood."

"Yes, blood. Blood and what, a full two minutes?"

Mary felt her body tense. "Are you saying that I should renounce the throne, sister? Is that what you would like me to do?"

"No," Ameria said far too quickly. "Just that if it is truly not the path for you, there is always another option." The twins stared at each other for several moments of silence. "I'm sorry, Mary," Ameria finally said. "I am sure you will make a wonderful queen."

"Of course she will," Coco said from beside Mary in an effort to break the tension. "Besides, Mary, you have to take the throne." He looked at her sideways with a large grin. "How else am I ever going to get to order all the other puppies around?"

"The other puppies?" Mary arched her eyebrows. "What makes you think that you will be able to order the other puppies around, Coco?"

"Because, when you are queen, I fully intend to be your king," he said with a hint of laughter. "All will bow before Coco, king of all the puppies!"

Coco sat up straight and gave Mary his best "regal" face. Both princesses burst into laughter.

Chapter III

~~~~~~❖~~~~~~

AMONG A WORLD OF RICHES, royalty, and power, the Temple of Kale stood as though a God among mortals. Hidden in the heights of the Rainbow Mountains, the path to the temple was shrouded by an ever persistent mist that danced in the light, reflecting every color imaginable as it twirled around the royal carriage. It was not until one reached the gates of the temple that the mist lifted, revealing all three of Kale's suns shining within the pale lavender sky.

In front of the temple, rising out of the bright blue grass kept well-trimmed by the temple groundskeepers, stood a long black iron fence with a tall gate. On either side of the gate stood two members of the Kalian Defense Team, the team of those chosen to protect the kingdoms from all dangers. They were an elite team, composed of sixty warriors chosen from among the thirteen temples. All were proven champions. The right to attend a temple was primarily based on the lineage of this team and placement was often heredity. Both of Mary's parents had been defendants, serving as the right and left hand of Master Leo. Before that, Mary's mother, Annabelle, served as the golden student of the Temple of Koloso while Mary's father had served as the silver student of Kale, to Master Leo's gold. The men had been partners throughout their many years of training and still held the record as the only undefeated champions in the history of the Kalian tournaments.

It was at the height of that championship year when the long friendship between the two warriors was forever shattered by one last legendary fight. Every year, twelve of the thirteen temples held annual tournaments. The hosted rounds in these standard tournaments were fought in pairs, with two chosen partners from each team facing off with a different set of partners from a competing temple.

However, every thirteen years, at the Temple of Ziazan, a thirteenth tournament was held. At this tournament, the champions of the previous twelve years were invited to compete on an individual basis for the title of the Master of Kale. The winner of this title was considered by all to be the greatest fighter in the land and often married into the royal family.

The year that Prince Eadmund and Master Leo earned the right to compete in this legendary tournament, they flew through the preliminary and final rounds until the only competitors left...were each other. The battle fought between the silver and golden students of Kale was a fight that, even all these years, still stood as the fight to which all others were compared. It was a fight that broke the bounds of skill, discipline, and friendship. Though they continued to serve together for years as members of the Kalian Defense Team, Mary had never seen the two men express the level of friendship that both assured her had existed before she was born.

The guards identified the carriage and waived the princesses through the large gate. It took several minutes for the golden horses to ascend the narrow path leading through the mountains to the temple. Mary turned towards the carriage window to gaze at the glittering temple that had served as her home for almost thirteen years.

Standing in the brilliance of the kingdom's three suns, the Temple of Kale was a vast, golden building which would have seemed even larger had it not been nestled against the backdrop of the massive Rainbow Mountains. Situated at the peak of one of the tallest mountains in the range, the golden walls reflected every caress of sunlight, forming blinding lights to the eyes of approaching travelers. The temples were closed off to the general public but for once a year when they played host to their annual temple tournament.

Tall columns lining the black marble walkway led to the temple doors. In the center of the walkway was a grand fountain, standing nearly twenty feet above the marble floor. A massive statue stood in the center of the fountain, a pair of gold horses with jeweled eyes. One of the horses had eyes of white diamond, while the other's eyes were black, symbolizing the temple Gods of light and darkness.

The two horses stood high, their legs pawing the air, nostrils flared eternally frozen in a lifeless trance. As Mary exited the carriage and walked towards the fountain, the eyes of the horses seemed to beckon her. The silent reverence with which the two sisters approached the ever watchful guardians was disturbed only by the running water, which ran in rainbow streams from the horses' mouths, splashing into the base of the fountain below.

"All these years and they still seem so real." Ameria spoke Mary's mind. The girls stood at the edge of the fountain for several moments, staring into the jeweled eyes of the silent guardians.

Then the moment was shattered when a voice rang out from the temple entrance. "Mary!"

Mary turned her gaze towards the large golden doors to see a pure white puppy running towards her.

"Hey, Mac!" Mary called to her friend and Coco's long time training partner. Mac wore a thin silver chain around his neck, the symbol of his silver temple status. Mary walked towards the puppy, meeting him halfway as Ameria trailed behind her. "Mac, you remember my sister?"

"Of course I do!" Mac said, looking up at Mary's blond twin. "Hi ya, princess!" the puppy said with a laugh.

"Hello yourself!" Ameria greeted the puppy enthusiastically. "Still haven't beat Coco, I see. What's up with that?"

"On the contrary, I have beaten him lots of times ...not my fault no one is ever paying attention when I do...I think it's a conspiracy."

"He lies!" Coco said, skittering around the corner.

"Do not! I totally saved you in the Kevera tournament. If there had just been two more seconds in the round, I would have completely..."

"Still going on about Kevera?" Coco interrupted, "That was months ago! What about the Dektra round where I totally saved you from the..."

"You did no such thing!" Mac shot back playfully. He paused, eyeing the two girls before offering a smirk. "Either way it seems we have these girls beat." Mac motioned to Mary's gown. "I love a woman in red."

Mary groaned. "I have got to get out of this dress."

"I second that," her sister replied.

"I have some clothes you can borrow," Mary offered.

"Great. Let's see if we can get to the living quarters before the entire temple sees us in this awful color."

The sisters walked quickly towards the entrance to the temple while the two puppies followed closely behind them, still arguing over who was the better fighter.

Chapter IV

◆•❖•◆

A HALF HOUR LATER, THE two sisters stood in Mary's room, showered and dressed in traditional temple attire. A symbol of their rank, both Ameria and Mariana were dressed in gold from their glittering shoes to the bands in their hair. With their long hair pulled back tightly, they wore long satin pants with matching sleeveless shirts that hung loosely around their bodies. Over this, both wore satin robes which bore the mark of Kale in the form of a five point star encased within a crowned shield. The star was divided into ten colors which represented the colors worn by the defendants in service to the temple Gods. The color of the shield corresponded to the rank of its wearer. In Mary's case, the mark blended with her robes of rank. One either side sat two wolves facing the shield, also etched in gold.

The sisters entered a narrow walkway that led to the training hall of Kale. The ancient hall was the oldest part of the temple, and legends told that it was built by the Gods themselves. The room lay directly under a large waterfall, which separated into two cascading streams sliding over both sides of the vaulted glass ceiling. When the light from Kale's suns touched the rushing water, the temple shimmered with all the colors of the rainbow, as though it were made of fragmented crystals, the magical colors ever changing with the flow of the water.

The inside of the room was the largest of any of the training temples, providing separate sections for each of the partnered teams. The various areas were separated by tall, rainbow curtains of silk. Each of the six areas were lined with posts of gold, embedded with stones of elaborate beauty which helped to reflect the dazzling array of lights.

The training areas were painted to match the rank of the corresponding students. Closest to the door was the training area of the lowest ranked students in the colors of purple and white on the left and yellow and black on the right.

Mary and Ameria walked passed these lower-ranked areas through a long, narrow walkway which lead to the center of the room that was carpeted in the colors of the temple ranks. They next walked by the section of the room that housed the blue and green training areas on the left and the red and pink areas on the right. Mary paused to offer a slight wave to her friend and teammate, Jace. Dressed in silks of red, Jace flashed Mary a warm smile as he worked through the steps of his rigorous training program.

As the princesses continued along the walkway, they came to a wall of solid gold that opened with a set of elaborate, jewel encrusted doors. Pulling on the ruby handle, Mary opened the door enough to cross the barrier which separated the highest of rank from the rest of the training area. Only two mats rested on this elite side of the temple's ancient room. On the left side, draped in silks of gold and silver, was the training area for the highest ranked students of Kale. On the other side, draped in silks of rainbow, was the training area reserved exclusively for the temple masters and the Golden and Silver Defendants. In the recorded history of the temple, only students who had earned these distinguished ranks had ever set foot inside the sacred ground.

The two equally ranked princesses entered the private section to find Mary's longtime partner standing in the middle of the gold and silver mat on the left side of the room. Dressed in robes of silver, Marcus had served as the silver member of Kale for as long as Mary had served as gold. He was taller than the twins, standing over six feet. He was handsome with dark brown eyes and tawny blond hair. His skin, always pale, appeared even lighter within the silver robes. He was a descendent from the Kalian bloodline and the nephew of Master Leo, the Temple Master of Kale and a former Golden Defendant.

Seeing the two princesses, Marcus walked towards the center of the room to greet them. When he reached them, he gave a slight bow in acknowledgement of their royal status.

"Welcome back, Mary," he said with a smile. "Greetings, Princess Ameria."

"Hello, Marcus."

"How was the palace?"

"Terrible," Ameria replied. "Our uncle was his usual, 'I'm the king so nothing else matters' self."

"Aw," Marcus said. "What did he do this time?"

"Declared that she would marry some non-temple lord from a neighboring kingdom."

Marcus' face failed to hide his surprise. "And you said, no?"

"Of course I said no!" Mary exclaimed. "Then I invoked the oath of Blood and Arms."

"Clever," Marcus replied, "promising to marry the Champion of Kale." He gave a sly smile. "So since I am planning to win that tournament, would you prefer a spring or summer wedding?"

"Strange," Ameria interjected. "My partner, Kyle, said to ask you the same question."

"A Kolosian king?" Marcus asked with a smirk. "Sure, that will be the day! Now seriously, Mary," he turned to the elder of the twins, "spring or summer?"

Mary rolled her eyes at her longtime partner while Ameria moved to the side of the golden ring. "Care to put it to the test?" Ameria asked the silver clad Kalian. "I can't remember the last time I had you in a round, Marcus."

Marcus moved to meet her. "Are you challenging me, princess?"

"Unless you're not up for it?" Ameria said in a teasing tone.

"As long as your sister doesn't mind," Marcus replied with a wink at Mary. "I wouldn't want my future bride getting jealous."

Mary groaned. "I know this breaks tradition, but," she shifted her gaze to her sister, "kick his ass, Ameria."

Marcus made a soft clicking sound with his tongue and shook his head playfully. "Cheering for a Kolosian. What will Leo think?"

"That someone finally taught you a lesson." Ameria answered for her. "Shall we do this?"

"Let's," Marcus replied.

The two champions walked to the center of the gold and silver mat. Then turned to face each other. They exchanged soft smiles before entering into their respective bows, bending at the waist, heads down, trusting the other not to attack before they had risen. When they rose, Marcus, as the lower-ranked of the two, would be allowed to make the first offensive move.

Marcus raised his head in perfect unison with his golden opponent and immediately launched into a kick with his left leg towards Ameria's right side. Ameria saw the movement and quickly moved to avoid the blow. Marcus hit only air.

Ameria spun around with a round kick of her own. Marcus raised his left arm and blocked, but was pushed several steps backwards from the strength of the blow. Ameria followed the kick with a series of three punches. Marcus blocked the first two with the sides of his arms, then summersaulted to his left to avoid the third altogether.

When Marcus stood on the far side of the ring, he drew a deep breath as he again turned to face the golden Kolosian.

Marcus threw two round kicks towards Ameria, neither of which came close to touching the ever-evading princess. He moved several steps forward, closing the distance between himself and Ameria.

Ameria switched to a defensive stance, raising both of her arms towards her upper body and transferring most of her weight to the back leg while slightly bending her knees. Marcus advanced closer. Ameria held her ground.

Marcus threw a powerful kick toward Ameria's left hip. Ameria's arm swept down, knocking away the blow with her left arm while throwing a punch with her right. She hit Marcus square in the stomach, knocking the breath from his lungs and causing him to take several steps back. Ameria used the moment to her advantage, following Marcus' backwards movement. She twisted her right hip as she spun into a kick. Her leg crashed into Marcus' side. His body twisted from the force of Ameria's movement and he collapsed to the floor.

Ameria took another step forward in an attempt to further her advantage. Marcus recovered more quickly than she expected, flipping onto his back and jumping to his feet. He threw a punch towards Ameria which she easily avoided. Marcus then stepped back from the princess. Switching his weight to his back leg and bending his knee slightly, Marcus threw another kick towards Ameria's right side. Ameria twisted to the side and brought her arm down on Marcus' leg and drove him to the ground, forcing her weight down upon him.

There was a loud crack. Marcus screamed as his body collided with the floor. His hands flew to his leg, which was twisted beneath him, the bone broken cleanly in two. Marcus grit his teeth, managing to suppress his second scream into a moan. "*Sutis*!" he cursed in Kalian.

"That should teach you," Ameria said. Marcus still lay on the floor, both hands clutched around his broken leg. Ameria gave a soft laugh then moved towards Marcus. "Come on, my friend. Let's get you out of this ring."

Mary moved into the ring. Together, the two sisters helped Marcus to stand, allowing him to put an arm around each of them. Balancing his weight between them, Marcus hobbled painfully towards the outer edge of the ring. "You know," Marcus said through gritted teeth. "Under other circumstances I would consider myself a lucky guy standing here between the two of you."

Both girls gave a soft laugh. "Don't tell me that you can't handle a little pain."

"Yeah, Marcus." Mary laughed. "Don't complain in front of the Kolosian. You'll ruin our reputation."

Mary moved to unhook the silver ropes on the side of the ring. Marcus hissed at the jarring movement. "Sorry," Mary said. She then moved back to Marcus, allowing him to re-balance himself between them. They hobbled forward and then stepped out of the ring.

Light surrounded the three fighters. At first, it seemed they were surrounded by tiny sparkles that danced in the light as though from a dozen crystals moving slowly in the air. The three stood still as the sparkles quickly became more clustered, moving past the two princesses to surround the injured fighter between them. The light lined Marcus' skin, outlining his form until he was wearing a thin sheet of light. As the light surrounded him, it grew brighter until it filled the entire room with a blinding flash that forced all three to close their eyes.

When the light finally faded and the twins opened their eyes, it was to find Marcus standing tall between them, his leg completely healed. "Gods," he said softly. "Sometimes I hate that we have to get all the way out of the ring for the healing power to work."

"Don't be a baby," Ameria teased. "You should have seen what I did to Kyle a few weeks ago. His arm was torn to the point where the only thing keeping it attached to his body was a few thin threads of skin. A light gust of wind in the wrong direction and it would have been lying on the ground next to him. All you had was a little bone showing."

"I hate how bright it gets," Mary commented. "One of these days that flash is going to seriously destroy my vision."

"I'm just grateful it works," Marcus said.

"I second that," Mary replied. Ameria nodded in agreement.

"Well, in the future I think I'll stick with Kyle." He motioned to Mary. "I'll let my future bride take care of you."

Mary rolled her eyes. Ameria said, "Deal."

"Now," Marcus said, "I do believe that it is time for lunch." He offered an arm to each princess. "May I escort you, my ladies?" Both girls took the offered arm and left the private section of the training temple. Halfway out of the room, Jace ran up to join them. Wearing the red silks of Kale, Jace stood third to Mary and Marcus' gold and silver positions. He was a distant cousin of the royal line and a future Lord of Flos.

"Hey," Jace greeted them. "What were the three of you doing in there? I saw the healing lights."

"Ameria taught Marcus a lesson," Mary replied, then laughed. "Too bad it didn't work."

"Well, Mary, if you can't teach him then..."

Mary nodded in agreement. "I know, but one can dream."

Jace laughed. "Here, Marcus. Why don't you let me take one of these beauties off your hands?" He held out his arm to Princess Ameria, which she quickly accepted and began walking down the hall in front of the other two. "Wish I could have seen the fight!" Jace informed the younger princess. "I always miss the best fights."

"So," Marcus whispered for his partner's ears alone. "You really did take the oath?"

Mary nodded slowly in confirmation. "It is my duty as future queen."

Marcus looked at her carefully. "Are those your words, Mary, or Master Leo's?"

Mary paused before replying in a restricted voice. "I will wed within temple law. With two Temple Champions on the throne, the ties between the crown and the temple will be reunited. The temple's authority will be put firmly back into place. No more of this petty squabbling that my uncle seems to have become so fond of over the years. His continued defiance of temple law would tear the kingdoms apart if I had not been his heir apparent."

"Ah, yes," Marcus said softly as they moved out of the training room and into the long, narrow hallway which would lead them back to the temple's living quarters. "I have heard the rumors. The twin children born of the Temple Champions while the king remains childless for choosing a bride outside of temple law. You don't actually believe it, do you?"

"What?"

"That the temple leaders cursed her to remain childless."

Mary rolled her eyes. "You of all people know that the temple leaders don't have that kind of power, Marcus. Whatever the reason is that my aunt has borne no children is between her and the Gods. No one else."

Chapter V

Two days later, Ameria climbed back into the royal carriage and began the long trek to what had become her home, the Temple of Koloso. Though located in the same mountains, the two temples were an entire day's ride by carriage. Ameria briefly thought of asking a defendant to transport her there. Blessed by the power of the Gods, defendants could transport themselves instantaneously between the temples with nothing more than a thought. In the end, Ameria decided against asking, instead preferring to take the scenic route with a pair of silver horses.

The journey through the dancing mist of the mountains was, to Ameria, one of the most mysterious and beautiful wonders she had ever beheld. The sparkles of rainbow light twirling through the never lifting mist made Ameria picture tiny fairies dancing upon the breeze, twisting and turning in delight to a melody only they could hear.

However, as the carriage moved closer to the equally famous temple, the lights began to disappear. Slowly, the carriage descendent from the height of the rainbow peaks, towards the base of the mountains. The wide valley in which the Temple of Koloso was located lay between several of the tallest peaks found within the range. The silver horses descended the rocky path with an unnatural swiftness. Temple horses were considered a gift from the Gods, and were tended full time by specially selected members of the temples.

All temple horses were born within the same stable located in the center of the Rainbow Mountains. The horses, much like the defendants and students they served, were assigned to specific temples based on the color of their luxurious coats. The color was matched to the color rank of the temples.

Golden horses served the Temple of Kale. Silver went to the Temple of Koloso. Red horses went to the Temple of Desoto and so forth. They were creatures of beauty and grace and treated with the utmost respect by students, temple masters, and visitors alike.

As the carriage descended through the mountains, the dancing lights faded further until they eventually disappeared altogether. As they approached the massive temple, Ameria found herself thinking that while the Kalian temple was a palace of glass, the Kolosian temple was a castle of dark stone.

Once, the valley which housed the Temple of Koloso had been an open field of beauty and sunlight. Over the millennia, the mountains had slowly shifted to shroud the temple in an ever increasing shadow. Normally, Ameria failed to notice the darkness in which others often claimed the temple was cloaked. However, after spending the last few days in the brilliance of the sunlight experienced by both the palace and the Temple of Kale, Ameria's entrance into the valley seemed bleak by comparison.

Ameria's carriage pulled up before the familiar sight, and Ameria exited the carriage, not bothering to wait for the driver to open the door. She walked briskly towards the front door of the temple, her heels echoing on the silver marble floor. She paused briefly to nod at the statue of the Gods, identical to the one that stood before the Temple of Kale, then continued to walk forward.

The guards who stood on the sides of the temple entrance parted the silver doors at her approach. The two men were dressed in black robes. The silver mark of Koloso, which was identical to that of Kale, save for its silver, as opposed to gold coloring, stood prominently against the dark material. The two men gave a bow as Ameria began to walk through the doors. "Welcome home, princess."

Ameria gave a curt, "Thank you," but did not slow her brisk pace as she entered temple. She continued down the long hallway and passed the living quarters without a single glance. She then walked through the narrow hallway which led into the main temple training area, featuring multicolored rings identical to those of Kale.

"Hey, Ameria!" Brandan, one of her fellow students, called to her from the side of the red curtains he was standing next to.

"Is Kyle in the training room?" Ameria asked.

"I think so," Brandan replied.

Ameria continued towards the tall, sliver doors at the end of the temple, which separated the top level of Kalian students from the rest of the group. As she stepped closer, she had to take several steps to the left in order to avoid the roaring fire that stood in the center of the room. Bright blue flames swirled in an elegant dance to a music meant only for the Gods.

The heat from the large fire filled the room with much needed warmth. The light reflected across the room with the help of a massive chandelier that hung above the flames, causing blue light to cascade through the room. Additional chandeliers holding large, silver candles, were positioned to the side of each training section of the temple, providing additional light. There were no windows in this part of the temple.

When Ameria finally reached the silver doors, she pushed them open and entered the private section of the training temple. Her partner, Kyle, stood at the end of the ring, facing the doors, leaning with his back against the edge of the silver ropes. Kyle stood well over six feet tall with shoulder-length brown hair that was so dark it was almost black. His skin was pale, marking his pure Kalian bloodline, and his eyes were a dark jade green.

He had high, sharp cheek bones and a thin frame that made him look even taller than his already impressive height. His silver temple robes shimmered in the firelight, as did the plain silver chain that he always wore around his neck. Kyle had served as Ameria's partner for nearly thirteen years. His father had also been a silver Kolosian student, and had later served as a Silver Defendant before retiring to serve as High Lord of Turbamentum. A position to which Kyle was the rightful heir.

"I knew it was you," he said with a small smile. "So, is it true? Will your sister marry by right of arms?"

"Yes, it is true. "

"Won't that be a little strange?" Ameria tilted her head in question. "I mean, having to marry your own sister after you win the tournament. I think it's kind of hot."

Ameria's eyes narrowed slightly. "You watch yourself, Kyle, or I might have to teach you a lesson."

Kyle offered her a wide smile. "Promises." Then Kyle moved forward and embraced his longtime partner. "I missed you."

"I missed you as well."

"I was starting to think that you had decided to switch temples. I heard you headed over to Kale."

"And serve as silver to my sister? You know me better than that."

Kyle shrugged. "Just trying to find a way to end my year on a golden streak."

Ameria laughed. "With Brandan, really?"

Kyle paused for a moment, and then shook his head. "Did you at least have some fun at our rival temple?"

Chapter VI

Mary was sitting at her desk reading through the latest book on Kalian history. Her room, as with everything else in her life, was draped entirely in gold. A large coverlet lay across the bed on the far side of her room atop gold satin sheets. Golden curtains were tied back on either side of the window, allowing the sunshine to filter in through the thin panel of glass. The sunlight danced across the room, creating a golden shimmer.

A knock at the door pulled Mary back to the present. "Come in," she called, closing the book before placing it on the left corner of her desk. The door opened and Jace entered the room. He was dressed in bright red temple robes, with the golden symbol of Kale across his left breast.

"Hello, Mary," Jace said with a smile.

"Hello."

"I heard about your trip. I was wondering how it felt to see your uncle again after all this time."

"He was the same as ever." Mary shrugged. "Still no respect for the temples."

"I think you should be careful," Jace said. "There is no way he can be happy about what you just did. Who was the guy they tried to marry you off to?"

"The son of some lord who's never seen a day of training in his life. I would never marry someone not of the temples, you know that."

"Even if it means marrying Kyle?" Jace asked skeptically. "You know that he's a top contender for that tournament."

"My sister's partner is the least of my worries."

Jace took a seat on the large sofa against the back wall of the room.

Mary moved to sit beside him. "We still have a couple of tournaments to get through. How's your training going? I know Katalin was having some trouble with the new techniques. Do you think she will get them down in time for next week's rounds? I could help her with them if you'd like?"

"She is starting to get them, though I am sure any help would be appreciated, if you're offering." He gave her a wide smile. "You could always fight with me instead. Then I'd be sure to qualify for finals."

Mary laughed. "You don't need my help to make it to the upper levels, Jace."

"I know that," Jace said. "But it's not enough to reach a Royal Championship rank."

Mary looked at him for several moments, trying to understand what he was saying, "You only need a Championship rank to be considered for the Defendant Team, Jace. And you're a Grand Champion, so you more than qualify."

"Yes, but I need a royal rank to fight in the thirteenth tournament."

Mary straightened. "Jace, I'm afraid I am not following you."

"Come on, Mary. I'm better than Kyle and just as good as Marcus."

"Jace," she said softly. "I can't allow you to fight against students of golden rank."

"Please, Mary! I...I just want a chance."

"Is this because I took the oath of Blood and Arms?"

Jace's lips clamped down to form a tight, thin line. Mary stared at him intently for several moments. "I'm the leader of this team, Jace. That means I'm responsible for the safety of each member when they enter that ring. You, against Royal Champions?"

Jace's face remained taut, but Mary knew him well enough to know that it was just the mask he hid behind. "Captain, I just want my shot, and with you, I could have it."

Mary stared into his light brown eyes for several moments. Then sighed. "Before I can say anything, Jace, I have to talk this over with Master Leo. Then I have to talk to Marcus. Marcus cannot fight below his rank and Katalin cannot cover him at the silver level. Therefore, they would have to sit out the next tournament."

Jace looked up at Mary. "You mean, you'll consider it?"

Mary spoke carefully in a low voice as she answered him. "It is not something I would recommend, Jace. If you truly want to try, I will talk to the others. However, Jace, there is one catch."

Jace stood from the sofa. "What is that?"

Mary looked up towards him from her seated position. "If Koloso is in the tournament, I will not raise you to the golden level. It's not up for discussion. If you don't agree then I will refuse to allow you to fight with me at all. Do you understand?"

Jace nodded.

"Say the words."

"I understand," Jace replied.

Mary offered him a smile before standing from the sofa. "Let me go speak with Marcus."

Mary walked down the hall to her partner's room. The hallway between the students' living quarters was painted in streaks of rainbow in a constant pattern of swirls in the order of the temple's ranking colors. Gold touched silver, which swept into red, pink, black, yellow, green, blue, white, and purple before finally swirling back into gold. All the students' rooms were identical save for the color, which matched the rank of the student who lived within them.

Marcus' room was as silver as Mary's was gold, except for black pillows which Marcus laid on top of his silver coverlet. Mary took a seat in one of the silver chairs that sat beside her partner's desk and relayed Jace's request. Marcus shrugged. To Mary's surprise he said, "If he wants to fight with you, I am fine sitting out the next round. We were undefeated last year, so the thirteenth tournament will land one of us a perfect record."

Mary tilted her head towards Marcus. "You don't seem very surprised at this request."

"I'm not. I had no doubt he would want a chance to compete, if the prize is your hand."

Mary shook her head. "Perhaps this isn't such a good idea. He won't win that tournament and if he competes, he would stand alone against a dozen champions of higher rank and skill."

"Mary, wait. I'm not saying that you lead him to believe anything, because you didn't. All I'm saying is..." he looked at her for a moment. "Let him try, Mary. Let him have a chance and then at least it will guarantee his placement onto the Defendant Team. It is where he belongs."

"It's where we all belong," Mary replied.

"You mean." He paused. "Instead of on the throne?"

Mary sighed. "No...yes...I don't know. There are just some days..." Her voice trailed off.

"What?" Marcus asked softly.

"Some days I wish that I had been born second."

"Have you thought about asking your uncle to make your sister his heir?"

"It crossed my mind," Mary's voice lowered to a soft whisper. "But my twin or not, I don't know if I could live with myself if I put a Kolosian on the throne."

"Yet if you become queen, then your sister will likely become the next Golden Defendant."

"I know." Mary groaned. "I'm just not sure which is worse. My sister as the Golden Defendant or sitting on the throne. I'm just not sure."

"I guess it really doesn't matter now," Marcus said with a hint of sadness in his voice. "You already took the oath."

"True," Mary replied. "But I always planned to do that, queen or not. The Gods demand it of every Kalian princess. Something my uncle seems to have forgotten long ago. I hope that I can get to the throne before he destroys all of our traditions." Mary shook her head then said in words so soft that Marcus had to lean closer to hear. "I thank the Gods that his wife bore him no children. Even Ameria would make a better queen that the child she would have raised."

"Yes," Marcus whispered back. "Thank the Gods for that."

Mary pulled back from Marcus. "So, I guess we need to go talk to Master Leo."

"So it would seem."

An hour later, Leo had given his consent to the fight.

Mary walked into one of the side rooms of the temple's living quarters. Once there, she stood before a large mirror in the center of the room. She moved her hand in front of the mirror, palm up and fingers spread. The clear surface began to glow with a silvery light. "I need to speak to the Temple of Desoto," Mary said. Moments later, Mary was facing the Temple Master of Desoto, Latie, who stared back at her from the other side of the mirror.

"Greetings, Master Latie," Mary addressed the revered temple master. She was a thin, tall woman dressed in robes of bright red, the color of the Desoto temple. She had brown eyes and her long blond hair was pulled behind her. Her skin held a slight tan which provided a healthy glow to her high cheek bones. In her youth, she had served as the golden student of Desoto and had, for a brief period of time, served as a Pink Defendant to Master Leo and Mary's own parents.

"Greetings, Princess of Kale. To what do I owe the honor of speaking with you today?"

"I would like to know if Koloso will be competing at the Royal Championship level of next week's tournament."

"No, Princess of Kale, they will not. I was just going over the roster yesterday attempting to finalize all the details."

"Great," Mary replied. "I need to make a change to our roster."

Latie sounded surprised. "I assure you, princess, in the absence of Koloso, the lords of our temple will provide adequate challenge."

"I have no doubt, Master Latie, and I look forward to answering their challenge."

Mary paused to draw breath. "However, I would like to make a change to the roster. Marcus has decided to graciously step aside so Jace, our red student, may compete at my side for a chance of winning a Royal Championship title. I would appreciate it if you move him up to the golden-silver level and take Lord Marcus and Lady Katalin off the roster."

"It shall be done, princess."

"Thank you, Master Latie. I look forward to seeing you next week at your temple."

"As I look forward to seeing you, Princess of Kale." The master gave a slight bow. "It shall be done."

Mary ended the conversation by once again waving her arm in front of the mirror, closing her hand as she did so. She walked down the rainbow halls to find Jace. She found him sitting on a sofa in one of the student common areas, speaking to Marcus. Both young men turned to face Mary as she entered the room. "Well, I've got some good news, and some bad news."

"Oh?" Marcus asked.

"The good news, Jace, is that Koloso will not be at the next tournament. The bad news is that every other golden student will be and we, my dear Jace," she motioned to her fellow student, "will have to beat every last one of them if we are going to make you a Royal Champion."

"Seriously." A smile broke across Jace's face. "I'm going to get to fight with you."

Mary nodded, returning the smile. "Yes, Jace. I will fight with you...though by the time we are done with the rounds, I am not so sure you will thank me for it."

"This is so...I mean, wow!"

He paused to draw a deep breath then managed to compose himself. "Thank you, Mary. I won't let you down." He leaned forward and wrapped Mary in a tight embrace.

Mary hugged him back and said, "Well, I say we go to the training temple and get some work done."

"Absolutely!"

Chapter VII

◆•▶•✧•◀•◆

THE TEMPLE OF DESOTO WAS in the Turbamentum province located just outside of the Rainbow Mountains. Six of Kale's teams were competing in the tournament. It was a half-day's ride by horse from the Temple of Kale to the Temple of Desoto, and it was such a beautiful day that Mary had elected to ride horseback instead of riding in a covered carriage. The higher ranking teams would not compete until the second day of the tournament, which would give them plenty of time to recover from the long ride. Mary's favorite horse was a golden stallion named Sherwyn.

They left early enough that only two of Kale's three suns had risen to fill the clear, purple sky. Mary urged her horse into a soft gallop and the two rode through the prism of multicolored lights which danced throughout the Rainbow Mountains. When they reached the lower part of the mountains and entered into a rare open field, Sherwyn increased his pace of his own accord and Mary lowered herself, intertwining her jet black hair with Sherwyn's golden mane. The wind whipped past them in a wild flurry and Sherwyn's pace increased further still.

Mary let out a joyous laugh as her horse pulled away from the others, enjoying the beauty of the warm spring day. She turned back and saw Jace racing to catch her, his horse whinnying a challenge as Jace surged forward. Mary slowed her mount to a hard gallop, allowing Jace to catch them before giving her mount back his head and the two raced side by side against the wind.

They rode for a good fifteen minutes before their horses began to tire, and Mary pulled Sherwyn to a walk. Jace joined her, slowing his mount in step beside his partner's. "I think we lost the others," Jace said, catching his breath.

Mary laughed. "Don't worry; they will be along soon enough. My goodness that was fun! I love riding."

"Yes." Jace laughed along with her. "What a rush!"

"I'll miss days like this," Mary replied. "Sometimes I think our training program robs us of days like these. Just being able to ride or play in total abandonment."

She had said the words lightheartedly, but Jace responded in a far more serious tone. "Mary you know..." He paused for a moment, as though considering his words. "Why did you take the oath? There had to be another way. Master Leo and Lord Louis would never have gone along with your uncle's demands."

Mary turned in the saddle toward her companion. "Jace," she said softly. "I was always going to take the oath. My uncle's action just sped up the process."

Mary studied Jace's handsome face. His features were as straight and unreadable as she had ever seen them. She pulled back on the reins and Sherwyn came to a complete stop. "Jace?" she asked quietly. "Do you want to tell me what is going on?"

Jace pulled back on his own reins and stopped a few feet in front of her. "I just..." He stopped again.

Mary drew a deep breath and exhaled slowly, "Jace, I'm a princess. There are things that are required and I..." She could feel herself squirming. "It's not like I asked for this, I was..."

A small scream interrupted her words. Both Mary and Jace turned, but saw nothing.

"Did you hear...?"

"Shhh," Mary shushed him. "Listen."

Several moments of silence followed, then they heard another sound, high-pitched but so faint that they could not make out the words. Mary made a soft clicking sound and Sherwyn moved forward at a brisk pace.

Jace followed without being told. The two rode towards the sound with the thunder of hooves preceding their arrival. As they rode forward, the rainbow mist lifted, and Mary realized that they were approaching a small town on the edge of the Rainbow Mountains.

As they approached, Mary took note of the small, simple homes that lined the sides of the village. The center of the town was an open air market. Fish hung from one of the booths. The crisp scent of fresh bread wafted from the bakery to Mary's left. She took little notice of these details, and instead continued quickly through the streets as another cry was heard.

The sound came from a group of middle-aged women standing on the outskirts of the small town. Mary motioned for Jace to halt, and the two students observed the situation from a distance. Three men stood around the women, taking turns removing various items from their homes. One woman burst into sobs when a man emerged from the doorway of a white house carrying a large bag.

The man was tall, though not as tall as many of the men Mary was accustomed to training with. He had dark brown hair that lay unkempt over his brow in short wisps. He was deeply tanned, as though he had spent too much time under the intense heat of the kingdom's multiple suns. The three men were similar enough that Mary thought they might be brothers.

One of the men re-entered the same house and emerged a few moments later carrying a bottle that Mary was too far away to identify. "No, please," the woman pleaded. "My son is sick. He..." The man grabbed the woman's arm and pulled so hard that she fell to the ground shrieking, though from fear or pain, Mary was uncertain.

"Princess."

Mary turned around at the unexpected voice. "Kyle?" she asked, surprised to be facing the silver student of Koloso. "What are you doing here?"

"I was riding with some of the younger students and rode ahead when I heard the screams." He glanced at the scene in front of them.

"Let's go!" Mary commanded, jerking the reins in her hand and spurring the horse forward with Kyle and Jace flanking her. The three young champions approached the scene swiftly, pulling to a stop only inches in front of the unknown men.

"What is going on here?" Mary demanded.

The man closest to Mary looked up, startled at the sudden appearance of the three young riders. "It's none of your business."

"Yes, it is," Mary said forcefully.

The other two men moved closer to the first. Mary could see their brown eyes and their black clothes were covered with dirt from their travels. The man had a splotchy beard of several days' growth and a thick mustache badly in need of trimming. His gaze was hard as he stared up at the riders. "They did not pay their royal fees. It's our job to collect." He gave a partial smile that showed his yellowed teeth.

Mary looked at the three cowering women. "Is this true?"

The tall woman who had been pleading for the contents of the white house stepped forward. Her face was smudged with dirt from where she had fallen and her simple blue garment was covered with brown dust. "We paid what we could, my lady. They wanted more."

Mary gazed back at Kyle and the two exchanged a quick glance. She looked at the men on the ground as Kyle nudged his silver horse forward to stand shoulder to shoulder with the princess, then waited for her to speak.

"In the name of the king and the temples of Kale and Koloso," Mary said. "You will lay down your swords and surrender yourself to temple authority."

"The hell we will!" one of the men on Mary's left yelled. "We are taking anything we wish." He moved several steps closer.

Mary sat perfectly still as he approached. Then, he made the mistake of reaching for Sherwyn's reins. The golden stallion rose on his back legs, raising his hooves in the air and knocked the thug to the ground. Mary jumped from her mount, drawing a sword from the side of her saddle as she did so.

The blade was a solid weight in her right hand. It was made of a rare silver metal found only in the heart of the Rainbow Mountains. The hilt of the blade was black stone with lines of gold interwoven into the handle and winding down the blade. The mark of Kale was clearly visible on the left side of the blade's handle, the golden symbol shimmering in the bright sunlight. She stood tall, holding her sword, and threw her outer robes to the ground to stand in full Kalian attire. Sherwyn moved to the side of the field, but not so far that Mary lost sight of him.

Beside her, Kyle and Jace also stood draped in their respective colors, swords drawn. Jace's blade was identical to Mary's but for the traces of red stones embedded into his hilt, as opposed to the gold in Mary's. Kyle's was made from the same silver metal, but held traces of silver on the handle as well, with the mark of Koloso glinting in the bright light.

"Oh, so you kids want to play," one of the men on Mary's right said with a laugh. His companions looked more uncertain. However, when their partner in crime pulled his weapon, they did as well. The blades were simple, made of a dull gray metal with a simple black handles.

The man lunged at Mary, swinging his blade hard towards the princess. She raised her arm and blocked the blow, but was forced to take several steps back under the weight of the larger opponent. It took the thug only one additional swing for Mary to realize that his swordplay was based on strength alone. Mary swirled around to easily avoid the next downward thrust and the man's forward momentum left him off balance.

Mary took advantage of his stumbling and twirled around him, swinging her sword towards her opponent's flank with as much speed as she could muster. The man began to turn around. Mary's sword flashed forward. He managed to stop the sword from hitting its intended target, but could not stop the blade from sinking into the flesh of his left arm.

He cried out at the sting of the blade and Mary stepped backwards into a defensive position. Blood flowed from the wound and ran onto the ground. Out of the corner of her eye, Mary saw Jace struggling with his larger opponent, while a quick glance to her left showed that Kyle had his fight under control.

Mary turned her attention back to her own challenger, who had risen to his feet. Holding his sword in the hand of the uninjured arm, the man charged Mary again. She held her ground for several seconds, and then stepped to the left. Her opponent raced past her, and Mary struck. Her blade bit into the handle of her challenger's sword, breaking the hilt and taking several of the thug's fingertips along with it. The sword clattered to the ground. The man fell, clutching his hand and screaming.

Mary moved her sword to the man's throat and kicked the fallen blade away from him. She looked around and saw that Kyle had successfully won his battle and had moved to help Jace, leaving the fallen man unconscious. At seeing his second companion defeated, the third man suddenly thought better of his actions and fell to his knees in surrender. Kyle grabbed his sword while Jace stood tall with his blade a few inches from the surrendering man.

The women looked up at the three young warriors with a look of awe. "Are you...defendants?" she asked Jace, who stood closest to the houses.

"No," he replied softly. "We are temple students. I am Jace of Kale, that is Lord Kyle of Koloso, and that," he pointed to his golden captain, "is Princess Mariana, the gold student of Kale."

Mary motioned to Jace, "Move that man over here by his friend."

"*Sutis!*" The man uttered a Kalian curse.

"Silence," Kyle told him, "or I shall cut out your tongue as well. That is the Crown Princess you are speaking too."

"Which defendants are responsible for this village?" Mary asked the women.

The women exchanged glances. The one with red hair gave a slight shrug of her shoulders. "What do you mean, princess?"

"Each province of the kingdom is protected by a group of defendants," Mary replied. "Which team guards this village?"

The eldest of the women stepped forward. She had long brown hair that was slowly fading to gray and her skin was beginning to wrinkle with age. "There is none, Your Highness. They haven't visited this village in a *repule*."

"Five years?" Mary asked in surprise.

"The king declared that all villages wanting to be under protection of the defendants would have to pay for the right. He took our name off the list of protection when we couldn't pay."

Mary looked at her fellow students, unsure of how to respond. Kyle took the liberty of tying up their beaten bandits and Jace moved to Mary's side. "I knew what my uncle was doing was wrong, but this... I never expected this."

"Do you have somewhere you can keep these men until we can send defendants to fetch them?"

"Yes, princess."

Mary nodded. "Kyle, would you mind escorting them to wherever this lady directs?"

"Yes, princess," Kyle replied, and offered a slight bow in her direction.

"I'll help," Jace said, running to Kyle's side as they gathered up the prisoners. Kyle's man had just regained consciousness and the uninjured man helped him to his feet.

A half hour later the three young champions were once again on horseback. They rode in great haste to the Temple of Desoto.

"Thanks for showing up," Mary said to her Kolosian counterpart.

"It was my pleasure, princess." Kyle replied. "I am just glad that I managed to show up in time. Ameria's going to be sorry she missed it."

Jace jumped into the conversation. "I loved that twisting move you did with the sword, Kyle. Do you think you could teach me?"

Kyle considered the younger man. "Well," he said thoughtfully, "considering we don't use swords in the tournament that we are competing in today." He shrugged and offered Jace a light smile. "Sure, I'll show you."

"Great!" Jace returned the smile, then looked at Mary. "Let's ride," he said, moving his horse from a medium gallop into a full run. Mary and Kyle glanced at each other for a moment before pulling on their reins and giving chase.

It was late evening when the three finally reached the palace of Desoto. Though not as grand as either of the student's own temples, no one could deny the beauty of the third Kalian temple. Located just outside of the mountains, Desoto was the sister Temple to Kale.

Desoto was the name of one of the heroes who fought alongside Kale and Koloso at the end of the last great war. He had been a champion of light and one of Kale's most trusted commanders. When the war was over, Kale honored his friend by naming him a lord of the temple. He was also charged with putting together a team to defend the realm from all future threats and was therefore, the first Golden Defendant. The temple upheld its legacy proudly. Five of its members were slated to compete in the upcoming thirteenth tournament, for which they would fight for not only the championship, but for Mary's hand.

The temple was primarily constructed of white marble. The large wall that surrounded the temple was made of a similar white stone, with a twinge of silver. Spiraling towers rose at various points along the wall, draped with long red banners that danced in the wind. Guards dressed in red cloth watched those towers day and night, protecting the students and leaders within. At the center of the wall stood a pair of tall, stone gates with long red banners. As they approached, one of the men must have recognized Mary's golden robes as he called, "Make way for the Princess of Kale!" The gates swung open.

Mary rode straight to the white marble steps of the temple. As she slowed her horse and dismounted in a single sweep of golden robes, her eyes paused to drink in the beauty of the Desoto temple. The temple, much like her own, was held above the ground by tall, pillars. Tiny droplets of red crystals were embedded into the milky marble like small drops of blood on a white cloak. The normally quiet grounds were alive with people arriving for the upcoming tournament, and hopeful and current champions alike walked up and down the marble steps, exploring the famous temple.

Mary walked up the marble steps with Kyle and Jace falling into line one step below her, as though to form a perfect honor guard. "We must find the defendant in charge," Mary said to the two men behind her.

Chapter VIII

AMERIA PULLED UP ON THE reins of her silver stallion. Though not the largest mount in the Kolosian stables, Argento was by far the most agile. With his slim frame and slender legs, Argento glided over the grassy slopes of the Rainbow Mountains with an ease that Ameria had found on few others of the stable's many horses. Argento's mane was pure silver, with a metallic glisten that would never be mistaken for gray. Ameria enjoyed her afternoon rides, racing through the valley of Koloso before climbing up and down the surrounding slopes. Usually, Ameria would have to keep her rides short, but with Kyle away training the younger students at the Desoto Tournament, she decided to take the afternoon off.

Ameria had left for her ride early, before the third sun had begun to rise. She had been riding for several hours, and now pulled her horse to a slow walk beside a gentle stream. They were on the edge of the Rainbow Mountains, and the magical mist that filled the air danced along the edge of the moving water. Pulling her horse to a complete stop, Ameria dismounted and removed the small saddle from Argento's back. The horse gave a soft whinny in thanks. Ameria watched the horse drink from the stream, before he moved to the side of the grassy bank and lay down in the deep blue grass.

Ameria pulled her bag from the left side of the discarded saddle. She had packed a light lunch of meat, cheese and bread. She had also packed a thick, black blanket which she spread out on the ground. She shrugged out of her golden robe and sat in her thin, satin slacks and matching short sleeve tunic. Ameria ate her lunch and then stretched out on the blanket. She closed her eyes, listening to the rush of the stream and the chirping of birds from the sparsely spaced trees behind her.

She was unsure how long she lay there, dozing by the stream, before her horse woke her, rubbing his nose against her left arm. She opened her eyes slowly, smiling up at the horse. All three suns were high above them in the purple sky. "Are you ready to go, Argento?" she asked softly. The horse moved to Ameria's left. Ameria sat up and watched as the horse trotted steadily towards the far field. "Argento?" The horse did not come to her call.

Ameria stood and followed her horse. She walked quickly up the hill. When she reached the top, Ameria was startled to see that she was not alone. Coming towards her at a slow pace were four riders all clad in black leather that must have been unbearably hot in the heat of the three suns. Three of the horses were a pale brown, while the fourth was as black as the leather of the man riding it.

A feeling of foreboding overcame the princess. She climbed back down the hilltop, and moved towards the trees beside the river. On her way she paused to grab her things. Once beside the trees, Ameria pulled the black blanket around her, wishing for possibly the first time in her life that she could trade her long, golden locks for her sister's dark hair. Though the trees were sparse, they were large with thick trunks that managed to hide most of her body.

Ameria sat quietly, hoping that the men would cross the river and be on their way. However, as the man on the black horse pulled up his reins, Ameria realized that luck was not going to be on her side.

The men did not appear to have seen her. Three of them dismounted their horses and bent down to drink from the river. Two of the men appeared to be in their late thirties or perhaps even their early forties. They both had pale brown hair with dark skin that had been burned by the suns. The third rider wore a black cloak and Ameria could not make out his face.

As Ameria turned her attention to the fourth horse, she realized that there was not one, but two forms in the saddle. A large black cloak covered them completely and neither dismounted. As she watched, one of the large bronzed men walked over and pulled the two riders from the saddle. The cloak fell away, and Ameria realized that they were in fact, children. A boy of about ten with brown hair and another boy who looked slightly older with dirty blond hair.

Both boys' hands were tied in front of them. The man who had pulled them down pushed them hard in the direction of the river. The younger of the two fell from the force of the shove. His brother, Ameria presumed, helped him to his feet. "Get on with it," the older man said in a deep, gruff voice. "You'll be no good to us if you don't survive the journey."

The other man gave a rough laugh. "They are hardly worth the journey. It might be better to just leave them here."

"No," the other man said, "I need them to work my lands. The gold we took from the village isn't nearly enough to justify this trip...especially split three ways."

"True, but there is another village on the way. Perhaps it will prove to be worth our while."

"I still think we should have taken the longer path. These mountains make me nervous." The third man who still had his back to Ameria spoke for the first time. "Too close to temple country."

"Would you relax," the brown haired man said. "There's not a temple for miles! And besides, we will be well out of the mountains before we hit the next village. You know that the defendants no longer guard these outer territories."

Ameria felt her eyes narrow. *Defendants not protecting the villages? What is going on?*

"We will stay here for a while," the cloaked man said. "Let the horses rest." As the men spread out blankets and started to unburden their horses, Ameria tried to decide what to do. All three men stood between her and the two boys.

The younger of the two began to cry softly. "I want to go home," he said as the elder attempted to comfort him.

Three against one were not the odds Ameria liked. The two uncloaked men easily had a hundred pounds on her. However, she could not just sit there and allow these men to take the obviously terrified children. She had her temple robes, but it was unlikely that these men would respond well to the symbol of authority.

Ameria stood quietly beside the tree, thankful for her hours of training as her muscles began to cramp from being forced to stand perfectly still. Ameria fought the sensations for the better part of an hour, until one of the men began to snore. Moving as slowly as she could, Ameria reached down to the saddle lying at her feet and drew her Kalian sword from the sheath hidden in its side.

The blade was made of silver metal found exclusively within the depths of the Rainbow Mountains and had been carried by Kolosian students for centuries. The hilt was formed of black stone with lines of gold interwoven into the handle. On the right side of the hilt, the silver mark of Koloso stood clearly against the black stone, shimmering in the bright sunlight. The blade felt solid in Ameria's right hand, becoming a mere extension of her arm.

She drew in a deep breath and moved from behind the trees. She stepped quickly toward the first man. Fearful of being outnumbered, she gave a silent prayer to the temple Gods. She approached the sleeping man and raised her sword. Stepping to the man's left, she moved the silver blade forward and quietly slit his throat.

The second man, who was nearby on a different blanket, bolted from his position with a cry. The man stood in a stupor as Ameria moved in on him. He barely recovered in time to block the first stroke of her blade.

The metals sang through the air disrupting the peaceful scene. Birds in the nearby trees let out a loud screech at the sound and took to the air. The bigger man returned Ameria's movement with one of his own, bringing his own black blade down on Ameria's silver one. Ameria parried, the two swords ringing throughout the field.

They separated and Ameria took the opportunity to chance a glance around her. The two boys were huddled near the river, but the third, cloaked man was nowhere to be seen. Ameria moved her blade, coming up at the man from below. His sword swung down, stopping Ameria's blade in its tracks. He pushed down hard, forcing Ameria to twist her arm in order to avoid dropping the sword. Ameria took several steps back again and the older man followed her. She raised her sword high, low, then high again, blocking each and every blow with far more outward ease than she was feeling.

They traded strokes for several more seconds, when the man suddenly twisted to the left, his foot slipping beneath him. Ameria pressed the advantage, moving her blade to his right. The blade sank into his side, breaking through skin and tearing into the muscle beneath. The blade would have gone farther, but Ameria pulled back as quickly as she had pressed forward. The man fell to the ground with a scream, his blood staining the blue grass beneath him.

With her opponent bleeding to death, Ameria turned to find the mysterious third man had reappeared. He had removed his outer cloak and jacket and now stood in a pair of black pants with a sleeveless black shirt. Ameria was surprised to find that he was younger than the others, appearing to be in his late twenties at most. He was taller than Ameria with eyes of deep green. His hair was jet black, and his skin was pale...Kalian pale, Ameria realized with a start.

She had fought the previous two men without speaking a word, but at seeing his Kalian features, she hesitated. "Who are you?" she asked. "What are you doing with these thugs?"

"I should likely thank you," the man said in a flat voice. "Now I won't have to split the spoils. If you leave now, we can just pretend this never happened."

"I can't do that," Ameria replied.

"Shame," he said. His lips curved upwards. "Let me guess, you're one of those temple brats."

"I am the golden student of Koloso."

"Koloso, hmm? I would have guessed Kale."

"Strange," Ameria replied. "I would have thought the same of you."

The man drew his sword. The hilt looked like carved bone and the blade was a gleaming silver that matched Ameria's own. The princess took several steps forward and moved in between the man and the young boys who ran towards the trees while Ameria braced her sword, wondering if the man in front of her would attempt to stop them. He didn't move, and the boys continued to run.

The man stepped forward, raising his sword high in front of him. Ameria held her ground, allowing her opponent to come to her. His sword swept down. She raised her arm and blocked the movement, managing to hold her footing under the weight of her opponent. She slashed her own blade down in a sweeping arch. The pale-skinned man blocked the blow. Their swords flew up, down and up again with each swing of the sword being blocked by the other.

The two swirled their blades through the air in an elegant and deadly dance. Ameria twisted her silver steel with all the speed and strength she possessed. The mysterious man matched her step for step. Ameria's breathing was labored. She had to constantly wipe the sweat from her brow to keep the water out of her eyes. The satin clung to her skin like a burning glove. Her opponent's labored breathing matched her own.

The pale man lunged forward. She was slow to counter, and the silver blade sliced down Ameria's arm. She cursed loudly and took several steps back. The cut wasn't deep, but stung nonetheless. Blood seeped to the surface of her arm, changing the cloth she wore from a brilliant gold to a murky orange.

Fighting through the pain, Ameria moved forward in a series of strikes. She swung left, then moved into a halfway downwards stoke which her opponent moved to block. Partway through the movement, Ameria reversed the direction of the blade, thrusting upwards. The blade slid across the man's upper torso, slicing him from shoulder to breast. He moved backwards fast enough to escape the full force of the blade. He groaned in pain as he stepped back, but rose too fast for Ameria to press her advantage.

Suddenly, Argento appeared from beyond the trees with two defendants behind him. Seeing the reinforcements, the man ran backwards and mounted his own black horse in a single sweep. Riding bareback, the horse ran through the water, breaking into a run. One of the defendants gave chase, while the other stopped beside the princess.

"My lady," a defendant Ameria did not recognize addressed her. "We saw the silver stallion without a rider and knew something was wrong. Are you injured?"

"Only a scratch," Ameria replied. "There were two young boys, did you see them?" The defendant shook his head. "Ride ahead," Ameria told him. "If he catches up with whoever that man was, it will take both your swords to capture him. They had some kids with them who ran towards the trees. I'm going to go look for them."

Argento ran up to Ameria and nuzzled her. "Hey," she said softly. "Thanks for bringing the help." She walked back to the trees and picked up the saddle. Once it was back on the horse, she slipped her sword in its sheath and rode towards the trees. They did not get far before seeing the two young boys.

Ameria motioned for them to come to her. "It's all right," she said softly, "you're safe now." She dismounted her horse and placed the boys in the saddle before walking Argento back to the stream. Both defendants were there waiting on her.

"I'm sorry, princess," the first man replied. He was a tall man, dressed in garbs of blue. "I lost track of the man when we reached the forest."

"What do you mean, lost track?"

"I'm not sure," the defendant replied. "One moment, he was ahead of me, then we reached the top of the hill. I only lost sight of him for a split second. Then he was just... gone."

"Gone?"

"It was as though he just vanished. I swear princess, I... I'm not sure what happened."

The princess turned her attention back to the two boys. "Where are you from?" she asked them.

"Riverta," the elder of the two replied. "Those men raided the village. When they didn't find much gold or jewels, they forced us to go with them."

Ameria turned toward the defendants. "Is that where you were coming from?"

The defendant in blue turned to the one in black and the two seemed to exchange a glance. "No," the Blue Defendant said. "We guard some towns in the center of the Rainbow Mountains. We were headed towards Desoto for the upcoming tournament when we saw your horse."

Ameria paused to think for several breaths. "Okay, I need to report what took place here to the head defendants, and I have no idea where Riverta is. So, I am going to accompany you to the Desoto temple and we can see the boys home from there."

"As you wish, my lady." Then the man in black motioned to the kidnappers lying on the ground. "What about them?"

The second defendant walked over to each of the men and felt for a pulse. He shook his head. "They must have bled out."

Ameria walked to the dead men's brown horses and untied the reins. She handed one of the horses over to the defendant, and saddled the other horse herself. She considered putting the boys on the second mount, but decided against it, not knowing the temperament of the horse. She slipped her foot into the stirrup and pulled herself astride the saddle. She fiddled with the reins for a few moments, testing the horse's responses before finally coaxing him into a soft trot and calling for the others to follow.

When they reached the temple a few hours later, the towering gates swung open at their approach. "Make way for the Princess of Koloso!" the tower defendants called. She paused long enough to hand the reins of her mount to a stable boy before ascending the white marble steps of the famous Desoto temple.

Chapter IX

Mary walked through the halls of the Temple of Desoto. The interior was an identical layout to the Temple of Kale, with the living quarters separated from the training rooms by a long, narrow corridor. Where the Temple of Kale was made of glass, the Temple of Desoto was made primarily of white marble. Embedded in the walls were deep red stones that sparkled in the light of the three suns.

At the end of the living quarters were several rooms which were reserved for meetings, guests, and a few offices for the temple masters, visiting lords or defendants. Mary walked past the first of the halls until she entered a large, circular room that held several offices. A number of men draped in red and white defendant robes stood outside the doors. Mary approached the defendant in red. He was tall, with short blond hair and light green eyes. Mary did not recognize him, but the silver emblem of Koloso stood out against his red satin robe. "My lord," Mary addressed the older man. "Are you the highest defendant present in the temple?"

"No, my lady," he said. "The Golden Defendant, Lord Edward, is here. He is in a meeting with some of the temple masters."

"I need to speak with him immediately. I had trouble on the road and heard some most disturbing news."

"What do you mean, princess?"

"I would prefer to speak with Lord Edward, though I welcome your presence when I do."

His face hardened and his lips stiffened into a thin line. "Do you mean you would rather speak to someone of another temple?" He motioned slightly towards the golden mark on her robe.

A third voice joined the conversation with a harsh laugh. "She means she would rather speak to the Golden Defendant, and to imply otherwise boarders on treason, Lord Stephen."

"Princess Ameria," the defendant replied. "Forgive me, I meant no disrespect."

"You are addressing your future queen, Stephen. Try to remember that."

"I'm sorry, my lady."

"Yes." Ameria dragged out the syllable, making the word sound almost sinister. "You are sorry. Now, I too wish to speak with Lord Edward, and your presence will not be welcome." She glanced at her sister. "I too had some trouble on the road, Mariana. I would be interested to know if our trouble was of a similar nature." She turned back to the defendant still standing by the door. "We will be in the central quarters. Tell Lord Edward that the Princesses of Kale are awaiting him."

"Yes, my lady. He will be sent for at once."

Ameria turned towards the hallway that led back to the living quarters. Mariana turned to follow her sister. The two walked in silence until they reached the large central room that stood as a communal location between the individual student rooms. Ameria took a seat on a long, red sofa while Mariana took a seat across from her.

"I thought you were not competing in this tournament." Mariana expressed her surprise at her sister's presence.

"I'm not."

"Oh good."

"Still afraid to fight me, dear sister?"

"With Jace at my side, you bet. I promised he could compete in this tournament with me, but only if you and Kyle were not in the rounds."

"Ah, wise decision. I fought a round with Brandan once under those same conditions." She flashed a smile at her sister. "We won, by the way."

Mariana raised her hand, palms out and fingers spread. "I never doubted you would."

"As I have no doubt you will. Still, it sure is something that you would risk that perfect reputation on a red student. The tournament I fought with Brandan was at one of the lesser tournaments so the possible loss would not have affected my undefeated record."

Mary shrugged. "Just because I don't want Jace in the same round as you, does not mean that he is not capable of holding his own. I consider you a special case."

"Then I guess I should consider myself honored," Ameria replied. A moment of silence passed between them. It was the unspoken question of which one was the greater champion. Instead of asking the question, the two sisters sat together and exchanged stories of their respective encounters which had brought them to the defendant's door.

They were deep in conversation when a voice interrupted them. "My princesses," Lord Stephen addressed them, emerging from the long hallway connecting to the room. Both girls turned towards the Red Defendant. "Lord Edward awaits your presence."

The princesses rose in a blur of gold silk and walked side by side down the hall, their golden robes touching lightly as they stepped together in perfect unison. They again entered the wide, circular area and were ushered into a room on the far left side. The room they stepped into was large, with deep red walls and matching furniture.

Along the back wall stood an elegantly carved mahogany desk. On the opposite side was a large fireplace of black marble and in front of the fireplace were two long, dark red sofas. Two defendants, one in gold and one in silver, stood in front of the sofa. The sisters took several steps toward the defendants and then entered into a traditional Kalian bow.

"Rise, Gold of Kale," Edward spoke to Mariana first. Then to Ameria, "Rise, Gold of Koloso." The two girls stood one after the other, sweeping their long hair behind them. Then, the two defendants standing before them entered into a more traditional bow, the Golden Defendant lowering his head and bending at the waist. The Silver Defendant, Lady Rebecca, lowered into a curtsy. Ameria deferred to her slightly older twin.

"Arise," Mariana instructed. The two defendants straightened.

"It's been a long time, Mary," the Silver Defendant addressed the Kalian princess.

"It has." Mary offered a smile to the older woman. "It is good to see you again, my lady." The Silver Defendant, formerly the golden student of Kale, was as pale as any member of the royal bloodline. She had dark brown hair and golden eyes. She was about Mary's height. Like all defendants, she wore a long satin robe that covered her from head to toe. The silver color of the robe marked her rank as the second highest defendant in the land while the golden mark over her left breast marked her rise from the Temple of Kale. She had served as one of Mary's teachers in her youth.

Rebecca's counterpart, Master Edward, wore a full-length robe of gold. Mary knew that under their solid-colored robes, both defendants wore silks of rainbow, in honor of the Gods they served. It was the key difference between the attire of temple students and full-fledged defendants.

On Master Edward's left breast was a tiny red bird, the mark of the Temple of Desoto, where Master Edward once served as the golden student of his temple. Though from another temple, Master Edward had served as a tutor to Mary on many occasions. The princess considered him to be one of the best and most honorable men she had ever known.

"Masters," Mariana began. "My sister and I respectively and separately encountered disturbing incidents on our journey towards the temple today." Mary moved and seated herself at the far end of the sofa, to which the others followed suit; the princesses on one sofa and the defendants on the other. She turned her gaze to Master Edward. "I was told today by a group of women I rescued that the defendants no long protect their village, because they could not pay their royal fees."

"I heard something similar when I went out for a ride," Ameria added. "We want to know if it's true. Have you stopped protecting the villages on the outskirts of the Rainbow Mountains?"

A moment of silence filled the room. "Princess Mariana," Edward said. "I am afraid I do not know what you speak of. No fee has ever been due to the defendants in order to qualify for protection."

Mary and Ameria exchanged a look and then proceeded to describe the locations of the various villages outside the mountains. Rebecca looked thoughtful. "I knew there were a few people who lived on the outskirts," she said. "Wait, the outskirts of the Rainbow Mountains?" Her body straightened slightly and she turned toward Edward.

"By the Gods," he said a little too loudly.

"No," Rebecca replied.

"What?" Ameria demanded, moving involuntarily towards the edge of the sofa.

"We've been having some trouble in Periculum. The king's men could not handle the problems in the city, so we switched some groups with the king's guard. It happened before I was in charge so when Periculum's problems were once again under control, the king's guard provided me with a list of all the villages in those areas."

"Gods," Rebecca gasped. "Are you saying that they charged taxes for..."

"Protection," Mary finished. "And erased the names of the villages that could not pay."

"He wouldn't," Edward said, tilting his head at the two princesses.

Mary and Ameria turned towards each other. "Our uncle," Mary said softly. "Do you really think our uncle would have ordered such a thing? To leave his own people in the hands of those..."

"Absolutely," Ameria replied.

The two girls turned back towards the defendants. "If this is true, my princesses," Rebecca said, as though afraid for the walls to hear her. "Then a grave evil is being committed throughout the realm."

Edward nodded. "We will send defendants to the mountains at once. We will let the people know that we are there for their protection and we shall ensure that all incidents such as the ones you encountered come to an end."

"Thank you, Master Edward," Ameria addressed him. "I saved two young boys on my way here from several bandits I encountered. I left them with two of your men and would request that they be escorted home to their families."

"Of course, princess," Edward replied. "We shall see it done. I will also speak with the other lords and temple masters on these matters and see if we cannot figure out what is going on."

"Thank you, masters," Mary said, standing from her seated position. "We will take our leave of you."

"Yes," Rebecca replied, standing to match Mary's height. "I shall find you after these matters have been addressed." She offered a half smile. "By the way, good luck with the tournament. Not that you will need it."

Mary returned the words with a smile. "I welcome it all the same, Master Rebecca. I hope to see you later for some more pleasant conversation."

"I will be sure to seek you out, princess." Mariana gave a bow at the neck before turning to leave the room, her sister following closely behind her. When the two were far enough down the hall that they could no longer be overheard,

Mary leaned close to her sister and whispered, "Our uncle wouldn't really have ordered those towns to go unprotected, would he?"

Ameria stopped walking and leaned her lips close to her sister's ear, resting her head on Mary's shoulder. "I think he would, Mary. I truly think he would."

Chapter X

------ ✦ ✦ ✦ ------

As the first sun began to slowly descend behind the distant mountains, the evening tournament began. Students had come from every temple in hopes of gaining the bragging rights associated with a championship win. Teams were paired by color, based on the rank of each pair. Though a student of lower rank, such as Jace, could move up a level to serve as a partner to a higher-ranked student, higher-ranked students were not permitted to step down.

Each level of competitors competed for a different title and chance to advance. The winner of the lowest ranking round was given the title of finalist. The winner of the blue and green round was called the grand finalist. The winner of the black and yellow round took the title of champion, red and pink were grand champions, and the winner of the gold and silver round were called both royal and tournament champions. It was a rare occurrence for a team to successfully win a round above their color level, however it did happen from time to time.

As Mary entered the wide room where the tournaments were taking place, she found a seat in the front of the stands beside Jace. "How are we doing?" she asked.

"Well," Jace replied. "Desoto won the finalist round, it was really pretty. The last fight couldn't have lasted more than two minutes. They fought color on color and won the competition with relative ease. Dektra actually came in second, and Koloso took third."

"Ouch," Mary replied. "I take it Rys and Lara had some trouble then?"

"Actually, they drew a first round against the Kolosian team, so they lost right out of the gate. Came in sixth place."

"How about Sam and Sara?" Mary asked.

"They actually took the Grand Finalist title for the green and blues, beating Koloso for the title. Then they held their own for several of the championship rounds," Jace gave a small sigh, "before getting knocked out by their own teammates."

"Kale versus Kale?"

Jace shrugged. "That's how the dice rolled. They came in fifth in the championship round, rather impressive I thought."

"How about our championship level team?" Mary asked of her black and yellow ranked teammates.

Jace motioned toward the fighting mats in front of the stand that had been painted in streaks of rainbow for the tournament purposes. "Well, they just knocked out Dektra and are on their way to a championship round." He motioned to the left side of the room. "Want to go give them a pep talk before they try and beat out the home team?"

"They are going up against Desoto?" Mary questioned the obvious.

"Yes, that team is good, captain. They will probably be one to watch in the upcoming year."

Mary gave a nod. "Save my seat, would you?"

"Sure thing," Jace replied as Mary made her way between the stands and down to the temple floor. She walked towards the left side of the room where Dan and Tyler were preparing to enter into the final fight of the championship level round. The two men both sported light brown locks clipped short and had eyes the color of golden honey. Though their families were from different kingdoms, they were first cousins by blood, as were many of the ruling families of Kale.

As she reached the two men, they offered her a slight bow. "Captain Mary," Dan said.

"I just came to wish you luck," Mary told the elder of the two.

"I felt really bad about having to knock out Sam and Sara," Tyler said. "They were doing so well after winning their own division."

Mary offered a small smile. "I was sorry to have missed it. Don't worry too much about having been forced to knock them out. Probably better you than the Kolosian team."

Dan nodded. "Or our sister temple that we are about to face. I'm really not sure if we are going to win this one."

"You had better," Mary informed him. "Otherwise, Coco will make fun of you for losing." A loud, deep voice rose over the crowd, calling for the competitors to enter the round. Mary flashed one last smile at her two teammates before she began walking back towards her seat.

From her seat beside Jace, Mary watched as the two teams entered the ring. Though Mary considered the golden student of Desoto, Davis, as close a friend as two competitors from rival temples could be, she was unfamiliar with the lower-ranked students from the temple.

The two teams gave a low bow of respect to each other and then turned and offered a second bow to those sitting in the stands. From somewhere on the side of the temple, an official's voice rang out. "For the last round of the championship level, I give you the teams of Kale and Desoto." Cheers rose up from various points of the temple. "Let the final round of the championship level begin!"

The teams jumped into immediate action. They matched up, black to black and yellow to yellow. Dan took several steps towards his Desoto opponent, then dropped into a defensive stance, bending his front leg slightly and bringing both of his arms up to chin level. He waited for his opponent to make the first move. He did not wait long.

A little taller than Dan, the yellow student of Desoto threw a downward punch towards Dan's face. Dan brought his hand, open palm up on the side of his opponent's wrist, pushing the intended punch high to hit only air. Meanwhile, Dan used his other arm to throw a punch of his own, hitting the taller man square in the chest, forcing him to take several steps backwards.

A few paces away Tyler, dressed in black, was shorter than his identically dressed opponent. Tyler twirled towards his opponent with a round kick, which the black Desotian jumped backwards to avoid. The Desotian moved forward and threw a kick of his own towards Tyler's left side. Tyler twisted, using the full length of his arm to stop the kick from connecting with his side. The two fighters turned and, for a moment, appeared to be engaged in a delicate dance as opposed to a fight. Then, Tyler threw a punch towards the Desoto student and the dance was broken.

Tyler's fist was caught at the wrist by the taller man and the student threw a punch towards Tyler which connected. The blow landed firmly on the side of Tyler's face, and a small amount of blood sprinkled over the rainbow swirls covering the mats below the competitor's feet. Tyler slipped towards the ground, reeling from the force of the blow, and the Desoto team member followed him to the ground, putting his weight into a movement against Tyler's right leg. A sickening crunch filled the room as Tyler's leg snapped in two. He gave a sharp cry of pain and his opponent abandoned him where he lay, turning his attention to the fight on his right.

Dan was holding his own against the other student, matching him move for move. His opponent threw a punch towards Dan's right side. Dan blocked the blow. Dan threw a punch of his own, moving his fist toward the Desotian's left side. His opponent blocked the move, pushing Dan's wrist back with his palm and moved his own fist toward Dan's face. Dan ducked, twisting his body around and slamming his elbow into the Desotian's chest, knocking the wind from his lungs. Dan slid to the ground and rolled right while his opponent fell towards the left.

As the uninjured party, Dan moved his feet almost instantly. His opponent was much slower, and Dan was on him before he could fully rise. Dan threw a kick that slammed into his opponent's left side, knocking him back towards the edge of the mat. Almost faster that Mary's eye could follow, Dan threw a second kick that connected with the left side of his opponent's face, snapping back his head and causing him to sprawl across the ground.

Engaged intently in his opponent, Dan barely saw the other Desotian entering the fight. He saw the kick heading towards his left side just in time to jump sideways. His body spun towards the ground and he twisted further, rolling across the ring and away from the new challenger. He rose near the edge of the rainbow mat and assumed his defensive stance against the higher-ranked opponent. Dan raised both arms near his face and stood still, letting his opponent come to him. The black ranking member of the Desoto temple closed the gap immediately.

The Desoto competitor half-kicked towards Dan's right side, then suddenly reversed direction, placing his foot back on the ground and kicking with his other leg in hopes of catching Dan off guard. Dan saw the reverse happen in time to avoid the movement, jumping towards his left. Dan blocked three more kicks, but he was tiring under the constant onslaught. Then, the other man came at Dan with a left kick. Dan turned right, and ran straight into the other man's fist.

    Dan lost consciousness in one, sweeping blow. Tournament officials moved into the ring and proceeded to carefully carry the three injured students out of the ring. The moment their bodies reached beyond the boundaries of the rainbow mat, small speckles of light began to surround them until they appeared covered in tiny droplets of sparkling water. The lights seemed to slide together and increased in intensity until the onlookers were forced to close their eyes against its brilliance.

    When the light faded, all four students stood tall before the on-looking crowd. Their broken bones were healed. The bruises had vanished. The blood on their clothes was gone. "Desoto wins the match and claims the title of champion!" The deep voice of the announcer resounded throughout the temple. The audience erupted with applause for the winning home team.

    "Well, that was an amazing fight!" the announcer's voice boomed. "But remember, don't go anywhere. Next up, the reds and pinks will fight for the grand championship. Then tomorrow, the puppy league takes the ring and let's not forget, the golden fight is still to come."

Chapter XI

Four hours later, Ameria watched from the stands seated next to her partner, Kyle, as her Kolosian teammate won the grand championship round. With no Kalian team in the round, the competition seemed less exciting than they normally were, with the two rival teams generally fighting it out to see which temple would have an extra team fighting for the title of Royal Champion. Desoto was once again the toughest challenger on the field, though Dektra gave both teams a run for their money.

At the end of the rounds though, it was Brandan and Rosa of Koloso going into the royal championship rounds with the higher-ranked gold and silver members of the temples. "It's probably not too late," Kyle said to his longtime partner. Ameria offered a small chuckle.

"Oh, yes, my sister would just love that. Have us join the fight at the last minute, finally put our skills to the test. Ruin our undefeated records just before the thirteenth tournament."

"No," Kyle corrected her, "you would only ruin one of your records."

Ameria laughed softly. "Do you really think that would be a fair round, without Marcus by her side?"

"Jace and I could always just stand back and watch."

"Without our dear parents here to watch." She sighed. "No, I would never hear the end of it, and I do mean never."

"Oh yes," Kyle said, giving Ameria his best crestfallen face, "they would harasses us until the end of time, wouldn't they?"

Ameria nodded with a grin.

"I do need to find your sister and her current partner though. I believe I promised Jace to teach him a couple of moves that he saw me do yesterday."

"Teaching a student from another temple?" Ameria conjured a shocked expression, raising her eyebrows and parting her lips slightly. "What would your captain think?"

"That Jace is not a threat to her or any she has trained." He paused, then added, "And to imply otherwise would result in me getting my ass kicked."

Ameria paused for a moment, then nodded. "Pretty much."

The two smiled as Kyle held out his arm. "May I escort you from the hall, my lady?"

Ameria nodded her consent and took his arm. They walked out of the training hall and down a series of long, marble hallways. They spent several minutes walking in circles before they found the other princess, sitting outside with Jace on the steps of a large, silver fountain. The bottom of the fountain was lined with the same red stones that were embedded in the temple, causing the fountain to appear as though it held a long stream of blood. It was one of the odd features that Ameria found both beautiful and disturbing.

"So Kyle!" Jace said a little too loudly as Kyle led Ameria over to the fountain of blood. "What do you say you and I sit this one out and let the sisters go at it instead?"

"Don't you start too!" Ameria said with a hint of humor in her voice.

To Ameria's surprise, Jace just grinned and looked at Kyle. "So, you couldn't convince her either?"

"No such luck, sorry Jace."

"Wait." Mary turned toward Jace. "You were both in on this? Jace has been trying to get me to ask you to join the rounds all day long!"

The two men gave identical grins. "We had to try," Kyle said.

Mary gently punched Jace's right arm. Jace's grin only got wider. "Just think, Mary. What happens if neither of you make it to the final round? Then we may never know which of you is better."

Mary and Ameria rolled their eyes simultaneously. Jace walked over to Kyle. "By the Gods, it's creepy when they do that."

"I know," Kyle replied. "They look so different, yet when they get annoyed with you at the same time..." He faked a shudder. "Must be a twin thing."

"All right guys, that's enough," Ameria said, but could not hide the laughter in her voice. "Now does Kyle really have some sword trick to show you, or was that just a ruse to gang up on us?"

"No way," Jace said. "The sword trick was really cool!"

"Indeed," Kyle said to his friend and rival. "Come with me. We will see if we can't find a side room where I can teach you."

"Do not keep him up all night, Kyle. He has a tournament to fight tomorrow."

"Yes, Mom," Kyle called back as the two men began walking back towards the hallway.

"Boys," Ameria said with a soft laugh. "What are we ever to do with them?"

Mary shrugged. "When you figure it out, please let me know."

"Sure thing," her sister said. Then she took a seat on the edge of the fountain. She dipped the fingertips of her left hand into the red water, and half-expected her fingers to turn as red as the water appeared. Yet when she lifted her hand, the water droplets clinging to her skin were as clear as crystals. "This water," Ameria said softly. "Still gets me every time."

"I know," Mary replied. "I've never really cared for this fountain. It's beautiful, yet..."

"Deadly," Ameria finished. "Kind of like life."

Ameria turned her dark green eyes to find her sister's sapphire gaze. "I forgot to ask, how are you, sister? I heard the men you fought today did not survive the fight."

"Two of them did not. The other got away." Her voice held a hint of something Mary could not place.

"Do you have something to tell me about this third man, sister?"

Ameria sat still for several moments and looked around. Realizing that they were moderately alone at the fountain, Ameria slid closer to her sister and leaned forward, lowering her voice to a whisper. "He was Kalian, Mary. I would bet my life on it. His skin was as pale as any royal, and he fought with a temple blade."

Mary's body visibly straightened. "Only members of the temples are allowed to carry the silver steel that runs through the veins of our swords."

"Yes, I know."

"You're saying that you fought a member of the temples today?"

"Mary, he matched me stroke for stroke, with a blade in my hand. Sliced all the way down my arm."

"With a blade?" Mary said, this time truly shocked. "I have seen you with a blade, sister. Yet I have never seen your equal."

"Something is very wrong, Mary. Very..."

"Excuse me, Princess Mariana, Princess Ameria," a voice interrupted the sisters' conversation. Both sisters turned to see several younger students, probably between the ages of five and nine, standing in front of the fountain steps.

"Yes." Mary turned towards the kids, placing an instant smile on her face.

"I know you're extremely busy," one of the little girls dressed in silver robes with golden hair shyly addressed the two champions. "But we were kind of wondering if...well if you might have...if you."

"If you would show us some moves!" a young, dark-headed boy asked excitedly.

Ameria smiled at the young boy. "What are your names?" she asked the children.

"I'm Rachel," the shy girl in silver said. "And this is Ryan." She motioned to the enthusiastic boy who had spoken. "We're gold and silver from the younger Desoto class. Master Latie said that it would be okay if we asked."

"And I'm Tanya!" said another young voice, this one from a young girl with light brown hair. "And this is Mary." She motioned to the girl with jet black hair.

"My parents said they named me after you," the girl said shyly.

"Oh, and what temple are you from?"

"Dektra," the golden-clothed girl said. "Tanya's my partner. Master Philip said it would be okay if we came and asked you as well."

"We would love to," Mary replied. "Let me see if we can find ourselves a room to borrow."

"Oh, Master Latie said we could use the golden training section of the temple," the blond girl spoke up. "Since we are all of gold and silver rank."

"Okay then," Ameria piped in with a smile. "Let's go."

Chapter XII

THE NEXT DAY, THE MATS were cleaned and the audience gathered once again as the Kalian Puppy League took to the ring. Mary was walking towards the main competition room when Coco suddenly appeared beside her. "Mary!" the puppy exclaimed.

"Hey, Coco," she replied, her spirits lifting at seeing her longtime friend. "Are you ready for your rounds?"

Coco gave a soft bark. "You seriously need to ask?" he responded with a ridiculous amount of confidence. "I am always ready, Mary! Now as to Mac…"

"Whatever he said is a lie!" The white puppy appeared beside them. "I am fully prepared to carry his tail all the way to the Royal Championship." He looked up at Mary mischievously. "Hey, do you think if I won enough championships, that I could fight in the thirteenth tournament. I'd make a great king!" He glanced at his longtime partner. "Just think, King Mac. You would have to do everything I say."

"Not even in your dreams!" Coco shot back. "Besides, Mac is a lame name for a king, no one would ever take you seriously. Now, King Coco…"

Mary could not help but laugh at the familiar bickering. "How about just focusing on this tournament today? Rev and Breeze are here, so you might actually have a bit of a challenge on your hands."

"Lose to a Kolosian?" Coco feigned a look of shock.

"The horror," Mac replied.

"High treason!"

"To the tournament!" Both puppies raced down the hall, Mary laughing behind them.

Half a day later, true to Mary's prediction, Coco and Mac faced off against Rev and Breeze in the Royal Championship round of the Desoto tournament. The four puppies were equally matched in size and strength. Rev, the golden member of Koloso's puppy league was a year older than Coco. His fur was a solid auburn color that held just a hint of red in the light of Kale's three suns.

His partner, Breeze, was a slender creature with white fur speckled with black dots. His tail was tipped black. His front paws were also solid black, though his back paws were white. Out of the past nine tournaments fought, Kale and

Koloso had come up against each other six times. Each team had won three, and this round promised to break the tie.

The fight lasted a mere ten minutes with the puppies on both sides barking, name calling, and wrestling each other towards the ground. After the puppies had left the ring, Coco and Mac took a bow and the crowd cheered their victory.

"Congratulations to Coco and Mac of Kale, Royal Champions and the winner of this year's Puppy League Desoto tournament!" The crowd erupted in cheers.

Coco rushed up the steps to where Mary was seated and jumped in her lap. "See," the puppy said proudly.

"I sure did," Mary replied, offering the puppy a hug. "Congrats, Coco." She looked down to see Mac standing at her feet.

"Told ya!" Mac said. "No Kolosian victories today!"

Coco jumped down beside his partner. "We showed them!" He looked up at Mary. "Your turn."

It would take at least an hour to reset the rainbow mats and another half hour to call all of the top competitors to the ring.

Mary went to find Jace. She found him in the hallway talking to Kyle. Kyle was leaning against the wall, his leg bent. Mary heard Kyle laughing as she approached. "Oh no," Mary said as she reached them. "What are you two plotting now?"

"Oh, nothing," Kyle replied with a grin. "Just discussing which one of us would look better with a crown on our head."

Mary rolled her eyes and sighed. "Not you too."

Kyle laughed. "A man can dream."

Mary motioned towards Jace. "Would you come with me for a moment?" she asked her partner.

"Yes," he replied.

Mary turned and walked down the hall while Jace and Kyle trailed after her. "Don't you have something better to do?" she asked the Kolosian.

"Nope, sure don't. I'm not fighting in this one, remember?"

Mary entered the room she had been given the night before and walked towards a small chest. It was gold, laced with several rubies along the front of the handle. She knelt and lifted the lid to reveal an interior lined with gold satin. She shuffled through several pieces of clothing, and then withdrew a silver cloth folded neatly and tied with a matching ribbon to hide the contents within.

She took the silver cloth in her hand and then moved towards Jace. "Something seems to be missing," she told him.

"My level of good looks," Kyle offered.

Jace looked around the room and back at Mary.

"You, Jace. Something is missing."

Jace's head tipped left, confused. "I...What is it?"

Mary shook her head, "I'm sorry Jace, there is just simply no way that you can fight alongside me."

"What?" Jace stammered. "I don't understand. You said we would..."

"I think what she means, Jace," Kyle interjected. "Is that you can't go fight a Royal Championship dressed like that. Could you imagine how embarrassed the other teams would feel?"

Jace turned his gaze to Mary. "I have a gift for you, Jace," she said, her face breaking into a wide smile as she held out the silver package.

Jace took the cloth from Mary and untied the ribbon. Silver garbs spilled into Jace's hand. He looked at Mary with wide eyes, his lips slightly parted. "This...this is silver."

"And today," Mary told Jace, "you are the silver member of Kale."

"She had it made just for you," Kyle told Jace from his spot near the door.

Jace was still standing with a stunned expression.

"You've earned it, Jace," Mary stated. "Marcus agreed that you should be allowed to wear the silver in his stead."

"I...wow, I... I won't let you down, Mary."

Mary's smile became even wider. "Just do your best, Jace."

"Congratulations, buddy." His Kolosian rival moved forward and wrapped one arm around the other man's shoulder in a half embrace.

"Thanks, Kyle," Jace replied.

"Now come on," Kyle said to Jace. "Let's get you into those new robes before you miss the tournament."

The two men turned together like old friends. Mary heard Jace's laughter as they walked down the hall. Then Mary moved forward and closed the door behind them before turning to change into her own golden competition robes.

When she was finished, she was wearing a long-sleeved golden top of satin, which hung loosely around her shoulders, allowing lots of flexibility, but was cinched tightly at the wrists, preventing the loose sleeves from getting in the way of the fight. She wore loose gold pants tied at the waist with a soft golden belt. The mark of Kale was on her left breast and her long black hair was pulled into a braid held by a thick, golden band. She wore thin slippers, but would remove them once she reached the mat, as competitors were required to go barefoot into competition rounds.

Mary walked into the hallway just in time for the announcement of the first draw. As the top four ranked teams would have an automatic bye in the first round, there would be at least four rounds before she had to actually enter the ring. Mary searched the crowd for Jace. She found him along the back wall, and by the look on his face, still laughing with his Kolosian counterpart. Mary walked towards them slowly, her eyes taking in the new silver garbs that now covered Jace from neck to ankle.

"They make a pretty pair, don't they?" Ameria appeared suddenly beside her.

Mary nodded. "They sure do."

"And one for each of us." Her sister laughed. "We should get a picture of this before he changes out of those silver robes. Something to commemorate the occasion"

Mary nodded in agreement. "Hopefully he will have a nice golden metal to commemorate it as well."

"We'll see," her sister said. "Don't forget, Rosa and Brandan advanced to fight in this tournament as well. Perhaps they will surprise us all."

Mary stopped walking and turned to look at the lists. "I don't know, Ameria. Their first round is against Postrema, so they probably won't have any problems, but after that they will be facing Dektra which means the second fight will be a difficult one to get past."

Ameria turned and looked for herself. "I guess we will have to wait and see."

The two continued across the room until they reached their partners. "Hey Kyle," Ameria addressed her partner. "Would you mind introducing me to your handsome friend, I don't think I've ever seen him before."

Jace laughed. "Hey, Ameria."

"Looking good in that silver, Jace." She eyed her sister. "I wonder how Marcus would look in red?"

"Not nearly as good as the two of you princesses did," Kyle interjected. "I saw the pictures of the royal dinner. You both looked gorgeous in those red gowns."

Both princesses turned their heads towards Kyle and gave him their best glare.

"If I were you, I would start running," Jace told his friend.

"I think you're right," Kyle replied before turning to run through the crowd.

"Are you ready to play with some real champions, Jace?"

"Absolutely!" he replied.

"Why don't we go grab a seat and watch a few rounds," Mary suggested.

"Okay, sure."

The four champions searched the rows until they managed to find seats together a few rows back. Only the bottom eight teams, including the Kolosian Grand Champions, would compete in the first set of rounds. Once the first set of four rounds was over, each of the winners would be paired with one of the top ranking teams who had received a bye in the first round. After that, the four winners of those rounds would advance to the semi-finals. The losers would fight each other for third place, while the winner would advance to the final round, and the Royal Championship.

True to Mary's prediction, Koloso's red and pink team defeated the lowest ranked of the gold and silver teams, from the Temple of Postrema, in the first round. Advancing with Koloso were the teams of Mortem, ranked sixth. Occidere, ranked seventh. And Proelium, who held the rank of eighth.

When the second level of lists went up, Mary turned towards her partner. "We're up against Occidere," she informed him. "It's not a bad pairing. Their silver student..." Mary searched her memory and then leaned closer to her partner. "Sorry, I can't remember his name. I don't compete against them very often."

"It's okay," Jace replied. "What about him?"

"He has a wicked right hook. Marcus once complained about getting hit on the left side of his face. He's a little on the bulky side and packs a lot of power into his punch. The trick is going to be to keep moving. If you can make him chase you, he will tire long before you do."

"All right, thanks," Jace said.

In the first round of the second level, Koloso faced off with the gold and silver members of Dektra. With Ameria and Kyle out of the tournament, Dektra was the third highest-ranking team behind Kale and Desoto. Koloso put on a good show, but eventually were defeated by the superior team from the Dektra temple.

A rough kick to the face sent Rosa unconscious to the floor and once she was down, Brandan did not stand a chance dealing with both competitors at once. A few well-placed kicks had Brandan holding his leg in multiple pieces and Dektra won the match. Then, Desoto advanced over Mortem in one of the shortest matches ever seen.

Knowing that her fight would be next, Mary left the stands and walked briskly down a series of hallways. The third door down held a small room, which was reserved for prayer. Lining the walls were small plaques holding the symbols for each of the thirteen Kalian temples. Mary walked to the one representing the Temple of Kale and knelt down before it. She offered a silent prayer to the temple Gods and then rose. She returned just in time to hear the announcer's call. "Occidere and Kale to the floor, please."

Mary walked towards the edge of the floor and waited as the announcer introduced the opposing team and then called the Kalians to the floor. "Fighting for Kale," the voice boomed, "Lord Jason, future Lord of Flos and the acting silver student of Kale, with Princess Mariana, Crown Princess of the realm, golden student of the Kalian temple and last year's undefeated champion." The crowd erupted into loud applause as Mary stepped into the ring. She took the customary bow in the direction of the opposing team, then turned toward the crowd and took a second bow directed at the many lords, ladies, and masters who sat among the spectators.

After rising, Mary drew a long breath and exhaled slowly. She slipped into a stance so familiar that it seemed a part of her. Keeping her arms close to her body, Mary raised her hands to protect her face. She then repositioned her legs so as to evenly distribute her weight between them. Beside her, Jace took a similar stance.

Mary heard the starting bell ring as though from a distance, and the fight began. Jace's opponent moved forward, closing the gap between them and launching an immediate round kick towards Jace's left side. Jace twirled around, twisting his body away from the oncoming kick. Jace managed to turn so fast that he grabbed the Occiderian student's leg while it was still in the air, and jerked his opponent's feet out from under him. Both men fell to the ground.

Mary took several steps towards her own golden ranked opponent. She threw her weight into a punch which the Occiderian student managed to block. Mary followed the punch with a fake kick to her opponent's right, then reversed and followed the kick immediately towards his left. Her shin connected with her opponent's side, and he collapsed to the floor. She grabbed his right arm as he fell. She twisted as hard as she could, dislocating his shoulder. He screamed in pain and Mary slammed her fist into the side of his head, knocking him out cold.

Nearby, Jace had managed to grapple his opponent's leg. Using both arms and his free leg, Jace twisted with all his might. A sickening crack was followed by a sharp scream and a single word, "Yield!"

Kyle ran into the ring and assisted Jace and then his injured opponent outside the ring. The healing lights worked their magic while the announcer's deep voice range out: "Kale advances!"

In the next round, Kevera advanced over Bellum, leaving Kale to face them in the semi-finals while in the other round, Dektra and Desoto faced off.

With a few creative moves in the kicking department, Desoto managed to defeat Dektra to enter the final round while in their own fight, Mary and Jace beat Kevera to also enter the final round.

Both top ranking teams received a brief respite while Kevera and Dektra fought for third. It was a very close match, but Dektra won. An hour recess was then called before the final match would commence. Jace, Mary, Kyle and Ameria entered a side training room and discussed some basic strategy concerning the upcoming last match. "The bottom line, Jace," Kyle offered, "is that the team from Desoto is very, very good. The best thing you can do is keep up the defense at all times, and stay away from Davis. Let Mary deal with him, no matter what."

Jace nodded. "I have no problem whatsoever with this plan."

Not long after, Mary was entering the ring against the gold and silver members of Desoto. Both parties took their respective bows, then the bell rang and the fight began. Davis' onslaught was relentless, and Mary found herself completely on the defensive. Deflecting her opponent's flurry of kicks, Mary extended an elbow in hopes of lessening their impact.

Jace was in a similar position, though Lance was not as fast as his golden partner. Jace had an easier time avoiding Lance's fists than Mary was having with Davis. When Davis tried to herd Mary towards Jace, Mary took a chance and launched a series of powerful kicks towards Davis, driving him back several steps and successfully adding more space between Davis and Jace.

Jace threw all of his weight into a deep spin, and was surprised when his leg hit its mark across the right side of Lance's face. Lance collapsed to the ground. Meanwhile, Mary continued her own advancement, switching from defensive to offensive. She ducked under a fist intended for her cheek and came up under Davis to land her fist against his face.

He reeled from the force, and Mary followed him, slamming her shoulder into his side with as much strength as she could muster. He spun, his footing beginning to slip. Mary grabbed his arm, and, twisting her body, she used the momentum to throw Davis to the ground.

Davis rolled away grimacing in pain. His shoulder was dislocated, but this did not stop him from struggling to regain a defensive stance. He jerked his own arm, popping it back into the socket, cursing as he did so. In too much pain to use his left arm, Davis backed towards the edge of the mat and waited for Mary to come to him.

Mary stepped forward and attempted to hit Davis on his injured side. Davis blocked the first blow, the second, third, but was unable to stop the fourth, which smacked hard against his cheek, throwing him off balance. This time he hit the ground, unable to use his injured arm to balance himself. Mary thrust her knee against Davis' hip, pressing her full weight upon him, effectively rendering his legs as useless as his injured arm.

"Do you yield?" she asked him.

"Would you?"

Mary smiled slightly, "No, I would not," she replied, before proceeding to bring her fist down against the point of his jaw, fracturing it. A few moments later, Davis succumbed to the pain, losing consciousness. When Mary finally rose, it was to find Jace standing over his own opponent, who was lying at his feet. She paused, surprised at Jace's success.

The crowd rose to its feet. They cheered, yelled, applauded. "Kale, Kale, Kale," came the chant from the left side of the crowd. Mary walked over to where her partner stood and pointed to him, before grabbing Jace's arm and raising it towards the sky. The chant quickly changed to "Jace, Jace, Jace!"

"Congratulations, my friend," Mary told her silver partner. "You are now a Royal Champion."

Kyle appeared beside Jace, draping an arm around him in celebration. "Couldn't have done it much better myself."

"Wow," Ameria added, making her way towards them. "Only way that fight could have been better is if you were Kolosian. Any interest in switching temples?"

Mary punched her sister lightly on the shoulder. "Get away from my partner," she said with a smile.

As soon as the announcers were able to get the crowd back under control, medals were handed out and Jace received his first golden award as a Royal and Tournament Champion. The foursome decided that they would stay at the Temple of Desoto for the night and then head out together the following morning. "Just in case we encounter any more trouble on the road," Kyle said.

"Yes," Mary replied. "Sounds like a good idea to me."

Chapter XIII

A FEW DAYS AFTER RETURNING to the Temple of Kale, the students were called by Master Leo to the center room for a meeting. Clothed in a golden robe that hid his rainbow silks beneath, Master Leo stood taller than his students. His medium length brown hair was beginning to turn silver around the edges. Somehow, the silver strands seemed to make the revered master look even more distinguished than he had been the first time Mary had met him, nearly fifteen years earlier.

"This is a little last minute," the master addressed his students. "But the High Lord of Usqub is throwing a charity tournament to help raise funds for things such as education and medical facilities. They have asked if the temples would mind sending a few fighters to compete in the tournament alongside some trained, non-temple students."

A moment of silence filled the room and then Katalin asked, "Master Leo, if they are going to put temple students with non-temple students, then how will they pair the matches?"

"The pairings will be randomized," Master Leo replied. "Normally, I would be hesitant to allow any of you to compete outside of the temples during a tournament season, but this is for a good cause. I thought a few of you might be willing to help them out."

"What are the differences between the temple rounds and non-temple rounds?" Sam, clothed in dark blue, asked from the back section of the room.

"What do you mean by non-temple?" Lara chimed in.

"Well," Leo replied, "by non-temple, I mean students who pursued their training by alternative means." He cleared his throat. "The first and most important change that you must abide by is that the fighting must be toned down. The healing powers of the temples do not exist in the non-temples, therefore when they fight, they only count the hits landed on a points-based system. Things such as breaking bones and fighting until the other is completely unconscious is frowned upon."

"Oh," Sara, Sam's partner, said from beside him. "Well, I guess I could deal with that. Would be nice to fight a round that didn't end in agonizing pain for one or more parties involved."

"Yeah," Katalin said. "I'd be up for a fight like that."

"You are such..." Sam searched for the words. "Girls."

"Why thank you," Sara replied. "And you are such a ... boy."

Katalin laughed softly. "I'll fight with you, Sara; if you like."

"That would be great." Sara turned towards Master Leo. "That is, if it's okay with you, master."

Leo nodded in her direction. "I have no problem with the pairing. The other thing I should mention..." He turned his head to focus his eyes on Mary. "The temple masters have agreed that the golden students should not be allowed to compete. We think it would be unfair to the non-temple students to pair them against our best."

Mary shrugged. "I don't mind, master."

"What about silver?" Marcus asked.

"You may compete if you wish, and if you can find someone willing to compete with you."

"I will!" Jace said enthusiastically. "I fought with Mary. I'd love to try fighting with Marcus as well."

Master Leo nodded. "Okay then, the four of you will represent Kale in the charity tournament."

The following week, the four temple students, along with Mary, saddled their horses and rode together to Usqub, which was far in the north, past the Temple of Occidere, where they stayed the night. Luckily, the suns shone brightly on both days of the ride, with only an occasional cloud in the otherwise clear purple sky. Mary and Jace raced down the slopes of the mountains, leaving the rest of the group barely in sight.

Sherwyn raced with the wind as they soared through valleys and over fields, down the mountains slopes and up the rocky cliffs as if he was running without his feet touching the ground. "I love riding," Mary said when they reached the top of a high hill. "What do you say we pause and wait for the others?"

"Sure," Jace said, pulling on his reins and moving his mount closer to Sherwyn's left side. "It is so beautiful up here," he commented, motioning towards the edge of the cliff that they were staring out over.

"I know," Mary replied softly. Several moments of silence followed as the two Kalians gazed into the horizon. The sky was a beautiful, soft purple and all three suns blazed high in the sky. A long lazy river curved its way through the valley below, cutting its way through a series of large trees with green bark and multicolored leaves of brilliant yellow, bright pink, and tasteful orange. The trees were surrounded by fields of flowers in dark reds and deep blues. Mary took a slow breath to inhale the fresh mountain air, flavored with a hint of flowers.

Mary turned towards Jace. "Do you want to know a secret, Jace?"

"Sure," Jace replied.

"Sometimes I think about taking my horse and my sword and just disappearing into these mountains. Fighting my way through these hills without a care in the world. No more tournaments, no more pressure, no more responsibilities." Mary closed her eyes and could almost see it. Riding through the towns, protecting the small villages from the thugs that terrorized them.

Riding all the way to the forbidden part of the Dark Forests where many had braved, yet none had ever returned.

"That doesn't surprise me, Mary," Jace responded. "I was born the son of a High Lord, but even that is not enough to give me even an image of the weight that must have been placed upon your shoulders from the moment you drew your first breath."

Mary continued to stare out into the horizon. "I never asked to be queen," she whispered back in a haunted tone.

"Mary," Jace said. "You can't possibly be forced to marry the winner of some..."

"I swore an oath, Jace."

"Screw your oath!" Mary had never heard so much anger in his voice. "It was unfair of them, they forced it upon you. You can't possibly want to..."

Mary turned and gave Jace the full weight of her gaze. "Jace." She worked to keep her voice soft and calm. "What are you trying to tell me?"

Jace met her gaze, and asked in a strangled voice, "Don't you feel...anything?"

Mary felt herself pressing her lips tightly together. She searched for the words that had been there a moment ago, but they seemed to have fled at the sound of Jace's voice.

"Jace," Mary said softly. "I don't want you in the final tournament."

"Why? I did well, very well."

"Yes, Jace, you did. But Jace," she shook her head attempting to form coherent thoughts. "Jace," she tried again. "Kyle was not in that tournament. Marcus was not in that tournament. My sister, four members of the actual Defendant Team and twelve years of other gold and silver champions will be competing at the Temple of Ziazan." She paused and searched his gaze again, leaning back slightly in her saddle. "I am better than you," Mary told him. "And for all I know, my sister might be better than I am."

"That's not true!" Jace responded before Mary cut him off.

"You don't know that, Jace. No one knows and let me tell you something else: her partner is better than you. I know that he seems nice. I know that he has taken you under his wing in more ways than one, but Jace, the next time he is in a ring, I want you to watch him. Generally people are so intent on watching my sister that they tend to miss just how good he is. If I was asked to place a bet between Kyle and Marcus..." Mary paused. She spoke her next words slowly in hopes of better communicating their severity. "I just might bet on Kyle."

Jace's eyes bore into Mary's, then looked down. It took a few moments for Mary to realize that he was fighting back tears. "Jace," Mary's voice softened.

"I love you, Mary," Jace uttered the forbidden words. "I...I love you. I am the son of a High Lord, my family is wealthy, and I am from the same temple as you. I have even proven myself enough to fight by your side. I want to marry you."

Tears filled Mary's eyes, and she let Jace see them. "Jace," she said. "I...I'm a princess. I'm the future qu..." She had to pause to draw breath. "I am not allowed to love you."

"But you are not saying that you don't?"

Mary slid out of her saddle and dismounted in a single, gliding motion. She walked closer to the edge of the cliff.

"I am a princess, Jason.," She used his full name. "An heir of Kale must sit upon the throne."

"You don't want to be queen, Mary. And your sister would take the throne in a heartbeat."

"Jason," she said painfully. "Don't force me to break both our hearts..." Her tone faded to a mere whisper on the wind. "If I could love someone, I would love you. But I am of the royal Kalian bloodline, and love, like freedom, like choice, is forbidden." She turned to face him. "Please, Jason. Can't you see?" The two stood on the edge of the cliff, lost in a sea of confusion.

"Hey, you two," Marcus' voice interrupted their moment.

"Nice of you two to wait for us," Katalin said. "We figured at the pace you were going you might have been at the temple already."

"Nope," Jace replied, forcing his voice to a cheerful pitch. "Decided to wait on you slowpokes."

"Well, we're here, so what do you say that we move on, preferably together this time."

Jace turned his horse back on the trail and began riding in a slow trot, before suddenly moving his mount back into a run. "We're only about twenty minutes away," Jace called. "Last one there is a Kolosian!"

Marcus laughed and urged his mount into a full run, catching up to Jace and racing towards an open field. Mary slid back into the saddle and gave chase, hoping the rush of the wind would hide her tears.

When they reached the town where they were to compete, they barely had time to unsaddle their horses and change before they were ushered off to a dinner being held for the competitors. By the time they got back to the allocated rooms, Mary was too tired to try and finish her conversation with Jace. The ride home would be a long one, and Mary figured that she would have optimal time to continue the conversation on the way back to the Temple of Kale.

The next day the tournament began. The five Kalian students spent the first few rounds studying the rules and watching how the students competed. "It appears that each time one team hits someone from another team, they gain a point," Marcus explained. "And when one team reaches a total of five points, that team wins the round."

Mary nodded in agreement. "Don't aim for the face either," Mary cautioned. "People are losing points for doing so."

Since Mary was not competing and did not want her presence to detract from the competitors, she had reluctantly abandoned her normal gold attire, and instead had donned a long pair of black slacks and a long-sleeved black shirt. She tucked her golden necklace beneath her shirt and pulled her hair back with a thin black band.

When Jace and Marcus were called down to the mats, the crowd roared with cheers and applause. Mary doubted that many of the spectators had ever seen a tournament with real Temple Champions. Jace and Marcus flew through the rounds, working hard to abide by the non-temple rules, though Marcus did lose a point or two when he misjudged the speed of his opponent and ended up smacking him in the face, and another when he used what the officials called "unnecessary force."

Katalin and Sara fought in four rounds throughout the day, while Marcus and Jace fought five. It was nearing the end of the day and all the competitors were told that there would be only two more rounds, and if anyone wanted their names withdrawn, they had only to ask.

Mary walked up to Jace. "What do you say we get out of here?" She looked around the room, expecting to see some of the spectators exit with the departure of several of the tournament teams, yet no one was moving. That seemed odd...

Mary glanced around the arena. She had a strange feeling in the pit of her stomach. Her eyes searched the room. Was someone watching her? Without any mark of her status, no one should have been watching. She gave the room a full sweep, but there were far too many people.

"Actually, Mary, we were going to stay, just in case we get called, though I doubt we will."

"I'm not sure that is a good idea, Jace. Perhaps we should just get out of here."

Jace tilted his head in her direction. "Why? Did something happen?"

"No," Mary replied, "but..." She glanced at the list of the competing teams. "Something seems off."

Jace rolled his eyes. "It is fine, Mary. One more round, random pairing and then we are out of here." He offered a slight smile.

"Okay," Mary replied quickly. Jace turned and walked back toward the ring. Mary glanced at the board again. Due to its unofficial status, the number of entries was far higher than a normal tournament, where only the qualified would have been allowed to compete. With the board cluttered and the team assignments randomized, Mary was unable to shift through the masses of names. She returned to her seat, trying to rid herself of the uneasiness she was feeling.

The first round called was a match between a local, non-temple student team and the blue and green students of Kevera. In a surprise upset, the non-temple students actually won the match against the higher-ranked temple students.

Mary was seated on the end of the second row when the announcer's voice cut through the crowd. "The silver and red team of Kale." Jace walked towards the edge of the ring with Marcus close behind him. He turned and offered Mary a small smile from across the room.

Then the announcer said the unthinkable. "Red and Silver of Kale vs. Red and Silver of Koloso." Mary's body tensed. Jace jerked his head to meet her gaze. Mary felt as though her blood had literally turned to ice. She rose from her seat and walked quickly towards the judge's table. She did not recognize any of the local men seated behind it. Mary cleared her throat and said, "Excuse me, sir."

"Yes?" The man seemed short in stature. His eyes were an ordinary brown and his face held no distinguishable characteristics.

"Sir," Mary addressed him. "This is meant to be a randomly drawn match, is it not? Do you really expect anyone to believe that you just happened to 'randomly' draw the top Kale and top Koloso teams to fight each other?"

A moment of silence followed before the man replied, "I assure you, my lady, pure coincidence."

Mary exhaled loudly. "We both know that is not true. You cannot do this. It's a publicity stunt. It's stupid, and if one of the champions were to be injured away from an actual temple, it would be your head."

"Sit down, ma'am," the short man replied angrily. "Or I will have you escorted out."

Mary turned from the table and walked towards Kale's side of the ring. Jason walked towards her. "I can end this round with a few well-placed words," Mary stated with an edge of anger penetrating through her usually cool voice. "We shouldn't do this. Neither Master Leo nor Master Jiro would approve."

"Mary," Jace replied, "look at the crowd. I'm not sure they would ever forgive us if we refuse to fight. I talked to Kyle. He said he'd be willing to go three circles then call a draw. The crowd gets a show and we don't utterly exhaust ourselves in the process. Then you and I will be out of here."

Jace beamed a smile. Mary looked at him uncertainly. "I don't like this, Jason." She again used the long form of his name.

"Come on, Mary. You said it yourself: I will never get the chance to face Kyle in a real match. Let me, just this once, with all these extra rules. Three rounds, five points or not, I promise."

Mary gritted her teeth, fighting the urge to call the whole thing off. Then she drew a long, slow breath. "Let me be very, very clear on this, Jace. If you do this, you do not, absolutely do not fight Kyle. You leave him to Marcus."

"But, Mary..."

"No buts, Jason. You will stay away from Kyle, or you will not fight."

"We're friends. It's just a little fun."

"I know you're friends, Jace. But you will stay away from him nonetheless. Is that understood? I want to hear you say that this is understood."

A heartbeat of silence passed between them when Jace finally said, "Okay, Mary, I'll stay away from Kyle."

Jace then seemed to shake himself and planted a smile on his face. "I'll be fine, Mary," he assured the princess. "Now go grab a seat and watch me and Marcus show Koloso why they are only ranked second."

Mary turned from her friend and did as he bid, reclaiming her seat on the end of the second row in the spectator's arena.

The two teams lined up face to face in the center of the ring and took their traditional bows. Then a mechanical bell was rung and the four champions moved into a standing position as the match between the two rival teams began.

The competitors faced off as Mary had instructed: red to red and silver to silver. Both members of the Kolosian team jumped into immediate action, launching left kicks faster than the untrained eye could follow. Yet instead of hitting their intended targets, the Kolosians hit only air. Jace threw a kick of his own to his opponent's right side and his foot landed perfectly on Brandan's ribcage. He twisted slightly from the blow, then managed to use the movement to his advantage by stepping backwards into the kick and punched Jace in the upper chest.

To Jace's right, Marcus continued to avoid Kyle's powerful series of kicks by jumping over, under and turning to the side of Kyle's never ending onslaught. It seemed that he would just attempt to avoid the fight through the entire round when suddenly, Marcus turned, moving not away from, but into Kyle's movement.

As Marcus moved past Kyle's dangerous leg, he twisted his body, using one arm to push down on Kyle's leg while the other threw a solid punch flat against Kyle's chest. As Kyle fell towards the ground, he reached out his arm, hitting Marcus just below the knee. However, the punch was not well-planned and did not have enough force to do anything other than throw Marcus off balance. Both Kyle and Marcus fell to the ground, Kyle on his stomach and Marcus flat on his back. Despite this, it was only seconds before both men had risen to their feet and the onslaught continued.

Meanwhile, Jace was doing more than his part at keeping Kyle's partner at bay, trading step for step with his Kolosian counterpart. A nicely twisted round kick sent Brandan spiraling to the ground, but he recovered before Jace had a chance to use the fall to his advantage. As the fighting began to increase in speed and ferocity, Mary began to wonder if she should have simply called off the round.

Jace managed to again knock down his opponent with a left kick right punch combination to Brandan's ribcage. Jace moved forward to take advantage of Brandan's unfortunate position and threw a punch aimed right at his opponent's upper chest, when seemingly out of nowhere, Kyle jumped across the ring and blocked the punch.

Momentarily surprised, Jace took several steps back. Marcus moved across the ring, following Kyle, while Kyle's partner recovered and suddenly moved between the two silver champions. Marcus engaged Brandan while Kyle aligned himself against Jace. Kyle threw a left punch in Jace's direction, which Jace deflected with the back of his right arm, pushing Kyle's fist safely aside. Jace threw a matching punch of his own, which Kyle stopped only a split second before it would have connected with his left shoulder. Jace threw a round kick towards Kyle's left side which Kyle moved to block. Jace then dropped his foot at the last moment, transferring his weight to his left foot while using the momentum of his movement to move quickly into a right kick, which connected with Kyle's upper ribcage, sending him to the ground.

Mary moved from her seat and tried to call off the round, but her voice was lost in the sea of cheers rising from the crowd. Jace moved in on his higher-ranked opponent and Mary's unease was suddenly replaced with a sense of pride. Jace threw a second punch and once again hit Kyle. Kyle took several steps back and launched a hard kick towards Jace's left side with a speed more worthy of a temple round than this unofficial bout. Jace blocked the first kick, but not the one that followed. Kyle's leg connected solidly with the side of Jace's head.

Jace's body collided with the ground. His head struck the hard mat beneath him with ferocious force. Several moments passed. Jace did not move. The other three fighters moved towards him. Mary raced down the stairs. When she reached the floor, she ran towards her friend. He wasn't breathing.

"Jace!" Mary called frantically sliding to her knees. It was in that instant, as Mary's hand touched the chest of her childhood friend that Mary knew. He would never again draw breath.

"Get the healers!" someone shouted from the crowd behind her. Tears streamed uncontrollably down Mary's face as her fingers traced their way up Jason's body. When she touched his head, blood covered her hand from his displaced skull. No healer, not even a Kalian one, could help him now. "Jason," Mary whispered. "Oh, Jace."

"Jace!" Kyle called out, leaning down to cradle his neck. "Gods, Jace, please." Kyle stood and again yelled for the healers.

Anger rose through Mary like ocean waves ripping through sand on the eve of the coming storm. She rose from the shell that only moments before had held her friend. She turned into a kick which landed squarely in Kyle's chest. The crowd around them raced back as the silver Kolosian struggled to regain his feet.

"Mary," Kyle pleaded. "Please, Mary, it was an accident."

"You killed him!" Mary screamed.

"Mary, please..."

Mary would have none of it. She spun in a sideways kick, connecting firmly with Kyle's left side. His body flew across the room. Mary followed Kyle, reaching him just as he regained his footing. She threw another kick to his left side. Kyle tried to block her, but was no match for her speed and ferocity. Mary raised Kyle's left arm with her own, allowing her next kick to slam into his body. He twisted from the force and threw a punch toward Mary's left.

Mary was faster. He hit only air. He threw three kicks her way; none of them so much as grazed the golden student of Kale as she maneuvered around and through Kyle's continuous movements effortlessly. Mary's leg again slammed into his left side.

Mary followed her kick with another. Kyle tried desperately to block Mary's movement, but once again failed to do so. Fellow team members watched in horror, unwilling to risk turning Mary's wrath upon themselves. When she finally threw Kyle completely to the ground, she followed him and laid in a series of blows with such ferocity that he was unable to lift a finger in his defense.

A hand finally touched Mary's shoulder. She shifted her weight into a backwards punch, trying to thwart Kyle's would-be rescuer. The punch was blocked and Mary was pulled away from Kyle. In an increasing fit of rage, Mary turned to throw yet another punch, then found her hand held firmly in her sister's grasp.

"Mary!" Ameria said. "Mary, please: stop this."

"No!" Mary screamed jerking her hand from her sister's grasp. "It was supposed to be an exhibition round. He's silver, Jace was red! What kind of honor is that? He has no honor. He killed him." Mary moved closer to Kyle and Ameria placed herself firmly between the two champions.

"It was an accident, Mary. You know it was an accident. Please, Mary."

"No!" Mary threw a kick, which her sister leaped to avoid. Instinct took over and Ameria grabbed Mary's right leg and twisted, driving Mary to the ground.

Ameria followed her sister, placing a knee down upon her in an attempt to pin Mary to the ground. Mary kicked with her free leg, forcing Ameria's body to topple to the side. Ameria rolled to the right while Mary scrambled to her feet. A moment later, her sister had recovered as well. The two sisters circled each other, matching step for step and blow for blow.

Ameria threw a forceful punch with her left arm. Mary blocked it a few inches from the right side of her face. Moments later, Ameria's fist landed solidly against Mary's side.

Her breath exploded in a gasp of pain. As Mary slipped toward the ground, she managed to catch Ameria's leg with her own, sending both champions to the mat in a tangled heap.

A single breath was all it took for both to regain their footing and the two sisters further engaged. Ameria threw three quick punches which Mary easily blocked. Mary took a step back, separating herself from her sister's onslaught before launching a front kick that threw Ameria back several feet. Mary attempted to close in on her sister when suddenly the Silver Defendant, Lady Rebecca, stepped between them.

"Mary!" the Silver Defendant demanded. "You will cease this fight. No good will come of it."

"No good?" Mary demanded. "No good! Putting that creature where he belongs will bring no good?" She motioned to where Kyle still lay motionless on the side of the ring. "I am treating that coward as he deserves!" Her voice receded in volume, though not in anger.

"Princess Mariana!" Lady Rebecca addressed her. "Fighting your sister will not change what has happened." Mary closed her eyes and attempted to breathe through her anguish. When she opened her eyes, more defendants were in the ring. Mary turned slowly and walked towards the table where the tournament judges still sat.

"This man," she said in a voice so tight it was almost a growl, "set the fight as a cheap publicity stunt, in violation of tournament rules, despite being warned of the consequences by his Crown Princess. I want him taken to the Palace Towers."

"Mary," the Silver Defendant replied. "This won't help…"

"He pulled a stunt that resulted in the death of a Royal Champion of Kale. I want him taken to the tower."

"Mary," Rebecca, the Silver Defendant, said in a soft voice. "You need to come with me and calm yourself."

"No!" Mary turned to face Rebecca. "You have no right to call me that, defendant. I am the Crown Princess of Kale, heir to the throne of this kingdom both in royal blood and by temple law. I am giving you an order! Take this man to the towers, now!" She turned her gaze back towards the table. "Take them all. Lock them in the tower of the palace. Do it, or I will have you locked up in their place."

A stunned silence followed as all watched, waiting to see if the defendants would obey her commands. Then, Lady Rebecca motioned to two of her teammates who moved forward and began to carry out the princesses' orders. The rest of the room stood in a profound silence, most still attempting to understand the events which had just transpired.

"Kyle, too," Mary said.

"What?"

"For the murder of a Kalian Royal Champion."

"Mary," Ameria moved quickly to her sister's side. "You are not thinking rationally. This was an accident. We all know the risk of stepping into these fights."

"And if it was Kyle?" Mary asked. "If it was your partner lying dead? Killed by Marcus? Would you think it was rational then, Ameria?"

Ameria took a small step back, holding her sister's intense gaze and finally stating, "Take Kyle to the tower. We will sort this out later."

With the order of the second princess, the defendants moved quickly. The tournament officials were gathered to be escorted to the palace tower.

In all the commotion, no one noted the additional presence of the creature that stood in the far corner of the room. Wearing a black cloak that covered all but his eyes, any who might have noticed the figure from afar would have thought it was just another of the numerous temple puppies who came to cheer their teammates.

Had one taken a closer look, they would have seen that there was something strange about this creature; something that would have sliced through even the bravest of hearts when gazing into its dark, glowing eyes. The creature's gaze was filled with a hint of glee at the events that had transpired. He had given up on the young Kalian many years ago, but now he was not so sure. His master would be most pleased.

Chapter XIV

MARY RODE HARD TO THE Temple of Bellum, from which she was transported magically to her home temple on the arm of Lady Rebecca. Once standing in the Temple of Kale, she walked numbly towards the private chambers of the high priest. Lady Rebecca followed behind her. Louis was waiting for them, and Mary fell to her knees as she entered the room.

"Mary," the high priest addressed the princess. "I am glad you are here. I am afraid I have some bad news."

"Lord Louis," Lady Rebecca interrupted. "Perhaps it should wait..."

"I'm afraid it cannot," Louis replied. "I am afraid this concerns you as well."

"What has happened?" Rebecca inquired.

"Mary," the high priest said gently. "Look at me." Mary raised her head slowly to meet his gaze from her kneeling position.

"Mary, I am honestly not sure how to tell you this," he drew a deep breath. "After you and your sister encountered trouble on the road to Desoto, Lord Edward sent patrols throughout the kingdoms in search of the man your sister described from her fight. Last week, we received a call from the Temple of Critous, claiming that a man who matched the description had been spotted in a neighboring village. Master Edward took a small group of defendants in search of the man."

"What happened?" The air seemed tight in Mary's chest.

"They rode out from the Temple of Critous to several nearby towns, two of which claimed to have seen the man. They split up when they reached the edge of the Dark Mountains, in order to cover more ground."

Louis shook his head. "They were ambushed, princess. The two riders with Master Edward were ripped from their horses. They were attacked by a pair of men. Only one of them actually survived to return to the temple."

"Master Edward?" Lady Rebecca asked while Mary remained silent, a sense of dread continued to make it difficult for her to draw steady breath.

"He fought the man he had been chasing. The same man, we believe that your sister faced off with. He..." Louis' words trailed off.

"No," Mary whispered. "Please, not Edward."

"Princess Mariana, Lady Rebecca." The high priest's voice was soft. "I am sorry, very sorry to tell you that Edward was killed in the Dark Mountains earlier today. He was killed in single combat."

Fresh tears flowed from Mary's eyes. She did not bother to wipe them away.

"My ladies," the high priest addressed them. "He died bravely, as a defendant should and will be mourned by the temples and commons alike."

"What happened with the survivor?" Rebecca asked. Her voice was tight and unsteady.

"When the survivor arrived back at the Temple of Critous, a group of defendants reentered the mountains. They recovered Lord Edwards' body, but have found no trace of the man who killed him."

The high priest looked solemnly at the Silver Defendant. "I will work towards making funeral arrangements, and make sure that the king and Prince Eadmund are made aware of the deaths."

"Jace's too." Mary's voice sounded horse.

"What?"

"There was a fight." Mary's voice came in broken pieces. "He died in the ring. He...I should have stopped it. I knew... Kyle killed him."

Louis fell silent, the horror of this news washing over him slowly. Lady Rebecca spoke, filling him in on the details of the fight. When Rebecca was finished, Louis drew a deep breath and addressed the Silver Defendant.

"Have his body brought here as well. The fallen defendants, along with Jason, will be honored together. Their bodies burned within the same funeral pier, so that they may arrive together at the gates of the Rainbow Halls."

"It will be done," Lady Rebecca stated.

"And for the time being, Lady Rebecca," Louis addressed the Silver Defendant, "I appoint you leader of the defendants, until the ceremony of succession can be performed." Louis turned his attention back to the princess.

"It was my fault," Mary said through bitter tears. "I let him go into that round. I let him die."

"Mary, he was a student of this temple and the Gods often call Champions to their side sooner than we would like. It is an honor that we train, live, and eventually die for. His fate was in the hands of the Gods, and now he will sit within their sacred halls. Go to your teammates, Mariana. Find solace in them. They will need you now both for your strength and leadership." Mary rose silently from her kneeling position and exited the room without a sound. Once the door was completely closed, Louis turned back to the Silver Defendant. "What is it, my lady? Speak."

"My Lord Louis," the defendant replied. "It's...I am not sure how to... and in the middle of all that has happened, this concern seems minor in comparison."

"Just tell me."

"I was afraid, my lord."

Louis looked up in confusion. "Afraid of what?"

"To get between them."

"What?"

"The twins, my lord. The twins were...amazing, terrifying. Mariana, she, she made Kyle look like an untrained child. She defeated one of the top five students in the land and she did it without even trying. Then when her sister stepped in... I haven't seen a fight like that since their father faced Leo and even then, if the sisters had been allowed to continue their fight, they might have put even Leo's fight to shame. I was afraid to get between them. They backed down when I addressed them, but if they had not..." Rebecca's eyes looked haunted. "I don't know if there is anyone, not even Leo, who could have stopped that fight."

The high priest looked up at Lady Rebecca intently. "Mary has always shown potential to reach the level of skill of which you speak, and she is undefeated in the temple fights." Louis tilted his head slightly. "But better than her master, she has never been."

"Yes," Rebecca answered. "But tell me this, my lord, has she ever truly fought to the peak of her ability against an opponent whose skill was equal to her own? I am not speaking about practice rounds where the masters enter only to teach, but a true fight where the competition requires her to be at more than her very best?"

Louis walked closer to the Silver Defendant as she said, "My Lord, she could be the next Golden Defendant. She could be the Golden Defendant, Champion of the Thirteenth Tournament, and the Kalian Queen. Her power would be..."

"Unlimited," the high priest finished for her.

Chapter XV

Mount Ziazan was the tallest peak in the entirety of the Rainbow Mountains. Situated directly between the Temples of Kale and Koloso, the mountain peak stood as the resting place for all those who bravely gave their lives in service to the temple Gods. It was holy ground, steeped in the spirits of the great masters who had come before and the whispers of those yet to come.

The mountain was a treacherous road, and only the best of the temple horses were trusted to carry their riders across the icy slopes near the top of the mountain. Mary rode silently beside Marcus, each on a golden mount. It was a slow ride taken in complete silence, as though even the creatures of the mountains mourned for the fallen champions. The horses walked slowly, their hearts as heavy as those of the riders they carried.

It was summer, so the ice had receded for most of the trip. The sky above them was a soft lavender with only a few sparse clouds strewn throughout the otherwise clear sky. The brilliance of all three of the kingdom's suns cascaded down upon Mary. Yet, even the intense, unobstructed light could not penetrate the ice that had formed firmly around Mary's heart.

Mary and Marcus rode near the front of the long procession. Behind them came a line of carriages escorting members from every temple and high ranking family found within the Kalian Kingdoms. They had come from near and far to mourn the passing of the universally beloved Golden Defendant.

Those who had elected to ride on horseback included Master Latie of Desato, and Master Philip of Dektra, who had both served alongside Edward on the defense team. Also on horseback was Master Jiro, the temple leader of Koloso, on a silver stallion.

Members of the Defendant Team were scattered throughout the crowd, each clearly marked by the long black cloak they wore over their colored defendant robes as a sign of mourning for their lost leader.

When the group reached the top of the mountain, they were hailed by a large, marble building. It was a tall, domed structure. Several members of the temples, including Master Louis and Master Leo, had arrived the day before to prepare for the funeral. The temple was a large structure of white marble at the end of a long dirt road. Banners from each of the thirteen temples lined the path leading to its outer doors.

As Mary reached the wide marble steps, she pulled Sherwyn to a stop. A young man dressed in rainbow robes emerged from the left side of the building and took the reins as Mary dismounted. "Welcome to the Temple of the Temple Gods, Golden Champion of Kale," the young man said with a soft bow. "I will take your horse to our stables."

"Thank you," Mary replied in a voice that failed to hide her weariness. The young boy waited for Marcus to dismount and then led both horses towards the far side of the mountain, where Mary knew a warm stable awaited.

The Temple of the Gods towered above the young champions. At the center of the Rainbow Mountains, the temple served strictly as a religious structure. Every year, students from other temples were chosen to serve a year at this sacred place, learning the history of the temple Gods and respect for the ways of the temple masters. Mary had spent her fifteenth year serving in the rainbow robes, while her sister had served a year later. Both sisters had achieved their undefeated status while the other had served.

Mary did not walk into the marble building, but instead stepped towards the right, walking slowly around the temple to the large structure beyond. Made of matching white marble, the structure stood apart from the rest of the temple.

A set of forty stairs stood on either side of the open aired building. Sitting in the center of the high marble floor at the top of the steps stood a cradle of wood and golden straw. The bodies of Lord Edward of Desato and Jason of Kale lay side by side in the center of the wooden funeral pyre.

Mary walked slowly until she reached the edge of the marble and then ascended the steps of the pyre. When she reached the top, she gave a low bow. Rising, Mary walked towards Jace's final resting place. He was wrapped in the golden cloaks of the Temple of Kale. Across his chest lay a large red cloth, signifying his rank. His hands clasped his long, silver sword with a black handle set with two large red stones on either side. Across from him lay Lord Edward, wrapped in red robes for the Temple of Desato, with a large golden cloth signifying his rank as the Golden Defendant across his chest. Like Jace, Edward's hands lay clutched around a silver and gold sword though, Mary noted, it was not the sword the defendant normally carried.

Tears filled Mary's eyes as she knelt beside their wooden grave. The marble floor lay before her, scarred by flames of heroes past. "I'm sorry, Jason," she whispered. Mary reached up and unclasped the thin golden chain from around her neck and placed it gently around Jason. "So the Gods will greet you as royalty of Kale." She started crying harder. "Be at peace."

Mary remained kneeling beside Jason until Marcus stepped beside her, and gently pulled her to her feet. "It is time, Mary." He looked up at the soft violet sky. "The Gods await them." They descended the stairs of the pyre and took several steps forward before turning to face the sacred grounds.

Louis and Master Leo were at the top of the marble steps. As Mary watched, they took a long strip of cloth with colors that swirled in the patterns of the Kalian ranks. The fabric was saturated in sweet smelling oils that Mary knew would soak into the cloth that draped the bodies of the two fallen champions. Master Leo moved to Jace's side of the pyre and gave a traditional temple bow, while on the opposite side, Master Latie of Desato did the same for the Golden Defendant.

Louis moved to the front and, raising his voice, addressed the large, silent crowd. "Today we have gathered to say farewell to fallen heroes." His voice was thick with sorrow. "The White Defendant of Bellum is being burned at the temple from which he rose, per his last request. He died in service to the realm."

Louis drew a deep breath and continued. "Lord Jason Far, son of a defendant, a Royal Champion of the Kalian tournaments, and the red student of Kale. We bestow upon him this day, the rank of defendant, so that he may join them and be welcomed as a champion in the realm of the temple Gods and greeted as a friend to Lord Kale!"

Mary swallowed her tears.

"And finally," a sudden gust of wind carried his voice through the crowd, "Master Edward of Desato, the Golden Defendant, has died in service to the realm. His name will live forever within the hearts of all defendants. Lord Edward served honorably until the moment of his last breath. He is survived by his son, who has already begun the path of following in his father's footsteps as the silver student of Desato." Louis allowed a moment of silence to pass. "Let us honor our fallen champions!"

As one, defendants, students, temple masters, and all those of the Kalian bloodline drew their swords, and held them high towards the purple sky. "Live to serve, die for honor!" they shouted in profound unison. "Glory to the Gods! Glory to the Lords of Kale! Glory to Lord Jason, the fallen Defendant of Kale! Glory to Master Edward, the fallen Golden Defendant!"

Master Leo and Master Latie lit the funeral pyre. The flames enveloped the bodies of their lords before the words of their fellow defendants had even begun to die upon their lips. The flames blended with the rainbow silks. The wind rose with a sudden howl. Smoke began to fill the air, yet the eyes of those gathered remained upon the burning pyre, each man and woman standing completely still, holding their swords towards the Gods.

Mary watched as the fire danced across the pyre, the wind swirling around the flames as though basking in their warmth. The higher the inferno rose, the more numb Mary became until eventually she felt nothing.

She stared into the fire until her eyes began to burn from the strain. On the other side of the pyre, through the raging flames, Mary caught sight of her sister. Dressed in silks of gold, her long blond hair blowing in the wind, Ameria all but blended with the twirling flames. Only her eyes separated her from the dance, her dark, sapphire eyes, like a drop of water among the flames. The two sisters stared at each other across the sea of fire, holding their silver blades towards the Gods.

The silence remained until the last of the embers faded to black. Then, the high priest rose and once again addressed the large, royal crowd. "My Lords and Ladies of Kale, I thank you for your attendance. Now, I must ask that the defendants step forward for the traditional walk of honor." One by one, the dark robed defendants turned from the pyre and walked towards the large building behind them.

When they reached the center point between the pyre and the building, they stopped, and began to form two lines with a single isle between them. When the last of the defendants entered the line, Louis' voice rang out again. "Who here claims the right of advancement in the death of Lord Edward, the Golden Defendant?"

A feminine voice rose out from the left side of the isle. "I, Lady Rebecca, the Silver Defendant to Lord Edward's gold, of the line of Kale and former golden student to the Temple of Kale, claim that right."

"Then place yourself at the beginning of the aisle, Lady of Kale. Defendants, prepare to swear your loyalty to the new leader, or challenge for the right of gold as you see fit."

Lady Rebecca of Kale stepped through the crowd to reach the end of the aisle opposite the high priest. Once there, she offered a low bow before removing her outer black robe to reveal the rainbow cloth beneath. She wore a shirt of rainbow satin with long sleeves that hung loosely on her arms, but cinched tight at the wrist. Her satin pants matched her top. Gold blended with silver, red, pink, black, yellow, green, blue, white and purple before finally shifting back to gold. Her blond hair hung in waves past her shoulders and down her back.

"May the Gods protect Edward's destined heir!" Louis' voice carried down the aisle. "Begin."

Lady Rebecca began a slow walk down the aisle, pausing to face each of the fifty-eight pairs of eyes lining both sides of her. "My Golden Defendant!" the first two defendants said in unison as she paused beside them. They then proceeded to enter into the traditional bow, dropping to one knee, with an arm on either side of them, fingertips touching the ground with their heads down. They remained in that position while Rebecca moved to the next pair. Defendant after defendant knelt on the ground after swearing their loyalty.

Then, a silver flash moved across the aisle faster than the eye could see as a blade lunged at Rebecca's throat. Rebecca blocked the blow just as quickly and returned the movement. Four upward strokes of Rebecca's arm, and her blade was at the challenger's throat. A single drop of blood stained the defendant's dark robe as he stepped back from Rebecca and entered into the same bow the others had taken. "My Golden Defendant!" His voice rang throughout the crowd.

Rebecca continued to walk slowly down the aisle until once again, there was a flash of silver on her left side. This time it was Lord Stephen who lunged forward. The kneeling defendants remained still, watching the scene play out before them. Lady Rebecca blocked Stephen's blade, then stepped sideways to avoid a second lunge.

The two fighters stood still for several heartbeats. The world seemed to hold its breath as the top two defendants faced off. Lord Stephen moved slightly to the left of the aisle, and cut towards Rebecca's side. She blocked the blow, twisting into the movement, throwing her opponent off balance. He managed to recover without falling, but not before Rebecca followed the movement with another. Stephen was barely able to block her next move as she raced into him with a series of powerful strokes. Rebecca's blade sliced down his arm, spilling blood down his wrist, the red blending with the black satin of his robe.

Stephen fought through the pain, spinning out of Rebecca's reach before returning with a series of strokes of his own. His blade sliced up and down in a fury as he threw his weight towards Rebecca's slimmer form. She slipped to one knee under the pressure before twisting away from Stephen, gasping for breath as she circled around her opponent, giving both an uneasy moment of respite. Then Stephen moved forward again. His blade sailed toward Rebecca as she suddenly twisted a step past the blade, twirling beyond the dangerous lunge.

She slipped to the ground, raising her blade above her head, square with Stephen's chest. Stephen froze just in time to stop his own weight from impaling him upon Rebecca's silver blade. He dropped his sword as Rebecca rose in a fluid movement, shifting her sword from Stephen's chest to his throat. She pushed the blade forward slightly. Stephen took a half step back before catching himself and standing perfectly still. Several moments of silence passed between the two defendants before Rebecca said, "Lord Stephen of Koloso, will you accept your place as silver to my gold, second in command of the Defendant Team?"

The two continued to stare at each other for several more moments before Lord Stephen finally took a step back and nodded his consent. He then dropped to kneel in a fluid movement, head down, his dark robes flowing around his body, his hands to the sides, fingertips touching the ground. "My Golden Defendant."

Lady Rebecca then moved forward and placed herself before Lord Louis. She entered the same bow that the other defendants held and placed herself at the mercy of the temple lord. "All hail, Lady Rebecca of Kale." Lord Louis' voice was clear as he stated the ancient words. "Arise, Lady Rebecca, as the Golden Defendant. Go with the grace of Kale and the blessing of the temples." Lady Rebecca stood as swiftly as she had knelt. "Arise also, Lord Stephen of Koloso, and take your place as the Silver Defendant. Serve at your golden leader's side with the grace of Kale and the blessing of the Kalian temples."

Lord Stephen stood beside his new leader. Lord Leo and Lord Jiro stepped forward and removed Lord Stephen's outer black robes. After bandaging his bleeding arm, they slipped a silver robe over Stephen's shoulders. Once adorned in his proper colors, Lord Stephen stepped forward with Master Leo and assisted Lady Rebecca into her robes of gold.

Master Leo addressed the new Golden Defendant. "Congratulations, Lady Rebecca. You have served your temple well."

"Thank you, Master Leo. Thank you, Lord Louis. I shall wear these robes with honor and swear to uphold the laws set forth by the Gods of Kale, and safeguard the realm from all threats from this day forward." She then turned and faced the line of kneeling defendants. "Arise, my fellow defendants."

They stood in a practiced unison, throwing off their black robes of mourning, which fell to the ground beside them. "All hail the Golden Defendant!"

Chapter XVI

----✦•≫•✺•≪•✦----

AFTER THE CEREMONY OF SUCCESSION was completed, Ameria turned towards the white marble building that stood as the Thirteenth of the Rainbow Temples. She walked up the marble steps and entered the main entryway of the temple. As the only temple dedicated solely to prayer, the Temple of Ziazan was distinguished by no particular color, but was instead painted in the same streaks of rainbow worn under the cloak of every defendant. As Ameria entered the sacred temple, it was by this elaborate array of colors that she was greeted. Large glass windows stood on both sides of the vast hallways, the filtered sun bringing out the brilliance of the brightest of the swirling colors, creating a dizzying effect. Ameria had achieved her undefeated status when she was fifteen, and had spent the following year serving at Ziazan while her sister had proceeded to win her own twelve consecutive championships.

Several large black chairs lined the hallway of the temple. Ameria seated herself on the left side of the room and awaited the arrival of Lord Stephen, the now Silver Defendant. She did not have to wait long as only moments after Ameria was seated, Lord Stephen stepped into the hallway. He offered a bow, bending quickly at the waist, before seating himself across from the princess.

"My lady," he addressed her.

"Princess," she hissed at him. "You address me as princess or Your Royal Highness, nothing less."

"In this temple..." Stephen began.

"I am still your princess! In this temple, in every temple, I am still your princess!"

The two stared at each other, but Stephen was the first to blink. "Forgive me, Princess Ameria."

"Never forget, Lord Stephen. My sister may one day be queen, but I will be the Golden Defendant. Then as my mother once served Leo, you shall serve me."

"You make it sound like this will happen in the near future. With all due respect, princess, you are still a student."

"A student whose fight you were afraid to stop."

Stephen paused before asking, "What are you talking about?"

"Do you take me for a fool?" The princess gave a harsh laugh. "I know you were there in the crowd the day Jace died. You watched my sister attack Kyle and then myself. You did nothing to interfere. You, my lord," she made the title sound like something foul, "were afraid of me. You are still afraid."

Stephen's hand slid toward the hilt of his sword.

"If you so much as begin to raise that blade at your princess, Lord Stephen, it will be your head." Master Jiro, High Master of the Temple of Koloso, appeared from behind the corner. He was a tall man, with shoulder-length blond hair that was slowly fading to silver. His jade green eyes flew to the princess. "Is everything all right, Your Highness?"

She offered her master a thinly pressed smile. "Everything is fine, master." Ameria gave a sigh. "I don't really feel like attending another funeral today."

"Lord Stephen?" the Kolosian master addressed the Silver Defendant.

"Yes, master. I was just leaving."

"Actually," Ameria cut in. "Lord Stephen was about to escort me to the Temple of Kevera and from there, he was going to escort me to the palace. Weren't you, Lord Stephen?"

Stephen dropped his eyes towards the ground. "Yes, my lad... Your Highness."

"Go wait for me in the center temple chambers and alert the temple to prepare for our arrival."

As the Silver Defendant turned and exited the room, Master Jiro turned towards Ameria and waited for an explanation.

Ameria waited for Stephen's footsteps to fade before turning to her master. "He is never where he should be." Her hands rose in a gesture of frustration. "There have been so many fights, so many moments where the Defendant Team needed their full strength, yet Lord Stephen was nowhere to be seen. Even after Lord Edward was killed and the defendants rode after his killer, they said Lord Stephen was the last to show."

Jiro's eyes narrowed. "I am surprised I had not heard this."

Ameria shrugged. "I was talking with a few of the group on the ride up here. They said Lord Stephen showed up with no explanation for his absence. I also find him belligerent, disrespectful, and with no value for temple traditions. I am ashamed to call him a fellow Kolosian. A man like that should not be placed in a position of such power." Ameria shook her head. "Once I win the thirteenth tournament, I plan to ensure he never sees gold."

Jiro considered the princess' words, then said, "Have you spoken to Princess Mariana?" Ameria shook her head. "Perhaps you should try. You are sisters."

"I'm not angry about the fight," Ameria told him. "If it had been the other way around, I would have done the same to Marcus."

"Do you really mean that?" He glanced at her with a look that Ameria could not quite place.

"Let's hope we never have to find out."

"Why don't you let me take you to the other temple?"

Ameria shook her head. "Stephen may be arrogant, but he is not stupid. He will transport me to the Temple of Kevera."

"The Temple of Proelium is closer to the palace," Jiro advised.

"I know, but I will likely be staying overnight and I like Kevera's accommodations better." She offered him a genuine smile.

"Ah, yes, the famous hot springs."

"And I have one with my name on it."

Jiro laughed softly. "Now I really think I should take you instead."

Ameria rose from the chair and offered a nod to her master. "I will return to the temple soon, Master Jiro."

"May the Gods protect you, princess." He stood and offered a slight bow.

"You as well, master." Ameria turned on the slick marble floor and walked down the hall. When she reached the central chambers, Stephen was seated on a black sofa. He rose as the princess entered the room. "I am ready to escort you to Kevera, Your Highness."

Ameria walked towards Stephen until he offered her his pale arm. Ameria linked her arm through his, and closed her eyes.

There was a bright flash, which caused Ameria to see multicolored lights even through her closed eyes and then suddenly she heard a feminine voice say, "Welcome to the Temple of Kevera, my princess and Lord Defendant."

Ameria opened her eyes slowly, her vision momentarily distorted. "Thank you," she replied as her vision began to clear.

The master of the Temple of Kevera was not as tall as Ameria, but what she lacked in height she made up in grace. Dressed in black robes of silk, the temple leader seemed to float across the room as she approached the new arrivals. Her long black hair blended with her robes as it flowed down her back, highlighted with dark red streaks with dye made from the Vera flower, a rare red blossom found only in the fields surrounding the Temple of Kevera. Ameria entered into a traditional temple bow of respect for the temple master and Stephen followed suit.

After the Kevera master motioned for both to rise, Ameria caught the dark brown eyes of the temple master. "Did you not attend the funeral, Master Nowfaleena?"

"I did, princess. One of the defendants was kind enough to escort me back to the temple soon after."

Ameria turned back towards the Silver Defendant. "You may go, Stephen. There are likely others in need of transportation to their various temples. You will return by morning. We ride at first sun."

"Thank you, Your Highness," he addressed her. A moment later there was another bright flash of light as Lord Stephen vanished from the room.

"I will have your room prepared, princess. Though I am afraid it is not quite ready yet."

"All I need is a place to sleep," Ameria assured the temple master. "And perhaps a visit to your fabled hot springs."

Nowfaleena laughed. "I assure you, princess, they are no fable. If you would just follow me this way," she moved towards the large door, "I think you will find them much to your liking."

A half hour later, Ameria was sinking down into the steaming hot water. Combined with a mixture of sweet smelling oils, the water offered a soothing, hypnotic effect. Ameria's thoughts wandered towards Jace. She had liked the kid. In fact, she had never found anyone to dislike the son of the Lord and Lady of Setra. Mary had lost control, it was true, yet no matter how hard she tried, Ameria could not find it in her heart to be angry with her sister. If it had been Brandan or Rosa…Ameria shivered and despite the steaming water could not seem to get warm.

The temple was made of black stone. Everything was dark, lit by large fires and small candles that sat upon dark, metal chandeliers. The windows were small, covered with thick black curtains that blew in the fierce winds on the edge of the mountains. Ameria lay in the springs listening to the evening wind until she eventually gave a soft sigh and climbed from the water. She dried her nude, pale body with a soft towel before wrapping herself in a thick black robe. She wandered down the hall to the small room that was hers for the night. She tossed and turned for several hours, and when she finally slept, it was to unquiet dreams.

The next morning, Ameria rose early. It would take several hours to reach the palace, and she was hesitant to take the road in the dark. As Ameria walked outside she found a large black horse saddled for her. She was surprised to see a small group of defendants, with Lord Stephen in the center. She walked down the temple steps and looked up at the Silver Defendant. "Lady Rebecca sent us as your honor guard. She felt you were too close to the Dark Mountains to ride without additional guards."

"I appreciate the companionship," Ameria told the defendants.

She had forgone her long robes for a simple golden, long sleeved top and matching pants. She pulled her silver Kolosian blade from her side and placed it into the side of her saddle, then she placed her foot into the stirrup and mounted the unfamiliar horse. She grabbed the reins, turning the horse left, and then right. She walked in a circle, attempting to quickly learn the responses of the unfamiliar horse.

"All right," she said after several minutes of testing the reins. "Let's go!"

She guided her horse into a soft gallop and the defendants behind her gave chase. After she became more comfortable with the stride of the horse, she increased his speed. The small group raced through the valleys, forests, and small hills as they rode towards the palace. Even with their speed, it was late evening before they reached the outer gates. "Make way for the princess!" Lord Stephen's commanding voice called to the tower guards. The gates swung open and the princess entered, but did not head towards the palace. Instead, she headed west and soon reached another set of tall gates. She pulled up on the reins, slowing her mount to a stop before the solid, black gates.

In front of the gate stood six men, dressed in the crimson of the King's guard. "State your name and business," one of the men called out.

"Princess Ameria of Kale, to see Lord Kyle of Koloso. I order you to let me through." Without a word, the man glanced behind him. Two of his fellow guards opened the gate. Ameria slid through and rode towards the far tower to where she knew her longtime partner was being held.

She passed through two additional sets of gates on her journey, each time having the gates opened before her. The king took no chances where the security of these prisoners was concerned.

When she finally reached the tower, she dismounted and passed the reins off to a crimson-cloaked guard.

"Lord Kyle is being held in the center of the tower," the guard informed her.

Another guard approached Ameria and motioned her forward. "This way."

The tower was almost as ancient as the story of Kale. Made of dark, gray stone, no one was sure when it was actually built. The guard grabbed a torch as they moved through the tower doors and began the long walk down the dark corridor and up the curved stairwell. When they reached the fourth flight, the guard opened a very old wooden door which creaked loudly as they walked into the gray hallway beyond.

"Stay close to the wall, Your Highness. This really is not the safest place for a princess." She followed his advice, staying on the far right wall, as far away from the prisoners' cells as she could. She caught glances of some of the prisoners in the dim light of the torch. Their clothes were often covered with dirt and small holes. Their hair was slick from being unwashed. Their eyes were hard. Some called out words Ameria cared not to repeat as they spotted the beautiful woman walking through their halls.

"My apologies, princess," the guard said softly. "Some of them haven't seen a woman in quite some time. Let alone one such as you."

Ameria did not answer, but instead simply ignored the calls as they walked through the halls. When they finally reached the end of the hallway, the guard motioned to Ameria. "He is in here, Your Highness."

"Thank you," she said. "Open the door so I may speak with him, then you may go."

"I'm sorry, princess. I am not allowed to leave you alone with the prisoner."

She turned towards him, her eyes flashing in the dark with a sudden anger. "I am the number one ranked fighter in the land. I think I can handle my own partner."

"Forgive me, princess." The guard's voice sounded unsure. "If you were injured it would be my head."

Ameria sighed. "Fine. You may stay nearby, but I wish to speak with him myself." She turned to face him fully, narrowing her sapphire eyes upon him intently. "You are not to speak a single word and if you ever breathe a word of what is spoken to anyone," she deepened the tone of her voice, "I will take your head myself. Understood?"

The guard's eyes were wide as he gazed at the princess.

"Open the door," she commanded. The guard moved to comply and a few moments later the door slid open with a loud *"woosh."* Ameria walked into the room to find Kyle lying on a small bed made of straw.

"So, what will it be today?" he asked without looking up. "Four day old mush or more of that rat soup?"

"How about getting your ass kicked?"

Kyle leapt into a seated position. "Ameria!" he exclaimed, then beamed her a smile. "I knew you wouldn't leave me to rot in here for long."

"Actually, I just might," Ameria said in a cold voice. She did not return the smile.

She stared Kyle down until the smile disappeared from his face. "Ameria," Kyle spoke slowly. "It was an accident. You have to know that it was an accident."

Ameria put up her right hand. Kyle stopped speaking. "Let me be very clear, Kyle. I know it was an accident. I know that you did not mean to kill him. This is absolutely not in dispute."

Kyle nodded and Ameria continued. "What I do not understand is why the hell you ended up fighting Jace in the first place." Venom seeped into her voice. "Why, in a strictly points-based tournament, you ended up in a fight with the team from Kale!"

"I'm sorry," Kyle said. "The other team started going and we started blocking and then we just...we were both fighting. Then Jace knocked down my partner and I..."

"Kyle," Ameria said through gritted teeth. "I do not give a shit what the other team did. I only care about what you did."

"I was trying to protect my partner and then..."

"You did protect your partner, Kyle. But then, instead of turning back to Marcus, you decided to fight Jace."

"Ameria, I..."

"You fought a lower rank. Not only a lower rank, but one you knew had no chance of defeating you in a fair fight. You know better, Kyle." Ameria shook her head. "Even if you had won, what honor would you have gained in victory?"

"Ameria, I..." He lowered his eyes to the ground. "I'm sorry, Ameria. Truly, I have no idea how things got so out of hand. It just, happened so fast."

"I do not want to hear your excuses," Ameria told him in a voice cold enough to freeze the brightest of flames. "We fight our equals for a reason, Kyle. You were the higher rank, and I trusted you to fight fairly and uphold the honor of the Kolosian temple." Her body visibly tensed and her neck curved slightly to the left, giving him a titled view of her dark blue eyes. "You are lucky that my sister declared your punishment. If it was up to me, far worse would have been done to you than simply locking you up." Ameria allowed a moment of silence to fill the room, then said quietly, "Your ego and arrogance cost a Royal Championship level competitor his life."

"I did not want to kill him. Jace was like a kid brother." Kyle slipped down to one knee in front of his princess. "Forgive me, princess. Please, it was never my intent. I never meant to hurt him."

"Once again, Kyle. I understand that. But you did pull a stupid, stupid stunt and the consequences were dire." Ameria fought to keep her voice steady. "I know that it all happened fast, but this does not change the fact that you allowed it to happen or that you must be punished for what you have done."

Kyle rose to his feet. "Ameria," he said softly. "I understand that I need to be disciplined, but please, my princess, my friend. Please don't leave me here."

Ameria gave Kyle the full weight of her sapphire gaze. "You deserve to be in here, Kyle. And even if you did not, I am not the one with the power to set you free. Write to my sister if you want out." With those words, she turned and called for the guard.

"Ameria!" Kyle called. "I would never hurt Jace."

"I know, Kyle," Ameria told him as the cell door slid open with a loud clang of metal. "I know." Ameria walked from the room. This time, she did not hear the jeers of the prisoners as she passed by. She numbly followed the guard down the dirty, ancient stairwell by light of the large torch he carried. As Ameria emerged from the tower, the last sun had fallen from the sky and shadows of impending night had cast themselves over the ground below.

When Ameria stepped onto the hard, barren ground, she turned to the man beside her. "I wish to speak with the captain."

The man nodded "He is already coming this way, Your Highness."

The Captain of the Tower Guard was a short, older man with skin that had been darkened by the suns over the years. He bowed to the princess as he approached, and Ameria waived him back to a standing position. His teeth were more yellow than white and his crimson robe was beginning to fray on the edges. "Your Highness," he addressed the princess.

"Have you been given any special instructions concerning Kyle, son of the High Lord of Turbamentum?"

"No special instructions, princess. But you don't work this tower as long as I have and not know that with one of his rank, special treatment is implied."

"I understand that, captain. However, I am going to make this explicit, so there will be no misunderstanding later." She glared down at the rather crude man. "No harm is to come to Lord Kyle. If it does, you will suffer his harms tenfold."

"With all due respect, princess. Is that a threat?"

"No, captain. It's a promise."

She turned and walked past the captain. Her horse had been brought around by one of the other guards. After checking to ensure that her sword was still safely tucked into the side of her saddle, Ameria mounted the large black horse and rode towards the palace.

Chapter XVII

Mary rose from her desk at the sound of a loud knock. She moved toward the carved, golden door and pulled it open to find Master Leo standing in robes of rainbow silk. The swirl of colors was almost as dazzling as the golden shimmer of Mary's room. The only disruption to the colorful pattern was the golden emblem of Kale on Leo's right breast and the tiny sword above the mark, symbolizing his former rank as the Golden Defendant.

Mary motioned the master forward and he entered the room with a thin smile and tired eyes. "To what do I owe this honor?" Mary questioned. Leo walked towards the desk and took a seat before motioning for Mary to do the same.

"Princess Mariana," Leo began.

"Uh-oh." Mary cringed. This wasn't going to be good.

"Mary," Leo tried again, "I am here to speak with you about Kyle."

"No," Mary replied curtly. "Just no."

"Now wait. It was an accident, Mariana. A tragic accident, and Jace knew the risks."

"He knew the risks of fighting with me," Mary corrected. "Not fighting in a point-based system where no real fighting was involved. Kyle broke the rules. For that alone he should be locked away."

"For how long, Mariana? How long must Kyle be locked away for an accident?"

Mary's eyes blazed with emerald flames. "Did my sister put you up to this?"

"Of course not! In fact, your sister is the only person who has not asked for her partner's release."

"Well, doesn't that say something," Mary replied heatedly. "Even my sister thinks he belongs in that cell."

Leo shook his head. "You of all people know that is not true, Mariana."

Mary turned her dark eyes upon Master Leo and gave him the full weight of her royal gaze. "He will rot in that place until Jace walks back smiling through my bedroom door!"

Leo let several moments of silence to fill the room, allowing Mary's words to slowly fade. "We were all grief-stricken by what happened to Jace, princess.

But it was an accident. If he had been imprisoned by anyone other than yourself, Kyle would be back at his temple by now."

If it was possible for Mary's eyes to hold more rage, they would have burst into flames. "Has my uncle ordered him released?"

"What?"

"Has the king, my uncle, ordered Kyle's release from the tower?"

"No."

"Then Kyle stays where he is, until he rots or the king says otherwise."

Master Leo drew a deep breath and then stood from the golden chair. "I hope you reconsider," Leo told her as he offered a slight bow. "Princess."

Leo left without another word. But as the door closed, another voice flowed softly through the room. "I know you loved him." Coco appeared as though from thin air.

"Everyone loved him," Mary replied.

"Not like you." When Mary did not bother to deny it, the puppy continued. "You couldn't have stopped him from fighting in those upper rounds, Mary."

"Of course I could have stopped him. I am the idiot who let him fight on that level in the first place."

Coco moved from the door and jumped up on the bed, looking up at Mary from the slightly higher position. "He would have found another way. He would have dropped to a lesser temple and been their silver if it meant even a dream of competing for your hand."

Fresh tears gathered in Mary's eyes. "I should have told him. My sister could have been queen. It's all she has ever wanted anyway. If Ameria had been proclaimed heir to the throne, Jace and I…"

"Still would have been separated by who you are," Coco stated.

"No. It would have become my sister's burden, not mine."

"Look at me, Mariana." The puppy moved as close to Mary as he could without falling off the bed. "Look me in the eye and tell me that you would give the throne to your Kolosian sister, to ride off with Jace into the sunset. Look into my eyes and tell me that you would give your sister the kingdom and put the fate of your people in her Kolosian hands. Tell me that your heart would allow you to do such a thing."

Mary glanced down at the suddenly wise puppy. She tried to tell him that she would trade the crown in a heartbeat for Jace's life. Yet the words would not seem to form on her suddenly thick tongue. "Damn you," she whispered as the brimming tears began to slowly slide down her cheeks.

Coco gazed up at her sadly. "You are a princess and a future queen. It is who you were born to be and, like it or not, it is your inescapable fate." More tears flowed from Mary's eyes. "You can't change your fate, Mariana; not even for love." Coco paused to draw a deep breath. "It is okay to hurt. It is okay to cry. But you cannot allow yourself to believe that throwing your destiny away would have saved him, any more than you can continue to punish Kyle for an accident. You are a future queen. Now you must act like one."

Coco sat with Mary for the better part of an hour before her tears finally began to cease. "I'm sorry, Mary. Truly sorry about Jace. But it's time to let Kyle go. Jace would not want him punished like this for an accident, and I think you know that." Mary gave a slight nod, but said nothing so Coco continued. "I will call for a defendant to transport you to the closest palace temple. From there you can ride to the palace." Coco did not wait for a response, but instead turned from the room, calling for the temple's guard as he walked down the rainbow halls.

An hour later, Princess Mary was standing outside the halls of Kevera where three defendants and one of the assistant temple leaders waited astride tall black horses to escort the princess to the palace. "It's a good horse," the temple leader, Nowfaleena, told Mary. "Though I must apologize, he is not the mount I would have originally chosen for you."

"Oh?" Mary asked.

"Your sister actually has him," Nowfaleena said.

"My sister?"

"Yes, she rode through a few days ago. I was told that she would be returning shortly. You will likely pass her on your journey."

"Do you know what my sister was doing here?" Mary asked.

"No, Your Highness. I did not think it was my place to ask. She only said she was going towards the palace."

Mary nodded. "Thank you, master. I am sure this horse will be fine. I should have him back to you in a few days' time."

"Keep him for as long as you have need, princess." Nowfaleena offered a slight bow which Mary returned. Then Mary slid her blade securely onto the side of the saddle and mounted in a single, graceful sweep. Jerking the reins, Mary's horse broke into a quick gallop and they raced as one into the field towards an ever-darkening sky.

Chapter XVIII

AMERIA RODE FROM THE PALACE with a heavy heart. Two riders trotted on either side of her black steed. Master Crite, the fifth ranking member of the Defendant Team, hailed from the Temple of Desoto. He was a short man with pale skin, sandy brown hair and matching brown eyes. Dressed in black, he wore short sleeves, exposing the long, thin scar that traced the length of his right arm. Mary knew that he must have received the scar from an enchanted blade, else the magic of the temples would have healed the mark long ago. The second rider was Captain Roth of the King's Guard. With darker hair and standing several inches taller than the defendant, Roth wore the deep crimson cloaks of the king's personal household.

The morning air was brisk and a cold wind blew across the hills, causing their robes to billow around them as they rode. Gray clouds filled the usually clear violet sky. "Looks like it might rain," Master Crite said. "Should we take shelter at a nearby village?"

"It does not look that bad," Captain Roth said. "We tend to get some sprinkles this time of year, but rarely full-blown storms."

"We need to get to the temple." Ameria eyed the sky uneasily. "Let's ride on."

Ameria gave a slight tug of her reins. Her horse surged forward. Two hours later, Ameria found herself wishing she had heeded Crite's voice of caution. Drenched to the bone and trapped in a relentless downpour, the three riders were forced to slow their ride to a crawl across the fields, unable to see more than a few feet in front of them.

The three riders finally came upon a large stone structure. It had likely been a house once, but based on its poor condition and dirt floors, the structure had not been used in quite some time. They carefully pushed open the splinters that had once been the structure's door and entered the room, leading their horses behind them.

The roof was leaking in several places and the water rushed to the floor, turning it to mud. Ameria walked the small room, searching for a dry corner. "Over here." She motioned the two men to the left side of the room. "The water hasn't reached here."

"Or here," Crite called from the other side. "I'll move the horses to this side and we can take the other."

Ameria nodded in his direction before taking several steps away from the relatively dry corner she had found and removing her drenched outer robes. She wrung the water out of the garment as best she could, then threw it over a thin beam to dry. She then proceeded to ring the water out of her golden hair before tying it back into a long braid. There was nothing to be done for the rest of her clothes as the water had soaked straight through the silk outer garments.

She started to walk back towards the opposite corner when Crite said, "Here, princess. I have an extra robe in my bag and it is much dryer than what you are wearing."

The princess took the robe gratefully. It was black and made of a cloth much thicker than her own.

"Thank you," she told him. "I am going to step out onto the doorstep to change."

"No, Princess Ameria. Allow us to go outside. Call us back in when you are ready."

The two men turned towards the door and stepped outside, pushing closed the few scraps of wood left of the door behind them. Ameria peeled the wet silk and satin from her skin as quickly as she could manage before wrapping the thicker black robe around her shoulders. Though slightly damp, the robe was much warmer and dryer than the clothes she had been wearing.

A clash of thunder filled the air as she wrapped the thick robe around her and the wind suddenly whipped through a small window across the room. It seemed to whisper, "Princess."

Ameria froze. The wind twirled around her with a faint howl. Ameria shook her head and finished tying the robe into place. "Princess," the wind howled again with a sinister quality.

"Hello?" she asked, her heart beating loudly. She held her breath, but heard only the thudding of her own heart.

Ameria jumped at the knock on the wood that had once been a door. "Princess," the captain's voice called. "May we come in now? It's a little wet out here."

"Yes!" Ameria called. "Sorry." The two men entered the room and the three began to look for comfortable positions on the cold, dirt floor. When Ameria finally began to drift towards sleep, she was utterly exhausted. As darkness slowly descended upon her, someone seemed to whisper. "Princess, princess..." Ameria stared into the darkness and there, she thought she saw something move in the shadows. Something as black as the night itself. "Princess...beware!"

Ameria woke with a start. The room was lit with the low touch of a sunless morning. She sat up and gazed around the room.

Both of the men stood near the entrance. "Princess." They gave a bow.

"The sky is still gray," Captain Roth said. "But at least the rain has stopped."

Ameria nodded. "Give me a moment to wake up and then we can be on our way. We can rest when we reach the temple." She walked groggily towards the men and gazed out at the gray sky. "It will be slow goings through the soggy ground."

"Yes," Master Crite said. "But at least we won't be drenched."

"Let's hope," Ameria said softly.

After taking a few minutes to compose themselves and re-pack their belongings, the three riders mounted their black horses and resumed the journey towards the Temple of Kevera. True to Ameria's prediction, it was a much slower ride than the day before. The ground was slick beneath the horses' hooves and mud clung to their black coats as they walked. Several rivers had risen to cover the bridges that crossed them and new routes had to be taken.

As they reached a crossroad in their path, Captain Roth said, "There is a path here through the forest. It will take a few minutes longer, but in theory the ground should be more solid than the open lands by the river."

The three riders turned their horses in the direction Roth motioned and entered a vast forest. The blue grass grew wild through the tall, untamed trees. The wood on this side of the kingdom was much darker than the colorful forests that painted the Rainbow Mountains. Here, the bark of the trees was a deep red edging toward black. The leaves were dark blues, greens and blacks. In the light of the three suns, Ameria supposed that the forest might have held a unique beauty, but against the gray sky, it seemed almost menacing.

Occasionally Ameria heard the chirp of a bird, but for the most part, the forest seemed quiet. Riding was slow as the forest was covered with thick patches of deep mud and fallen limbs from the wind of the previous night's storm. Ameria was continually forced to dismount and lead her horse around the various obstacles they encountered.

After several hours of slow riding, Ameria inquired as to how much farther they would be riding in the forest.

"Still a ways to go, princess," Master Crite replied. "But don't worry. We should be at the temple by nightfall."

"Okay, then," Ameria said. "Do you know if there is somewhere we might let the horses rest for a few moments, and perhaps get some water?"

"Yes, my lady." Crite replied. There is a stream up ahead. I will show you."

Ameria estimated that they rode another ten minutes before coming upon the low stream. She dismounted, her shoes sinking into the mud as she removed the bridle from her horse before leading him towards the stream. Ameria took several steps from the horse and placed her own hands in the clear flowing water. She cupped her palms and moved her hands towards her lips, drinking thirstily.

Master Crite stepped beside her and handed her a small flask. She filled the flask with the crisp, clear water. "Thank you," she told him. "I am sorry I got us into this. I should have listened and sought shelter when you advised me to do so."

Crite shrugged. "None of us knew how bad the storm would become. Besides, I have done worse than sleep on the ground in my day."

"Well," Ameria said with a slight smile. "I must say...I think it was a first for me."

Crite returned the smile. "Yes, I figured as much. What did you think of it?"

Ameria made a face. "There are worse fates, but personally, it is not an experience I hope to repeat anytime soon."

"Nor I," Crite replied. "Here." He handed Ameria a second flask. "Would you mind filling this one as well? I'm going to go grab something from the saddle bag."

"No problem," Ameria replied. She turned and once again leaned down towards the river. When the flask was almost filled, the water turned red.

"What?" Ameria glanced up to find Master Crite lying on the ground a few feet from her. There was a hole in his chest. Ameria whipped her head around, but not fast enough. Something crashed into the back of her skull. Pain exploded. Bile rose in her throat and her ears rang.

She tried to rise, but was hit again, this time on the left side of her head. She lay on the ground in excruciating pain. She moved her hand up to the side of her head; blood was running from her ear. Her vision blurred and she could do nothing but lie there. She saw several blurred shapes moving towards her, but could not make out her attacker. Then a voice sang through her ringing ears. "Sorry, princess," the voice said. "The twins of Kale must not be permitted to live."

Twins of Kale? Ameria struggled to move from her balled position, but it was all she could do to keep from vomiting. Another blow to her head and she started to lose consciousness. She saw the glint of something silver. *A blade?* she wondered. Her eyes started to close of their own accord. Someone screamed. *So,* she thought, *this is what it is like to die.*

Chapter XIX

Princess Mariana was not happy. Caught in a sudden storm the previous night, she had been drenched to the bone. They managed to find limited shelter in a small, cramped cave they had found embedded in the side of a larger hill. After sleeping on the hard, cold stone another day of riding was the last thing she desired. Mary made a mental note to "thank" Coco, who had elected to remain at the nice, warm Temple of Kale.

Next time I take any trip, he is so going with me, she thought.

Now, the five riders were forced to work their way slowly through the muddy terrain. As she maneuvered her horse carefully over branches and around the deeper puddles, Mary found herself missing Sherwyn, who had never needed such careful guidance. Still, it wasn't the horse's fault, and Mary patiently led him through the treacherous trail.

"We should go through the forest," the accompanying master from Kevera told the group. "In the midst of all these rising waters, it is the safer way to travel." The riders turned their horses left and entered the dark forest.

Mary gazed at the trees looming above her and wondered what Coco would say. Probably something like, "Wow, creepy. I'll take my chances by the river." Perhaps it was good after all that the puppy had not accompanied them.

The riders continued further into the forest. Mary noticed several birds flittering through the trees, occasionally swooping down in search of the bugs that had been displaced from their underground burrows by the pouring rain. As Mary maneuvered her way around a low tree that had fallen across the trail, one of the birds jumped onto an eye-level branch on Mary's right side. "Chirp, chirp."

Mary pulled up on the reins. "Well, hello there." It was a small bird with dark blue and emerald green feathers across its back. Its small chest was a slightly lighter blue, and it had deep, black eyes. "Aren't you pretty." Mary spoke softly and remained as still as she could, so not to spook the bird.

"Chirp, chirp, chirp." The bird tilted its head at Mary.

"I'm sorry," she said softly. "I don't think I have any food for you."

"Chirp, princess, chirp."

Mary jerked back involuntarily.

"Did you just?" She turned to see if anyone else had heard, but the other riders were several paces ahead. She looked back at the bird. "Did you say, 'princess'?"

"Chirp, chirp."

She sat still for several more seconds, then shook her head. "Talking birds," she whispered softly. "I must be tired."

"Chirp, princess, chirp. Beware, beware!"

"Beware?" she asked. Beware of..."

Mary's horse collapsed under her with a dreadful cry. Its body tumbled toward the ground. Mary twisted her body, more training than thought, throwing herself towards the left in a desperate attempt to avoid being crushed.

Her side smashed into a tree and she felt a sharp pain in her right ankle. The horse gave another terrible screech as his body collided with the ground. Mary lay still for several moments, the wind completely knocked out of her. She was not sure which hurt worse; her ankle or her likely bruised ribs. She managed to raise her head.

Three of Mary's fellow riders stood to her left, swords drawn. "What is going..." she started to ask. Then, the Master of Kevera lunged at the defendant dressed in blue.

Their blades sang through the air. "Protect the princess!" the Blue Defendant called to his companions. As if in slow motion, Mary watched a second defendant, dressed in green, draw his own blade. The Green Defendant walked towards the blue, and buried his silver sword between his partner's shoulder blades.

Mary attempted to climb to her feet, but was taken aback by the searing pain in her ankle. She looked at her leg for the first time. A large piece of dark red wood had completely pierced the ankle and was protruding through the opposite side. Without removing the wood, Mary used her hands to crawl towards her fallen horse.

Blood painted the ground where the horse had fallen; a sword had sliced through the muscle of its neck. Crawling through the pool of blood, Mary reached for the saddle bag. The third defendant bravely fought the other attackers, but dressed in white and the lowest ranked of the group, he was clearly outmatched. "Run, princess," he screamed at her, as the two advancing warriors slowly pushed the defendant back towards the princess.

Mary grabbed her sword from her saddle bag then reached down towards her ankle. She could not possibly hope to fight with the spike in her leg. She wrapped her hands around the spike, and pulled with all her strength. Mary screamed as she yanked the wood from her ankle, her blood pouring forth to mix with that of her fallen horse. Her head swam from the pain. She stumbled to her feet, putting as much of her weight onto her good foot as she could.

Mary lifted her sword and limped forward just in time to deflect the stroke of a silver sword intended for the White Defendant's throat. She brought the blade down again, protecting the White Defendant's right side. She felt lightheaded. *How much blood am I losing?*

Mary's blade swiped right, colliding with the Green Defendant's own silver steel. She then raised her blade in an upwards stroke, attempting to cut his throat. He parried just in time to stop her. Then, Mary raised her sword again but this time, as the Green Defendant moved to again protect his face, Mary instead pushed forward at a much lower angle. Her Kalian blade sliced into the Green Defendant's lower belly, and he collapsed to the ground with a scream, his entrails spilling out. Mary turned to help the White Defendant, when the side of her face was splattered with blood.

The White Defendant collapsed, the artery in his neck split wide by the Kevera master's blade. Mary stumbled back, her injured ankle slipping in the slick blood spreading beneath her. She fell to the ground and crawled to her right, towards a tall tree, placing her back against the trunk and struggling to stand. More blood gushed from her ankle. Mary turned to face her last attacker, and realized that even more men had appeared. Cloaked in long, dark robes Mary could not see their faces. She raised her blade as two of the men moved forward.

"I am the Gods' chosen," she warned. "Fight me at your peril."

The two new men did not answer, but simply closed in on the princess. Mary raised her blade in front of her, holding the long sword at a slight angle. Two swords came down. Mary turned the blade sideways, blocking both movements, slicing her hand open in the process. She let out a low hiss and collapsed to her knees.

She blocked the next two blows on her knees, then sent her silver blade sailing toward the man on her right. The blade sliced through cloth to bite into the flesh beneath. Blood rose to the surface of the man's leg. He took several steps back, cursing in pain.

Another man took his place. Mary looked out in fear at the gathering group of dark robed warriors. How many were there? Six? Nine? Mary could not see well enough to be sure.

Mary rolled forward, managing to cut into the leg of another of the hooded figure, but was unable to stop the next blade from slicing down her arm. More blood spilled down Mary's body and her vision dimmed. Dropping back to her knees, her swings became less steady. It took all her strength to remain upright and a few moments later, the blade slipped from her blood soaked hands.

Someone dressed in red satin stepped forward from amongst the hooded men. "May the temple Gods protect me, or greet me in the Rainbow Halls," Mary whispered the Kalian prayer.

Her knees gave out and she fell to the ground at the tall man's feet. A silver blade appeared before her, undoubted in its purpose. "Long live the twins," the man said in a deep voice.

I know that voice, Mary thought. A shrill scream rang through the air, and then everything went black.

Chapter XX

Princess Ameria listened to the sound of high-pitched screams. She tried to open her eyes, but seemed to lack the strength. More screams filled the air. She tried again, this time managing to half open her left eye. Something moved in the shadows. It raced among the group of faceless men in front of her. Ameria's eye closed again. The screams began to fade. She fought against the comforting darkness, forcing her eyes open once again. The shadowy figure walked towards her. It moved through the forest as though made of the very shadows the tall trees cast upon the ground.

"Ameria," a soft voice seemed to call from afar. "Ameria stay with us. Just close your eyes and sleep."

For one moment, Ameria thought she could see a woman. Young and beautiful with a lightness to her step that Ameria had never known. She moved her head ever so slightly to her left...was that Mary walking hand in hand with Jace?

Then as suddenly as it had appeared, the vision vanished and Ameria was staring into the formless figure of a shadow that closed in upon her. "No," it whispered in the sinister voice of the wind. "Wake, princess," the shadow hissed. "Wake!"

Ameria's eyes opened. Her heart pounded to life. Pain skewered her head. She gulped several deep breaths of air, but all she could smell was blood. "I'm going to be sick." She rolled her body to her side, wondering if the bones in her head were shifting as she moved. The world spun. She jerked her body back forcefully to keep from vomiting all over herself, then lay face down, curling her arms under her injured head.

The air reeked of blood. *How much did I lose?* she wondered, but was unable to so much as raise her head.

She closed her eyes and remained trapped on the forest floor as night descended. She must have fallen asleep again, because when she opened her eyes, early morning light was just beginning to shine through the tall trees.

The pounding had lessened and Ameria managed to very slowly raise herself to a seated position. The smell of blood still filled the air.

Pieces of bodies littered the ground. Flesh torn from limbs, heads sat beside fresh corpses. Splintered bone protruded from arms and legs pulled off at the joint. Ameria's robe was soaked in blood and darker things. She struggled to her feet. More flesh splattered the ground behind her. A head sat in a tree, the flesh of its right cheek torn off. Ameria stumbled backwards and screamed as her foot crunched the bone of a torn hand beneath it. She twirled around, fighting to keep her balance.

Ameria screamed again and forced her injured body to move forward, her feet sliding in the stream of blood and sinking into the occasional piece of flesh beneath her. When she finally reached the edge of the stream, she jerked the robe from her body and stumbled into the cold water. The water chilled her skin, forcing a gasp from her throat at the sudden change in temperature. Tiny pin pricks crawled their way up her body like a thousand stinging ants, but she forced herself to lower her head into the cold water, scrubbing at her stained skin.

When she finally emerged, Ameria fought her way to the opposite side of the stream. She lowered her shaking, nude body into the tall grass and began to sob.

Chapter XXI

———◆•❦•◆———

Princess Mariana cringed on the floor of the forest, listening to the screams as she awaited the stroke that would claim her life. Her body shook on the cold ground. Then the screams began to fade and the voices grew dim. *Am I dead?* she wondered. She opened her eyes. The trees had vanished and Mary was suddenly standing in the center of a vast open field filled with sunlight.

Mary climbed to her knees, and was surprised to see a pale hand held out to her. Allowing its owner to pull her to her feet, Mary rose to find herself staring into Jace's soft brown eyes. Dressed in crisp robes of rainbow silk, Jace stood taller than he ever had in life. She glanced down and found to her surprise that she was dressed in a sheer gown of gold, made of a material so light that she hardly knew it was there.

"Shh," Jace told her, his voice soft. He reached his hand below her chin and gently tilted Mary's face to meet his gaze. "No tears, Mariana. No tears." The sound of his voice washed over her like a cool breeze, carrying her brimming tears with them.

"Jace."

He gave her one of his best smiles. "Walk with me, Mary." He reached for her hand and she wound her fingers around his. The grass was a brilliant blue and the sky above was a perfect lavender, dotted by light clouds of every color of the rainbow. A single sun filled the sky, cascading the colors of the spectrum down upon the land and putting even the glory of the Rainbow Mountains to shame. Flowers lined their path in an exotic display of colors which could only be found in the realm of dreams.

Mary suddenly stopped walking and turned towards Jace. "I love you," she said quickly. "I should have told you. I should have told you all the time. I should have..."

Jace gave her another soft smile. "I know, Mary. I love you as well. I have missed you. You know it wasn't your fault." Mary did not answer. "And it wasn't Kyle's fault either, Mary."

Mary shook her head trying to understand. "Where am I? I should be afraid, but..."

"Fear does not exist here, Mariana. " He reached up and cupped the side of her face with his right palm. Jace leaned forward to plant a soft kiss upon the princess' lips, when a dark shadow fell over the land. Mary opened her eyes, staring past Jace into the land beyond.

"Ameria?" Was that her sister, standing on the opposite side of the large field?

The shadows began to move as though they were a living thing. The soft wind transformed into a storm, racing towards Mary at a speed faster than she could understand. The wind bit at her skin. The shadows gathered before her and said, "Wake, princess. You will wake!"

"Jace!"

Mariana jerked into a seated position. Pain seared through her ankle. A head sat on either side of her. She let out a loud, involuntary shriek. Her hand slid behind her to assist in crawling backwards. Her fingers touched another head. She jerked backwards, sliding across the forest floor in a river of blood.

She struggled into a standing position and turned to her right. She found the bodies that the heads belonged to. They were shredded along the forest floor, ripped to long, bloody pieces. Mary screamed. In the nearby tree was another head that she recognized as one of her attackers.

"Help!" she called to the silence of the forest. "For the love of the Gods please help!"

Her arm was sliced down the center and covered with blood, not all of which was her own. Her ankle throbbed continuously as she hobbled away from the gory scene.

"Who's there?" she screamed. "Who did this?"

She heard the rustle of leaves and jerked her head to the left. "Hello?" she called out. "Who's there?"

No one answered. The forest turned eerily quiet. "Please," Mary pleaded. Only silence followed.

Mary was not sure how long she sat on the edge of the bloodbath before finding the courage to move. Her clothes were covered with blood, dirt and bits of human flesh. Her injured ankle was filthy. It would get infected if she did not find a way to clean and wrap it, if it wasn't infected already.

Mary fought her way to her feet and limped back towards the bloody scene. Luckily her fallen horse was on the far side of the circle, so Mary was not forced to walk back into the center of the circle of corpses.

When Mary reached the horse, she leaned down towards the saddle and grabbed both her and the Kevera master's bags. She was surprised to see that her sword was tucked safely into the scabbard attached to the saddle. Had someone put it back?

Mary snatched the sword and bag from the saddle and limped slowly away from the scene. The trail they had been following was nothing more than a rocky, muddy path. Mary's heart lurched as she realized that she had no idea where she was. She searched the sky but without the suns, was faced with only a single, gray sheet.

Mary limped slowly down the path, often pausing to catch her breath beside a nearby tree. She managed to get away from the scene and was grateful that she did not have to walk far before coming upon a small body of water. The water was clear in color and Mary lowered herself down thirstily.

She removed the clothes from her body and slipped into the stream. The water was cold and stung as it seeped into the gaping cuts on her arm and ankle. She rinsed as much of the blood as she could from her pale skin, being careful to clean the large hole in her ankle as best as she could.

She then pulled herself from the water and dug through the large bag. She was surprised to find not only antiseptic and bandages, but a large black robe as well. The blood had not penetrated the thick skin of the bag, so the supplies were relatively clean. Mary took the large blue bandage and tore it into several strips. She wrapped the cloth around her ankle, hissing in pain as she was forced to tighten it around her injured foot.

Mary took the other strip and tied it around the widest part of the gash in her arm. It had thankfully stopped bleeding, but Mary was still lightheaded enough to know that she must have lost a lot of blood. She was also very cold. She struggled to a standing position, putting her weight on her good foot and proceeded to wrap the thick black robe around her. She rung the water from her long black hair.

She sat on the bank for several moments, trying to think. "Sitting here won't help anything," she said aloud to herself. Then thought, *But traveling in a dark forest doesn't sound very appealing either. I really should make a fire and start again in the morning. If you freeze to death you'll never get out of here.*

Mary searched the bags and found a fire starter. It was a thin piece of red wood which, when snapped, would spark a hot flame. She spent the next half hour stumbling around the forest searching for stray pieces of wood. When she had gathered enough, she withdrew one of the fire sticks and snapped it in half over the gathered kindling. A bright blue flame blazed to life and spread slowly over the pile. The heat from the blue flame was hotter than normal, and Mary moved closer, drinking in the sudden warmth. Night had fully descended over the forest and Mary used a shirt that had been in the bag as a makeshift pillow and lowered herself into the tall grass by the fire. She lay there for a long time, staring into the flames with her golden sword at her side.

The fire dimmed and Mary's eyes began to close. "Long live the twins," the menacing voice whispered through her dreams.

When Mary opened her eyes, morning light had long since filtered its way through the tall trees. Leaves rustled to her left. Her hand flew to her sword. She rose from the ground to a seated position. At the edge of the clearing sat a tall man on a large black horse. The man wore a long-sleeved black shirt and pants that appeared to be made of thin black leather. His short hair was as dark as Mary's own. His horse moved slowly through the tall blue grass toward the princess.

"Hello," the man called to Mary. He stopped several paces from her and dismounted. Mary was surprised to see that his skin was as pale as hers. He looked perhaps sixteen, if not younger. "Do you need some help, my lady?"

Mary searched quickly through the possible answers, but considering her injured leg, she had little choice but to say, "Yes, please. Please help. "

"What are you doing out here, my lady? These woods are no place for anyone to be in alone."

"We got caught in the rain," she said. "My escort was attacked. I'm not sure what happened to them. We had taken the forest path to avoid the overflowing rivers. Then I was thrown from my horse. I have no idea where I am." She took a hard swallow. "Please, sir. I...can you help me?"

"Have no fear, my lady," the young man replied. "My name is Ryan and this is Sky." He motioned to his black horse who gave a soft whinny at the sound of his name. He approached her slowly. "Are you injured?"

Mary nodded. "It's my ankle."

His eyes slid over her. "Looks like your arm as well."

Mary looked down at her left arm, only a small portion of the gash covered by the strip of bandage. "Oh, that's nothing compared to the ankle."

He reached a pale hand toward her and Mary accepted gratefully. She stumbled as she tried to balance her weight. Ryan stepped closer. "Here," he said. "Put your arms around me."

She shifted her sword to her side and tied it into the folds of her robe. "Really that's not necessary."

Ryan ignored her and wrapped his arms around her thin frame. "Hold on." Mary slipped her arms around his neck just in time. Ryan picked Mary up and carried her to his horse. He lifted her easily onto the side of the saddle. She placed her hand around the horse's neck and used her upper body weight to swing her leg onto the opposite side of the saddle. Ryan then climbed on in front of her.

"I will happily escort you out of the forest, but I really think we should see about getting those injuries properly cleaned first. There is a small village about half an hour from here where we can get your wounds cleaned and see about getting you some warmer clothes. It gets very cold in these mountain passes."

"Mountains?" Mary asked confused. Sky started walking slowly along the trail.

"Yes," Ryan replied. "You are in the Dark Mountains. Where did you think you were?"

"I...I don't know," she said softly. Silence followed as Mary digested this new information.

It must have continued longer than she thought, because the tall man asked. "Are you okay, my lady?"

"Yes, sorry."

"What is your name?"

"Ana," Mariana used the second half of her name.

"Well, Miss Ana, the village is just over that far hill. We will stop there and get that ankle looked after."

Mary nodded. "Okay, thank you." A few minutes later, they reached the top of the large hill and Mary saw several houses nestled into a small clearing in the forest. The village was small, with no more than twenty houses built of wide, wooden logs. They rode closer to the town and two men holding long, black blades walked towards them.

"Pete!" Ryan called to one of the two men. "It's just me."

"Oh," the man, dressed in black clothes almost identical to Ryan's called out. "Who's with you?"

"She was lost in the woods, hurt her leg pretty bad. I thought I would have Mother take a look."

"Your mother is the healer?" Mary asked.

"Yes, she sure is."

As they rode closer to the guard, Mary was surprised to see that their skin was as pale as her own. *Kalian?* she wondered. Ryan dismounted the horse and exchanged a slight hug with the other man. Pete had sandy brown hair and pale skin. Both men sported the same dark green eyes, height and thin facial bone structure. "Ana, this is Pete. He is my..."

"Brother," Mary finished for him. "You must be brothers."

"Yes," Pete replied. "The older brother."

"Only by two years!" Ryan exclaimed. "Besides," he flashed Mary a smile, "you look closer to my age anyway." He then turned back towards Pete. "Where is Mother?"

"I think she was putting together some herbs in the temple."

Temple? Mary wondered as Ryan grabbed the reins and walked beside the horse, leading Mary into the small village. They walked past several houses and through an open air market. Several merchants sat by their small booths selling everything from fresh fish to small jewels. Many of them called out as they passed by. "Hey Ryan! How have you been? How about something nice for the pretty girl?" Ryan gave a slight wave, but continued leading the horse through the small village at a steady pace.

The eventually reached a large, domed building with doors carved of gold and jewels to match the finest of the Kalian temples. "Which temple is this?" Mary asked.

"It's not one of the main temples," he told her. "It's just our...place of worship to the temple Gods." A series of stone steps led to the large building. Ryan stopped the horse at the edge of the stairs. "Here. Allow me."

He reached up and gently lifted her down from the horse before once again gathering her in his strong arms. She moved her sword carefully as not to cut either of them with the sharp blade. Holding her as though she weighed nothing, Ryan carried the princess up the stone steps and through the golden doors.

The interior of the temple was draped in thick gray carpets. The walls were of a smooth stone that was to light to be a true black, but also too dark to be considered blue. Ryan continued to hold Mary in his arms as they walked down the stone hallways until they reached a large door near the end of the corridor.

"Mother!"

"Ryan?" a voice called back from the other end of the hall. "I'm in here!"

Ryan opened the door and stepped inside. The large room was made of the same stone. The carpet was deep blue. Several large columns lined the walls, each embedded with swirling patterns of gold. They glistened in the light of a large fire that blazed along the back wall. On the left stood several shelves full of plants, kept warm by the roaring fire.

A tall woman stepped forward. "Ryan, I was beginning to..." Her words died upon her lips. Ryan's mother had long brown hair that fanned across her back, stopping just above the waist. It hung loosely around her in the same soft waves. Her eyes were a misty green, far softer than those of her children. She was thin with sharp, high cheek bones. "Who is this?" his mother asked.

"I found her near the lake. She got caught in the storm." He shuffled Mary in his arms so that her bandaged ankle was exposed.

"Of course," his mother said with a soft smile. "Take her into the next room and I will grab some fresh bandages."

Ryan turned and carried Mary back into the main corridor and then into a small bedroom. The walls of the room were a soft crème and the floor was covered with gray carpet. "Whose room is this?"

"Mine," Ryan replied. A faded red blanket covered the small bed. "It's not much," he said.

"It is fine," Mary said quickly. Ryan sat her down on the old bed, which gave a small creak. "I don't want to get blood on your blanket."

"Don't worry about it," Ryan replied. "It's so old, it really should be thrown out anyway."

Ryan's mother walked into the room behind them. She carried with her several bottles of ointments and had long strips of bandages slung over her left arm.

She placed the bottles on a small wooden desk behind her and held the bandages out for Ryan to take. She carefully unwrapped the bandage Mary had made. The princess winced as the woman pulled the bloody cloth away from her torn skin.

"By the Gods, girl," the woman exclaimed when she finally saw the large hole in Mary's ankle. "You did do a number on this leg, didn't you?"

"Yes, ma'am. A piece of wood pierced it straight through."

"Must have been some fall," she told Mary, eyeing the cuts down her arm.

"It was."

"We need to make sure that it doesn't become infected," the woman told Mary as she walked back towards the desk. "This will wash out the area, but it will sting."

Mary nodded and dug her fingers into the blankets beneath her. Sting was an understatement. Mary gasped harshly as the searing liquid burned through her tattered flesh. She moaned loudly and her breath came in short, hard gasps.

"I'm impressed," Ryan said. "Didn't even scream."

"Okay," the woman said. "Now I am going to put some salve around the injury...don't worry it should actually feel rather soothing." She applied a smooth white cream that, true to her prediction, cooled the burning of Mary's skin. She then wrapped Mary's foot, starting at the heel and stopping several inches above the ankle. "It looks like the foot will heal in time." Then the woman turned to

Mary's arm, repeating the process. When she was finished, Mary rose shakily form the bed.

"Thank you..."

"Angela," the woman replied. "But most call me Angie."

Mary nodded. "Thank you, Angie. For your kindness."

"It is starting to get late and the trail out of the forest is a long one. It would likely be best that you stay with us tonight, as a guest and leave early in the morning. That way it will still be light for your escort's return journey."

Mary paused. By now, the Royal Guard was likely searching for her, along with the majority of the defendants. However, not knowing who to trust and not wanting to encounter trouble in the dead of night, Mary nodded her consent.

"Wonderful," Angie told her. "I was about to begin preparing dinner."

"You will stay here tonight," Ryan stated. Mary parted her lips to protest, he raised his hand. "I insist. My brother, the one you have yet to meet, will not be home tonight. I will borrow his room."

"I'll see about getting you some clean clothes as well," Angie told the princess. "I have some gowns that I think should fit."

An hour later, Mary was seated at a long, wooden table. She had taken a lukewarm bath and had been given a simple cotton gown of light blue. The sleeves were a little long for her, but she compensated by rolling them back. The gown reached her ankles and flowed lightly around her as she moved. A large, black pot of warm soup graced the center of the table and Ryan filled a small white bowl for her. "It's not much," he said.

"It's wonderful," Mary assured him. The warm soup soothed Mary's throat, which had become raw from her earlier screams. She was starving and had to constantly remind herself to eat slowly, lest the introduction of food upset her stomach. After two helpings of the soup and a little bread, she was exhausted.

"Here." Ryan moved closer to her as the meal ended. "Allow me."

"No, I can walk..."

Ryan ignored her and carried her back down the hall to the bedroom.

"You really don't have to keep carrying me everywhere."

"I don't mind." He smiled. "Makes me feel heroic."

It sounded like something Jace would have said. Mary gave a soft laugh, and then stopped. Ryan placed her on the bed.

"You look sad, my lady."

Mary shook her head. "I just...haven't laughed in a while."

His dark green eyes studied her face. "Well, that's too bad," he said. "You have a beautiful smile." Mary smiled. "If you need anything, I am just down the hall."

Mary lay down and drew the faded blanket around her body. As soon as she found a comfortable position, she fell into a dreamless sleep.

Chapter XXII

Princess Ameria awoke naked on the side of the river bank. She must have cried herself to sleep. She moved slowly to a seated position. Her head still pounded. Even the stray rays of light not trapped by the tall trees above seemed too bright for her eyes. She moved her hand upward and touched her head gingerly. Her hand came away with dried blood. She moved her hands down the rest of her form, tracing her fingertips over and around her throat, down her sides and legs. From what Ameria could tell, she had sustained no injury other than that to her head. She crawled back towards the river, but the water was not clear enough to see her reflection.

Using her arms, she pushed herself unsteadily to her feet. The world swayed. She closed her eyes and stood still for several moments until the world righted enough for her to take a few steps forward. The black cloak still lay on the side of the river, but Ameria could not bring herself to touch the blood-caked garment. Instead, she forced herself to face the scene of the slaughter.

Crite's body was lying closest to her, farther away from the worst of the blood bath. Ameria approached him slowly, looking for the bag that he had been carrying. She found it still draped over his arm. Ameria reached down carefully and grasped the thin bag, pulling it from Crite's lifeless body.

She opened the bag, wincing as her finger touched something sticky. Yet the golden cloth that she pulled from the thick pouch, though still slightly damp from the rain, was blessedly free of blood. Ameria tore a thin piece of cloth from the bottom of her golden robe and then tossed the bag several feet behind her. She turned back to Crite's unmoving form.

"I'm sorry," she whispered to her fallen protector. She turned the master over and, with some difficulty, she managed to maneuver the large man onto his back in the soft grass.

She searched the river bank and found his silver blade lying only a few feet away. She grasped the blade and placed it on Crite's chest, then she reached down and closed his dark eyes. She took the strip of golden cloth she had torn off her robe and tied it around the top of the sword. "I will find who did this," she promised. "Rest now. Glory to those who die in service to the Gods and Kalian temples."

Flakes of blood once again smeared Ameria's skin from touching Crite's body, so she stumbled back towards the river and washed it from her flesh. Once moderately clean, Ameria slipped into the damp golden robes before grabbing her own silver blade, tying the scabbard around her waist and squinting towards the sky.

The suns were high in the sky and Ameria made a guess as to which direction she should be walking, though she realized with a touch of fear that she had no idea where she was. Nevertheless, she could not stay here in the forest so close to the scene of the slaughter. That much blood was bound to attract the attention of animals, many of which Ameria preferred not to come into contact with.

She forced herself to turn back to the gory forest floor in an attempt to see if she recognized anyone, but her mind rebelled against the sight, as though refusing to believe that the piles of torn flesh had once been living Kalians. She turned back, her stomach queasy and her head still pounding.

Ameria began a slow trek down the rocky path, having to occasionally maneuver her way around fallen branches and thick vegetation. By the time the suns began to set, Ameria was not sure which hurt worse, her head or her feet. The fact that her head still felt as bad as it did concerned her greatly. Her nose started bleeding on two different occasions during the walk and Ameria had yet to see a single form of recognizable civilization.

As evening cast its shadow over the forest, the bugs began to gather as well. Swatting the first of the many bugs she would find that evening, Ameria swore, "When I get out of this forest, I am going to burn it to the ground! Right down to the very last acorn."

She swatted another bug, "One big pile of ash," she promised. As Ameria continued her slow progress, her fear was slowly replaced with anger. "I don't know who did this," she said to no one. "But by the Gods, I will have someone's head!"

The golden satin clung to Ameria's skin, sticky with sweat. She was thirsty, having left the flask by the river and having yet to find another source of water. It was another two hours before she did come upon another small body of water. True darkness was just beginning to creep over the forest floor, and Ameria decided she should stop for the night. She knelt beside the stream and drank her fill before slowly walking the area, gathering a small amount of sticks that would have to serve as wood for a fire.

She pulled a fire stick from her bag and broke it over the pile. Blue hot flames sprang to life and cascaded over the wood. Ameria placed the bag under her head as a makeshift, though rather uncomfortable, pillow. As she tried to position herself on the forest floor, her nose once again started to gush with dark blood.

"Damn!" she cursed, moving her head in an attempt to keep the blood from landing on her bag. She quickly tore a piece of cloth off of the sleeve of her robe and used it to plug the left side of her nose. She tilted her head forward, so as not to let the blood drain into the back of her throat. The blood quickly soaked through the thin satin cloth. It took several minutes for the blood to slow, and even longer for it to cease. She took the rag and tossed it to the side before slowly walking back towards the stream. She washed her face and hands and then moved back to the blue flames, placing herself as close to their warmth as she dared.

Throughout the day, the pounding in Ameria's head had only grown worse. Ameria feared that she was hurt much more than she could see. Exhausted, Ameria fell into a deep sleep.

Ameria was suddenly standing in a field of flowers under a clear violet sky with a strange, blue sun. Her torn robes had been replaced by a thin, white gown that flowed around her as though it was light as air, stopping just above her ankles. She was barefoot. In the center of the field was a small fountain of white marble.

As Ameria ascended the cool marble steps, she caught sight of her reflection, and her breath stopped in her throat. The dress she wore had a square neckline and the long sleeves flowed gently around her arms. She was crowned with tiny white flowers that had been gently laced through her long blond hair. Her eyes held a light which she had never seen.

She had no idea how long she stood before the fountain when she suddenly heard soft laughter. Glancing up, she saw a tall, beautiful woman with long black hair, wearing a dress that matched her own. "Welcome, princess," the woman said in a clear, soft voice that was the very essence of joy. The young woman stretched her hand toward Ameria and gave a soft, crystal laugh. "Come, princess. The fields await you."

Ameria laughed with the strange woman and took her hand. The woman pulled Ameria forward, towards the field of flowers with a sense of joy slowly filling her senses. The next thing the princess knew, they were running, racing among the endless fields in a world where Ameria suddenly knew, would hold never ending flowers. "Wait," Ameria suddenly whispered.

The woman turned her deep blue eyes toward the princess. "No waiting, princess," she said softly. "No more waiting, ever again."

Ameria drew her hand back from the dark-haired woman. "No," she said softly again. "This isn't right. Something is wrong."

"Hurry, princess. If you hurry, he may not find you. If you hurry, nothing will ever be wrong again."

Ameria froze. "The twins of Kale," the voice whispered in the back of her mind. The sky suddenly darkened. A low, thunderous growl echoed behind her. Ameria's heart lurched into her throat.

"Stay with us," the woman pleaded. The growl grew deafening. Ameria fought to find the courage to turn around when a searing pain bit the flesh of her left arm. Ameria screamed. Her eyes flew open and she was staring into the dark eyes of a gray wolf. It was gnawing on her left arm.

Ameria jerked involuntarily, but the wolf had its teeth sunk deep into her flesh and she only succeeded in tearing it further. She screamed again. The wolf's teeth were stained red with her blood. Two more sets of eyes suddenly appeared in the darkness and Ameria's heart sank.

She groped to her side and used her right hand to grab her silver blade. She swung it weakly at the wolf. The wolf let go of her arm to avoid the blade, but

Ameria's injuries spilled her blood over the ground. The other two wolves advanced as the pack worked together to make its move. The fire had receded to mere embers and the forest had grown dark around her. She needed to bind her arm, but feared putting down the blade with the advancing wolves.

Ameria swung the sword again with her good arm and let out an animalistic cry in hopes of scaring off the advancing wolves. Blood continued to run down her arm and she feared she would faint from blood loss.

Another of the wolves advanced. Ameria moved to the side as fast as she could. The wolf was faster. Its teeth sank into her leg and more of Ameria's blood spilled forth. She let out a shriek of pain and screamed, "Help me!" into the darkness of the forest. For the second time on this journey, Ameria feared falling into a sleep from which she would never awake.

As her vision blurred, Ameria gave a silent prayer. The wolves surrounded her now, but remained at a slight distance, as though they knew she was about to lose consciousness. *At least that will be one small mercy*, Ameria thought.

A low growl filled the air, deeper than those of the wolves who had been attacking her. The wolves gave a soft whimper and suddenly the eyes around her vanished. The wind began to blow around her with a harsh ferocity. Ameria tried to focus, but could not see anything in the darkness. The voice of the wind once again whispered in the same sinister tone she had heard before. "You will live, princess. You will live."

Something bit simultaneously into her left and right wrists. Ameria somehow found the strength to scream once again. The world twisted in on itself; trees spun, leaves danced, and the stars appeared to be under her, with the ground above. Pain burned through her veins like poisonous venom.

Then, the powerful clench on her wrists vanished and Ameria found herself lying on the ground in agony outside the Temple of Koloso. Ameria began to scream.

Chapter XXIII

Princess Mariana woke as the first rays of light came cascading through the small glass window. Mary sat up and groaned as she moved her ankle. She glanced under the bed. The blade that she had tucked tightly into the mattress was still there. She let out a sigh of relief. Someone had left a small brush lying on the side of the wooden desk. She grabbed it, smoothing out her long black hair. She limped from the room and walked down the long hallway. About halfway down, Angie saw her and greeted her with a smile.

"Ryan is through that door." She motioned to Mary's immediate left. Mary walked towards the indicated door. The large room held a series of mats, not that different from the sets found in a normal temple. They were in far worse condition though, with tears at their edges. Curtains hung in tatters around several of the sections. Mary imagined that once this room had been as fine as any of the Kalian temples, but now it stood only as an old, tired building.

Ryan must not have heard Mary enter the room, as he stood with his back to her on one of the training mats at the far end. The mat he stood on was a dull red that looked like it had seen more than its fair share of beatings over the years. Mary walked quietly towards Ryan. He held a silver sword forged of steel which Mary knew all too well. It was a temple blade.

Mary wiped at her eyes in disbelief. Surely, this was not the same man who had fought her sister on the plains of the Rainbow Mountains? Mary watched Ryan closely as he lunged forward with his blade, his stance a little too narrow for the type of sword he carried.

She continued to watch for several moments. He had a well-trained technique, but his form could use some work and he seemed to lack the level of confidence usually found in expert swordsmen. Mary shook her head. Ameria had described the man she fought as a true master of the blade. Ryan's movements did not fit that description.

"Widen your stance," she called to him, limping closer. He glanced at her, startled. "The blade you are holding is heavy, and when it collides with another blade, it will become even heavier. If your stance is too narrow, then you will find yourself thrown off-balance. It could cost you dearly in a fight."

"Are you a sword master?" he asked.

"Not a master," Mary answered. "But I have trained under several."

"Wow, that must have been amazing. My brother teaches me when he has the time."

"Your brother? Not the one I met outside?"

"No." Ryan shook his head, his black hair tossing slightly as he moved. "My other one."

Mary nodded, the sense of unease sliding into the pit of her stomach. "Too bad you are injured," Ryan said. "Would love to have a go with someone who has trained under actual masters."

Mary nodded. "Well, if you can get me out of this forest, I would love to oblige you."

"Oh, yes," he said. "I will go get the horse and we can be on our way."

"Thank you," she said softly.

Mary walked back towards her room and once again ran into Ryan's mother. "We washed your robe, but it is still a bit damp. You are welcome to keep the gown if you wish. It hasn't fit me in years. Kind of nice to see it in use again."

"I would like to thank you for your hospitality," Mary offered a low bow to the older woman. "Is there anything I can do to repay your kindness?"

"It was our pleasure, Ana. I hope your injury heals smoothly, though if I had to guess where you are headed, I doubt there will be any problem with that leg by this time tomorrow."

Mary's heart beat faster.

"I saw your sword, my lady. It is a temple blade."

"You mean like the one your son carries?"

Angie fell silent.

"What are a group of Kalians doing in the center of the forest? Why is this temple not a part of the Kalian lines?"

"If you want to repay our kindness, you will speak of our village to no one. I don't know exactly who you are, but I recognize a sword of Kale when I see it. I do not want that world here."

Mary was taken aback by the sudden anger in the older woman's voice.

"Do you understand me, daughter of Kale? Speak of this temple, this village, to no one."

"It's princess," Mary mumbled. "Princess of Kale."

The woman's eyes grew wide. "No," she whispered. "He said the princess had blond hair. Yours is black."

"He?" Mary questioned.

"Quiet!" the woman shushed her. "Ryan has saddled the horse. Go now, princess. Go and never return to this place again. Do you hear me? Never return to this place again!" She turned towards Mary's right and entered the next door down the hall, closing the door behind her.

Bewildered, Mary limped down the hall as quickly as she could, grabbing her sword from under the mattress. She once again tucked the blade into her robes as best she could and began to walk down the long hallway. When she reached the entrance of the temple, Ryan was waiting for her at the bottom of the steps.

Ryan picked her up gently and carried her down the steps before placing her onto the black horse. "Hello, Sky," she said softly to the horse. The three suns of Kale blazed high in the violet sky, finally free from all but a few sparse, scattered clouds. "Today is a much better day for riding, isn't it?" she asked the horse quietly.

Ryan mounted the horse in front of her. Mary slid her arms around his waist and the two began to ride from the village back towards the forest. As they reached the edge of the small houses, Ameria saw another horse riding towards them. The horse was bright red, its coat gleaming in the brilliance of the sunlight. The rider's black hair was cropped short. Muscles were visible across his broad shoulders. They rode closer and as the horses began to cross paths, Mary caught sight of the man's dark green eyes and knew without a doubt in her mind; this was the man her sister had fought on the side of the Rainbow Mountains.

The eldest of the three brothers wore a sleeveless, loose neck shirt that bared the top of his chest. A thin scar ran across his upper torso, starting at the shoulder and disappearing into the shirt beneath; the exact place Ameria had described her blade slicing into him.

Two swords rested in the side of his saddle. The hilt of the first sword appeared to be carved of bone lined with a stronger metal to prevent it from breaking.

The hilt of the second sword was gold stone lined with small red jewels along the inside of the handle. The red mark of Desoto sparkled in the sunlight. The last time Ameria had seen that sword had been at the side of the late Golden Defendant, Lord Edward.

"Ryan," the older brother demanded. "What is this?"

"She was lost in the rain," Ryan started to explain.

"You brought her here!" Rage filled the other man's voice. "Here!"

"What was I supposed to do?" Ryan asked. "She was too hurt to walk. I couldn't leave her in the middle of the woods."

"Yes, you could have," the older man exclaimed. "Who is she?"

Ryan shrugged. "What does it matter? She needed help."

"Outsiders are not allowed into the..."

"Take it up with mother, Alec," Ryan replied curtly. "Mother tended to her injuries and told me to escort her home."

Alec's eyes narrowed and Mary met his green eyes head on. "Brave little thing, aren't you?"

For a spilt second, Mary considered her options. Even on her best day, Mary was not the sword progeny that her sister was. Injured, she was even less so. Plus, she doubted that the man's two brothers were going to stand idly by while she tried to kill him. The man did not seem to recognize her as the princess and therefore this fight would have to happen another day.

Even with this realization, she did not look away, giving the man the full weight of her royal gaze and silently promising that her eyes would be one of the last things her friend's killer would ever see.

"No," the man said. "This one does not scare easily. I'd be careful, brother. She has a look of death in her emerald eyes."

With those words, Alec kicked the sides of his horse and rode towards the small village. Ryan moved his horse toward the forest, and spent the better part of the next few hours apologizing for his brother's rude behavior.

"I'm so sorry," he said repeatedly. "My brother is a brute, no question. Always riding off, coming home with things that don't belong to him. I honestly have no idea what he does all day." Ryan shook his head sadly. "Sometimes he leaves for weeks at a time. No explanation, no goodbyes, you just wake up and he's gone. He comes back weeks later, never tells anyone where he has gone."

"Sounds frustrating," was the best Mary had to offer. "Tell me, Ryan, are we in the Kingdom of Flos?"

"No, Agnus."

"Agnus?" Mary repeated. "My Gods I must have gotten way off course!"

"Where should we be heading, my Lady?"

"Can you take me to Critous?"

"Sure," he said. "Do you live near there?"

"No," Mary replied. "But I know some people who do."

"Okay. It's about a half-day's ride."

The two riders worked their way forward. It took them another two hours to get out of the forest. Then the ride became much faster as the horse was able to run through the open fields without fear of running into fallen trees or hidden creatures.

The two raced down gentle hills and large fields, once again restored to their former glory by the warmth of Kale's three suns. When Mary and Ryan reached a large field near a low stream, they paused a while, allowing the horse to drink and rest.

Ryan laid out a large green blanket over the blue grass and lifted Mary onto it gently. He pulled a pair of cheese sandwiches from the small saddle bag.

"Thanks," Mary said, "I was getting hungry."

"No problem. This is actually one of my favorite fields. It's so dark in the forest, sometimes I just need to get out here to enjoy some sunlight." His black horse gave a soft whinny as he found a blue patch of grass to graze on. "Sky likes it to," Ryan said with a smile that Mary returned. "I was wondering, Ana. If you felt like telling me what really happened to you yesterday."

Mary drew a breath and her eyes trailed downwards. "I have a confession," she said softly.

"Oh?" Ryan said, his smile widening into a grin. "Let me guess. You think I am irresistibly handsome?"

Mary laughed. "Well, there is that. But the other part is that well..."

"It can't be that bad?"

"My name is actually Mariana," she said. "And most people call me Mary, not Ana. Actually, come to think of it, no one calls me Ana. I was lost and scared when you found me yesterday and didn't really trust you enough to tell you my name. And you have been so kind to me. I'm sorry."

"That's okay," Ryan told her. "If I had been lost and hurt, I might not have told you my real name either."

"I told you I had an escort and that they were attacked."

Ryan nodded.

"Well, actually the escorts were the men who attacked. They led me into the woods, then they turned on each other. I am honestly not sure..." She shook her head and turned her gaze towards the field of flowers against the violet sky. "It really is beautiful."

They sat in silence for the better part of an hour, watching the gentle wind blow through the flowers across the valley. Then Ryan called Sky back to him, gathered Mary into his arms and placed her on the saddle once again.

When they began to get closer to Critous, Mary said, "One more confession, Ryan. If you wouldn't mind, I would like to go directly to the temple."

"The temple?" he asked. "It's my understanding that they don't generally open their doors for riders."

"Trust me, Ryan. They will open their doors for me." The two rode towards the Temple of Critous, which was located on the outskirts of the Dark Mountains. Ranked tenth among the temples, the gate was formed of a pale purple stone and draped with the purple banners of the temple it represented. "Slow down to a walk," Mary cautioned Ryan. "They won't be expecting me this far north." Then she whispered, "Time for another confession."

Chapter XXIV

AMERIA HEARD VOICES IN THE distance. Her world still spun before her eyes, but she called out nevertheless, "Help! Help me!"

"Did you hear?" one voice said.

"Over there," said another.

"Miss, are you... oh my Gods!"

"Miss, what happened? I...there's blood everywhere. Quick, run to the temple and get help."

"Hold on miss." A hand lightly brushed her hair back from her face.

"Ameria!" the voice said with a touch of panic. "It's Princess Ameria."

Cold hands touched Ameria's torn arm and she screamed at the pain of the slight movement. Her world still seemed to be spinning. She couldn't focus. "Should we move her?" the first voice asked.

"Ameria, its Brandan." The second voice identified itself. Something tightened high on her left arm. She shrieked, and could not see through the sea of tears streaming from her eyes. "I'm sorry, Ameria. We have to stop the bleeding."

"Ameria, Kev is here. We have to tighten another band around your leg. Do you understand?"

Ameria could not form the answer. Her body shook in pain. The forms around her moved in quick, blurry motions. Something cinched tightly around her leg. She hissed loudly, but managed to repress another scream.

"Ameria," Brandan said again. "I'm going to pick you up and carry you into the temple. I'll be as careful as possible."

"Do you think that's a good idea?" Kev asked beside him.

"She has to get back to the temple. She's loosing too much blood. If we stand here she could bleed to death. Ameria, come on, it's Brandan. Tell me you can hear me. Say my name, say Brandan."

Ameria forced his name through her lips. The smell of blood was nauseating. There was no part of her body not saturated in pain. "Bran...dan," she managed to whisper. "I'll get...get sick."

"Doesn't matter," Brandan said. "I'm going to pick you up now and I'll be as careful as I can, but..." His voice trailed off and he did not wait for Ameria to answer. Arms slid around the center of her back and under her long legs. He rose slowly, but she moaned in pain anyway. She reached up and placed her arms around Brandan's neck as best she could. Every step across the dark valley was agony and she was sobbing long before they reached the temple doors. The journey up the marble steps was the most painful of all and by the time they reached the top, she was shrieking.

"Get Master Jiro," Brandan told Kev. "Run."

Ameria's throat was raw and scratchy. "Brandan, Hurry."

Brandan lengthened his stride and raced straight down the hall, ignoring the looks of the other temple students and questions that followed him. The large doors to the training room were closed and Brandan shouted, "Open the damn doors, now!"

The moment they stepped within the large doors, the tiny crystals of light began to gather around Ameria's crippled body. As the lights grew brighter, Ameria felt an instant pang of relief as the pounding in her head ceased for the first time since her attack. Ameria closed her eyes against the light's brilliance. The torn flesh of her arm was quickly mended and she heard a slick, sickening sound as the bones in her skull slid slowly back into their proper place.

Then her relief turned to agony. A searing pain ripped through her hands drawing another scream from her raw throat. Her wrists were on fire. She squirmed in Brandan's arms and he tightened his grip in an effort not to drop her. She fought harder. They collided with the ground, still blinded by the brilliance of the lights surrounding them.

When the light finally faded, Ameria was still screaming. The injuries on her leg and arm had been healed, but those on her wrists were still there. They were thin, long marks that ran from the center of her hand to several inches above the wrist. It was like a thin, jagged blade had been drawn across her skin, yet in the center of both of her pale wrists, was a deep puncture wound. The lights had scorched her skin around the marks, leaving her hands red and burnt. Her fingers trembled as she attempted to curl them against the palm of her hand.

She looked up to see Master Jiro standing in the doorway, a look of fear across his face as he viewed her once perfect skin.

Chapter XXV

MASTER LESTER OF THE CRITOUS temple bowed before his future sovereign. When he was informed that the strange rider at the gate was, in fact, Princess Mariana, he had left directly from his chambers to wait for her at the foot of the dark stone steps. He was an older man of medium height, with short gray hair. He was draped in dark purple robes, the color of his temple. His eyes were dark brown with many creases around them, marking his more than thirty years as the head Master of the Temple of Critous.

"Welcome, princess," he said, unprepared for the arrival of such a high ranking guest. "I am sorry, my lady, but I received no notice of your coming."

"Nor would you have," the princess responded. "I did not expect to be here. However, I find myself in need of your assistance, Master Lester."

"Of course, princess. Anything within my power to give."

"Ryan, why don't we dismount? One of the temple students will take care of Sky and Master Lester will show us to the temple training room." Ryan did not reply, but pulled up on the reins and did as the princess bid. Once dismounted, he reached up and took Mary gently into his arms. She wrapped her arms around him, not bothering to protest.

"This way," the Critous Master beckoned. They followed him through a series of stone hallways. Amethysts were embedded into the walls, creating a glint of violet sparks throughout the various corridors. When they reached the doors of the temple training room, Mary told Ryan to carry her into the room with a quick warning. "The room will get very bright. Make sure to close your eyes; the lights will fade quickly."

They stepped inside the temple training area, and the specks of light gathered round, healing Mary's injuries. "Wow," Ryan said as the lights faded. "I'm not sure I've ever felt so..."

"Rejuvenated," Mary finished for him, explaining that the lights were a powerful source of healing.

"Princess," Master Lester interrupted. "What happened, my lady? The call went out that you never arrived at the palace. The defendants have been searching everywhere."

She considered the old master for several moments and then said. "It's a long story, master. I need you to call Lady Rebecca. I need her here immediately."

The master nodded his consent. "She will be sent for at once, princess."

"Ryan," she said softly. "You can put me down now." Ryan placed her on the ground gently and Mary knelt to untie the bandage from her now perfect ankle. "Look, if you want."

Ryan knelt and glanced at the ankle. He ran a finger lightly over the smooth skin. "It's like it was never injured." He looked up at her. "That's incredible!"

Mary offered a small smile. "You haven't seen anything yet. Let's go to the central room and wait for Rebecca."

The two walked quickly through the amethyst-encrusted halls and entered a large room near the center of the temple. The walls of the temple were the same as the halls beyond, and the two large sofas lining the left side of the room were draped in purple sheets of satin. "What's with all the purple?"

Mary gave a soft laugh. "You really don't get out of that forest much, do you?"

Ryan shrugged. "Not for anything more than running through some fields."

"Well then, you are about to learn a lot in the next few minutes." Mary gave another laugh and spent the better part of the next half hour answering Ryan's various questions about the temples. They were interrupted when a tall woman dressed from head to toe in robes of golden silk entered the room. Mary stood immediately and gave a traditional temple bow before Lady Rebecca, the Golden Defendant of Kale. Ryan saw Mary enter the bow and attempted rather unsteadily to copy her uncomfortable stance.

"Rise," Lady Rebecca said quickly. "By the Gods, princess! Where have you been? What happened? I've sent search parties to the far reaches of the kingdom!"

"I am fine, my lady," the princess replied. "Thanks in large part to the help of this young man." She motioned to Ryan. "Ryan, I would like to introduce you to Lady Rebecca of Kale, the Golden Defendant of the Realm."

Ryan's eyes went wide as he turned towards the golden lady. "The Golden," he stumbled over the words, "Defendant! By the Gods!" he exclaimed and then gave a bow at the waist. "It's such an honor! I didn't know, I...I've always wanted to meet a defendant."

"If you helped our princess," Lady Rebecca replied, "then the honor is mine."

"I need to get to the Temple of Kale," Mary told Rebecca.

"They said you were injured. Were you attacked? Where are the others who were with you?"

"The others were behind the attack," Mary said firmly. "My own honor guard turned on me; one or two did not, but they were killed by those who did. There was a storm and we had to travel in the forest and that is where they ambushed us. Must have been..." She closed her eyes, but all she saw was the piles of countless bodies strewn over the ground. "I don't honestly know how many there were. At least twenty, perhaps more."

Lady Rebecca looked on in horror. "Are you sure? I mean, are you..."

"I know what I saw," Mary replied. "I need to get to Kale, now. I need to speak with Master Leo and I need you to take Ryan with us, if," she turned to the young man, "you will agree to accompany me?"

The young man did not hesitate. "Yes, Ana...I mean, princess."

"I will escort you both immediately," Lady Rebecca informed them. She held out a hand to Ryan, which he quickly took in his own. Mary grabbed her other hand. There was a flash of light not too different from the crystal healing lights in the training chambers and suddenly all three of them stood inside the main training room of the Temple of Kale.

Mariana started towards Master Leo's chambers, when she suddenly turned to Lady Rebecca and asked, "Where is my sister?"

Lady Rebecca turned her eyes to the ground. "There has been no word of your sister, princess. She disappeared the same night you did."

Mary's heart sank. She turned to leave the room and then suddenly stopped and turned back towards the Golden Defendant. "Lady Rebecca," she said. "I need you to go to the palace and order the release of Kyle, my sister's partner. Tell him to go join the search for my sister and that I would like to see him once she is safe."

"Yes, Princess Mariana." Rebecca gave a low bow. "It shall be done."

With that order, Mary left the room with Ryan closely at her heels. She walked down the halls until she ran into Tyler and asked, "Where is Master Leo?"

"In chambers with Lord Louis," Tyler replied.

"Thank you."

She changed directions only slightly and soon reached the chambers doors of the temple leader. She did not knock, but simply threw open the doors, motioning for Ryan to follow behind her.

Both turned as the princess entered the room. "Mary!" Louis called in surprise.

Master Leo did not speak, but instead took three long strides forward and gathered the young princess into his arms. "You're safe!"

"Where have you been?" Louis asked into an exasperated voice. "What happened? I had a dream of you covered in blood."

Mary looked at Louis. "We were attacked," Mary told the puppy before launching into the long story.

"If what you say is true," Louis said in a solemn voice, "then how are you still alive?"

Mary met his gaze head on. "When I awoke," she said in a harsh whisper, "they were all dead. Not just dead, slaughtered. It was a bloodbath."

"And did this young man," Louis motioned to Ryan, "have something to do with this slaughter?"

"No. I have no idea what or who was responsible. I woke up covered in blood and there was not a soul in sight. Not one living soul."

Chapter XXVI

AMERIA WOKE FROM THE DREAM at the sound of the opening door. She jumped at the sound. Her eyes flew open. Kyle knelt on the floor beside the bed on which she lay. "Kyle?" Ameria said in a confused voice. She attempted to move to a seated position, then gasped. Her wrists were wrapped in long, white bandages which covered the thick, foul smelling gel that had been placed on them by the healer called in from the palace.

"Princess," Kyle said, not rising from his kneeling position on the floor. "Princess, please, forgive me. If I had listened to you, if I had not been imprisoned, then you never would have been between the palace and temple that night. You wouldn't have been in that forest, you..."

"Kyle, stop." Her voice sounded tired. She cleared her throat and attempted to find a more commanding tone. "Rise, Kyle. Rise and look at me."

Kyle stood and faced the princess.

"Help me."

Kyle stepped closer to the bed and placed his arms around her torso, helping Ameria rise to a seated position on the edge of the bed. He handed her one of the pillows that she had been lying on and she carefully placed both of her wrists on the pillow in her lap.

"Listen to me, Kyle," Ameria said softly. "This," she nodded downwards, motioning towards her arms, "this was not your fault. If it had not been in the woods, it would have been in some field or some other wood or outside some tournament. This was a planned attack. It was not your fault."

Kyle cast his jade eyes down, unable to face his longtime partner. "But if I had been with you..."

"Then you would have died," said a second voice from behind him. Mary entered the room behind Kyle. "Hello, Ameria," she addressed her sister.

"Hello, sister."

"Kyle," Mary addressed him. "My sister is correct. This was a carefully planned attack. There were twenty to thirty men involved, all of them experienced swordsmen. Had you been there, you would have died."

"It was not your fault," Ameria said again.

Kyle glanced into Ameria's crystal blue eyes. "Please," he said. "Forgive me."

Ameria shook her head and glanced at her sister. "It's not my place to forgive you, Kyle."

Kyle turned to face Mary and bowed at the waist. "Forgive me."

Mary considered her words for several moments and then nodded towards her sister. "Kyle," she said in a voice devoid of emotion. "I want you to go to the training temple and wait for me there." A heartbeat of silence fell before Kyle gave a nod and walked from the room, leaving Mary to face her sister alone.

"Ameria," Mary said softly as the door closed behind Kyle. "By the Gods, Ameria. I am so sorry, sister. What...what happened?"

A profound silence filled the space between them before Ameria whispered, "I died."

Mary's heart suddenly began to thud inside her chest with a strength that was staggering.

"I was dead, sister." Ameria's eyes pierced through Mary's deep green gaze. "And so were you."

The room seemed cold. "No," Mary replied in a voice that was barely a whisper. "No, I was not dead. Wounded, yes, but..."

"I saw you, in the field with Jace."

Mary stared at her in bewilderment. Her pulse began to pound fiercely against her left temple.

"I knew you had been fond of the boy, but to love him?" Ameria shook her head. "I would have thought better of you, sister, than to allow him to believe he was worthy of the love of a Kalian princess."

"You have no idea what you are talking about." Anger seeped into Mary's voice.

"I saw you in that field, Mary. It was more than enough to give away the secrets of your heart. You loved him."

"What does it matter." The pounding of Mary's heart increased and the room felt as though it were spinning. "Jace is dead."

"As were we."

Mary shook her head. "No, Ameria. It was a dream."

"No, sister. We were dead and should lie in the realm beyond. Something brought us back."

"Ameria, you injured your head. You don't know what you are saying."

"It killed them. All those who raised their blades against us; shredded by their hands. A dark, formless shadow; granters of life and death." Ameria raised her arms. "A creature of shadow with a twisted sense of humor."

"Ameria," Mary interrupted. "We are alive. Whatever killed them saved our lives."

"To what end?" Ameria demanded. "To leave me scared and crippled?" She stared directly into her sister's eyes. "I would rather be dead."

"Ameria do not say that. I am so glad that you are alive."

Ameria held up her bandaged hands. "Yes," she whispered. "And glad you are not me."

"That's not true, Ameria. You are my sister. I would gladly have spared you this pain if I could."

"Liar," Ameria hissed, her voice suddenly laced with venom. "You would never sacrifice your hands. Your prized, fighting hands. Not for all the world."

They stared at each other with blazing eyes, Mary refusing to believe the truth of her sister's words. The room was now in a full spin. "I will check in on you later, sister."

"As you wish, Your Highness." Ameria made the title sound like something foul.

Mary stumbled out of the golden room and into the dark hallway. When she rounded the corner, she paused and pushed her back against the wall. Tears sprang to her eyes. She sank down against the wall, and buried her head in her hands. *I was dead*, her sister's words echoed through her mind. *And so were you.*

"No," Mary whispered. "No, no."

"Princess?"

Mary turned her tear stained face up to find Master Jiro standing in front of her. Mary looked up at the Kolosian master.

"I think I have some hot beverages in my office."

Mary shook her head, forcing her tears to vanish from her eyes. "Kyle is waiting on me."

"I think he can wait a little longer. Please, princess." He held his hand out and Mary took it graciously.

Master Jiro walked a few steps forward and Mary followed him down a series of black stone hallways. Bits of shimmering silver were embedded in the walls. They entered Jiro's private study, which had a large black desk against the back wall and a large, roaring fire against another. Shadows of the blue flames danced across the wall like spirits called forth from an ancient prophecy. Jiro motioned Mary to one of the large, black chairs by the fire. Mary did not realize how cold she was until she approached the flames. She sank down into the soft cushions and Jiro prepared her a hot cup of Raspin.

A few minutes later, Jiro handed her a second glass. "Be careful, it's hot."

"Thank you," Mary replied, before turning her gaze back to the dancing blue flames.

"I have no idea what she said to you," Master Jiro began. "And I honestly don't know what each of you experienced out there, but deep down she loves you. You are sisters. You are blood."

Mary surprised herself by letting out a harsh laugh. "Sisters? Yes, by blood most royal. How could one forget the cursed royal blood?"

"Cursed?" he asked. "Is it so cursed to be a future queen?"

A moment of silence passed and then Mary surprised herself again. "I blamed him...Kyle, for Jace's death. I blamed him. But really, I am the only one to blame. Had I been born anyone but a princess, I could have...I should have...but, I was a princess. And I could not. The blood wasn't good enough."

"Your blood?"

Mary shook her head with dry eyes. "No. Not mine. His. His blood was not royal enough to love a princess of Kale. He lost his life because of some notion that my blood was better than his."

Mary dug her long nails into the palm of her left hand until she drew blood. She raised her hand in front of the Kolosian master. "Here, royal blood; does it look so different than his?" Mary gave a harsh laugh. "Don't you see? I killed him."

"It was destiny, Mariana. And that is the one thing that no one can escape. Not even a princess."

Mary's gaze shifted from the flame to the man sitting beside her. His silver robes shimmered in the firelight, not with the same gleam as Mary's golden ones, but strangely beautiful just the same. She looked up into his green eyes, so like her own. "It was our fate to die," she whispered. "Our fate and yet...here we are."

"Yes," Jiro answered. "Yet here you are."

Then she confessed the one part of the story she had failed to tell anyone else. "Something saved us, master. But it was...dark." She searched for a better word, but found none. "It was darkness itself." The two fell into a well of silence as the blue flames continued to dance across the walls.

"There is a story," Master Jiro said. "A story about twins of the ancient bloodline; the same bloodline that flows through your veins."

"What story?"

Jiro nodded. "It does not surprise me that you would not know of it, my lady. It is little more than myth, an old legend all but lost to our history."

He straightened in his chair. "It is said that twins of the bloodline are...special. That they are meant for a special destiny and that when these twins are born, forces gather to protect them. To what purpose or end, is a question lost to time. There are many stories, some good, and some horrible and of their actual truth, I know not." He drew a deep breath and exhaled slowly. "I only know what I believe, princess."

"And what is that?"

"I believe that you and your sister have always been protected by something... powerful. Be it fate, destiny or something else, something darker... I know not."

Mary tilted her head slightly. "I am not sure I understand."

"Tell me, princess. Do you know the names of the last set of twins born of your bloodline?"

"Kale and Koloso."

"And before that?"

Mary shook her head.

"Desoto and Dektra." Mary stared at him. "And before that," he continued, "it was Kevera and Mortem."

"All the temples?" Mary asked, startled. "I thought the temples were named after Kale's generals in the Dark Wars."

"Ah, yes, and most of them were," Jiro replied. "It was once tradition to name children after heroes of the past, a tradition that has generally faded along with much of the Kalian history." He cleared his throat. "Most were named after the heroes of the past and the most famous of those, were the twins of your bloodline."

"I don't understand. What does this have to do with me?"

"I am not certain," Jiro replied. "Perhaps nothing, perhaps everything. All I know is that twins born of your line have a tendency to have long affairs with the history books, and most achieve a level of fame that others only dream."

Mary shook her head. "I don't want that, master. I just want to serve the realm, in whatever manner it will have me."

"As the queen?" he asked. "Or as the Golden Defendant?"

Mary felt her body tense. "Which would you have me to be, master?"

"I would have nothing, princess. I only ask the question."

"I am the rightful heir to the throne, from the Temple of Kale."

Jiro nodded. "Yes, my lady. It is true. But you are also the most elegant fighter I have ever seen. Not since your mother have I seen such a combination of skill and grace." He looked at her, and broached the forbidden topic. "You could be the Golden Defendant and someday lead your temple with the same skill and grace that Master Leo has always displayed. You would be Princess Mariana of the Kalian bloodline, Golden Defendant and Master of the Temple of Kale, and without the heavy weight of the golden crown, be free of the restrictions of your royal blood."

Mary stared at him, attempting to respond, but finding herself unable to do so. It was as though he had reached into her soul and found her deepest fantasy. A realistic chance to be free of the curse of the crown and royal blood, and all she had to do was hand the title over to her twin. Mary could almost see her dreams dancing across the walls in the light of the flames.

She closed her eyes and pictured herself garbed in the golden robes of a temple master, the mark of the defendants upon her breast. She saw herself seated in Leo's golden chambers, now her own, advising Master Louis on the latest temple matter.

"Is it true, Master Mary," a young boy dressed in golden robes asked of her, "that you once fought the queen in the thirteenth tournament?"

She smiled down on the young boy. "Yes, I did."

"Was it hard to fight the heir to the throne?"

"My sister was my greatest opponent," she found herself replying. "The fight was, after all, the stuff of legends. But why would you ask?"

"Because I will face the Kolosian prince next week," the boy replied.

Mary opened her eyes, startled, and gazed at Master Jiro seated across from her. He sipped slowly on his own glass of Raspin in his metallic silver robes. The firelight caught the gleam of the silver mark of Koloso embedded into his robes. *The Kolosian prince*, the nameless boy's words seemed to glide across the room. She raised her gaze to meet Master Jiro's jade green eyes.

"You would just love that, wouldn't you? At long last, a Kolosian seated on the Kalian throne. Did my mother put you up to this? Did my sister?" Mary rose from her seat and gathered herself to her full height, towering above Jiro in his seated position. "I am the Crown Princess of Kale!" Her voice carried throughout the dim chamber. "And if Ameria wants my crown she will have to take it from me herself. Do you understand?"

Jiro moved from the chair to the floor where he knelt to one knee. "Forgive me, princess. I did not mean to offend. I only remind you, my lady, that if you choose to be queen, then your sister will undoubtedly become the Golden Defendant."

"Silence!" Mary commanded. "My sister made it perfectly clear that she desired my throne, but I will not give it up. No Kolosian shall ever sit upon my throne. Not while I breathe."

He remained kneeling on the floor as Mary walked towards the black desk on the opposite side of the room and placed her empty Raspin glass on it. "Thank you for the drink, Master Jiro. I think I have left Kyle waiting long enough."

Mary exited the room at a brisk pace and began to maneuver her way down the many corridors which led from the living quarters into the Kolosian training rooms. She hardly noticed the beauty of the walls surrounding her as she raced past the lower ranks of the training area and threw open the sacred doors to enter the gold and silver training section of the Kolosian temple. Kyle was waiting for her in the center of the training mat and entered into the traditional bow as she approached.

"Rise."

Kyle rose in a sweep of silver robes.

"Draw your sword."

Kyle hesitated.

"Now."

Kyle drew the silver-handled sword at his side, which was encrusted with two silver horses, one on each side of the Kalian blade. The silver horse, according to legend, had first appeared in the hills of Desoto, the land over which Kyle would one day preside. Mary pulled her long black hair back with a thin golden clip before drawing her own golden-handled silver blade from her side.

"Princess, what are we doing?"

"Crossing blades," Mary replied. She stepped forward and lunged at Kyle, putting most of her weight behind the movement. Kyle jumped to the side, causing Mary's momentum to carry her several steps forward in order to avoid falling. She turned to her left to once again face Kyle. "Cross blades with me."

Kyle shook his head, "I will not fight you, princess. Not like this."

"Yes, you will, Kyle."

"No, I..."

"I am the Crown Princess of Kale!" She was suddenly screaming. "I do not make requests; I am your future sovereign, now cross blades with me!"

Kyle looked uncertain, but he stood his ground against Mary's next lunge, blocking the blade. She moved forward again, slicing towards Kyle's left side. He twisted his body towards the blade, meeting the stroke head on, pushing them both backwards from the backlash. Kyle recovered but did not move to follow her, instead holding his ground, widening his stance for better balance. Mary swung her blade down again, aiming the tip at his midsection. Kyle moved his own blade up, easily deflecting her strike.

Kyle finally moved forward, parrying Mary's next stoke and swinging his own blade at her right side. She twisted, evading the silver sword. Sweat began to seep through Mary's robes, causing them to cling uncomfortably to her skin. Kyle moved forward and the sound of their clashing blades reverberated throughout the temple walls. As he recovered, Mary took several steps back. She wiped the sweat from her brow before it could threaten her vision.

He followed her, driving her towards the edge of the silver side of the temple mat. Mary struck out again, stopping her backwards progress, but was unable to gain any ground. Kyle swung his blade from above, using his height to his advantage, and she dropped to a knee, bringing her blade up to meet the downward stroke above her head. The swords sang once again and Mary rolled to her right, towards the center of the mat. Then, she sprang to her feet in a single, fluid movement.

Kyle followed her. No sooner had Mary stood, than she was once again blocking his deadly blade. She moved to her left, but was too slow in the movement, exposing her arm. Kyle took quick advantage, sinking his blade into her exposed skin. Then he immediately stepped away from her. Blood began to mix with the sweat staining her golden robes. "Mary, I think that's enough."

In response, Mary moved forward with her uninjured sword hand and swung her blade towards Kyle's side. He stopped Mary's sword. She twirled around the mat to his right side and tried again. Kyle evaded the movement with a quick step backwards. She pushed him back several more steps until they had once again reached the center of the mat. Blood began to drip from the edge of her golden cloth onto the silver mat below. She advanced with another series of thrusts: left, right, left and then, suddenly, Kyle's sword was at her throat. "Enough!" Kyle said, holding the blade just shy of her pale skin.

A heartbeat passed. Kyle stepped back. His sword fell to the ground with a soft clatter, the silver blade appearing almost dull against the golden floor. "Please, princess. That's enough."

Mary turned towards Kyle. "With a sword," she said softly, "my sister is better than I. Without a sword, it is a fair fight, but with a sword." Mary shook her head, slipping down onto the golden mat beneath her. Her heart raced, the air of the room burned her throat. "The only person I have ever seen match my sister's blade is you, her partner." She drew a deep, painful breath. "You want my forgiveness, then I need something from you."

Kyle took a seat on the mat across from her, fighting for breath. "Name it, princess."

"I met the man who killed Lord Edward."

Kyle stared intensely at the princess.

"I want to kill him." Her voice was firm. "I want to kill him, but my sister said that he matched her blade for blade and if that is true, then he is better than me." She stared into Kyle's eyes head on. "I want you to train me, Kyle. I want you to teach me the sword so that the next time I see this man, who rides flauntingly with Lord Edward's blade at his side...this man who killed our lord, my friend, our Golden Defendant....I want you to teach me the sword, Kyle, so that next time I see this man...I can cut his heart out."

Chapter XXVII

AMERIA'S SWORD CLATTERED TO THE floor. "*Sutis*!" She cursed.

"It is okay, princess," Master Jiro tried to sooth her. "It's only been a few weeks."

"Thirteen! It has been thirteen weeks, and I still can barely hold the sword, let alone actually use one."

"Ameria, your hand is getting stronger. These things take time."

"Time!" Ameria raged. "The tournament is coming! How am I supposed to win the tournament with these?" She held up her hands. The scars were prominently shown. Whatever had punctured her hands had cut cleanly through every tendon and ligament her fingers had to offer. Her hands would not bend properly and she had little movement in several fingers. The healers, who treated her hands, had made the mistake of telling the princess that she should feel grateful to have any movement at all. Ameria had the men who spoke forcefully thrown from the temple grounds, promising death if she ever saw them again.

Her hands trembled at the slightest strain, but Ameria fought through it, attempting in vain to keep up with her training. With kicks and general workouts she was as skilled as ever, but when it came to anything involving her hands, she was just shy of helpless. The princess, who had for so many years been a silhouette of control, had transformed into an emotional avalanche, one moment seeming her old self and the next sinking into a bottomless pit of anger and despair.

Kyle, who stood in the room behind her, had to choke down his own anger as he watched the once proud sword master struggle to do so much as grip her thin blade. "Ameria," Kyle volunteered. "Why don't we practice a few kicks? I could use the practice."

Ameria swirled around and glowered at him. "You think I can't do it, don't you? You think I'll never hold a sword again. My own partner!"

"Ameria," Kyle tried to sound reasonable, "you know that is not true. I really could use the practice."

"Why?" she demanded. "Is my sister not keeping you on your toes, *partner*? Perhaps if you spent as much time helping me as you do courting my sister, I would be able to hold my sword by now!"

"Ameria," Kyle pleaded, "you know that's not true. You don't understand."

"Oh yes I do!" Ameria turned in a swirl of gold and stepped forward, moving her dark blue eyes only inches from his green ones. "You don't want me to recover, do you?"

"Ameria!" Kyle stammered. "How could you think that?"

"I know your game. With me out, you're in. You won't defeat Mary. Oh no, you're not good enough for that." She smiled, but it did not reach her eyes. "With me out, you will take silver to her gold. Defendant or no, my uncle will die before she ever rises to the rank of a Golden Defendant and with her trapped on the throne, it leaves you free to run the team in her stead. You, King Kyle, the Golden Defendant. And me? A disabled husk hidden from view in the backroom of the palace, probably married off to whatever man will take me so that his children will gain a royal title!"

"My lady," Kyle began.

Ameria slapped him across the face, then shrieked from the pain in her hand. "*Sutis*! Gods *Sutis*!" she cursed before turning and running from the room.

The last thing she heard was Master Jiro asking, "Are you okay, Kyle?"

"Yes," he replied softly.

Two hours later, Ameria was still in a fury. She had paced the stone floor of her room so often in the last few weeks, she was surprised that the floor had not given way beneath her feet. She rarely slept, tossing and turning from the terrible nightmares experienced when she tried. Sometimes she would wake up thankful to be alive, while others she would curse the Gods for answering her prayers. *If they had just ignored me*, she thought bitterly, *then at least this humiliation would be over*.

When she was not in the training rooms, Ameria wore long, golden gloves to hide her hideous flesh. The scars were large, reaching from her wrists past the center of her hands. Even so, Ameria thought she might have been able to tolerate them, had it not been for the burns that splattered her skin. Whatever had bitten her hands had punctured them completely, leaving the hideous scars on both sides.

Despite all the questioning by the king's inquisitors and the investigations taking place within the temples and defendant team, no one seemed to have a clue as to who was responsible for the attempted assassination of the two royal sisters. Ameria hid behind the walls of her Temple, refusing all visitors both personal and professional. Only her fellow Kolosians were allowed to see her at all, and during her training, only Kyle and Jiro had been allowed into the rooms.

Her sister had come several times, but Ameria closed the door on her, screaming to be left alone. It made Ameria physically ill to look at Mary. Mary, who had gone through the same trauma, but had miraculously come out of the situation unscathed. Mary, who would not only become queen, but was now all but guaranteed to win the Kalian tournament. It seemed that even the Gods now favored the older sibling...even Kyle.

From the moment she had been injured, her lifelong partner had suddenly started spending an immense amount of time at the Temple of Kale. "I've lost everything!" Ameria yelled at everyone and no one. "Everything!" She flung her arms, casting off the golden gloves. She starred at her marred skin. Tears filled her eyes, but she fought them. "I can't even grip a sword," she whispered.

Ameria lay down on her large bed and sank down into the golden covers. "I will not cry."

Chapter XXVIII

The song of swords echoed down the golden halls. Exhausted, with sweat pouring down her body, Mary parried Kyle's next swing at a far slower pace than she would have liked.

He lowered his sword. "Okay, princess. We've been at this for hours; I think it's time for a break."

Mary nodded. "Yes, I think I could use something to eat."

"And I, for one, could use a shower." Kyle responded.

"Why don't you use my shower?" Marcus offered from behind them.

"Sure, that would be great. Thank you."

"No problem. You know the way. Feel free to grab a spare robe from the closet."

"Sure, thanks," Kyle said again before turning to leave the private section of the training rooms. Marcus and Mary turned to follow him.

"I thought you were going to train with me today," Marcus commented quietly to his partner.

"Sorry," Mary replied. "Lost track of time."

"Seems to happen a lot lately."

Mary stopped walking and turned to face her partner. "Are you upset with me?"

Marcus shook his head a little too quickly. "Just making sure you still know who your real partner is, Mary."

Mary inhaled sharply. "We will train tomorrow, okay? Promise."

"Fine." Marcus nodded.

As they exited the large gold doors separating the golden training area from the rest of the temple, Mary walked towards the red mat where Ryan was speaking with Master Leo. Leo had been training Ryan at Mary's request. Katalin, promoted to the rank of red when Jace died, had been acting as an additional coach and sparring partner for the young man. As the team had yet to replace their vacant space, Ryan had been given the purple chambers of the temple, which Lara had traded in for the higher rank of white when Jace died.

Ryan showed tremendous talent for the sword and Mary wondered again how he had managed to remain hidden all this time. Had he been born within one of the main kingdoms, Mary was sure he would have been brought into one of the temples for training, though it was highly doubtful it would have been this particular temple. Ryan's mother had surprised Mary by granting her consent for her son to remain by the princess' side. Officially, Ryan was not a student of the Temple of Kale, as it was unprecedented to allow anyone who had not been raised within its walls to enter into the training program.

Mary had been asked by Master Leo several weeks before to view the younger class and see if one of the students should be deemed worthy to be promoted to tournament level. Yet the idea of doing so left Mary with a foul taste. The spot to which Leo was referring still belonged to Jace and no one on the team seemed eager to see it filled.

Mary walked to the mats where Leo stood speaking with Ryan. Lara, dressed in white, stepped forward to greet her. "Princess Mary. I was wondering if I could make a request?"

"You may."

"I...well, you see, I know that you are not participating in all of the Kalian twelve this year, since you were undefeated last year. But it's my understanding that your sister is injured and since that's the case, you might actually be considering fighting next week at the Temple of Kevera?"

Mary nodded. "Yes, I was considering it."

"Well, if that's true, then there are only nine of us which means that I won't have a partner. I've won most of the rounds this year, so I was thinking."

"You would like me to sit out so you can fight with Rys?"

Lara shook her head. "No, that's not it at all. I was thinking that, since I'm fighting in the lower brackets and that makes it kind of low key, that perhaps Ryan might join me in the ring?"

"Ryan?" Mary looked thoughtfully at Lara. "Have you spoken to Master Leo about this?"

"No, my lady. I wanted to speak with you first. I know that he is your guest and I know that it's a little unprecedented, but..."

Mary shook her head. "You would have to ask Master Leo," she told the younger girl.

The two walked to the edge of the mat. Leo was demonstrating several upward strokes of the blade which Mary recognized all too well. "Master," Mary called. He turned around to glance in her direction. "Lara knows that particular sequence. Why don't you let him try them out on her for a few minutes?"

Leo nodded his consent and Lara moved into the red and pink training area. Leo walked towards the princess and exited the mats. "I'm assuming you would like to speak with me, princess?"

"Yes." Mary took several steps away from the mat to ensure that they were out of hearing range of the other two students. She filled Leo in on Lara's request.

"Well." The temple master looked thoughtful. "There is no rule expressly forbidding such a substitution. As long as he goes with the official backing of the temple."

Mary nodded, but then paused. "I don't know if it's a good idea."

"Why is that?"

Mary shifted her weight from her left to her right, and then back to her left. "It's not step by step training. He will be going up against people who have done this for years. Including the team from Koloso."

"That is true, Mary. But this young man has been trained as well. Certainly not to the extent of you or Marcus, but more than enough to hold his own against the lower ranks. Plus, remember, he is younger than you. Had he been trained within the temples, he would just now be reaching the proper age to achieve a tournament rank."

Mary shrugged. "I achieved tournament rank when I was younger than him."

"Yes, Mary, but, as you know, you were a special case."

"All the same."

Leo's eyes searched her face. "Ryan is not Jace, Mary. And this is not placing him against one such as you or Kyle. He would be fighting in the lowest tournament rank we have to offer. I've seen him fight with Lara. He would do well with her, I think. And she does need a partner."

"I could just sit this one out."

"And put Katalin in the same round as Kyle?" Leo shook his head. "Even with Marcus, that is not a good idea." Mary," Leo paused for breath, "just because something bad happened to Jason, does not mean that something will happen to Ryan."

"I know that," Mary snapped. "Don't you think I know that?"

Chapter XXIX

―――※―――

"Are you really going to fight without Ameria?" Brandan, the fourth ranking student of Koloso, asked.

"Are you really happy wearing that pale pink all the time?" Kyle replied.

Brandan shrugged. "If you wear gold at this next one, then I can move up to red and Kev can wear pink."

"You would have me discount my partner's rightful rank, just so you can get out of pink?"

"Not discount!" Brandan said, aghast. "Just, if she is not fighting then you would officially be representing us as the golden student for that tournament. And besides." Brandan shot a wide grin in Kev's general direction. "Kev actually looks good in pink."

"Not half as good as you," the third man shot back.

Kyle laughed despite himself and the voice of the other two men quickly joined him. The three Kolosians were seated in one of the temple lounges, surrounded by the golden walls of the Temple of Kale. Dressed in pink and black respectively, Brandan and Kev were seated on golden cushions. The windows of the Temple of Kale were open wide as the light of the kingdom's three suns filled the room with warmth. Across from them, Breeze lounged on a chair, his eyes closed lightly with his black paws stretched out in front of him, clearly enjoying the sunlight which was a rarity at the Temple of Koloso.

"Man." Kev stretched his body in the warmth of the suns. "Sometimes I think we went to the wrong temple. There's got to be a spare hill somewhere nearby. Couldn't we just move our temple to the top of one of them?"

"Oh sure." Brandan laughed. "I'll wave my arms and 'poof!' The temple will magically appear at the top of the hill."

Kyle rolled his eyes. "What exactly are you all doing here?"

Kev cleared his throat. "Honestly, you have been spending so much time here in the last few months, we really did want to know if you are planning to fight in the Dektra Tournament." He motioned to Kyle's silver robe, which bore the golden mark of Kale. "Or will you be fighting for a different team?"

Kyle sighed. "My own robe is being cleaned. Look guys, this is nothing personal. The princess has asked for my assistance on a few projects over the last few weeks. I owe it to her to help."

"So you are fighting with her in the next tournament?" Brandan asked.

"No!" Kyle said quickly. "It is nothing like that at all. If Ameria wants to enter the ring, I will fight with her, and if she does not, I will move Rosa up to the top level with me."

Kev gave an exasperated sigh. "So much for that."

"What?"

"Just think, Brandan," Kev continued. "Forget getting out of pink. You could have worn silver if Kyle was fighting with the Kalian princess!"

A moment of silence passed before Brandan suddenly said, "Oh man, why didn't I think of that? Kyle I totally think you should stay here and fight with Mary!"

Kyle glared at his teammate. "Brandan," he said in a warning tone. "I..."

"Does it smell bad in here to you?" a high-pitched voice interrupted.

Someone inhaled deeply. "Yeah," came the reply from yet another voice. "It smells like the distinct scent of losers."

"Not just any losers," the chocolate-colored puppy rounded the corner.

"Nope, worse," a white puppy answered his partner, entering the room right behind him.

"Kolosian losers!" Coco and Mac said in cheerful unison.

"Don't you have something better to do?" Kyle asked the two puppies.

"Than to bug you?" Coco tilted his head to stare up at Kyle. "We're not scheduled to beat you for another few weeks, so nope, not really."

"Hey ya, Breeze," Coco said to the black and white spotted Kolosian puppy lying in the sun.

"Hello, Coco," Breeze replied, twisting his head to adjust the silver chain he wore around his neck.

"We've got better rooms for sun sleeping than this one. We'll show ya, if you want?"

Breeze stood slowly from his stretched position and glanced towards Kyle.

"Go on, Breeze," Kyle said. "I'll be here for a few more days, so if you'd like to stay that's fine with me, if it's fine with them." He motioned towards Coco and Mac.

"Come on, Breeze!" Coco exclaimed. "We'll show you the best sunshine room in the whole temple. You'll never want to go back to that dark place ever again! I could use a partner who could actually help me win a fight once in a while."

"What he means," Mac cut in, "is that he needs someone to kick his butt, so that I will finally have a partner who doesn't keep dragging me down."

"Come on Breeze," Coco called. "At least we'll get away from this Kolosian stench!"

"Straight down the hallway and fourth door to the left, last one there is a Postrema!" The three puppies took off down the golden hall like long lost friends. Kyle shook his head, but could not suppress a smile.

Chapter XXX

RYAN STOOD TALL IN HIS purple robes, as he prepared to take the ring for the first time in his life. "Just remember," Mary cautioned him again. "Stick to your own color. Purple to purple. Let Lara handle the other..."

"I've got it, Mary. Don't worry."

"You don't 'got it' until you say it."

Ryan gave a small sigh in the same manner Jace used to, and said, "I will follow Lara's lead. I will stay within my own color group. I promise."

Mary attempted to smile, but found she lacked the courage, so instead she gave a small nod. "Good luck, and may the Gods look favorably upon your fight today."

"Thank you." Ryan gave a bow at the waist and then suddenly dropped to his knees, attempting to replicate the temple Bow.

"Really, there is no need for that." Mary motioned for him to rise.

"I want to," he said from his knelling position on the floor. "I'm fighting for the Kalian temple. That makes you my captain...at least for today."

Mary paused a moment and then nodded. "Okay, then. Rise, Ryan of Kale." He rose rather ungracefully, his body unaccustomed to the kneeling position required by the temples.

The tournament had officially started an hour before when the bottom eight teams had entered the first rounds. The top four teams had been given a bye and the second round of matches were about to start.

Mary glanced at the chart and took note of the four advancing teams. It looked like the teams from Kevera, Mortem, Critous, and Bellum would be advancing. No real surprise there.

"The Temple of Kale and the Temple of Bellum," the announcer called to the audience. Ryan turned to find Lara as the two headed towards the roped off tournament mats. Mary moved to the side of the ring, to the benches usually reserved for the coaches of the fighting teams. Coco was standing on the edge of the wide seats and Mary sat down beside him. "His first fight! Is he excited? He does know that if he loses to a Bellum, then I get a free license to tease him about it till the end of time, doesn't he?"

Mary gave Coco her best glare. Coco sobered at Mary's expression. "He will be fine, Mary. It's a low-level match, and if something were to happen, we are inside the temples. Drag him to the edge of the mat. He'll be fine."

Mary took some comfort in these words, and then her thoughts wandered to her sister, Ameria, who had not been healed by the magic of Kale, but instead was left maimed and disfigured; Mary shivered. Dozens had been interrogated, imprisoned, and removed from positions of power, yet the source behind their attacks remained nameless. Mary, who had once loved the adventure of her long rides, now found herself afraid to venture far beyond the temple walls.

She had spent every free moment of her time either helping Ryan with his training or working with Kyle. Master Leo was very impressed with her improvement with the blade and she had disarmed both Leo and Kyle several times in the last few weeks, something she had never before been able to do. Kyle had also graciously stepped in and helped Ryan with his swordplay. Ryan continually impressed the silver Kolosian with his aptitude and skill.

"Hey Mary," Kyle's voice interrupted her thoughts. "May I take a seat?"

"Actually," Marcus interrupted. "That is my seat." Marcus moved forward, shoving past Kyle to take the seat beside Mary. "Shouldn't you be supporting your own team?" he asked the silver Kolosian.

"Not until they are in the ring," Kyle replied.

"It is bad enough that you have been training their opponent." he grumbled. "Now you are going to publically cheer for Kale as well?"

"I would think you would be grateful," Kyle remarked. "After all, it is your team I was helping out."

Marcus stood. "No one asked you to," he spoke through gritted teeth.

"Actually, yes, they did."

"Well, it certainly wasn't me."

"Marcus," Mary intervened. "Enough."

Marcus turned to Mary with heated eyes. "Siding with the Kolosian again?"

Mary stood and took several steps forward, all three stepping away from the chairs behind them. "Marcus, I am not siding with anyone. You are both behaving like..."

"He is not your partner, Mary. But I am beginning to think you would like him to be."

"Don't be ridiculous, Marcus," she stated in a low tone. "Now that is quite enough." She drew a deep breath, calming her nerves. "Now, why don't you go find Master Leo and make sure there are no last minute instructions?" He looked at her and then back to Kyle. "Please," she added. Marcus left reluctantly.

Mary sighed and then turned back to find that the previously empty seat had been taken during the exchange. "Coco," Mary asked the puppy. "Do you mind moving over one?"

"Sure," Coco replied. "But I'll have to move upwind. I can't enter the ring smelling like a Kolosian! It might rub off."

"Don't you have a fight of your own to prepare for?" Kyle asked the chocolate puppy.

"Not until after the Grand Championship round," Coco replied.

"Ah." Coco moved down and Kyle took his place on the other side of the princess.

Meanwhile, the purple and white teams stepped onto the mat. They offered a respectful bow in each other's direction and then took their individual stances. A bell rang out, reverberating along the temple walls, and the match began.

Never taking her eyes off the fight, Mary asked of the man seated beside her, "How is my sister?"

Kyle sighed. "Angry. As one might expect."

Mary nodded. "I think when this tournament is over I will try to see her again."

"I doubt she will let you in."

Ryan was facing off with his color coordinated opponent. He blocked a punch aimed for his left side and then completed a beautiful round kick with his left foot that landed squarely into his opponent's side, knocking the purple Bellum student halfway across the ring. He rolled several times before flipping back to his feet.

"If Ameria doesn't wish to see me," Mary continued the conversation. "Then I guess I will just have to sit there until she changes her mind."

"Might take a while."

"Doesn't matter. She is my sister. I have to at least try."

"You have tried, you know that you have tried, don't you?"

"Not hard enough," came her reply. "Oh." She motioned towards the fight. "That was a thing of beauty."

The Bellum student had attempted to kick Ryan's left side. Ryan had leaned back away from the movement, but instead of jumping completely clear, he had slid towards the ground under the kick, brought up his arm, and caught his opponent's leg in mid-motion. He twisted the leg as he rose, spinning the Bellum student to collide with the white mat. The crowd started to cheer Ryan's name while behind them, Lara had successfully managed to throw her own opponent completely out of the ring.

"He made that look effortless!" Kyle exclaimed.

The Bellum student tried to rise, but Ryan knocked him down before he had completely reclaimed his footing. Lara moved closer, but remained just out of reach, allowing Ryan the freedom to finish his first fight alone. Ryan's opponent rolled several steps away and rose to his feet. Ryan followed him across the ring. The purple-ranked Bellum threw a punch squarely at Ryan's face. Ryan brought one arm up and pressed the back of his hand against his opponent's wrist, pushing his the other man's arm up and away from him. With his other hand, he landed a punch to his opponent's chest. The Bellum student collapsed, gasping for breath. He did not rise, effectively yielding the round.

Mary let out a loud whistle and Kyle clapped his hand. "Way to go, Ryan!"

Lara embraced her partner with a loud thank you, but her voice was overridden by the cheer of the crowd behind them. Ryan reached out and helped the Bellum student to the side of the ring. The lights gathered and shimmered, leaving all four students standing unharmed by the time they dimmed.

Mary stood still at the bench as Ryan walked towards her, but Coco raced ahead to congratulate him. "Way to go, Ryan!" the puppy exclaimed happily.

"Thanks, Coco," Ryan knelt and gave him a gentle scratch behind the ears before rising and walking to Mary.

"Congratulations," Mary told him, feeling even more relieved than she had imagined.

Despite this initial sense of relief, Mary felt even more insecure in the next round when the Kale team squared off with its sister team from Desoto. Yet with immense skill and an unnatural grace, Lara and Ryan prevailed against them as well, advancing to the final round. On the other side of the chart, Kevera and Koloso had each respectively triumphed over Dektra and Mortem, leaving the number five team, Kevera, to face off against Koloso. Kevera managed to hold off the Kolosian team for the better part of ten minutes before the Kolosians drove one of the Keverans out of the ring, leaving Koloso with a two to one advantage. The fight ended a few minutes later, with Koloso advancing to the final round.

"We will now take a short break," the announcer's voice called over the crowd. "Desoto and Kevera will fight for the honor of third place, while our top two teams catch their breath. Then, a special treat as Kale and Koloso face off!"

"I guess that's my cue to go show some team loyalty." Kyle turned towards Ryan. "Good luck, sorry my teammates are going to beat you. At least try to give them a run for their money."

"He'll give them a run," Coco piped up. "They will run straight from the ring and back to their dark, dreary loser-temple!"

Mary offered Ryan a smile. "Are you ready for this round?"

Ryan nodded. "I know they're good and yes." He held up his hands, "I will only fight the purple guy."

Mary nodded and twenty minutes later, retook her seat on the side bench. Ryan and Lara entered the ring on the opposite side of Cal and Setrick, the purple and white team from Koloso. The two teams bowed to each other as a sign of respect and then the fight began.

Kolosians were trained to be more offensive than defensive fighters. This was not to say that they couldn't block a punch, but rather that they were generally the first to make a move in the majority of rounds. Such was the case in this particular round, with Cal throwing the first kick towards Lara.

Lara jumped out of the way and Cal ended up spinning into a full circle from the power of his movement. He landed, feet flat on the ground and hands up to guard his face and upper chest. Lara took advantage of this stance by attempting to sweep his lower leg with her own. Cal jumped to his left to avoid the movement and Lara followed him across the purple floor.

Across from them, Setrick had moved in on Ryan with a powerful thrust of his arm towards Ryan's left shoulder. Ryan leaned to the right to avoid the intended impact. Setrick followed and moved his other fist towards Ryan's right.

Ryan was unable to avoid the second strike, and he stumbled back several paces. He recovered just in time to counter Setrick's next punch with one of his own, landing his fist squarely into his opponent's shoulder. A sickening crack was heard as Setrick's arm popped out of its socket.

Meanwhile, Lara was continuing to counter Cal's every move. The two seemed evenly matched. Lara stuck to her defensive strategy, attempting to wear Cal down for several minutes before finally deciding to launch a series of attacks. Lara threw a kick to Cal's left and it was suddenly his turn to block. He slapped her ankle away with the back of his arm and then took a defensive posture, standing firmly in place with his fists up to guard his upper body.

Setrick threw a kick with his left leg, but without the use of his arm, he was off balance and the strike was easily avoided. A quick kick towards Setrick's left side had him reeling to the ground, falling partially on his injured arm. He cried out in pain and, this time, remained down on the mat.

On the other side, Lara landed a successful kick on Cal's right, sending him to the floor. He recovered before Lara could press her advantage and entered into a series of ferocious kicks. Lara blocked one, two, three, but the fourth sent her flying to the ground. Dazed, Lara could only look up as Cal's foot sailed towards the center of her chest...and was thrown aside by Ryan's hand crashing into Cal's knee. Cal fell to the ground beside Lara and she rose to her feet with the room still spinning. Cal remained on the ground clutching his leg. "Thanks," Lara told her partner as the announcer called the round for Kale.

A cheer reverberated through the crowd as the Kalians claimed the victory for the round. Several of Koloso's team members rushed forward and moved their fallen teammates to the side of the ring while Ryan and Lara walked to where Mary was seated. "I'm sorry," Ryan said once within speaking range of the princess. "I know you said to stay within the same color, but he was going to…"

Mary shook her head. "It is okay, Ryan. It was good that you protected your teammate. It is what being a part of a team is all about. The important thing is that you did well and, until your own opponent was down, you stuck with my directives." She offered him what might have been her first real smile of the night. "Congratulations, Ryan. You did our temple proud."

"And it's not over!" Coco piped up. "You have to go beat the Postrema in the next round." Coco's voice became louder as he noticed Kyle had walked up beside them. "And losing to a Postrema is almost as bad as smelling like a Kolosian!"

Ryan did not lose to the Postrema. Nor did he loose to the team he fought next. Since Ameria was injured, leaving Koloso one member short, Koloso had no one entered in the blue and green rounds, which lead most to believe that Kale's higher-ranked team would face an easy victory. In a surprise upset, Desoto defeated Kale's upper ranked team in the semi-final round, leaving an even more surprising final round of Desoto versus Kale's lower-ranked team in the championship final match.

Lara held her ground skillfully throughout the match, but it was Ryan who impressed, driving his opponent out early in the round and then moving to join his partner. With the two to one advantage, the green clothed student from Desoto was forced to block a string of movements from both sides and was soon driven from the ring by the lower-ranked pair. The crowd went wild with the victory, delighted to witness the unprecedented advancement of the lower-ranked team.

They followed their victory by defeating the black and yellow team from Saktatio and entering the championship round in their place. They also defeated Mortem, advancing to the quarter finals. It was not until that round that Koloso put a stop to their wondrous advancement. With a series of vigorous kicks, Lara crumpled to the ground within the first three minutes of the round with her right leg snapped cleanly in two. She cried out in pain, clutching her leg, tears springing to her eyes.

Her defeat left both higher-ranked students free to pursue Ryan. They worked as a unit and within a few strokes it was over. A kick to Ryan's right side knocked the breath from his lungs and a second made sure he was unable to recover. He collapsed in a heap and was unable to draw enough breath through his cracked ribs to rise again. Mary ran to the floor and tried to lift Ryan towards the side of the ring. She was struggling under the weight, when Marcus appeared beside her. Together they moved Ryan to the side of the ring and closed their eyes against the blinding light. Moments later, Ryan gazed at Mary with glassy eyes.

"So does this mean Coco will be making fun of me after all?"

Mary stood with a smile. "Just ask him about last year's Kevera tournament, it should shut him up." Marcus laughed and released Ryan from his grasp, allowing him to regain his own feet. "You did exceptionally well, Ryan. Far better than anyone imagined. It is a rare thing to win a round above one's level and to advance to an even higher level; virtually unheard of." Mary let go of Ryan's arm and took a step back, putting space between them.

Dan, dressed in black, came forward and gave Ryan a high-five. "Don't worry, Ryan. We'll get those Kolosians for you."

"As long as the Kevera Team doesn't get to them first," his partner, Sara, added. Sara was dressed in yellow robes, brighter than Mary's gold, yet somehow lacking the sheen and luster that was prominent within Mary's golden fabric.

"Doubtful," Dan replied. "The Kolosian team is on fire today. We will probably have to take them down ourselves."

True to Dan's prediction, it was Kale vs. Koloso in the final match, in which Dan kept his promise and defeated the Kolosian team after a respectable ten minutes of fierce exchanges between the two sets of champions. After being declared the winner of the championship round, they successfully defeated Occidere and Critous before succumbing to the superior skill displayed by the Temple of Desoto. Once again it was Kale vs. Koloso in the final. Koloso advanced, taking the title of Grand Champions.

Despite all the surprises and upsets featured in the lower levels of the tournament, the Royal Championship rounds played out like clockwork. The bottom eight teams were eliminated by the semi-finals leaving the top four to fight for the title of Tournament and Royal Champion. Mary and Marcus faced off and successfully defeated the gold and silver members from the Temple of Desoto while Kyle and Rosa defeated the Dektra Team, leaving the top two teams to face each other in the finals.

After each of the semi-final rounds, a break was called while the puppy teams from Kale and Koloso faced off. Coco and Mac won the day and their egos seemed to grow before Mary's eyes, if that was even possible.

The ring was cleared. The teams from Kale and Koloso were called to the floor. As Mary walked onto the mats she offered Kyle a bow of respect. "Is there some reason you haven't surrendered yet?" she asked the silver Kolosian.

Kyle shook his head. "I figure the best way to learn how to defeat you is to try."

With the ring of the bell, Mary's eyes focused exclusively on Kyle as she attempted to drown out the rest of the world. The crowd seemed utterly silent as the two fighters began to circle each other. To their left, Rosa had entered into a series of kicks against Marcus, but Mary hardly noticed, not daring to take her eyes off the tall warrior in front of her. Kyle threw a round kick towards Mary, but she took two quick steps to her left, easily avoiding his foot. Kyle threw a punch towards her right, and she blocked it, raising her arm in just the nick of time.

Mary twisted into a kick. Kyle blocked her leg with a stinging impact, tossing her away so violently that he threw himself off balance. It was a struggle, but Mary managed not to fall. Her leg started to throb. Kyle threw himself at her, landing a punch to the side of her arm, hard enough to bruise. Mary countered with a kick of her own. Kyle moved left to stop her, but was too slow and her uninjured leg slammed into his ribcage, cracking several ribs as it did so. Kyle let out a gasp of pain, moving one hand to clutch his side.

Mary was startled by the sound of the breaking ribs. She froze for several heartbeats before turning back to strike Kyle again, but by that time, he had placed himself momentarily outside of her range. Mary followed him, but remained at a kicking distance, keeping her injured arm closer to her body than she normally would.

Kyle was having trouble breathing through his broken ribs. He fought through the pain to take enough of a stance to hold his ground. Mary threw a punch toward his uninjured side, but he blocked her arm with his own, forcing her arm up, causing Mary to miss him completely. Kyle came in with a punch of his own, hitting Mary's left side, and it was her turn to gasp as her own ribs cracked. Mary took several steps back, winded and wincing in pain. She tasted bile, but managed to choke it down as she retook her defensive stance.

Kyle launched another kick towards Mary. She blocked, but the momentum was too much and both champions fell to the ground, thrown off balance by the power of Kyle's movements. Mary caught herself, preventing her injured side from colliding with the mat, but in doing so, she caused further damage to her injured arm. She let out a vicious hiss from the sudden impact, but managed to pull herself to her feet.

Kyle also rose from the mat, though his movements lacked their legendary gracefulness. Mary's fist suddenly collided with the left side of his face, sending him to the ground. He caught himself with his arms and coughed. Blood splattered the golden mat. A tooth rolled to the floor in front of him. He coughed again, spitting more blood as the stinging pain roared through his jaw. He wondered if it was broken. He managed to rise to his feet slowly.

Mary froze at the sight of the blood. The smell assaulted her senses and suddenly she seemed to stumble. She closed her eyes to clear her vision, but when she opened them, everything was covered with blood. Kyle's leg collided into her uninjured side, snapping her back into reality, but he ended up spinning in a full circle, unprepared for Mary's lack of action against him. Mary collapsed to the floor. She was slow to rise.

She launched a sideways kick. Kyle caught her leg in midair. Kyle twisted her leg into an unnatural position popping it from its socket. Mary screamed in sudden agony, and lashed out, hitting the back of his head as she squirmed in pain. The two fighters collapsed to the floor in a heap of twisted limbs, with Kyle blacking out.

The force of the impact made Mary's stomach churn. Kyle's body lay unmoving on top of her and she struggled to crawl out with a shriek that would have filled the room had the roar of the crowd not been so deafening. She scrambled hysterically away from the blood and vomited on the golden floor.

The announcer called the match for Kale, but Mary was in too much of a panic to care. She lay on the floor clutching her leg with her uninjured arm and let out a soft scream when Marcus tried to move her. "Come on, Mary," her longtime partner said in a soothing voice. He reached for her again. Mary scrambled away as though he were a snake. "Mary, what are you doing?"

It was only when Ryan stepped out from behind Marcus that Mary allowed anyone to touch her. "Hey, Mary," Ryan said softly. "I know it hurts, but we have to get you out of this ring." He gathered the princess in his arms in the same fashion which he had carried her through her last injury and walked slowly towards the edge of the ring. Mary buried her face in his cloak to muffle her sobs.

The light worked its magic and healed Mary's injuries, yet she remained clinging to Ryan's purple robes, as she fought to regain her control. It took several moments for her to compose herself enough to dry her tears and disentangle herself from his arms, more thankful than ever that the majority of the scene had been covered by the noise of the cheering crowd.

On the opposite side of the ring, Brandan and Kev had carried their unconscious leader off the mats, where he was revived by the same bright lights that had healed Mary's injuries. "You almost had her!" Kev informed him. "I mean, really, I have never seen anyone come so close to beating her. It was incredible. It..." But Kyle was not listening. Instead, he searched the crowd for the princess.

He finally spotted her moving away from the crowd towards the far hallway leading from the main competition area into the living residence beyond.

Leaving Kev still chattering away, Kyle maneuvered his way through the crowds as Mary disappeared down the almost empty hallway. He increased his pace, but she was out of the hallway and at the front door of the temple before he reached her. "Mary!" he shouted, entering into a run. "Mary!"

Mary reached for the door and Kyle placed his weight against it, pushing it closed with his left hand. Mary's face was expressionless as she said, "Move."

"I can't do that, Mary."

In response, Mary grabbed Kyle's arm just above the wrist and twisted it away from the door. She shoved him with an impressive amount of strength, sending him crashing into the wall on the backside of the door and momentary knocking the wind from his lungs. "Mary!" he called, but his voice came out as little more than a gasp.

She raced down the marble steps headed for the stables, ignoring the calls of the pages who stood ready to assist her. She rushed downhill to the stables and found her horse, Sherwyn. Not bothering with a saddle, Mary mounted the golden stallion and yelled for the guards to open the gates.

Realizing that the princess was going to ride out, Kyle raced to his own silver stallion. He jumped onto the horse, without waiting for the saddle. "Mary!" he called.

She ignored him, guiding her horse towards the gates, which opened at her command. When she dug her heels into the sides of her horse, Sherwyn broke into a run, entering the mists of the Rainbow Mountains.

Kyle gave chase, cursing softly at his lack of a saddle. He chased after her, urging his silver stallion even faster, and yet he still seemed to be losing ground. He managed to keep her in sight and continued the chase, though for how many miles, he did not know.

The horse raced forward. The chilled wind blew through Mary's long black hair and stung her skin. She pushed on, attempting to outrun the nightmares that nipped at her heels. She lowered her head, leaning into the horse until Sherwyn's mane touched the side of her face. She closed her eyes and for one moment, the entire world dissolved into the feel of the harsh wind and the sound of Sherwyn's pounding hooves.

Mary had no idea how long they rode before Sherwyn's pace began to slow. They continued to walk for several moments before Mary finally said, "Whoa," and pulled softly on Sherwyn's golden mane, bringing him to a complete stop. The sky above her was cloudless and all three suns filled the violet sky. Her eyes stung from the wind and her cheeks were streaked with tears. She tensed at the sound of pounding hooves and pressed firmly on Sherwyn's neck, signaling him to turn around.

The silver horse rode in behind them, Kyle's shoulder length black hair wind-blown and his own green eyes stinging from the intensity of the ride. Kyle coaxed his horse to a stop a few feet in front of Mary's and paused, waiting for her to speak.

Mary stared at Kyle for several moments, and then exploded. "What do you want?" she screamed and her voice carried over the clear, empty hills surrounding them. "Say it, Kyle. Say it!"

Kyle shook his head, and Mary's rage continued.

"It was pathetic, absolutely pathetic! I...that was...not, not..."

"Not what?" Kyle asked her in as calm a tone as he could manage.

"Not worthy! That was not worthy. I was not worthy."

"Mary, it wasn't you."

"If you knew that, then why keep going? Why didn't you stop?"

"Because I know you, Mary!" His own voice rose in intensity. "I saw the look on your face, I've seen it before. It is the same look I have seen on Ameria's face every day since the attack. I saw the look and if it had been anyone else, I would have stopped, but I know you, Mary!"

Kyle moved his mount alongside the princess, placing himself directly across from her. "I didn't let you win, Mary. I fought like hell to beat you, because had I not, you never would have forgiven either of us. I gave you exactly what you needed; the only scenario you could live with."

Mary stared at him in a silence that seemed to stretch through the very hands of time. "Thank you," she whispered, but the gratitude did not reach her eyes.

Chapter XXXI

------※------

The two men rode through the hills in silence. The sun had long ago set, yet no stars appeared in the darkened sky. A ferocious wind howled through an unnatural fog which had surrounded them throughout their ride. "There's a storm coming," one man whispered to the other. "Something is wrong."

"You are not going to spout off more superstitious nonsense, are you? I'm not sure I can stand it again."

"Superstitious," he exclaimed. "If it's superstitious, then what, by the Gods, are we doing here?"

"Shh," said the other. "Do you want some passerby to hear you?"

The man lowered his voice and adjusted his cloak, pulling it tighter against the cold. "It's not the passerby we should be worried about," he said, once again in a whisper.

"It's impossible," the second man said.

"Then how do you explain it? We sent nearly twenty men after each of them. Twenty of the best fighters in the land, and yet, the twins survived. How do you explain it?"

"Dumb luck, I suppose. They said one of them came out of the woods with help."

"So in other words, the princesses were lost in the middle of the Dark Forest and happened to run into a random group of fighters good enough to take down our warriors at the exact moment that we orchestrated our attack?"

"The defense team found them, you know they found them," the second man said. "They found them just in time and saved them. Sheer dumb luck."

"Both of them?" The first shook his head. "No, it's the legend. You know it's the legend. Why else would they have wanted us to order an attack on the princesses?"

"Quiet!" the second man shouted. "They want them out of the tournament, that's all. And when we reach the temple, we will take care of this ourselves. I don't want to hear another word on this superstitious..." His horse came to a sudden stop.

"What the?" He kicked the horse with his heel. The horse started walking backwards. Beside him, the other man's horse reared, tossing his rider to the ground.

"They've heard us!" the man on the ground said in a panic. "They're coming!" His horse turned and raced back the way they had come, disappearing into the mist.

"Quiet, you fool. No one's here. No one." The sound of thunder roared through the night. The second horse started to thrash, forcing the man to fight to keep his seat. The horse rose, pawing the air once, twice, the man was losing his grip; the third time, he fell to the ground next to his partner. His horse vanished as quickly as the other. "It's the storm," the first man said, but his heart was racing. "Just the storm."

Yet even as he stared, something moved in the darkness, something darker than the moonless night. The thing was shifting in patches, with no fluidity to its movements. His partner was kneeling on the ground, shaking with fear. "They're here!" he screamed.

"Move, you fool! Run, this way!"

The other man did not move. "You won't outrun them," he whispered. "And they show no mercy."

A glint of light shone in the darkness, like a reflection of a single, sinister flame. Lightning lit the sky. Both men screamed. It would be the last sound they would ever make.

Chapter XXXII

―━◆▸✦◂◆━―

Screams rang down, surrounding Ameria in a suffocating wave. She lay trapped on the cold, hard floor, held fast by an invisible force. A growing pool of blood slid down the smooth, marble floor. Ameria fought against her unseen chains, to no avail. The blood touched her outstretched hand, painting her pale skin scarlet with a warm, wet touch.

Ameria woke with a scream that was swallowed by the roar of thunder. The howling wind beat the rain against the window like the sound of lost souls attempting to escape the raging storm. In the left corner of her room, the once bright fire had dimmed to glowing embers. Drawing a deep, slow breath Ameria pulled the covers over her to compensate for the low fire. She rolled to her right, adjusting her head on the gold, satin pillows. She closed her eyes for several moments before turning back towards the fire, then gasped as she stared into a pair of sinister, inhuman eyes.

Ameria jerked back across the bed as a flash of lightning lit the room. She froze. To the side of the bed stood a creature. From afar, it might have resembled a wolf, but looking into its eyes, Ameria knew that it was not. It was taller, standing nearly six feet high on all fours. Its fur was pure black, blending into the darkness of the room. Long, sharp teeth protruded from the side of its open mouth, its warm breath searing Ameria's pale flesh.

The shaggy fur stood in contrast to its thin, sleek body. But it was the eyes that held Ameria captive. His slanted, cat-like eyes reflected in the darkness like a clear stone glittering in a flame. The creature's eyes narrowed until they were only thin slits, and became even more sinister as it glared at the young princess. It leaned forward, its white teeth aligning more evenly with Ameria's pale throat.

Fear gripped the princess, leaving her helpless in its paralyzing grasp. The creature gave a deep, low growl from the back of its throat. She fought to find her voice. "I'm dreaming,"

"No," the creature answered. His voice was deep and low, more a slow growl than a voice. "You are not dreaming, Princess Ameria."

Another flash of lightning lit the room.

She remained trapped in her paralysis. "Who are you?"

Thunder roared through the room, causing Ameria's terrified heart to beat even faster, thrumming through her head with a deafening ferocity. The flame from the fire rose to life unaided, flooding the room with a low light. Ameria stared into the flames reflected in the creature's slanted eyes, and then she knew. The creature gave a low, deep growl. "Hail, Princess of Kale. Hail, Princess of Koloso. Hail, Princess of both."

Ameria fought to breathe over the insistent pounding of her heart. "You are a wraith." She could barely hear her own voice.

"Yes, twin and heir to the ancient bloodline. Yes."

"It was you," she whispered. "You killed them."

"Yes."

"Why?"

"I protect the twins of the ancient line," he said, his voice never rising from his deep, low growl. "Twins of the ancient bloodline. Fear to the fearless. Hope to the hopeless. Mercy to those who hate you. Death to those who love you. That is your destiny, Princess of Kale, Princess of Koloso, heir to both. "

"I don't understand."

"You will, princess." His eyes widened as he moved closer to her.

Ameria felt her breath catch in her throat, unable to breathe through petrifying fear. His breath caressed the skin of her scared hands.

"It will not do." His breath became warmer with each word he spoke. "No, it will not do." Her skin started to crawl and then burn. Ameria whimpered in the searing heat, but managed not to cry out. "So strong. So young. So...beautiful." Her pain reached an almost unbearable level, yet the creature only stared. The heat increased and flames burst forth to dance along Ameria's skin. She screamed, jerking her hands towards her. The flames vanished before her eyes.

The souls in the wind continued to cry out against the raging storm. Thunder shook the room. "The hour is drawing near," he growled and this time the sound filled every corner of the room. "Beware, princess. Beware."

"Even you?" Her voice was a mere breath.

"Especially me."

Lightning filled the room again and the wraith offered a growl that made the storm seem tame, his reflected eyes filled with a sense of wild glee that frightened Ameria more than his sinister manner had done only moments before. He moved forward suddenly, his teeth opened towards Ameria's exposed throat. The wraith stopped a fraction of an inch from her skin; the sound of the wraith's snapping teeth rang through the air. The unnatural flames of the fire died instantly. The wraith gave a harsh laugh, before disappearing into the darkness, as though swallowed by shadows of the night.

Ameria did not know how long she lay there, waiting for her body to override its fear enough to move from the bed. She rose unsteadily as she forced herself to slip from the covers. She gazed around the room, half expecting to see the wraith reappear. She stepped away from the bed, and nearly fell when she tripped over a large object on the floor. She cursed, the racing of her heart reignited by the near fall.

She walked towards the side of the room more carefully and placed several pieces of wood onto the fire. The blue fire blazed to life, illuminating the darkness of the room. She blinked several times and walked back to the bed.

Lying on the ground was a long, silver sword. The hilt of the blade was black, encrusted with a pair of dark red jewels which Ameria had never seen before. She reached down for the sword with her scarred hand. Her fingers curled around the blade. Ameria squeezed her hand and cautiously lifted the sword waiting expectantly for it to slip from her fingers. It did not. Ameria raised her arm and found the blade to be a solid weight in her hand, though not as heavy as the sword she normally carried. She twisted the silver blade. The movement felt natural. She moved the sword forcefully in an upward stoke, and her fingers held true. She could once again wield the blade.

Beside the sword lay a silver sheath. Ameria placed the sword on the bed and knelt down. The sheath was lighter than the sword, but was still weighed down by silver and jewels. Symbols lined both sides of the sheath. As Ameria pulled it closer, she recognized the mark of Kale.

Across the Rainbow Mountains where the same storm raged, Mariana held a matching sword of gold, with a golden sheath. It bore the mark of Koloso.

Chapter XXXIII

An insistent pounding woke Lord Louis from unquiet dreams. He removed himself from the bed and walked to the door. The pounding grew more insistent, getting louder and faster with every clap of thunder. "Come in," he called. The door flew open. He was surprised to see not one of the temple masters, but Princess Ameria, dressed only in a thin, golden gown. Her long golden hair hung loosely around her frame. Her eyes were slightly bloodshot, as though she had not slept all night. "What is it, Princess Ameria?"

"My lord, I apologize for disturbing you in the dead of night." Ameria moved farther into the dark room, and towards the large fireplace against the wall opposite the bed. The fire still burned brightly.

When Ameria reached the edge of the room, she turned and drew something from her side. "My lord," she addressed the temple leader, "I come for answers." She then held out a long blade encased in a silver sheath. "Is this," she motioned to the jewel encrusted blade, "the sword of Kale?"

Louis moved closer to examine the blade, and then gave a slight gasp. The red jewels embedded in the handle of the blade glistened in the firelight. The silver gleamed as though it had the power to turn reflected light into a living thing that seemed to dance throughout the room. He leaned forward and gently touched the side of the blade with his paw.

As he touched the silver blade, Louis saw a man. He was tall, broad across the shoulders with the pale, pale skin that would forever dominate those of his bloodline. His short blond hair and sapphire blue eyes reminded Louis of the bluest part of the sea.

Louis moved his head to see a row of men, clad in black standing before the young man, but the golden-haired man was not afraid. He drew his sword...this sword from the sheath on his side. Moments later, the high priest knew, those men moving towards Kale would be dead.

Louis jerked back from the blade as though it were a snake. "Where did you get that?" He looked up to meet the gaze of the princess. "Ameria," he said again. "Where did you get that sword?"

Ameria ignored his question. "What color is the sword of Koloso?" Another clash of thunder drowned out the silence of the room. "What rank did Koloso hold?"

"Gold," Louis replied reluctantly. "The sword of Koloso is Gold. The silver sword in your hand is the sword of Kale."

"No." Mary appeared from out of the darkness. "It can't be. Kale was gold. His temple is the temple of kings."

"Mary," Louis said softly.

"Tell me the truth," Mary demanded. Then, with more anger, "Why?"

"People need their heroes, Mary. Don't." He shook his head. "Don't look at me like that. It's not as bad as you think. Kale was a hero. He saved his kingdom."

"I don't understand." Ameria replied.

"Tell me the story, of Kale and Koloso, Ameria. Tell me the story as you know it."

"Why should I? Everyone knows that story."

"Please, Ameria."

She met his gaze in challenge. "Kale, heir to the throne, and his younger brother, Koloso, were betrayed by a rogue defendant. This rogue raised an army and spilt the team's loyalty. His army swept like a plague across the land, sowing seeds of distrust and disloyalty. Kale sent out his best champions, Dektra and Desoto. Both were killed by the rogue. Then Koloso rode out on his own, against his older brother's wishes, and met the same fate before Kale himself rose from the throne and challenged the traitor to one on one combat. Kale slew the traitor avenging the death of his captains and younger brother. Then Kale wiped the traitors' names from all the history books so that his name would be forever lost."

Ameria drew a deep breath, and then trained her gaze into the eyes of the high priest. "But what I don't understand, is why is the sword of Kale, this sword," she help up the blade, "silver?"

"And this one," Mary added from behind them, "the sword of Koloso, gold?"

"Because Koloso was the elder of the two," Louis stated with a sigh. "Koloso was the elder brother, and Kale was the younger."

"Then why have we...has everyone been taught different? Why are the heirs not trained in the Temple of Koloso?"

"Because Kale was the one who survived to be king. Kale was the one who lived to rule. Kale was the one, and the story had been changed for the public long before I was born. And in the end, my princesses, this should not matter."

"What you are saying is that, as the eldest, I am the heir of Koloso and she is the heir of Kale? All of these years and you have had us believing we owed our birthrights to the wrong brother? I am the heir to the brother who died."

"And I to the one who lived." Ameria's voice echoed her sister's.

"It should not matter," Louis said to the two sisters. "You are not the heir of Kale or Koloso, Mary. You are heir to the king and to Master Leo, the once Golden Defendant. And you, Ameria, are your mother's heir and as such, heir to the leadership of the defendants. Kale and Koloso...they are just old stories."

The two sisters caught each other's eyes in a glance of emeralds and ice. Then why did the wraith switch the swords? Mary was about to ask the question aloud, when there came another knock at the door.

"Yes?" Louis called. "Can no one sleep tonight?"

The door swung open and a defendant dressed in black entered the room. "Forgive me, Lord Louis," the man addressed Louis, then he recognized the two figures standing beside the fire. "Forgive me as well, Princess Mariana and Ameria."

"What is it?" Louis asked.

"I have a message from the palace. The prince has summoned Master Leo and Princess Mary to come immediately. It's a matter of grave urgency which the prince states that he cannot issue the details through a messenger."

Chapter XXXIV

━━━◆❧✦☙◆━━━

Defendants gathered the horses from the stables of Kale and Koloso, and now sat outside the Temple of Critous upon horses of silver and gold. The prince had summoned not only his daughters, but Master Leo, Lord Louis, Master Jiro, Lady Rebecca and Lord Stephen. Ryan, Marcus, Kyle, Brandan, and Kev had also elected to accompany the princesses, while Coco, Mac, and Breeze rode in a small carriage pulled by two golden mares.

Despite the obvious tension at the cryptic nature of the prince's message, the gathering of riders was a magnificent sight. Draped in long clothes of silk in vibrant colors of rank, the top five ranking defendants rode at the flank of the Golden Defendant, two on each side. The students of Kale and Koloso rode in the center, their robes of gold, silver, red and purple blowing in the wind while the two highest ranking of the temple masters brought up the rear. The horses raced forward, carrying the powerful group through the hills and plains towards the gates of the Royal Palace. Mary had not seen such a gathering since the funeral of the pervious Golden Defendant.

Ameria wore thick golden gloves to hide the scars which still covered her hands. Not knowing that she once again had mobility of her fingers, Kyle had offered to let her ride with him. Ameria had declined, but felt Kyle's gaze shifting to her constantly. Ameria was not sure why she had not told her partner of the wraith's visit, but to her knowledge, Mary had not told anyone either. On any other horse this ride would have taken all day, but with the magical speed and stamina of the gold and silver stallions and mares, the ride only took a few hours.

The gates of the palace opened long before the group reached them, the extraordinary array of their colors and ranks visible for miles. They rode through the gates as one, not slowing until they reached the marble steps which led to the palace doors.

Several lords were awaiting them, including a distinguished looking older man with Kalian skin, short brown hair that was slowly becoming streaked with gray, and his son's jade green eyes. Dressed in robes of silver, a mark of the status he once held as the Silver Defendant, the High Lord of Turbamentum, looked as distinguished as the pure Kalian blood which flowed through his veins.

As the highest ranking of the waiting lords, it was this man who stepped first from amongst the crowd and entered into a traditional Kalian bow. Lady Rebecca motioned the two princesses to the front. They rode forward with their partners a few steps behind them. Mary took the lead. "Greetings, Lord Chiro of Turbamentum."

"Greetings, Your Royal Highnesses, Princess Mariana and Princess Ameria. Greetings to Lady Rebecca and the fellow defendants who ride by her side as well." The group spread out slightly, so that those standing on the steps could better see who was included in the princesses' riding party. Lord Chiro rose to his feet with a word from Mariana and acknowledged the fellow masters who had ridden near the parties' rear. Kyle kept his horse steady by Mary and Ameria's side, and said, "Hello, Father."

"Greetings, Kyle." Lord Chiro acknowledged his only son. "I had hoped to see you on this day."

"Why have we been summoned?" Mary asked the lord.

"I do not know, Your Highness," Lord Chiro answered. "My lord, Prince Eadmund has commanded us to come, and here we stand. He waits in his chambers for the arrival of his daughters."

Mary and Ameria dismounted in perfect symmetry and turned to their group. "Lady Rebecca, Master Leo, Lord Louis, and Lord Jiro," Mary addressed them. "Would you please accompany us to my father's chambers?"

They ascended the steps without speaking, simply dismounting from their own gold and silver mounts and gathered behind the princesses. As they stepped forward, Mary's hand went to the golden hilt of her new blade. It was lighter than her usual sword, and Mary had almost decided not to carry it. But the Gods had given it to her for a reason and after her last trip to the palace; she dared not leave it behind.

Lady Rebecca walked ahead of Mary and was the first to reach the two guardsmen standing at the door. "The prince summoned us," she told the guard.

The men glanced at each other "We were told that he needed to speak to the princesses alone, before he could speak with anyone else."

"These summons are strange," the Golden Defendant said. "I do not like their cryptic nature and someone recently attempted to assassinate the princesses. I will go in as their bodyguard, or the prince will not see them."

The door opened behind the guardsmen. Prince Eadmund stood in the doorway. He looked tired. Dark circles were visible under his blue eyes. His graying hair appeared unkempt. His silver robes were crumpled. "It is all right," the prince stated. "Enter quickly." The small group slipped into the room, Rebecca and Leo insisting on entering first, while Master Jiro opted to stand outside the door. Once inside, Mary and Ameria bowed to their father and remained in a kneeling position until ordered to rise.

"Father," Mary said to the tall man in front of her.

"Hello, Mariana." He nodded towards the group. "Ameria, Leo, Louis, and, of course, Rebecca. I must say this is some honor guard you have assembled."

"This isn't even half of it."

"Yes, I figured you would all ride together. I apologize for the cryptic delivery of the message, but I needed you all here." The prince cleared his throat.

"Your uncle is not well, Mariana. He has not been well for, well, for quite some time. Two days ago he took a turn for the worse. They don't expect him to live much longer which means, Mary, that within four days, or perhaps a week's time, you will be the new queen."

Mary stared at her father as though she could not understand the language he was speaking. "Do you understand me, Mary," he said gently. "In a few days, you will be the new queen of the Kalian line."

Mary continued to stare at him.

"Are you sure?" Ameria questioned from beside her. "What is wrong with him? Why has he not been taken to the temples?"

"The healers have been called, but this is a disease, Ameria, and as you know, the healing powers of the temples only work on physical injuries. Not illness."

"Wait." Mary glanced around the room and suddenly, there were too many people there. "I want to speak with you alone, Father."

The Golden Defendant shook her head. "That is out of the question, you cannot be left alone outside the walls of a temple, especially not with this news."

"Then leave my sister in the room with me."

"No, princess. It is not a good idea, not until you are queen."

Mary let out a short breath of frustration. "Fine," she said. "Will you consent to leaving the room, if I choose a master to remain?"

The Golden Defendant looked thoughtful for a moment, then nodded. "Then send in Master Jiro," Mary announced the surprising choice.

"As you wish, my lady." The defendants left the room while Master Jiro entered, surprised as the others at being Princess Mary's named choice.

Princess Ameria turned to her sister and a moment of silence passed between them before Ameria finally said, "I will leave the two of you to your privacy."

"Walk that way." The prince pointed to the private chambers beyond. "Your mother would love to see you." Without a word, Ameria turned towards the far door and exited the room, leaving Mary alone with her father and Master Jiro.

"Father," Mary addressed the prince, "if the king is dying, then you should be crowned, not me. He named me heir only because of the similarities of your age. Since he is now dying much sooner than you thought, then you, Father, should be king and I crowned your heir, instead of my uncle's."

Her father gave her a hard stare for several moments. "Answer me this, daughter. Why of all the lords at your beck and call, did you ask for Master Jiro, instead of your own master?"

Mary drew a deep breath and let it out slowly, considering how honest her answer should be. "Master Leo has made plans for my days on the throne since before I was born. I think you know that, Father."

"What is it you want, Mariana?"

Mary parted her lips, but no sound came out. She swallowed hard.

"I am a Princess of Kale, Father. I only wish to do what is best for the realm. I am seventeen years old, was named heir under the pretense that I would have at least another ten years to learn the ways of the court, a world of which I know little and have been even less a part of. I am a trained defendant, Father, and only one tournament away from proving myself worthy of the team on which both you and my mother once served. Would you really take it away from me?"

Mary shook her head. Her voice was raw. "I am not ready to be queen, but I am ready to be a defendant. You on the other hand, have already been a defendant, and you would be a wise king for the realm." Mary sank into a temple bow. "I will honor every vow, Father. I will marry a tournament champion and we shall one day rule by right of arms and blood. I shall reunite the temples and the royal lines. But please, Father, not yet."

Prince Eadmund stared at his daughter. "Seventeen," he whispered. "I cannot imagine what a burden it must be. It was one I was always thankful never to have."

"Then don't take this from me," she pleaded.

"Answer me this, Mary. If I walked out this door right now and asked your sister to take the throne, what would she say?"

"Yes," Mary said without hesitation. "She would say yes."

"And would you, as her older sister, follow her rule?"

"Yes," Mary said again. "Yes, I would."

"Then why should I not tell my brother to name Ameria his heir?"

"Because then she would not fight in the final tournament." Mary raised her head and caught her father's blue gaze, so like her sister's. "The queen cannot fight in that tournament, and you, along with the rest of the realm, would never know which of us is better."

It seemed the most pointless of all the arguments that Mary could think of, yet she knew, it was the only one that mattered.

"You crown me queen, Father, and a Kolosian will win the thirteenth tournament. The Temple of Koloso will become the most revered temple in the realm and your grandchildren will be Kolosian-trained."

A hint of anger filtered through Prince Eadmund's eyes. Mary knew in that moment, that upon her uncle's death, neither princess would be crowned queen.

Chapter XXXV

Kyle dismounted his silver stallion and handed the reins off to one of the waiting pages by the palace steps. With his silken robes shimmering in the sunlight, he walked up the white marble steps until he reached his father's side. Chiro turned towards his son with intense curiosity. "It has been a long time, son," he said to Kyle. "And I find you riding by the side of both princesses. This is good news"

"I always ride beside the princess, Father." Kyle shrugged. "Sometimes I think you forget that I am her partner."

"Yes, the Kolosian Princess." Chiro sighed. "Is it true that she can no longer fight?"

Kyle narrowed his eyes. "That is not public knowledge. How did you?"

"I have my sources." Chiro shook his head. "Had I been a more clever man, I would have sent you to Kale."

"You are a clever man, Father. You sent me to Koloso because you assumed both princesses would be sent to Kale and had that been the case, I would have worn red instead of the gold you sought."

"Nevertheless," Chiro said quietly, walking his son to a more isolated corner of the palace grounds so not to be overheard. "You do realize that you have the potential to come in behind the princess, especially with Ameria out of the match."

"She will be in the match, Father!" Kyle insisted. "I don't know what you have heard, or who the hell told you, but Ameria will compete in that round."

"Yes, but if she does not, then you have an opportunity to claim the prize and the crown."

"Father." Kyle took a step back from the older man. "You don't know this. Even if Ameria were not in the round, which I assure you she will be, there are dozens of champions and actual defendants from over the years who might outshine me. Plus, Marcus will be in the round, and he has trained with Mary step for step."

"Marcus? Oh, yes, the silver Kalian. I have seen him fight, he will be your most difficult challenge, but in the end, I am sure you will prevail to golden status."

"Golden?" Kyle was confused. "You said silver, where did this gold business come in?"

The powerful lord gave his son a thin-lipped smile. He gazed around the room, ensuring that no one was within close proximity and then leaned down towards Kyle's ear. "I hear the king is dying and that Mary will be crowned queen before the week is out. Which means..."

"That she won't be able to compete," Kyle whispered back, then gave a deep laugh.

His father's smile became a glare. "You have just been placed a heartbeat from becoming the number one contender in the thirteenth tournament, and becoming king for your victory, yet you laugh?"

"Yes, Father."

"Explain quickly, before I find you ungrateful."

"Father," Kyle said. "If there is one thing Mary will never do, it is give up that tournament."

"If she is queen, then she has no choice."

"Then she will not be queen." Kyle shook his head. "There is nothing that Mary would give up the crown for, no life in the entire kingdom she would not sacrifice, no power that she would not give up, except that tournament. You are a fool, Father. The princesses will fight in the tournament, if it costs them their souls."

Chapter XXXVI

———◆►◘◄◆———

AMERIA SAT BESIDE HER MOTHER in her golden robes which sparkled in the sunlight that filtered through the tall windows of Princess Annabelle's private chambers. The older woman was dressed in a floor-length crimson gown of velvet with long sleeves which covered her pale arms. She sat in a black, straight-backed chair with her back towards the large windows. Ameria sat beside her, her golden hair pulled behind her with a thin gold band. Her mother turned to better see her daughter. The two women gazed at each other with matching light blue eyes.

"So, daughter," Annabelle addressed the younger princess. "What do you think those Kalians are plotting? Your father and sister?"

Ameria shrugged. "I tire of guessing, Mother. Why don't you tell me?"

"That you should be queen," her mother said matter-of-factly. "But then again, what do I know? I am just a Kolosian who married into this line." She leaned towards the edge of her seat. "The question is, Ameria, does you sister want the throne?"

Ameria inhaled deeply. "No, but don't worry, Mother. She is a Princess of Kale and therefore, will do her duty. Do you honestly sit here and plot against your own child?"

"My child...oh yes, I suppose she is my child. Though to be the mother of a Kalian, I never would have imagined such a thing."

"Every heir to the throne goes to Kale," Ameria said. "Why in the world would you have expected Mary to be any different?"

"Because her father was only silver! It was her right to go to Koloso where her mother had once stood gold."

"Come, Mother," Ameria said with a sigh. "Surely after all these years you and Father are not still having this same argument. Is it not enough that I claimed your title?"

"I would prefer for you to claim your uncle's," her mother said angrily.

"The glorious rivalry," Ameria stood from her chair. "Can't you give it a rest? The king...my uncle, is dying!" Ameria took several paces forward and then back, making a small circle in front of the chair before eventually walking to the window, staring out at the purple sky. "It's too beautiful a day for the death of a king."

Her mother remained seated. Her deep red gown pooled around her as though she were a work of art, a golden chain sparkling in the sunlight with the silver mark of Koloso as a small pendant at the end.

"Forgive me, my child." Her mother said. "It is tragic, to lose a king. I did not mean to sound unsympathetic. I only think of your future. Death is a part of life. It is only the living that must worry about what comes next."

"Fields of flowers," Ameria whispered.

"Excuse me?"

"Nothing," Ameria shook herself out of her trance and walked back towards her mother.

Chapter XXXVII

KYLE LEANED AGAINST ONE OF the large marble pillars outside the palace doors. He was not used to being excluded from the inner circle surrounding the princesses, however, it was understandable, considering the rank of those who had accompanied her. He had been standing outside for the better part of three hours. His satin robes were clinging annoyingly, and his pale skin was beginning to redden in the constant stream of light from Kale's three suns.

The crowd of people surrounding him continued to grow as lords from the highest to the lowest ranks began to gather. The lords of Flos and Agnus stood conversing with his father while lesser lords stood nearby in hopes that those of higher rank would make use of them. Temple masters had been called from each of their respective temples accompanied by the highest ranked of their students. Davis and Seth had just arrived from the Temple of Desoto and Kyle gave a wave in the direction of his gold and silver counterparts as they stood on either side of Latie, their temple master. Latie conversed with Master Philip of Dektra and Master Lester of Critous in the elegant manner which only the temple masters seemed to possess.

Despite this, Kyle felt alone in the crowded area in front of the palace, wondering how the princesses would respond to the news of their uncle's illness. It was no secret to Kyle that the sisters bore little love for their uncle, yet his status alone and the reminder that even one such as a king is still born mortal would sit heavily upon the shoulders of the two princesses. Kyle had little doubt that the king was in fact dying, though more by the assurance of his father's spies than from the gathering crowd.

Kyle shifted again around the large pillar, attempting to stand in its shadow, in hopes of deflecting some of the suns' burning rays. Several of the palace guard walked through the crowd dressed in robes of deep crimson, several shades darker than the bright scarlet adopted by the temple defendant and students.

"Hello, Kyle." Davis suddenly appeared beside him draped in his golden Desoto robes.

"Hello, Davis." Kyle offered a tired smile.

"You look exhausted."

"Long day."

"Do you know what is going on?"

"When you know, so will I," Kyle lied.

"I'm not sure I've ever seen this many people inside the palace walls. Usually the security is so tight that you're lucky to see two people out here at a time, let alone this huge group."

"I know," Kyle replied. "A little crazy."

"Yeah."

The two men paused for several moments and then Davis said, "So, are you ready for the thirteenth tournament?"

"You know it," Kyle replied. "I will see you there, I expect?"

"Of course. Can't let you marry the princess without at least having to put on a show for it. Besides, it will be interesting to see you without Ameria by your side."

"And you without Seth." Kyle motioned toward Davis' silver-robed partner who was still standing at the side of Master Latie.

"Yes. I figure a good performance will at least get me considered for a spot on the Defendant Team. They haven't promoted anyone so far this year because they are waiting to see who shines in the tournament."

Kyle nodded. "You are the golden student of Desoto," he told his technically higher-ranked companion. "I foresee no problems with you earning a spot on the team."

"Thanks," Davis replied. "I just hope to serve the realm."

"As do we all." The two men gave a bow of respect in the other's direction. Then Davis turned and walked back towards his partner just as two members of the palace guard stepped from within the doors.

"Attention everyone!" they shouted above the clamoring of the crowd. "Attention!" All eyes turned towards the speakers. "His royal majesty, the king, has asked to see the following people: The leaders of the Kalian temples, the top five defendants, the High Lords of Usqub, Turbamentum, Serenitas, Flos, Agnus, and Periculum and the Master of the Temple of Ziazan."

Those named began to move swiftly towards the palace doors while Kyle leaned back against his pillar in disappointment. After the named group had been cleared, the palace guard walked towards him. "Lord Kyle, Princess Mariana has requested your presence."

"Mariana?" he asked for clarification.

"Yes, my lord."

Kyle began walking towards the palace doors, when he spotted Ryan near the side of the steps. The young man stood clad in the purple robes of Kale, though Kyle doubted after his first tournament fight, that he would remain ranked so low for long.

He was speaking with two tall figures who Kyle did not recognize, both clad in silver robes of status. He allowed his gaze to linger on the taller of the two, and saw the mark of Mortem on his left breast. He had pale skin with black hair. Had Mortem promoted someone to silver?

"Lord Kyle," the guardsman interrupted his thoughts.

"Did Mary ask for Ryan or Marcus as well?"

"No, my lord. Only you."

Kyle followed the palace guard down a series of hallways until they came to a large wooden door on the north side of the palace. "You may go in," the guard said to Kyle. "She is waiting for you."

Kyle entered the room and found Mary standing against the large glass window staring out into the sky. "Princess."

"My uncle is dying." Mary did not turn around.

"And your father will be crowned king," Kyle said it a statement.

"Yes."

"By your own plea."

"Yes." Mary continued to gaze out the window.

"You are not surprised that I know this?"

"No."

Kyle stared at the princess for several moments and then sank to his knees. "Princess Mariana," he said firmly. "I am at your command, my lady."

Mary turned slowly. "What makes you think I need you at my command?" she asked, motioning for him to rise.

"I hear your screams."

The blade rose in Mary's hand. She crossed the room in a blur and pressed the cold steel against Kyle's throat. "You have no idea what you hear." A small trickle of blood rose to the surface of Kyle's pale skin.

Kyle stood perfectly still. "I have no idea what terror plagues you, my Lady. But I am at your service for whatever you may need."

"I have the entire Defendant Team at my call. All the power of the temples, at my call," her words were vicious. "What makes you think that I need you, Lord Kyle?"

"Then why call for me, princess?"

Mary's green eyes narrowed and the room seemed to grow darker before Kyle's eyes. Clouds gathered across the violet sky, covering the light of the three suns. Mary pulled back the golden blade and held it to her side. She stared into Kyle's eyes, so like her own.

"Princess," Kyle spoke slowly, "I will do anything you ask."

Mary stepped forward, closing the distance between them until she could feel the caress of his warm breath on her skin. "Drown out my dreams, Kyle. Drown them out, because I don't want them. I am a pawn in some great plan, some destiny of which I wish no part, yet am unable to escape." Her voice sounded hollow. "Drown them out, Kyle."

"Princess, I do not have the power to make you forget," he said solemnly.

"Kyle," she whispered leaning forward, slowly closing the distance between them.

"Anything within my power, princess."

Chapter XXXVIII

Ameria sat with her parents. Just moments after the king had made the formal announcement that due to his niece's youth, his brother, Prince Eadmund, would succeed him as king, the argument began. "If she passed up the throne," Princess Annabelle argued with her husband. "Then Ameria should become the heir."

Eadmund shook his head. "Mary did not pass up the throne. Her uncle and I decided that since his health took a turn so much earlier than expected, that it would be better if I became king. That is all there is to it."

"You Kalians! You just can't fathom..."

"Don't you mean your wonderful lord and husband by whose good graces you shall soon be crowned queen?"

Annabelle glowered at Eadmund. "At least I didn't raise a daughter who would refuse the throne."

"Well, if you had ever taken the time to get to know Mary, maybe this wouldn't have been an issue."

"Okay, you two," Ameria interrupted before either parent could reply. "Play nice."

Ameria rose from her chair and offered a low bow to her parents. "I think I will go search for my sister." She walked quickly towards the door in hopes that she would be gone before either parent offered an objection. Once outside the hallway, she did not search for Mary's chambers, but instead wandered outside towards the steps of the palace. The guardsmen gave a bow as she approached the large doors leading to the exterior marble steps, but they made no move to caution her against stepping outside.

She searched for Kyle, but did not see him among the massive crowd. Growing larger by the minute, it was hard to pick out anyone from among the sea of faces and brightly colored robes. Members of the Palace Guard moved throughout, helping to keep order as best they could while beyond the crowd, Ameria spied several defendants riding quickly out the open palace gates, with Lady Rebecca at the head of the group. Probably going to spread the word of the king's impending death to the other defendants.

Turning back to the sea of faces standing before her, Ameria's gaze eventually settled on Marcus. She maneuvered her way through the crowd to reach his side. "Hey, Marcus. Have you seen Kyle?"

"He was called inside, my lady."

"Inside? With his father?"

"I don't think so. I think Mary asked for him."

"Mary?" Ameria shook her head. "More secret meetings, I presume?"

"So it would seem," Marcus replied unhappily. He turned back towards Ameria. "I am glad you walked over here, Princess Ameria. I never had the chance to express my sympathy over your attack. I wanted to..."

Ameria waved softly with her gloved hand. "None needed, Marcus."

"All the same."

"I thank you for the concern, but honestly, it does not matter. Have you seen any of my other teammates?" She scanned the room looking for a recognizable face when she caught a glimpse of a tall man with black hair moving through the crowd. His green eyes caught her gaze a moment before he swiftly turned away from her. Ameria's eyes followed the stranger.

"Marcus, who is..." She lost him in the crowd.

"What is it, Ameria?"

"I thought I saw..." She shook her head and once again scanned the crowd. Seeing nothing, Ameria turned back to Marcus. "I guess I'm seeing things."

"Saw what?"

"There was a man in silver. I couldn't place him, but he looked so familiar."

Marcus shrugged. "Perhaps because he is someone we have fought before?"

"As I said." Ameria turned towards her longtime rival. "Probably nothing."

Ameria scanned the crowd again and then saw the same distinctive face, only it couldn't be the same. "That man in purple over there, who is he?"

Marcus glanced in his direction. "Oh, you mean Ryan? He is the new purple student of Kale. He helped save Mary when she was attacked in the forest and has been training under Master Leo ever since."

"She brought him to the temple with her? That does not sound like my sister."

"He did help save her life," Marcus replied. "I think she feels that she owes him a debt."

"I feel like I have seen him before."

"Well, you shouldn't have. At least I don't think you should have." Ameria stared at Ryan. "Would you like me to introduce you to him, princess?"

"No, that's all right. I'm sure I will meet him in good time. I think I am going to go find my sister. Would you like to come with me, Marcus?"

Marcus nodded and the two champions moved back towards the marble steps when the guardsmen approached the steps again. "Master Leo, Master Jiro, and Lord Louis have asked for all students of gold and silver rank to join them in the palace. All gold and silver students! Everyone else, the king thanks you all for your patience and the palace guards will be out momentarily to assist you all in finding arrangements for the next few nights outside the palace walls."

Ameria and Marcus increased their pace and reached the top of the stairs before the others. "Did that order include me?" she asked.

"I do not know, princess. I can ask if you wish."

"No need, I will go with them and find out."

The group entered the wide palace corridors and walked through a series of hallways to the far side of the massive palace. With most of the king's guards outside dealing with the crowd, the interior of the palace seemed to be guarded rather sparsely, considering how many high ranking lords and students were within.

They continued into a large room with deep crimson walls and glass windows on all sides. The room was dim. Large gray clouds blocked the sunshine that was normally filtered through the massive windows. Across the room stood all thirteen Temple masters, along with Lord Louis. It was Louis who addressed the crowd of champions telling of the king's impending death and the change to the immediate line of succession. Only half-listening to the news she had already been informed of, Ameria's eyes circled the room searching for the silver student she had seen earlier; he was not there.

With a feeling of unease, Ameria's hand gripped the handle of her silver sword in a gesture of comfort. Something about that face troubled her. Her sister and Kyle were also missing from the group of gathered students.

"However, let me remind you all," the puppy's voice snapped Ameria's attention back to the crowd of temple leaders. "Do not allow this to interfere with your training. The death of a king or not, the thirteenth tournament is coming and will, as required by ancient Kalian law, commence on time."

Ameria felt a chill from a non-existent wind and that familiar voice whispered, *"Beware, princess. Beware."*

Chapter XXXIX

On the opposite side of the palace, two figures draped in silver robes walked silently down the marble halls of the palace. With pale, Kalian skin and green eyes, neither man looked out of place among the massive crowd summoned to the king's court. When the gold and silver students had been called to enter the palace walls, it had been all too easy for the two men to slip in among them and vanish within the sparsely guarded hallways. With the stolen plans of the palace committed to memory, the older of the two moved towards the left side of the hallway, placing his back firmly against the wall before turning to peek around the corner.

Two members of the King's Guard stood before the tall silver doors. The older of the strangers held up two fingers, alerting his companion to the number. The second man offered a single nod, then both turned and walked towards the doors. "We have a message from the Golden Defendant," the elder of the two men said in a deep voice.

One of the guards stepped forward. "I'd be happy to deliver the message for you."

"I was instructed to deliver it in person."

The guard eyed the mark on the chest of the two men. "I would have thought that such a message would be delivered from one of the upper level temples."

"Trust me," the older stranger replied. "The message is from him."

"Him?" The guard's hand went to his sword, but it was too late.

The long silver blade entered the man's chest, slicing up to penetrate his right lung. He fell with a sickening thud, gurgling and coughing blood as he drew his last breath. Almost simultaneously, the second man in silver moved towards the other guard, slicing through his arm as the guard went for his sword. Blood spewed from the opened artery in his arm and he tried to cry out a warning, when the blade cut his throat. The guard fell to the ground without making a sound. He died instantly, a pool of blood staining the marble beneath his fallen form.

"Now they die," one brother said to the other.

"For Father," said the other.

The two men pushed opened the large silver doors in front of them and entered the room. Inside stood two men. One dressed in robes of silver and the other in crimson robes of state. "I know that this is difficult to speak of, my lord. However, we must arrange for the impending funeral."

"I am aware..." Prince Eadmund's words died on his lips as the two silver students entered the room. "May I help... Nathan?"

"Nathan is dead," the eldest of the two said before placing his sword in front of him, blood still dripping from the silver metal. "And soon you will join him."

"That is Lord Edward's sword!" the prince exclaimed. "Where did you get that?"

"From the same place I am going to claim yours, Your Highness."

Eadmund stared at him bewildered. "Alec?" he asked. "You're Alec, aren't you? By the Gods, you look like your father."

"You do not get to mention my father!" the younger man raged. "You never again get to speak of my father!"

Alec raised his stolen blade and moved slowly towards the prince. Eadmund, ever the defendant, reached for the sword that hung at his side, drawing the blade.

The statesman spoke from the left side of the prince. "This is treason! To raise a blade against the future king comes with a death sentence."

"Yes," Alec said. "But you won't be there to see it."

"Leave him out of this," Eadmund said. "Come now, Alec. You don't have to do this. Your father and I were friends. He wouldn't want this..."

"You betrayed him," Alec said in a shockingly cold voice. "And now, you are going to die." Alec's blade sliced in a downward stroke towards the prince. Prince Eadmund blocked the blade with his own in a deafening clash of Kalian steel. The second man stood by the door watching silently, allowing his brother to fight this battle alone.

Alec's blade rose again. Eadmund blocked. Alec swung left, and Eadmund jumped right. Alec swung again, two times, three, four. Eadmund began to feel his strength wane under the powerful onslaught of the younger man. Alec moved his blade towards Eadmund's left and this time, the sharp metal sank into Eadmund's arm.

Injured and exhausted, Eadmund struggled to stop Alec's next onslaught, falling to his knees as their swords collided. He scrambled back several feet from Alec, gasping for breath and cursing himself for not keeping up his training. Not that he was sure it would have mattered. His opponent was amazingly skilled with the blade.

"Alec!" Eadmund tried reasoning with him once again. "Listen to me, son. I don't know what you have been told but..."

Alec's sword arched down towards Eadmund once again and Eadmund raised his own blade to block it. The door to the prince's chamber opened and a passing guard rushed inside. Alec's brother, still standing beside the door, sank his blade into the chest of the newcomer, killing him in a single stroke. "He won't be the last," one brother cautioned the other.

The sound of clashing swords raced along the walls as Alec blocked one of Eadmund's movements. The two men circled each other, gripping the heavy blades with both hands. Eadmund was beginning to feel woozy from blood loss.

His movements began to slow. He barely stopped the second swing of Alec's sword and then Eadmund stood still, waiting.

Alec's sword swung upwards, and his body turned to the left, knocking the prince from his defensive stance. The silver metal thrust into Eadmund's stomach, spilling his intestines. Alec moved the blade up, slicing through Eadmund's side. The prince gasped. His hands moved to his lower stomach. Blood filled his lungs. He fell face down with a horrible gurgling sound.

Alec turned from the fallen prince towards the statesman huddled in the far corner of the room. He let out a scream as Alec approached him and sliced open his throat with a single swipe of his blade. "Let's go find the other," he said to his brother. Alec reached down and wiped his blade on the bottom of the dead statesman's crimson tunic. He stared back at the dead prince one last time.

Chapter XL

A SERIES OF SCREAMS RANG down the halls. Mary moved toward the door, but Kyle pushed past her. He was almost to the tall door, when it opened. Kyle's sword was in his hand before Mary could fully see the palace guard who stood on the opposite side. Kyle's blade stopped just shy of the guard's throat.

"Princess Mariana!" the guard called, freezing at the touch of Kyle's blade.

"Kyle, step back," Mary ordered the silver Kolosian. Kyle obeyed and the guard dropped to a knee in front of them. "Princess," he said. "Princess."

"What? What is it?"

"My...my princess. I am not sure how to..."

Master Jiro entered from behind the door with Master Leo by his side. "Mary," Leo addressed her before entering into a low bow himself.

"Is my uncle..." Mary started to ask, but was unable to complete the sentence.

"No, my lady. Your uncle lives still." He paused and Mary stared down at him, wondering if there had ever been a point in her life where Master Leo had ever bowed to her before this moment.

"Leo, what is it? You're scaring me."

"Princess Mariana, I am not sure how to be the bearer of this news."

Mary felt her heart skip in fear. "What is it, Leo?"

"My lady," his voice held resounding sadness. "I am so sorry, my princess. Your father, Crown Prince Eadmund Dektra of the Kalian line and temple, is dead."

Mary stared at Leo without comprehension. "What?"

"I am sorry, my lady."

"What?" Her eyes skipped from Master Leo to Master Jiro, who met her gaze with sad, confirming eyes.

She turned, and started to slip to the ground. Kyle caught her, embracing her tightly. Mary did not cry, but instead hung numbly in Kyle's arms, forcing him to support her entire weight. "How did the prince die?" Kyle asked in an empty voice.

It was Master Jiro, still kneeling on the floor, who said, "He was murdered, my lord." Mary did not say a word, but merely sat encircled in Kyle's arms. Kyle carefully repositioned the princess more firmly in his arms, holding her as though she were a child. He then walked towards the far wall and sat down on the couch, continuing to hold her tightly against him.

"Do you need the princess?" Kyle asked the two masters kneeling on the floor.

"We are locking down both princesses," Master Leo said firmly. "She is not to leave this room until we determine the threat is contained."

"Is the person who killed Prince Eadmund dead as well?" Kyle asked in a cold, businesslike voice.

"We have not yet found the one responsible, my lord. But we have closed the palace gates and every person will be interrogated. They will not escape, you have my word."

Kyle nodded. "Fine, lock down the princesses. Do not allow anyone inside this room unless Mariana herself orders it so."

The two masters bowed their heads as Master Leo rose and headed for the exit. "I shall go now and lead this investigation myself."

Mary rocked back and forth gently against Kyle's chest. "No," she whispered. "No, no, no..."

"Leo," Kyle said as the Kalian master reached the door. "Send for Ryan."

"I don't know if that is a good idea, Kyle. Not after what happened..."

"Send for him anyway."

Leo nodded and left the room.

"Go outside, Master Jiro," Kyle said.

"I think someone should stay..."

"She can't cry with you in the room," Kyle said matter-of-factly.

Mary heard footsteps and then the soft thud of the heavy door closing behind the two men.

"They're gone, Mary. It is just us now."

Mary sat frozen in his arms. "Mary, did you hear me? It's just us Mary. Just us." Mary did not move but remained silent in the stillness.

Kyle raised Mary to a seated position, her body moving slowly as though she were weightless. Kyle looked into her eyes and slapped her left forearm hard.

Mary cried out in sudden pain and stood, her sword drawn in a trained reaction. Kyle did not move, but instead stared into the enraged eyes of the princess.

"That's better," he told her. "Be angry, Mary. Be sad. Be furious. But you should not, cannot, do nothing."

Mary brought down her sword towards Kyle, and Kyle moved back from the blade. He drew his silver sword against Mary's gold. "Come on, Mary. This is what you have been training for." Mary raced towards Kyle, her blade held out to her side. The gold and silver metal danced in the air and sang in a symphony of clashing metal.

Mary's blade twisted in the air. Kyle stood firm and met her attack head on. "That's it, princess," Kyle said as their blades met once again. Mary swung her blade toward his left side while he spun to block it. She tried again. Kyle twisted his body, turning just out of the reach of the blade's deadly tip

Master Jiro rushed back into the room. Mary said, "Don't!" Jiro froze by the door. Mary's sword crashed down upon Kyle's. Kyle ducked under the blade before rolling across the floor out of her reach. He jumped up, planting both feet firmly on the ground waiting for her next move.

Mary flew across the room, but Kyle was ready. He stopped her sword at a safe distance from his upper chest. Kyle swung his blade down towards the princess, using his height to his advantage, and she brought her own blade up towards him. Both blades reached the other's neck. The two champions froze. "Draw," Kyle whispered.

The two stared at each other for several moments as their blades cooled the hot flesh of the other's throat. Then Mary lowered her sword and stepped back from Kyle. She threw her blade at the large window behind her, completely shattering the glass. She stepped through the glass and into the cold air beyond, gazing up at the dark clouds that filled the skies. She let out a single, deep-throated scream as she stared toward the temple Gods.

Chapter XLI

PRINCESS AMERIA DID NOT CRY at the news of her father's death. She did not rage at the Gods. Instead, she raged at the guards who would not permit her to leave the room to go hunt her father's killer. "I do not care what Master Leo ordered!" she raged. "I am your princess!" Yet she knew that for all her screaming, it would do no good. "Are you, at least, protecting my mother?" she demanded of her captors.

"Yes, Princess Ameria. Your mother is being well-guarded."

Ameria paced the large room like a caged animal. Her mind raced with a thousand angry thoughts of all the enemies that could have possibility benefitted from killing her father. Most of the names were from those considered most loyal to the crown and temples. *Anyone who qualifies for the thirteenth tournament would benefit from killing the prince*, she thought, shifting through dozens of faces and countless names. *Anyone who wanted my sister out of the match...* She gave a harsh laugh. *Which I guess makes me the prime suspect.*

Just because she had never been close to her Kalian father did not mean that she did not love and respect him. She was royal because of his blood, not her mother's, and for that, she would always be grateful. Ameria began to re-circle the room, which had been emptied with the exception of Philip, dressed in robes of pink marking his as the Master of Dektra, and Lester, the Master of Critous in robes of purple.

She mentally shifted through more names and faces when suddenly her mind came back to the tall silver student whom she had lost among the crowd. Had she ever seen him before? She shifted through her memories. Tall, black hair, Kolosian skin, dark green eyes...her mind raced.

"How did they kill my father?" she demanded.

"I think, princess, that these are details you need from Master Leo."

"Forget Leo!" she told him. "I am your princess and I am asking you: how, exactly, did my father die?"

"He..."

"Did he die by the blade?"

He nodded and Ameria suddenly stopped pacing. Tall, pale skin, green eyes. "I have fought my father with a blade before," she said suddenly. "It would have taken a true sword master to kill my father with the blade."

"Yes, my lady. Prince Eadmund was very good with the sword."

Ameria looked up at him. "I saw who killed him."

"You what?"

"I saw who killed him. I fought him several months ago, he matched me stroke for stroke with the blade. By the Gods!" Ameria felt as though she were going to vomit. "I stared right at him! Right at him! He's wearing silver robes, dressed as a silver student from one of the lower temples. He probably walked right into the palace when the leaders called all the gold and silver students."

She looked at Lester. "Quickly, go tell Leo. He has short black hair, dark green eyes, and he is wearing silver student robes."

Ameria felt another chill on the air, "Beware," it seemed to whisper for her ears alone.

"Go, run!"

Lester turned to the door and raced out in search of the Kalian master. Ameria turned and seated herself on the couch near the fireplace. "It's cold in here," she said softly. "Do you think we could start a fire?"

"I will ask for some wood," Master Philip said. He opened the door and ordered the guards to start a fire for the princess. A few minutes later, blue flames rose from the center of the fireplace, yet the chill continued to seep deeper into Ameria's bones. Master Philip stood beside the couch in silence.

"I am sorry for your loss, princess," Master Phillip finally said in a soft voice. "I had the privilege of training beside your father on several occasions. I rarely saw anyone more courageous...except, perhaps for your mother."

"Thank you," Ameria said softly.

Phillip moved closer to Ameria, standing directly behind the couch on which she was seated. "You and your sister were all he could ever hope for and more." Master Philip put his hand gently on Ameria's shoulder and squeezed softly. She did not reach for his hand, but neither did she move it away. "He loved you very much."

"Thank you," she said again. "I know that he counted you among his closest friends."

"Yes." Philip's voice was thick with sorrow. "I am sad that your father is gone, but also, in a bittersweet way, perhaps it worked out for the best."

"Not you too," Ameria whispered. "Don't say you are glad that my sister won't be in that tournament."

"Oh no, princess, not that at all. I only meant..." his voice trailed off. He removed his hand from Ameria's shoulder. "I only meant that he would not live to see this." His voice was soft.

"What?" Ameria asked in confusion.

A wind rose within the room, as though someone had thrown open the closed windows. The once whisper rose to a scream, *"Beware princess!"* Ameria heard the scraping sound of metal as the blade was drawn from Phillip's sheath. She jerked forward, throwing her body across the room. Phillip's blade slashed into the cushion where Ameria had been seated only moments before.

Ameria scrambled across the room, but Phillip was between her and the tall door in the opposite corner. "I'm sorry, princess. It's not fair, I know, killing you when you are so injured that you cannot even grip a blade."

"It was you," Ameria whispered. "You organized the attack on us in the woods."

"One of many, princess." He slowly closed the distance between them. "I do this for the realm. The prophecy cannot come to pass. The Heirs of Kale must die."

"Prophesy? What prophecy?"

She stood her ground against the wall, placing her hand firmly on her sword hilt, her heart racing. He moved ever closer, his silver blade held before him. Ameria offered a silent prayer and pushed her back hard against the wall. Philip advanced towards her. "So brave. So Kalian," he whispered. "Your father would be proud."

"You're a Temple master. Why would you do this?"

Philip stood directly before the princess, his silver blade encrusted with dark pink stones on both side of its hilt. "The twins of Kale must not be permitted to live. Princess of Kale. Princess of Koloso. Heir to Both."

Ameria pulled her sword from its sheath a fraction of a second before Philip's blade crashed down upon her. She stopped his blade midair.

She twisted her arm, pushing Philip's arm to the side. The blade slipped from Philip's grasp and clattered to the floor as Ameria plunged her silver blade through the temple master's chest in a single stroke. He gasped. His hands clutched her blade piercing his heart. "No, it's impossible," he whispered.

A deep growl filled the darkness. The wraith stepped out of the shadows, his eyes like two single flames burning through the night. Philip's body fell to the ground as he began to die. "No," he whispered as his eyes took in the dark creature standing at the side of the princess. "Too late," he whispered.

His body fell still, never to draw breath again. Ameria withdrew her sword from his chest and turned slowly to look into the eyes of the wraith. "Well done, princess." His voice hissed across the room. The blue flames danced across his reflective eyes in a glint of light before the wraith vanished back into the shadows. "Well done."

Chapter XLII

~~~~~~

Mary walked from the room with Kyle on one side of her and Master Jiro on the other. A large, mixed group of defendants and palace guards stood outside the doors. They parted to make way for the princess.

"Where are we going, princess?" Master Jiro asked as they began to walk down the hall.

"To see my sister."

"Master Leo said..."

"My father is dead and the king is dying. That makes me queen in all but name. I need to find my sister."

"Did you find Ryan?" Kyle asked the silver temple master.

"I sent a guard for him, but he has yet to return."

"That is strange," Kyle said softly.

Mary shook her head, not pausing in her forward momentum. She was met halfway down the hallway by her sister, who seemed to be walking as quickly in Mary's direction. Strands of Ameria's long golden hair lay matted against her face. Her cheeks were flushed with rouge and her golden robes seemed to cling to her skin. Something stained the sleeve of her normally crisp robes. Mary studied the reddish tint of the satin as she closed the distance between them.

"Is that blood on your sleeve?" she asked Ameria.

"Yes, but not mine."

"Whose?"

"Master Phillip," Ameria answered. "He tried to kill me." Mary stared at her uncomprehendingly. "He was behind the assassination attempts in the woods."

"Master Phillip? What are you talking about? He's a temple master! Of your sister temple!" The room seemed to be spinning. "I don't..." Mary put her hand against the crimson palace wall and leaned her head down. "I don't understand."

"Breathe, princess," Kyle said, moving to her side. She drew several deep breaths. Then she raised her head and looked at Master Jiro.

"I have no idea what is going on, my princess. But I swear to you, I am going to find out."

"No," Mary replied, keeping her hand on the wall. "We are going to find out."

"Princesses, I must insist that you both return to a room where you can be protected."

"No," Ameria added her voice to the conversation. "No more hiding. Someone is trying to kill us and I, for one, am not going to stand around waiting on them. I know who killed our father, Ameria. I saw him." She shook her head and cursed in a string of Kalian terms. "I thought I recognized them, but I did not put it together in time."

"Who? Who are we looking for?"

"It was that guy I fought on the edge of the Rainbow Mountains. The one who was so good with the blade."

Mary felt her heart sink even further. "You mean the one who killed Lord Edward?"

"Yes!" Ameria hissed. "He's here, wearing silver robes."

Ameria gazed around the hallway and said, "I think I know how to find them." Kyle gave her a quizzical look, but she motioned him forward. "Follow me...quickly."

Mary moved towards the hallway and Kyle raced forward, matching her step for step. "Where are we going?"

"We have to find Ryan."

"Ryan? Why?"

"I have no time to explain." The group raced down hallway after hallway until they finally reached the outer doors of the palace. A dozen men both from the Royal Guard and the Defendant Team stood guard before the tall doors.

"Open the doors," Mary ordered. Two of the men followed her command. The princesses, Kyle, and Master Jiro stepped forward. At the sight of the two royals, the gathered crowd fell to silence. "Ryan!" Mary called to the crowd. "I need to speak with Ryan!"

No one moved. Mary scanned the crowd searching for the young man's purple robes. "I don't see him," Kyle said softly. Then to the crowd, "Has anyone seen Ryan? He's the purple student of Kale?"

"I think he went inside the palace," Brandan called out.

Mary turned and stared back at the tall doors behind her.

"What is going on, Mary?" Kyle demanded.

"We have to find him."

"But why? Is he in danger?"

"Something like that."

Mary re-entered the palace and then felt a terrible pain in her head, as though someone had struck her. She stumbled against the wall and would have fallen, had Kyle not grabbed her arm to steady her. "Mary, what..."

Two silver blades clashed mere inches before Mary's eyes. She jerked backwards, and Kyle stepped with her, preventing her from falling. Mary stared forward; there was no one in front of her. No blades, no fight. "Mary what is going on?"

She shook her head. "Someone is under attack."

"But you and Ameria are both here. Who else would they be after?"

"Mother!" Ameria said.

The two caught each other's gaze a spilt second before entering into a full run. Various corridors became mere blurs as the two princesses raced toward the far side of the palace towards their mother's chambers. Yet when they burst through the doors, they found their mother sitting quietly alone.

Mary paused and drew a deep breath. Swords once again clashed before her eyes. She let out a small scream.

"What is going on?" their mother demanded.

"We have to find Ryan," Mary said with a hint of near desperation in her voice.

"Why, Mary?"

"We have to!" She gazed around the room blindly. "What am I missing?" she asked of no one.

She turned and faced the wall of glass windows behind her, and saw the figure in the shadows. Without a word, she stepped closer to the glass, somehow understanding that she was the only one who would see it. "*Not you,*" the wraith whispered. "*Not you.*"

Mary stared back at the wraith.

"The blade, princess."

"The blade?"

"Yes."

Mary turned her gaze to the sword hanging on her left hip. The golden handle glittered in the firelight. She turned to glance at her sister and Kyle. They stood speaking softly to her mother, both hands lightly touching the tip of their deadly swords. There were very few people who Mary would call true masters of the blade, but Ameria and Kyle were one of them. As were those who had taught them: Lord Edward and at a younger age, their father. What was missing? She gazed down at her own sword once again and then into the eyes of the wraith. As the knowledge of the wraith's words suddenly dawned on her, Mary turned towards the others.

"Where is Master Leo?"

Chapter XLIII

MASTER LEO WAS HELPING WITH the search of the palace grounds and had just checked in on the men guarding the gate. He was beginning to walk back towards the palace, when two men dressed in silver robes approached him from across the grassy field. Leo walked quickly towards the two men meeting them halfway. "Any news?" he asked.

"Not yet, but there is about to be," the taller of the two men stated. He was taller even than Leo, his black hair cropped closely and his deep green eyes holding a glint that sent a chill down the Kalian master's spine.

"What do you mean?"

"The Temple of Kale is about to need a new master."

The man who had spoken unsheathed his long, silver blade and suddenly, it dawned on Leo. "You're the one who killed Prince Eadmund."

The stranger smiled. "Yes, I had that honor. And now, I will also have the honor of killing you."

Alec moved forward, his silver blade lunging for Leo's neck. Master Leo jumped to the side, moving himself out of the weapon's range and pulled his own silver sword from his side. Leo gazed into the dark green eyes of his opponent and finally said, "I see you carry your father's blade."

"Seems only fitting, does it not? You will be killed by the same blade that once saved your life."

"Alec." Leo stood still. He glanced back to the second man standing in silence behind Alec. "Brothers?" Leo guessed.

Alec brought his blade down upon Leo's with a thunderous force. Sparks flew from the clashing metal. Alec's sword flew towards Leo's left side, but Leo brought up his own sword, blocking the movement and forcing Alec to take several steps backwards, fighting to keep a hold on his blade. Alec recovered his grip far too quickly for Leo's benefit and sprang forward again. This time his blade moved in an upwards stroke towards Leo's stomach. Leo leapt back. Alec's blade sliced through midair.

Alec swung towards Leo's left side. Leo blocked the blade, half-turning to move his sword toward Alec's arm. Alec turned away from Leo's movement. The sword-master's blade sliced through the silver fabric covering Alec's arm, but did not bite into the flesh. Alec took a single step back, adjusting the blade in his hand. Then he stepped towards Leo.

Leo struck upwards toward Alec's left again, but Alec blocked the movement with a loud clash of silver. Their blades continued to collide, creating a ghastly music to which their bodies danced in a deadly circle of silver, gold, and steel. Alec twirled towards Leo's left and drew blood to Leo's shoulder. Leo drove forward and, with a powerful kick, sent him spiraling across the grassy field, breaking several ribs in the process.

Alec rose less steadily, his side screaming in pain, but he managed to fight past it and dashed towards the golden Kalian master. Surprised at how quickly Alec moved with the broken ribs, Leo managed to stop the blade from slicing into his neck, but was unable to stop Alec from cutting into his sword hand. Blood covered the hilt of Leo's sword, causing the metal to become slick. Leo placed both hands on the blade for better control, but his shoulder was injured from Alec's first infliction and his arm proved less than reliable.

Alec brought his blade down towards Leo's left side and this time the blade sank home, splitting Leo's flesh and breaking through his ribcage with a sickening sound. Master Leo collapsed, Alec's blade sliding along the inside of his chest.

"No!" a voice called. Alec turned around to find Princess Mariana racing towards him with Kyle by her side. Peter turned towards the newcomers, freeing his sword, but froze as recognition dawned. "Ana?" he asked in surprise. "What are you doing here, Ana?"

Mary stopped as she reached him, and Kyle dashed ahead. Peter moved to stop Kyle, but Mary jumped forward, placing herself between the two men, allowing Kyle to rush past her towards Alec. "Hello, Peter," Mary said quietly. "Helping your brother with his dirty work now?"

"What are you doing here, Ana?" His eyes took in her Kalian robes. "You're the golden student of Kale?" he asked in an astonished tone.

"Yes. And it's Mariana, Peter. Crown Princess Mariana."

He stared at her for several moments while across from them, Kyle's silver blade crossed with Alec's in a fierce clash. "I don't want to hurt you," Peter finally said.

"You just helped put a blade through my master's side, Peter. Too late for that."

Mary moved towards Peter, and their blades met high in the air. She drove forward, aiming for Peter's upper chest, but he brought his blade down on Mary's, driving the tips harmlessly towards the ground. The two blades rose, circled and met again soundly in the air between them. The blades sang as they met again and again throughout the dance both fighters seemed to know so well.

Across from her, Kyle struggled to hold his ground against the swordmaster. He felt like he was fighting Ameria, blocking stroke after stroke of Alec's deadly blade. Alec swung high and Kyle ducked under him, rolling in the grass several feet and then jumping to his feet to avoid another of Alec's downward strikes. Master Leo lay on the ground between Mary and Kyle's battles.

Peter blocked another of Mary's movements, but just barely. Despite years of training, Peter was not his brother and Mary was proving more than worthy of her reputation as an undefeated champion of the Kalian line. Peter attempted to strike her right arm, but Mary was faster. She twirled around him as though she were a choreographed dancer, and sent him flying off balance with a powerful shove to his left shoulder.

Kyle hissed as Alec's blade bit into the skin of his left arm. The cut wasn't deep, but it stung and was way too close for comfort. A mere second slower and Kyle was relatively sure that he would have been missing an arm. He jumped back several steps, attempting to put distance between them, but Alec was having none of it and pursued Kyle across the field. Kyle prepared to meet Alec's blade once again.

Mary caught Kyle's fight out of the corner of her eye and could tell that he needed help. Regretting that she had sent her sister to the opposite side of the palace grounds, Mary twirled around her own opponent once again and managed to block another sideways stroke of Peter's blade. Mary moved her sword in a downward stroke towards Peter. He moved to block her when Mary changed directions, driving her blade up. The sharp metal sank deeply into the underside of Peter's arm leaving it attached by only a few thin threads of flesh. He screamed and sank to the ground. Blood poured from Peter's arm. His silver robes bled to black and the grass beneath him was stained with a stream of hot blood.

Mary looked up and turned towards Kyle. Alec's blade was at his pale throat. Beside them, stood Ryan, holding onto the reins of two silver stallions.

Chapter XLIV

―─◆─▶─※─◀─◆─―

MARY TURNED WITH SILENT EYES and walked towards Alec. He stared at her from across the field, watching her with a deadly calm. She walked slowly, closing the distance between them as her heartbeat likened to the insistent ticking of an unwanted clock. She stopped several paces from the pair, her sword gripped tightly in her pale hand, its blade painted red with his brother's blood.

"Brave little thing." Alec turned his dark gaze upon her.

"I am the captain and golden ranked member of the Temple of Kale," Mary said.

"Am I supposed to be scared of that?"

"I want my partner."

"Partner?" Alec offered a twisted smile. "So the Temple of Kale and Koloso are working together now?"

"Only against a common enemy," Mary replied coolly.

"Common? Oh, I think I am far from common."

"He killed the prince," Kyle said from behind Alec's blade. "Don't let him go."

"This is not the fight you want," Mary said, raising her sword as the fresh blood dripped to the ground. "Only I can give you that."

"I could always slit his throat, and then yours."

"Mary," Ryan said.

"Silence!" his brother commanded.

Mary turned her jade eyes on the younger man. "Your brother is bleeding to death, Ryan. Go to him. Tie off his arm, or he will die."

Ryan looked at her uncertainly and glanced at the silver horses. "Take the horses with you. You will need to get Peter into the saddle."

Ryan looked at his brother. Alec said nothing, so Ryan moved forward quickly and walked towards Mary, leading the horses behind him. Alec did not move his blade from Kyle's throat. Mary turned her jeweled gaze back to the elder brother.

"I killed your prince." His voice was almost a hiss. "You cannot let me go. It would be your head."

She met his gaze head on, shocked to realize that after all of this planning, he still had no idea who she was. "My father is dead and both my king and master lie dying." Her voice was strangely calm. "That makes it my call."

"No," a second voice said firmly. Mary turned to find her sister standing beside her. "No. He killed Lord Edward. He killed our father. He killed your master. He tried to kill your sister. He goes nowhere."

"He has a blade at Kyle's throat." Mary's voice was still calm.

"I don't care. That man cannot be permitted to live, Mary. He dies today, by my hand." Ameria began to cross the distance between them.

"He will kill Kyle," Mary cautioned.

Ameria stopped walking and looked at her partner, whose throat was still touching Alec's silver blade. "Don't let him leave, Ameria," Kyle said and then let out a sharp hiss as Alec's blade bit ever so lightly into his throat. Alec actually stood behind Kyle, using his body as a shield.

"You owe me a rematch," Ameria said coldly. "What do you say? You've killed a prince, a Golden Defendant, and a temple master. Why not add a golden student to your roster? Silver is not worthy of your blade.

"Tempting," the man said. "Yet every moment we stand here, I feel your reinforcements coming. Even I cannot defeat the entire defendant team."

"Give us Kyle," Mary said. "Give us Kyle, you take your brother. That will be that."

"No," Ameria hissed. "Let Kyle go and fight me instead. Your brothers can leave. It is not their life I want."

"The promise of a Kolosian? Now what the hell is that worth?"

"The word of two princesses," Ameria said.

"Princesses?" He changed his gaze from one sister to the other. "You are the twins?"

"Ameria, let them go! Let Kyle go," Mary directed her words at Alec. "Let him go and you have my word, you and your brothers can go."

Ryan stood several feet behind the two sisters, having successfully bound his brother's arm and had maneuvered him into the saddle of a silver stallion. Ryan stopped both horses behind them, waiting for instructions on how this scene would play out.

"Ameria!" Mary called again. "I do not need another death on my hands."

Ameria whirled on her sister with wild eyes and walked several paces towards the silver horses. "And what do you think will happen if we allow them to live?" she demanded. "They have tried to kill us twice! How long until they succeed?"

"They won't," Mary said. "We will hunt them down, I swear it. But not at the cost of Kyle's life."

"Over my dead body," Ameria yelled suddenly, raising her silver blade towards where Ryan held the reins of his injured brother's horse. Ryan stared in terror unable to move from the oncoming swing. Ameria's blade raced forward, but was stopped a breath away from Ryan's neck by the flash of Mary's gold. The two ancient blades collided in a spark of gold and silver.

"Mary!" Ameria screamed. "Move!"

"Not if it will cost Kyle's life to do so. We have lost too many."

"And I will not be next!" Ameria screamed.

Kyle used that moment to throw himself backwards, practically falling onto the man behind him. Alec's sword slipped away from Kyle's throat and both men collided with the ground in a heap, knocking the wind from their lungs. Kyle threw a punch desperately, his hand making contact with Alec's left cheek. He scrambled away from Alec and stumbled towards the two princesses.

Ryan mounted the silver horse behind his brother and led the single horse forward, racing towards Alec. Ryan dismounted as he reached his brother. Seeing Kyle free, the two sisters raced forward. Ryan jumped off the horse and said, "Get on, Alec!"

Alec mounted the horse in a single stride behind Peter. "Go!" Ryan shouted.

Alec kicked the side of the horse, and the silver stallion raced towards the palace gates.

Ameria let out a wordless scream as Alec rode away. "The gates are closed!" Ameria said. "They have to be closed."

Mary did not hear her sister's cries. She rushed across the field to where her master lay. "Leo!" she screamed, falling into the dirt beside him. "Leo!"

He was breathing, but it came out as a wheezing, gasping sound. She looked at his left side where Alec's blade has slipped between his ribs and, as Mary could see, into his lung. "Leo!" tears filled her eyes. "You're going to be okay," she stammered, knowing it was a lie.

Her sister had managed to calm down the second silver stallion and was attempting to mount it and give chase to Alec. "No!" Mary screamed. "Ride to the palace!" she screamed. "Get help."

Mary took off her outer robe and tried to maneuver it around Leo's torn side. Kyle appeared beside her and helped her lift Leo enough so that she could slide the golden cloth under him. The blue grass surrounding him was now brown. The sky was growing darker by the minute. She pulled the silk as tightly as she could, but knew that it would do nothing for his injured lung.

He spat blood as he fought for each breath. "I can take you to the temple." She floundered. "We can ride, right now. We can, ride..."

"You wouldn't get there in time," Kyle said softly.

"Please," she said in desperation. "Please, help me. Help me!"

"Mary," Leo gasped with shallow breaths.

"Master," Mary said. Raindrops seemed to be falling on Leo's broken form, yet it was not raining.

"Mary, it was Nathan. Nathan...ask your mother; Nathan."

"Shh, don't talk," Mary shushed him. "Please, Leo. We are going to help you. The healers will be here any minute and you'll be just fine. Please."

"Mary, Mary..."

"No, please, Leo. Please, I need you. You're the only real father I have ever known. I...I can't do this without you." Mary put her face on his chest, begging him to live.

"I love you, Mariana. You were...the da...daughter I never had."

"Leo, please, please."

His eyes became more and more glassy and then he looked at her. "What a Golden Defendant you would make." Then his breath released in a horrible gasp and she felt his heart stop beating. "No," she whispered. "No, no, no…"

Chapter XLV

Ameria raced her horse through the crowd and up the steps of the palace. She dismounted in a single, liquid movement. Master Jiro, in his long silver robes, met her at the door. "Master Leo is near the gate," she said without meeting his gaze. "He's dying."

"What?" Jiro stared at her in disbelief.

"Send the healer, for what little good that will do. And probably Marcus, too; if Leo dies before you get there, my sister will be a mess." She walked down the hall.

"Wait!" Jiro followed her. "What is….what the hell happened?"

"You mean other than my sister allowing our father's killer to escape?" Ameria did not slow her pace. "Send the healer," she said again. "Not that it will do any good."

"Ameria stop!"

"I am going to the king's room."

"The king is ill and all of this news has just made it worse. He is in no condition to see…"

"He will see me!"

Ameria reached the doors to the King's chambers. Four members of the Royal Guard stood before it. "I will see the king," she said.

"I am sorry, princess," the man closest to the door with dingy blond hair and golden eyes addressed the young woman. "The king is not to be disturbed."

Ameria stepped to the nearest guard and launched an elegant, round kick, knocking him into the far wall with such force that he crumpled under the impact. She twisted out of that kick and drove her elbow into the left side of another. The guard gasped, the air knocked from his lungs as Ameria followed her movement with a fist to the left side of his face, cracking his jaw. She turned in a defensive stance back to the other two men and shifted her icy gaze to the blond who had spoken. "I will see my uncle, now!"

The man hesitated for only a moment, and then opened the large doors behind him. Ameria walked into the room.

The room was dark. Long, crimson curtains of velvet draped the large mass of windows in the king's chambers. The bed stood on the far side of the room with thick velvet blankets laying atop, matching the curtains perfectly. In the far corner sat a woman in a thin, golden floor-length gown with long sleeves that hung loosely at her wrists. The satin fabric was wrinkled as though she has slept in the gown for many a night. She turned her bloodshot eyes in Ameria's direction.

"What are you doing here?" the queen demanded.

Ameria walked towards the bed where her uncle lay under several layers of crimson covers. He coughed softly at her approach and struggled to raise himself on the crimson pillows beneath him. "Ameria," the king said, spying his golden-haired niece. "Where is your sister?"

"You cannot be here!" the queen cried. "Where are the guards?"

Ameria ignored her aunt and answered her uncle's question. "Mariana is with Master Leo," Ameria said in a flat voice. "We thought the assassins were after us. We were wrong."

"What do you mean?"

"They were after my father and Leo." Ameria filled him in on the events that had just transpired.

"Is Master Leo still alive?"

"I saw the injury when I approached the fight. I do not believe he will live long enough to be healed. However," She gazed into her uncle's emerald eyes, a perfect match for her sister's, "one of the killers remained behind. I want him captured and interrogated, immediately. Then I want to lead the search for his brothers. They will all die."

The king nodded his consent.

Chapter XLVI

IT TOOK BOTH KYLE AND Marcus to pry Mary away from Leo's body. When she calmed down enough to stop fighting them, Kyle took her in his arms.

"We should take her to the palace," Marcus advised.

"No." Kyle shook his head. "We can't have everyone seeing her like this. My father has a house just outside the palace walls. I will take her there."

A carriage was quickly called for. At its arrival, Kyle lifted Mary inside and they rode towards the manor. A few onlookers stared as the royal carriage passed by, but Mary did not care. She simply clung to Kyle's silver robe and sobbed an endless sea of tears. "No, no, no," she whispered over and over again. When they arrived, Kyle carried her into one of the bedrooms and placed her gently on satin blankets. He tried again to soothe her, but Mary proved inconsolable.

The princess cried until she had no tears left to shed and then fell silent. For two days, she neither spoke nor ate. The silver Kolosian remained by her side, sleeping in a chair beside her, keeping silent watch over her still form.

It was on the morning of the third day that Kyle realized that he could allow her to grieve no longer. He woke her with the morning sun. "Mary," Kyle spoke softly. She opened her green eyes slowly.

"I'm sorry, princess." Kyle addressed her. "I would let you sleep longer, but you have to know what is going on."

"I don't care," she said with a voice of pure sorrow.

"It's about Ryan." Kyle cleared his throat. "He helped his brothers escape and I fear the king is going to kill him."

Mary stared up in confusion. "What?"

"Your uncle, the king. He lives still, and he is going to sentence Ryan to death for assisting in the escape of his brothers. I thought you needed to know."

"What did he tell my uncle?" Mary demanded, sounding like herself for the first time since Leo died.

"Ryan swore he did not know what they were doing. He stated that they came to inform him that their mother was ill and that they needed a horse to return home quickly. He went to borrow some horses and signed them out properly. When he started walking back, he saw the fight."

"Do you believe the story?" Mary sounded uncertain.

Kyle looked intently at the princess. "I do not know, Mary. I mean, he helped them escape."

Mary stared at him. "That part, I believe. I let my father's killer escape to save you. And technically, I am not even supposed to like you."

"I guess it's a good thing you do."

Mary gave a deep sigh and rose from the bed. "I'll take a bath."

Kyle nodded, calling several maids into the room to draw a bath for the princess. A few minutes later, Mary walked into the side room and closed the large wooden door behind her. She removed her filthy robes and stepped into the steaming water awaiting her. She could not remember the last time simple hot water had felt so wonderful. Yet inside, her heart still ached. *What a Golden Defendant you would make*, his words seemed to echo across the silent room.

Are you saying I should give up the crown? She wondered.

"My lady," Kyle's voice interrupted her thoughts from the other side of the door.

"Yes?" Mary asked.

"The servants delivered fresh towels. Would you like me to have them brought in to you?"

Mary glanced over the edge of the large marble tub and then said, "Why don't you just put them on the counter yourself?"

The door opened quietly and Mary watched as Kyle stepped into the room with downcast eyes and placed the towels quickly on the edge of the counter. "I can't reach them way over there," she informed him. "Would you please move them a little closer?"

Kyle did not hesitate. He took several steps forward and placed the towels closer to the edge of the large tub.

"Here." Mary straightened and began to wring the water from the strands of her long dark hair. "Hold it out for me?"

Kyle did not say a word, but merely opened the towel, and then stared down to meet her jade green eyes. She drew a deep breath and stood quickly, water cascading down her body as she stepped over the marble and into the towel, thankful that her skin was red enough from the heat of the water that he could not see her blush. She wrapped the large towel around her body. She felt exhilarated, half-crazed. "Thank you," she whispered as she leaned closer towards Kyle.

"I am at your service, princess."

She repeated his previously spoken words, "Anything within your power."

"Yes," he answered as she pressed her lips to his. He remained still under her caress. She stepped even closer, kissing him again. This time, he mirrored the kiss, but otherwise remained still, allowing her complete control. She pulled back and stared into his dark eyes. "Let's go save Ryan."

Chapter XLVII

―――◆―◘―✻―◘―◆―――

THE KING HAD BEEN CARRIED into the throne room by several men to take his seat on the throne before his court. His cheeks were unnaturally pale. His cough was constant. He had been advised to remain in bed, but had stubbornly risen, much to the queen's dismay. Princess Ameria stood by her uncle's side, ignoring the queen's insistent concerns.

The room was massive. The walls were not painted of the same crimson that graced much of the palace, but instead were painted silver. Two silver thrones sat in front of the farthest wall of the throne room, which was made entirely of glass. On a normal day, the room would be inundated with the brilliance of Kale's three suns and those who looked on the king would squint against the glare of the light surrounding him. However, the suns had not shown since the day the prince and Kalian master had died. The sky remained covered in a constant shroud of dark clouds, casting the land in shadow.

Ryan had been dragged into the Royal Throne Room. The purple of the Kalian robe he still wore was dark enough to hide much of the blood that had soaked through the satin cloth. His left cheek sported a deep, purple bruise and his eye was almost entirely swollen shut. On the other side of his face, a long, thin cut ran from just below the corner of his eye to his ear. His hands were bound behind him with a coarse rope stained red with his blood.

"So far," the king addressed the boy who stood bound before the throne. "I have refused to allow these men to do anything that would result in permanent, disabling damage. Tell me where your brothers are, and you may find me receptive to the idea of mercy." He let out an awful cough. "Refuse again, and they shall be given free rein to do whatever is necessary to get the location from you."

Ryan remained bravely silent, refusing to give in.

"So be it," the king said. "Take this man back to the tower and employ any means necessary to extract the location of his brothers. If he dies in the process…so be it."

Ryan stared in silence, but could not keep the fear from his eyes. The guards escorting him turned him roughly towards the tall silver doors behind them as Mary entered the room. Dressed in robes of gold, the Kalian princess wore her crown upon her brow, which stood starkly visible against her long, free-flowing black hair. Behind her stood Kyle, wearing crisp robes of silver, his shoulder-length black hair pulled tightly behind him with a thin silver clasp. He stood tall and clean shaven, following never more nor fewer than a single step behind the princess.

"Mary," Ryan stammered.

Mary turned toward the king. "Your Majesty," she addressed the frail man.

"Your Highness," the King replied. "I see you are finally wearing your crown."

"It seemed an appropriate thing to do, when attending a formal session of court."

"These matters do not concern you, princess," the queen said from the side of the throne.

"I beg your pardon, my lady. I shall soon be queen. Every decision of this court concerns me." She shifted her gaze towards Ryan. "That boy is a member of the Kalian temple. His fate therefore, lies in my hands, Your Majesties, not yours."

"That boy," her sister's anger filled the room, "killed the Crown Prince of the realm. His fate lies with the king and the king has declared his death."

"You do not know that, Ameria."

"Yes, I do! How dare you question what I know happened. They attacked our father and your master... and escaped!"

"Then take your anger out on me, sister. Not the boy."

One of the crimson robes statesmen entered the conversation. "Even if he was Kalian, his life would have lay with Master Leo, not you."

"Except Master Leo is dead," Mary replied. "And until a new master is instated, all decisions concerning the team lie with the golden student of the temple."

Ameria stepped down from the silver steps of the throne and walked toward her sister, her heels echoing across the silver marble beneath her. "What are you doing, Mary?" Ameria's blue eyes focused exclusively on her sister. "How do you think those men even got into the palace? He was there during the fight. He got them the horses to escape. They never would have made it out of the palace had he not assisted them."

"Ameria, there is no blood on his hands."

"No, he let his brothers bloody their hands, while he watched and arranged their escape!" Ameria shook her head. "The guards at the gate were all dead. Did you know that? Of course you didn't! His brother killed the guards at the gate, including two defendants!"

Mary stared at her sister, unsure of how to proceed. She turned to gaze at Ryan's bruised and beaten face. Did he help his brothers enter the palace? Did he know what they planned to do? Her heart ached at the realization that she did not know the answer.

"Ameria," Mary tried again. "You don't know what happened here. You don't know if he knew."

Ameria sighed in disgust. "I know he helped you in those woods, but Mary," she shook her head, "how do you know that he did not help you for the express purpose of getting into the palace?"

Mary shook her head slowly. "You don't know everything, Ameria. You don't know the entire story."

"Then tell me!"

Mary gazed at her sister unable to bring herself to confess that she had known whose brother Ryan was.

Ameria turned towards the men holding Ryan. "Get him out of here," Ameria commanded. "You heard the orders of your king."

"Your Majesty, I implore you." Mary returned her attention back to her dying uncle. "Uncle, please do not allow this to happen. Give me a chance to prove what really happened."

"I'm sorry, Mary. Unless he will reveal the location of his brothers, I have no choice."

The guards began to lead Ryan from the room when the young man called out to her, "I swear, Mary. I did not let them in the palace and when I did see them, I had no idea what they had done."

"Silence," one of the guardsmen slapped him across the cheek. Mary watched them lead Ryan from the room.

"Uncle, please. I just need time."

"Not unless he gives up his brothers."

"Would you?" Mary asked the king. "Would you have given up your brother? Would my father have given up you? Would any Kalian do something of such dishonor?"

The king started coughing and raised a pale cloth to his lips. When the coughing ceased, the cloth was filled with bright red blood.

Mary left the throne room without a word and Kyle, after offering a quick bow to his sovereign, turned to follow her.

"Kyle," Ameria called his name. "Don't follow her, Kyle. No good can possibly come of it." Kyle paused and then turned and bowed to the princess before following Mary out the door.

Mary walked down a long series of corridors before she finally reached her mother's private chambers. A large fire filled the dark room with a deep, blue light. Two large, silver couches graced the space directly in front of the fire. As regal as ever, Princess Annabelle sat near the fire in a full-length black gown. The front of her gown dipped into a simple scooped neck that stopped at a modest height above her breasts. A thin silver crown was nestled in her long hair and a thin golden necklace encircled her pale throat. She turned toward her eldest daughter.

"Mariana," her mother greeted her with the soft spoken, patient manner for which she was respected far and wide.

"Mother," Mary said, pausing as she approached.

"Please sit down, daughter."

Mary complied with the request, taking a seat on the couch opposite of her mother, pulling her sword from her side as she did so and placing the golden sheath upon the satin cushion beside her. Kyle stepped to the side of the couch, standing beside the princess.

"It is a tragedy, what has happened." Princess Annabelle offered her sympathy to Mariana. "I am sorry, daughter, for the loss of your master. Leo was truly a great man, defendant, and Kalian master. The realm mourns his passing."

"Should you not be speaking of my father instead?"

Annabelle offered a slight smile. "Is it really necessary to speak of the virtues of your father?"

"No more so than it is to speak of those of Master Leo."

Annabelle nodded. "Very true, daughter."

"I am sorry for the loss of your husband, Mother."

"And I, for the loss of your father."

The two stared at each other in silence before Mary finally managed to break through the ice surrounding them. "Mother...." She cleared her throat. "Princess," she tried again, the word sounding far more natural than Mother. "When Master Leonardo Desato died, he said I should speak with you. He said the name, Nathan, and said I should ask you who that was."

Annabelle's expression changed with a sharp intake of breath. Her lips parted and her body visibly tensed. "Nathan?" her mother asked. "Are you sure he said 'Nathan'?"

Mary nodded.

"Why would he want you to know about Nathan? I don't..."

"The men who came today killed both Leo and the prince and one of them was the same man who killed Lord Edward." Mary drew a deep breath and exhaled slowly before launching into her confession. "The boy who helped me when I was lost in the woods; I knew his brother had killed Edward. I knew that my sister had fought him in the Rainbow Mountains. I knew, and I let the boy come into the temple anyway. He saved me, it was the least I could do."

"The woods!" her mother exclaimed. "Nathan...wait. Are those Angie's children?"

Mary jumped from the couch, grabbing her sheathed sword as she did so. "How do you know their mother's name?"

"Nathan... By the Gods!"

"But that is not his name," Mary said. "The man who killed father, his name is Alec."

Annabelle felt her world spinning out of control. "Alec," she whispered softly.

"Who is he, Mother? You have to tell me. If you don't, they are going to torture his little brother to death, and his brother doesn't deserve it."

"Nathan was a lord. He fell from grace and betrayed his oath. Your fa..." She had to draw a deep breath. "Your father and Master Leo banished him."

Mary sighed and turned her head up towards the ceiling. "And Alec is his son," Mary finished for her. "They are all his sons."

"I would assume so, yes," her mother replied. "You don't have time for this story, Mariana. What you need to know is that Nathan was a powerful, dangerous man. He was a class behind the four of us; Eadmund, Leo, Jiro and I. He served as the silver student of Koloso." Her mother's normally clear eyes glazed over, as though she were seeing it all again. "His wife was the golden student, his partner. They were sword-masters above all else. I had never and likely shall never see their equal with a blade. If they taught their sons, they are likely just as deadly."

"So they are of the Kalian bloodline. And the blades they carry were their parents'."

"I would imagine so, Mariana."

"Then why would they not have known who I was when I came across the temple?"

"I don't know. I have no idea."

"So after all of these years, this man's children came for vengeance against those who banished their father?"

"If it is them, then yes, that would be the reason."

Mary stared at her mother. "Thank you, my lady. I must go now, but I will come back for the rest of this story."

Her mother nodded and Mary walked towards the door. Kyle followed her down a series of hallways until Mary reached the chambers that had been set aside for her. "Kyle," she whispered in a hushed tone. "Go find Marcus for me, and anyone else who you feel owes their loyalty to you, and not my sister."

"What are you going to do princess?"

"I cannot allow Ryan to die if he is innocent."

"And if he is not?" Kyle asked her.

Mary met his gaze head on. "If he is guilty," she spoke slowly. "Then I will kill him myself."

Chapter XLVIII

A FEW HOURS LATER, MARY was standing in a small circle surrounded by a close knit group of Kalians and Kolosians. Marcus had come at his partner's call, flanked by Sam in his robes of green and Dan in his robes of black. With Kyle came Brandan and Kev, in red and black respectively. "No one does this by anything other than their own free will," Mariana instructed the small knit group. "There will be no judgments whatsoever of anyone who refuses."

"We are Kalians, captain." Dan, with his brown hair and matching eyes flashed the princess a smile. "We can't let these Kolosians show us up now."

"This is not a contest, Dan," Mary answered him. "There are very serious consequences to what we are about to do."

"We are with you, Mary," his cousin, Sam, answered for him. "It doesn't matter that he hasn't been with us for very long. Ryan fought in the tournament with us. That makes him as Kalian as the rest of us."

"And we can't possibly stand by and watch the Kalians prove braver than us," Kev piped in.

"Okay," Mary said. "I want everyone to go back to their rooms and change out of your temple attire. Ask the maids for black. Tell them it is in order to go into mourning for the prince and Master Leo. They always keep plain black clothes on hand for such occasions. Meet back here at nightfall."

The group broke up and slipped from the room, staggering their exits so not to draw too much attention. "Mary," Kyle offered after the last visitor had left the room. "There is no need for all of this, you know. I could go alone tonight and get him out. No one else would have to risk themselves, including you."

Mary stared at Kyle with unsure eyes, and then asked. "Why are you doing this, Kyle?"

"What do you mean?"

"You are Ameria's partner, not mine. Why are you doing this?"

"I swore to serve you."

"Whatever is in your power to give," she echoed his previously spoken words. "But why, Kyle? You are her partner, not mine."

"As Marcus is yours. Yet upon learning of your uncle's fate, you asked for me, not Marcus."

Mary stared at him intently.

"How did you know who Ryan's brother was?" Kyle asked on a different line.

"What?"

"How did you know?"

Mary met his gaze. "I saw Alec with Lord Edward's sword, and the scar he bore, exactly where Ameria described it."

"And you brought Ryan into the palace anyway?"

"I had to," she said softly. "He was innocent of his brother's crimes and..."

"And was your only link to later find Edward's killer," Kyle finished for her.

"Yes," Mary admitted.

"You were keeping him so you could kill his brother."

"Yes. When I had mastered the sword well enough to kill him."

"And that is why you asked for me."

"Yes," Mary replied.

"And now?" he moved closer to the princess. "What are you doing now?"

"I think he is innocent."

"So we save him."

"No," Mary replied. "Not 'we.'"

Kyle crossed his arms across his chest. "What do you mean?"

"You can't go, Kyle."

"And why not?"

"Because if I die tonight, my sister will become queen, and you are her chosen king."

His arms fell to his side as he stared at the young princess standing before him. "And you want me to marry your sister?"

"Yes," Mary said softly. "If I die tonight, then yes, I want you to marry my sister. She needs you...and so does the kingdom."

He closed the distance between them. Mary took several steps back, but Kyle followed her movements, until her back was against the crimson wall behind her. "I could stop this whole thing," Kyle whispered. "One word to the palace guard and the king will lock you in this room."

"No," Mary whispered, heat flaring through her face. "You wouldn't do that, Kyle. You cannot do that."

"And why would I not?" he asked. "Give me one reason not to."

Mary searched his dark eyes. "Because I will never forgive you if he dies."

Kyle kissed her, pressing her body against the wall. Mary pulled away from him, but Kyle moved his arm against her left shoulder, pinning her to the wall. Then he kissed her again. This time she kissed him back, opening her lips to his. She had no idea how long they stood there. When Kyle finally drew back, Mary followed him, but stopped when Kyle said, "Mariana."

"I asked for you, Kyle, because I knew you would protect the kingdom before you protected me. Something I continually fail to do."

"Mariana," he said again.

"I may not live through the night," Mary said, her voice momentarily frantic, but then calmed. "And even if I live, I am sworn to marry a nameless champion.

A promise I could have avoided, had I known that my uncle would die so soon. Had I known...had I known."

"Give her the throne, princess." Kyle shook his head. "I know how you react, I know what you say. I know that you are the rightful heir and I know that she is a Kolosian. I know, I know, I know." An unfamiliar anger began to seep into Kyle's usually calm tone. "But, Mary! You do not want the throne and Ameria does not want the Golden Defendant position! Trade with her, princess. Give her the throne, it is what you want."

"Don't you think I want that?" she asked in a raw voice. "Don't you think I would give anything to... to just be..." She shook her head. "It's my right, my duty, my...my curse!"

Kyle looked at her from the several steps between them and finally said. "I know, princess. I know."

Kyle crossed the room slowly and walked out the door of Mary's room. "I will be back," he told her as he closed the large door. Kyle turned and found himself standing toe to toe with Marcus. The silver Kalian matched Kyle's height, his light brown hair brushing just past his broad shoulders. "May I help you, Marcus?"

The silver member of the Temple of Kale gave his Kolosian counterpart the full weight of his gaze. "Yes, Lord Kyle," Marcus replied. "You can stay away from the princess."

"Excuse me?"

"That woman is my partner, Kyle, not yours." His voice cut sharply through the still air around them. "And I intend to keep it that way."

"With all due respect, Lord Marcus," Kyle replied. "That woman is your princess, and shall be addressed as such, even by one with a rank such as ours." Kyle's hand tightened on the hilt of his silver blade.

"She is my partner, Lord Kyle, and I suggest you go back to your own, because you shall not have mine. I do not fear you, neither here nor in any tournament."

Kyle stared at his longtime rival for several heartbeats. "Then I shall look forward to meeting you in that tournament, Lord Marcus." Kyle gave a soft tilt of his head toward the silver Kalian. "Now, if you will excuse me, I believe we both have a job to do." Kyle stepped sideways around the other man and walked down the hall. Marcus remained silent, watching long after Kyle had disappeared around the corner before turning to enter Mariana's room.

The princess looked up, surprised to see her partner. "What is it, Marcus?" She asked. "Is Ryan...?"

"You kissed him," Marcus said in a firm, matter-of-fact tone. "Are you in love with the silver Kolosian?"

Mariana moved her head back in surprise. "I don't think that it is..."

"It is my business." Marcus walked across the room, quickly closing the gap between them. "You are my partner, Mariana. You have always been my partner. If you are in love with Lord Kyle, it is my business."

"Marcus, you are out of line."

He reached for Mary's arm and she stepped back, out of his reach. "Marcus what are you doing?"

"I have fought by your side every single day for twelve years, princess. We are partners, we are Kalian, and I am telling you now, my lady, that I intend to fight for your hand."

He leaned closer towards the princess and this time she did not pull away. "When you loved Jace, it was one thing. Jace was not strong enough to be my rival, nor powerful enough to be your king. You knew that and, as such, I knew you would eventually come to terms with Jace on your own. But Kyle is another matter, my lady, and if you think I am going to stand by and watch him take you from me, you could not be more wrong."

Mary gazed up into his deep eyes as though in a trance. "Marcus," she whispered as his face leaned towards hers.

His lips stopped just short of her own. "I will not kiss you, my lady. But I want to be clear: I am your partner, Mariana. And I have every intention of being your king." He dropped into a low bow before turning back towards the door. The princess watched him leave breathlessly; the only sound was the echoing of his black boots along the palace floor.

Chapter XLIX

―――◆◄☼►◆―――

MARY CHANGED FROM HER OUTER robes of status into more simple clothes of mourning. She wore a long-sleeved black cotton shirt that fit comfortably and long black slacks which fit loosely at the waist, but clung to the legs, which minimized the sound of moving fabric. She pulled her hair back with a plain, black band. Kyle was the first to return to Mary's room, dressed in matching black attire. Together, they prepared for the arrival of the rest of their group, when someone knocked on the door to Mary's chambers.

Mary waited cautiously as the door opened. Lord Sethrick entered the room, dressed in his silver robes, marking his status as the Silver Defendant. Surprised at seeing the high ranking lord, it took both students several moments to enter into the traditional Kalian bow before the defendant.

"Princess. Lord Kyle," Sethrick instructed the two kneeling champions. "Princess Mariana," Lord Sethrick began. "Your presence is requested in the throne room immediately."

"What for?" the princess questioned the defendant.

"I am not at liberty to say, Your Highness."

Mariana rose from the ground in an elegant, practiced movement and walked towards the door before the Silver Defendant. Her heartbeat quickened and Mary gave a nervous glance to Kyle. He moved to follow her. The two warriors walked down a series of hallways before they once again arrived at the tall, silver doors to the throne room. Entering the large chamber, Mary's mother stood in her black velvet gown. At Annabelle's side stood the queen, wearing a black, floor-length, long sleeved gown of silk. A few feet from them stood Lady Rebecca wearing her golden robes befitting her status as the golden member of the defendants.

Mary walked forward to face her mother and queen before reluctantly asking the higher-ranked of the two women, "You summoned me, my queen?"

"Yes," the queen responded. Mary waited impatiently, but the queen did not continue. Mary shifted her gaze to her mother.

"We have called you here, Mariana, in the presence of these few, to inform you of grave news." Mary's heart skipped a beat before her mother continued. "Princess Mariana, it is my duty to inform you that your uncle, King Darek Dektra, fourth of his name in the Kalian line, is dead and that you, Princess Mariana, are his next legitimate heir."

"Technically, the king stated that you would not be crowned until your twentieth birthday," the queen began.

"However, since there is no legitimate heir of proper age," her mother interrupted.

Mary stared at the three women standing before her. "You mean, I'm queen?"

"Not until you are actually crowned," her aunt began.

"Yes," her mother again interrupted. "At only seventeen, you are too young to officially take the crown; however since I am now the Queen Mother, the answer is yes, Mariana. For all intents and purposes, you are the queen."

"Where is the signet ring?" Kyle asked from behind the princess.

Katerin looked reluctantly at the Kolosian and slowly held out her hand. "Here," she said in a voice that was as sour as any Mary had ever heard. The queen opened her hand to reveal the king's golden ring, embedded with the mark of Kale below a golden crown. Mary took the ring from the queen and handed it directly to Kyle. "Run."

Kyle waited for no further instruction before running from the room and disappearing out the tall, golden doors.

Chapter L

⊷ ⋈✱⋈ ⊶

Kyle raced from the throne room down the long hallway and out the palace doors. Sprinting around several corners of the vast field to find Kev waiting for him with multiple black horses. "Kyle?" he asked in confusion. "Where are the others?"

"Change of plans, Kev," Kyle told his fellow Kolosian.

Kyle held up the golden ring.

Kev's eyes widened. "Is that what I think it is?"

Kyle nodded and mounted one of the tall black horses that Kev had brought from the stables. "The king changed his mind?"

"No."

The tone of Kyle's voice was all that Kev needed to understand what had occurred. "She's the queen."

Kyle nodded. "Take the rest of the horses back to the stable," he instructed his teammate. "Then tell the others what has taken place. I have to get Ryan."

Kyle tapped both sides of his mount and urged the black stallion into a run. He raced towards the gates of the farthest tower. Night had fully settled over the land. Clouds blocked both moon and stars from offering any light in the darkness. Kyle slid lower towards his horse's mane, his black clothes blending with the silky black coat of his steed.

When they reached the tower, Kyle pulled his mount to a stop and shouted towards the guards. "Open in the name of the Crown Princess!" Two men with lit torches stepped forward and moved towards Kyle. When they came close enough to see his face, they asked, "Name?"

"Lord Kyle, silver student of the Temple of Koloso, riding in the name of Crown Princess Mariana." He opened his hand and showed the golden ring that lay within his grasp. "Open in the name of the new queen."

At the sight of the golden ring, both men stepped back and called for the gates to be opened. The tall gates swung open in the darkness. "The captain will meet you on the tower steps."

Kyle slipped the royal signet onto his left hand, so that he would not drop it in his rush to reach the tower. His horse raced forward and followed the light of the torch-lit path towards the steps of the tower where Kyle had previously been imprisoned. Kyle dismounted his horse in front of the tower steps and walked towards a tall man dressed in black from head to toe.

Kyle recognized him as one of his former captors, Lord Vetril. He was an older gentleman, with short gray hair and a touch of gray stubble on his lower chin. His skin appeared more pale than normal against the starless night. He raised a torch high to better see as Kyle approached him. "Lord Vetril," Kyle addressed the older man. He held up his hand, allowing the well-recognized ring to shine in the torch light. "I bring an urgent message from the throne."

Eying the ring, Vetril turned his gaze to Kyle's green eyes. "Must be pretty damn important for the king to have given you that token."

"You have a prisoner being interrogated. His name is Ryan. I have orders from the throne to immediately escort him from the tower."

The prison captain looked at Kyle quizzically. "Why would the king order you to remove him from the tower, when the princess came with orders to lead his inquisition personally?"

"The princess?" Kyle asked. "Princess Ameria is here?"

"In the lower levels of the interrogation rooms. Conducting it herself."

A sense of dread chilled Kyle to the bone. "Take me to them, NOW!"

The man walked several paces ahead of Kyle, leading the way into the darkened depths of the tower dungeon. Left, right, left, deeper and deeper into the bowels of darkness, the prison captain led the silver Kolosian. Kyle heard the sound of screams long before they reached their final destination. They entered the room in the lower dungeon. Kyle took a deep breath, but regretted it as the smell of blood and the general dankness of the lower dungeon more thoroughly settled upon him. Kyle followed Vetril into the room, yet was still unprepared for what he found.

Ryan stood in the center of the room, bared to the waist. His arms were held above his head by thick, silver chains. Blood cascaded down his chest and back in thin, long streams that stained his skin before collecting in small pools at his feet. His left eye was swollen completely shut. Black and purple bruises covered his sides. His lips were caked with blood and it looked as though the bones on the right side of his cheek were not where they should have been.

Two men with matching brown hair stood behind Ryan, both dressed in black from head to toe. Kyle heard the crack of the whip before he saw it, striking in three consecutive lines across Ryan's skin.

"Kyle?"

Kyle turned to find Ameria standing in the far corner of the room watching the scene play out before her. "Ameria," he stammered.

"What are you doing here, Kyle?"

"I could ask you the same question." He addressed the princess.

Ameria shrugged. "Ensuring this is done properly."

"You need to return to the palace, Ameria."

"Why, Kyle?"

Kyle flashed the king's ring.

The features of Ameria's face tightened. "What the hell are you doing with that?"

"You need to return to the palace, princess."

"Not until you tell me what the hell is going on? Why do you have my uncle's ring?"

"It is not my place to say, princess. Except that I was sent here from the throne room and you need to return to the palace."

Ameria turned back to where Ryan hung in chains. "Fine," she said. "But I will be back shortly to finish this. I will get what I want out of him." She returned her gaze to Kyle. "One way or another." Ameria pushed past Kyle and walked towards the door, grabbing a torch on the way. He waited several moments while the princess left and then he turned to face to the men responsible for Ryan's torment.

"I have orders from the Crown for his immediate release," he told the two men, once again showing the ring.

"Why did you not tell the princess?" the inquisitor asked.

"That is none of your concern. Give me the keys to those chains."

Kyle was handed a small, silver key and hurried to remove Ryan's chains, catching him as he fell. There was nowhere that Kyle could touch that was not covered in bruises and cuts.

"Ryan, it's Kyle." He tried to soothe the younger man. "Mary sent me. I am going to get you out of here." Blood continued to seep from Ryan's skin and Kyle began to wonder just how much he had lost.

Kyle moved Ryan towards a cot in the corner of the room. Ryan tried to keep from screaming at the agony of every movement. "I need you to lie down, Ryan. I need to check your injuries." Ryan was limping and as Kyle helped him onto the cot, he realized it was because his leg was broken; the bone protruded from the skin in the lower portion of his right leg and his left was twisted into a most unnatural angle.

Blood seeped from Ryan's body into the black cloth of Kyle's borrowed clothes. There was so much blood. Kyle did not know where to begin. "Kyle?" a voice called. Kyle glanced up to see Brandan entering the room. "Mary sent me after you. She thought you might need help."

Kyle shook his head. "These injuries are massive and he is losing blood."

"What can I do?"

"Help me tie off the worst of them." There was a particularly deep cut on Ryan's left leg that worried Kyle more than several of the others. Blood was racing from the cut at an alarming rate. "Ryan," Kyle said softly. "I'm sorry, Ryan, but I am going to need to cauterize this one." He motioned to the leg gently. "If I don't, you will bleed to death long before I can get to any of the other injuries."

Kyle walked quickly towards a table of chemicals kept on hand in these rooms for just such a purpose. He searched through the various bottles while Brandan found a clean rag and tied it around Ryan's upper arm, where the skin had been split.

Kyle cleaned his silver blade with the clear liquid, and then grabbed an unburnt torch from the wall and pulled out a fresh fire pack from beside it. He broke the stick over the torch, igniting a bright blue flame. He placed the tip of his Kolosian blade above the flame while Brandan continued to bandage several smaller injuries on Ryan's tortured body.

"Should you use a blade?" Brandan asked.

"It's steel from the Temple of Ziazan," Kyle replied. "It will work better than anything else." Brandan nodded.

Kyle searched and finally found a thick strip of cloth. He walked to where Brandan was tending to Ryan. "Ryan," Kyle said, sounding far more confident than he felt, "I need you to bite down on this. I have to stop the bleeding." Ryan looked at Kyle in fear. "Brandan, give him your hand."

Brandan moved his hand into Ryan's and said, "Squeeze it all you want, buddy. Just hang on, okay?"

Ryan took the offered hand and allowed Kyle to position the strip between his teeth. "Okay, Ryan. I'm going to count to three, okay? Deep breath." Kyle removed his now red hot blade from the blue flames and positioned it towards Ryan's injury. "One." He carefully touched the hot blade to Ryan's leg, catching the boy off-guard, searing his leg to stop the bleeding. The smell of burnt flesh filled the air. Kyle had to fight to contain the contents of his stomach as Ryan screamed.

Kyle then proceeded to bandage Ryan's leg. He screamed as the cloth touched his injury, and Kyle found himself wishing that Ryan would pass out from the pain. Instead, he continued to moan in agony.

"It's okay, Ryan," Brandan tried to reassure him. Then he glanced at Kyle. "He doesn't look so good."

"Let's get him out of here."

Brandan and Kyle maneuvered the younger man between them and half-led, half-carried him down the corridors and up the steps of the tower. "Get our horses," Kyle issued the instruction. Moments later the demand was answered and two black stallions were led forward.

Kyle mounted his horse and had Brandan help position Ryan in front of him. "Hold on Ryan," he said firmly. "Follow me, Brandan. Quickly!"

Brandan mounted the other horse in a single stride and the horses raced forward. The gates to the tower swung open. They ran straight from the tower to the palace gates, where Kyle pulled his horse to a stop and motioned for Brandan to do the same. "Hold the horse," Kyle said quickly.

Brandan dismounted his own steed and ran over to Kyle, holding his horse still while Kyle climbed down and entered the palace stables. He walked quickly past the various stalls until he finally found Sherwyn inside one of the larger stalls reserved exclusively for the golden horses of Kale.

"Hey there," Kyle said softly to the golden stallion, who gave a soft neigh of recognition as he saw Kyle approach. "I could use your help tonight, boy. Mary could use your help."

Kyle fetched a large black blanket and saddle and placed it on Sherwyn's back, quickly attaching his golden bridle and reins. He led the horse to the edge of the stables where Brandan was waiting with Ryan.

Kyle helped Ryan from the black horse to the golden stallion and then turned to address Brandan.

"I need you to take this," he held up the golden signet ring, "and put in on your left hand. It will open the gates and any other doors you may encounter on your way. This is Mary's horse, Sherwyn, the fastest of all the golden stallions. I need you to ride from here directly to the Temple of Procelium, and there state that by order of the crown, and the golden student of Kale, this man is to be treated in the temple training rooms. Stop for nothing and ride quickly, he has lost so much blood. I am not certain he will survive."

"But Kyle," Brandan stammered as he climbed onto the horse behind Ryan. "I'm not sure."

"If he does survive," Kyle cautioned. "Then he is not to leave your sight. Do you hear me? He is not to leave your sight."

"Kyle," Brandan tried again. "I don't think I can..."

"I need you to do this, Brandan. Ride quickly, stop for nothing. Use the ring to order the gates open. Say by order of the crown if you can. Otherwise, say it is on direct orders of Queen Mariana Dektra, first of her name of the Kalian bloodline. Now go!"

Kyle lightly slapped the horse. Sherwyn raced toward the gates. "May the temple Gods protect you!" Kyle called after them as they vanished around the corner.

By the Gods of all that is, Kyle prayed silently, *do not let that boy be guilty*.

Chapter LI

———✦·✧·✦———

One glance at the deserted throne room was all it took for Princess Ameria to realize that something was wrong. The room was lit by a large, blue fire. Mary stood alone at the far end opposite the throne, gazing out through the large glass wall into the starless night beyond. Dressed in a long sleeved black shirt and matching black pants, she all but blended in with the dark shadows of the room that were occasionally interrupted by the swirl of blue firelight.

"What happened?" Ameria asked.

"Hello, Ameria." Mary turned from the window to face her sister. "Where have you been, sister?"

"At the tower, overseeing the interrogation of the prisoner."

"You were what?"

"Someone had to make sure they were doing it right," Ameria replied, meeting her sister's heated tone with her own icy words.

"Did you kill him?" Mary demanded.

"Not yet. But I guarantee that death will be welcomed after what he has been through."

"Damn you, Ameria!" Mary shook her head, trying not to picture all the things that Ryan might have endured at the mercy of her twin. "He is being released," Mary finally said. "Right now."

"What do you mean, he is being released?"

Then it dawned on her. "So that is what Kyle was doing? Sneaking him out, in direct violation to the king's orders? That is beyond bold, Mary. Even for you. Where is our uncle? We will see what he has to say about this?"

"I think what you mean to say, Ameria, is that it is a bold move, Your Majesty."

Ameria froze, staring at her sister with blank eyes. "What?"

Mary paused, instantly regretting her words and then turned her deep green eyes upon her sister's blue. "Our beloved uncle, the king, died tonight, sister. I am sorry to be the one to tell you."

"Our uncle is dead?"

"Yes, Ameria. Our uncle is dead."

"That means you..."

"Stand as the next queen of the Kalian bloodline." She paused, allowing her words to settle over the room, then continued. "Master Louis is finishing last prayers with the queen and temple masters as we speak. Messengers are being sent throughout the land. His body shall be burnt the day after tomorrow with the dawn, and then those from the temple shall travel from the palace to the Temple of Ziazan to attend the funeral of Master Leo and Prince Eadmund, whose bodies will be sent to the Rainbow Halls the following day."

"Who will rule the land during the mourning period?" Ameria asked.

"Our mother has assumed the position of Queen Regent, much to our aunt's dismay."

"So let me understand this, Mariana. Our uncle has been dead for less than an hour, and your first act as queen, apparently, was to contradict the last orders, our uncle, the king, will ever issue to this great kingdom?"

"I am not saying that Ryan may not yet deserve the punishment you wished upon him, Ameria. I am simply saying that he has not been proven guilty and until such a time when he is, he cannot be punished as you wish him to be."

"He allowed our father's killer to escape!" Ameria's voice came across with a fire that threatened to scorch the very air between them.

"No, Ameria. I did that. I chose Kyle's life over stopping him. I chose to try and save Leo instead of giving chase."

"And you were a fool!" Ameria raged. "A traitor to the crown you now covet!"

"I made a choice, the only one I could live with. What you are doing to Ryan, you are doing without proof! His only proven guilt is loving his brothers!"

"What the hell was he doing in the Temple of Kale in the first place?" Ameria suddenly demanded. "What was he doing there?"

"I knew!" Mary confessed. "All right? I knew that he was the brother of the man who killed Lord Edward. I saw his brother riding with Edward's blade and I took Ryan to the temple with me." Mary shook her head. "Don't you see? He is our only link to them."

"And you lead him straight into the palace walls! You are not worthy of the crown, Mariana! You might as well have killed our father yourself!"

Mariana's golden blade was in her hand before she realized she had reached for it. "I did no such thing," she replied. "I kept him near me so I could find my way back to his brother."

"And instead," Ameria's voice was fire to Mary's ice, "you killed our father! You killed Leo!"

"I did not!" Mary responded as Ameria drew her own silver blade.

"You are weak, Mariana. You have always been weak. It's the reason father was hesitant to see you on the throne."

"Father did not want me to take the throne, because he couldn't stomach the idea of seeing you at the head of the Defendant Team!" Mary snapped, then raised her sword just in time to stop the first swing of Ameria's deadly silver blade.

The clang of metal filled the room as the ancient blades met. The flickering light of the blue flames which lit the room danced upon the edge of their swords, leaping from the golden metal to the silver, and then back to gold. The sisters stood still with their blades crossed, facing off on the edge of a moonless night.

Both sisters took a single step back and stared across the dancing flames. "I see they healed your hands."

"Yes," Ameria replied. "It seems even the Gods knew that you did not stand fit to rule."

Ameria once again swung her silver sword toward Mary's slender throat. Mary raised her golden blade and blocked Ameria's movement. Ameria swung to Mary's left. Mary's parry sent them both spiraling to their right. Mary then switched to the offense, moving her sword toward Ameria's right side. Ameria moved her own sword to block Mary's, and Mary suddenly jerked her blade up toward the side of her sister's face. Ameria jumped back, avoiding the golden metal by a mere fraction.

Ameria lunged at her sister again, putting all her strength behind the movement. Mary struggled under the force as their blades met, feeling herself pushed several steps back by the sheer power of Ameria's attack. Mary pushed back against her twin, regaining her footing without ever uncrossing their blades. The swords of silver and gold danced up, danced down, and up again, shattering the silence of the room with the deafening ring of their song.

Mary watched her sister closely. Ameria's left shoulder moved back slightly, and Mary sidestepped Ameria's next movement before she even got close. Ameria's frame turned right and Mary twisted, leaning back. Again, Ameria's sword touched only air. Mary moved her own sword forward. The blade slid across Ameria's right arm, slicing through the golden fabric and producing a shallow cut to the skin. Ameria hissed and twisted her blade, slicing through Mary's black shirt as she attempted to pull her sword away from her sister's. Blood rose to the surface of the twins' matching wounds.

"What, by the Gods, is going on?" a masculine voice interrupted their duel. Mary registered the sound of Kyle's voice, but dared not turn her gaze away from her sister's thin frame.

"Mary? Ameria! What, in the name of all the Gods, is happening?" Kyle demanded again.

Ameria's frame shifted to the left, and Mary brought her sword up to a defensive level, blocking Ameria's next assault. The two sisters circled each other. Mary said, "Get out of here, Kyle!"

"Yes, you heard your queen," Ameria said mockingly. "Better obey her, Kyle. It will be the last command she ever gives."

Ameria brought her blade down toward Mary's shoulder. Mary stepped away from the intended blow and spun around, slamming her elbow into Ameria's upper body. Ameria lost her balance and fell to the ground.

Mary brought her blade down towards Ameria, but she rolled across the floor. Mary's blade struck the silver marble floor and the sound echoed through the room. Mary raised her sword and turned to once again face her twin, who had quickly regained her footing.

Mary's breathing was becoming more labored. The unfamiliar black cloth clung as though molded to her skin. The black cotton shirt was more comfortable than her normal satin robes, but was still soaked with an immense amount of sweat. Her left arm was bleeding from where Ameria's blade had bit into her skin.

"Mary, Ameria, stop it!" Kyle pleaded again. "For Gods' sake, you are sisters!"

"I claim no sister who allowed my father's murderer to go free," Ameria hissed across the room.

"And I claim no sister who would torture a man without proof of his wrongdoing!"

The twins flew towards each other in a moment of blind fury, their blades moving faster than either realized was possible. Pure instinct took over as the swords flew up and down in a series of strokes and parries. Mary stopped her sister's blade only inches from the left side of her face, then felt her own blade bite into the satin fabric covering Ameria's right arm.

"Stop this!" Kyle's voice rang out as though from a distance.

The two sisters turned as one, their swords an extension of their souls. The force behind their blades sent them spinning in the other's direction and they used their momentum to bring their blades towards each other again. They felt their blades pass through the undeniable feel of flesh. A scream split the air.

Both sisters stepped back in a daze. Kyle lay crumpled on the ground at their feet. "Kyle," Mary said in disbelief.

The blades had done their work with deadly precision. Kyle's face was covered with blood, the flesh of his left cheek was split open, driving straight through the thin, angular bones and into his left eye. The second had sliced into the right side of his neck. Blood cascaded onto the silver floor beneath their feet, spreading around the two sisters like a dark pool.

Ameria's scream rang throughout the room and down the hallway beyond.

"Kyle!" Mary rushed forward and fell to her knees beside his fallen form. Blood spewed from a severed artery. Ameria knelt beside her sister. She ripped her outer robe from her body, pressing the material against the gash in Kyle's neck. The golden cloth changed to a deep red before her eyes.

"Why?" was all Mary could manage to say. A river of blood began to flow across the silver floor, saturating the thin material of Mary's black slacks and painting the pale skin beneath. Her stomach churned at the sight of his ruined face, the vision of his left eye forever destroyed by the stroke of her blade. Ameria ripped more of her golden robes and pressed the fresh cloth on top of the bloody rag. It took only moments for the new strip to match the color of the blood soaked cloth beneath it.

Mary's heart throbbed against her temple with such force the room began to spin. "Kyle," she whispered, the weight of their actions crushing against her until it was difficult to breathe. She realized for a moment that she was on the verge of blacking out, and forced herself to draw a breath, pressing a deep gulp of air past her lips to drop painfully into her lungs.

Ameria was speaking, but Mary seemed unable to understand her words. Kyle's body began to tremble as the stream of blood surrounding them became as vast as an ocean, spreading easily across the slick, marble floor.

"Don't die," she whispered, hot tears streaking across her face. "Please Kyle, don't..."

"Stay with me!" her sister's voice cascaded over her own. "Please, Kyle."

His body began to tremble more violently in Ameria's arms. He gasped for air, but seemed to lack the strength to draw a full breath.

"Help us!" Mary screamed towards the tall doors of the throne room. Mary took Kyle's hand in her own. The grip was weak, then slack. "Kyle?" Mary asked gazing down through the tears that would not cease.

A harsh sob escaped Ameria's lips.

"Kyle?" Mary whispered again. His breathing had stopped.

"No!" Ameria cried. She leaned down and pressed her lips against Kyle's, blowing air into his lungs. When she rose, she looked at her sister. "Help me," she pleaded. Then dipped her head back down and once again attempted to breathe life back into Kyle's still form. Mary remained still, clutching his lifeless hand in her own.

Master Jiro's voice flowed entered the room. "By the Gods, what happened?" Neither sister answered, Ameria continued her efforts while Mary sat silently, her body trembling.

"Kyle?" Jiro's voice was a mix of sorrow and disbelief.

"Breathe!" Ameria demanded. "Please, for the love of all the Gods, breathe!"

"Don't go," Mary's own voice whispered across the silent room. "Please, Kyle." Mary leaned her face down against his chest, her hair dipping into the pool of blood beneath her. "Don't go." A harsh sob escaped her lips as she buried her face against his chest.

"By all the Gods of Kale," Ameria said again. "Breathe!"

"He's gone," Jiro's deep voice came from behind them. "I am so sorry, Your Highnesses. He is gone."

"No," Mary whispered, raising her head and looking up at her sister. "Not the Gods."

She stood. Blood dripped from her long black hair, sliding along the sides of her face and neck, painting her skin scarlet. She drew her golden sword from the wet floor and walked along the slick marble towards the glass wall of the throne room. Mariana raised her blood-soaked blade and closed her eyes. The blade shattered the glass wall before her into a thousand tiny shards. She stepped through the glass, Ameria's sobs echoing behind her.

She walked quickly towards the grassy field beyond, and eventually broke into a run. The monuments that honored the Gods had once stood proudly before the palace, but had been slowly moved farther to the east side of the grounds, as they did not please the king's temple-less queen.

When Mary reached the tall statues, she knelt before them on one knee and swept her blood-soaked hair to the left side of her face, exposing the back of her neck to the cold night air. A harsh wind blew as she lowered both arms straight on either side of her body, allowing only the tips of her fingers to touch the ground. She did not pray to the Gods. "Proteus," the unfamiliar name fell from her ruby lips as though she had known it all her life. "Proteus!"

The howl of the wind grew louder and a flash of lightning split the dark sky. She closed her eyes tightly, lowering her face to fully expose the back of her slender throat. The wind blew harder. Then a warm, wet breath touched the back of Mary's neck. "Princess of Kale," the wraith's voice crawled across her pale skin. "Princess of Koloso."

Mary raised her gaze. The wraith towered over her kneeling form. Its eyes appeared silver, as though reflecting the light of the moon that had long ago vanished behind the dark clouds. His sharp, jagged teeth were inches from her exposed, blood covered flesh.

"You are afraid, princess." His eyes remained motionless in the darkness.

"Help me." Her voice came out as a mere whisper.

"How?" he hissed.

"Save him."

"Your sister's partner? The man who killed the one you loved?"

Mary's eyes blinked against the harsh wind and for a moment, she was staring into Jace's light brown eyes. His laughter echoed in the wind. She forced her eyes open, breathing hard at the sudden image.

"Fear to the fearless. Hope to the hopeless. Mercy to those who hate you. Death." He paused on the word. "Death, princess. Death to those who love you, Princess of Kale, Princess of Koloso, Heir to Both."

She stared into the wraith's silver eyes and said, "Save him."

"Even if it would cost the lives of others? Some whom you love just as deeply?"

A hundred faces flashed before Mary's eyes as she struggled to process his words. She blinked back tears and again saw Kyle's body lying lifeless in her sister's arms. "Save him."

The wraith tilted his head slightly and then let out a harsh laugh. "So be it, princess. But Remember: Death comes for us all, in the end."

The wraith gave a low laugh and vanished before Mariana's eyes. She sat on the ground praying silently before rising to walk back toward the palace. She walked slowly, stumbling in the darkness, her arm still bleeding from where Ameria's blade had sliced it open.

She did not walk towards the doors, but instead walked back over the broken shards of glass to re-enter the throne room. Ameria was still kneeling on the floor in a pool of blood, but Kyle had risen and stood staring into the blue flames of the fire, his back to Mary as she approached him. She did not speak, but instead walked forward, her steps echoing across the silver floor.

Kyle remained facing the fire as she approached. The princess stopped just shy of reaching him before dropping down to one knee. She knelt in a pool of his blood with only the crackling of the fire breaking the silence of the room. "Mariana," Kyle finally spoke, his voice tight with restricted emotion. He turned slowly to face her. A long, jagged scar ran along the left side of his once perfect face, running both above and below his untouched jade green eye. "What have you done, Mariana?"

Mary stared at his face and her voice grew tight in her throat. "Kyle, I..."

"She called the Gods," Ameria answered, standing from her keeling position in a single movement, her golden robes dyed red with blood. As she stood, Mary saw the still form of a man dressed in silver robes lying lifeless on the floor behind her. "And the Gods answered."

Mary did not need to move forward to know - it was Marcus.

Chapter LII

―――◆◄━◆✱◆━►◆―――

Two days later, the twin sisters stood side by side at the funeral of King Darek Dektra, fourth of his name in the Kalian bloodline. His body was burnt on the Pyre of Kings, a large, black marble structure which stood on the far side of the palace grounds, out of sight of the palace. Lords and ladies had come from the far reaches of the kingdom to attend the funeral. Princess Annabelle had attempted to speak to Mary of her future reign, but Mary refused to listen, instead silently donning a full-length gown of black satin. Her sister wore a matching gown and the two walked in a mutual silence which they had maintained since Marcus' death.

Master Jiro had informed Mary quietly that Marcus had entered the room at Ameria's screams, assisting Jiro in prying her away from Kyle's body. "Then," Jiro had continued, "Marcus gasped, and his body went limp. He..." Jiro's eyes had lost contact with Mary's. "He never drew another breath."

Mary had locked herself into seclusion until the morning of the funeral. The crowd seemed vast as the king's body was carried out of the palace by several of those he had known best. Dressed in robes of crimson and a golden crown, the king held no sword as he was raised onto the funeral pyre. Since he had not been trained in the temples, he was not permitted to carry one into the realm beyond.

With a few sparse words of his reign, the king's body was lit aflame. Defendants and royals alike knelt to one knee as the flames spread over the king's crimson robes. A profound silence settled over the crowd until long after the flames had vanished. Then, Lord Louis dismissed the crowd with a quiet tone. As the crowd began to disperse, defendants rose and gathered in a large circle near the left side of the grassy fields. Mary moved to join them when her sister broke their previously mutual silence. "I cannot allow you to become queen."

"You want to have this argument now?"

"I know you are grieving and I know what you are going through. But yes, Mariana, now."

"You have no idea what I am going through!" She struggled to control the volume of her voice.

"Fine, I don't. But sister, if you cannot handle this conversation, then you cannot handle the throne." Mary looked at her twin with a sense of utter disbelief. Ameria continued, "I cannot allow you to become queen."

"And I cannot hand you the throne, Ameria."

"I know."

"Then what do you propose?" She turned, giving her sister the full weight of her gaze for the first time since their blades had collided into Kyle's body.

"You swore the oath of Blood and Arms."

"Yes."

"That means, you swore that the kingdom would be ruled by royal blood and the champion of the thirteenth tournament." She moved closer to her sister, her voice becoming more intense with every word. "If I am that champion, then you will give me the crown."

Mary stared at her sister, allowing the threat of Ameria's words to wash over her. "The thirteenth tournament."

"For the crown," Ameria said.

"For the crown."

"And if I am crowned queen, Mariana, then Ryan's life belongs to me."

"You can't..."

"That is the deal. That or we can fight this out right now, and the one who lives will rule the kingdom. The crown...and Ryan's life."

The two stared at each other as though no one else existed. Then Mariana nodded. "For the crown," she echoed her sister, "and Ryan's life."

They walked in silence towards the defendants and, soon after, mounted their respective horses. Sherwyn and Kev had returned the previous night to attend the funeral. Ryan had survived the ride and his injuries had been healed by the magic of the temples. Defendants had escorted Ryan back to the Temple of Kale.

The champions rode their respective mounts to the Temple of Proelium, where defendants transported them to the Temple of Koloso. Once there, the princesses changed back into their temple robes, before beginning the long trek up the icy slopes of the Rainbow Mountains which surrounded the Temple of Ziazan. The flags of the temples had been placed along the dirt pathway leading to the creamy white Temple of the Gods. With an anguished heart, Mary dismounted her golden stallion. She handed Sherwyn's reins to one of the temple students, who was dressed in swirling rainbow robes that displayed the order of the temple colors in repeating patterns.

Mary did not enter the marble temple, but instead walked slowly towards the tall, open-aired structure which stood to its side. Two sets of forty steps led up to a white marble floor which was scorched black in scattered places from the numerous fires it had seen over the centuries of welcoming fallen defendants. Mary stood at the edge of the marble steps for what seemed like decades, unable to bring herself to ascend them. Suddenly, Coco appeared beside her, looking solemn in his golden robes. He took several steps forward and then turned back to Mary, waiting for her to follow.

The princess took a deep, trembling breath, then forced herself to follow the white and brown puppy up the steps. When she reached the top, she paused. Master Jiro stood before the body of the fallen Kalian leader. Upon seeing the princess, he walked slowly across the marble and offered Mary his arm. She took it reluctantly. Jiro lead her forward towards the body of the fallen Kalian master.

Lord and Master Leonardo Desato lay peaceful in death, his eyes closed and the constant lines of worry finally gone from his handsome face. He was dressed in robes of gold, signifying his rise from the Temple of Kale and a matching golden cloth lay across the center of his chest, representing both his former rank as the Golden Defendant and as the Temple Master of Kale. His hands were clasped around his silver blade, the hilt of which was inlaid with gold and the mark of Kale etched into both sides of the hilt.

On the opposite side of him lay Prince Eadmund Dektra, also draped in robes of gold. Across his chest lay a silver cloth, marking his rank as the silver student of Kale and the once Silver Defendant. His hands were also clasped around his Kalian blade. His hilt was silver with the mark of Kale etched in gold upon the right side of the blade. On the other side was a small crown, signifying his status as a prince of the realm. Mary knelt between her two fathers.

"I am so sorry," she whispered. "So, very sorry."

"Mariana," a quiet, masculine voice called. She turned expecting to see Master Jiro, but instead found herself staring into Kyle's scarred face. "Mariana, it is time."

She rose from her kneeling position and approached Master Leo's silent form. She reached down and placed her hand over Leo's, her fingers finding the hilt of his sword. "I ask the Gods to hear my vow," she whispered to the fallen Kalian master. "I shall kill the man who did this." She drew a deep breath and slowly let go. "Goodbye, Father."

Then she turned to face the final pyre. Wrapped in robes of gold with a cloth of silver, Marcus lay as though a younger version of Mary's father. Her own silver blade lay upon his chest, his hands clutched around the golden hilt. "He always complained that I had the better sword," she had informed Master Jiro. "Let him take it with him to the realm beyond." She motioned to the new golden blade at her side. "It was meant to go with him."

Kyle remained silent as she stared at Marcus' body, then he took her arm and slowly led her forward. She silently forced herself to kneel before him, Kyle following her to his knees, shadowing her motions. "You should have let them take me." Kyle spoke quietly.

"No," Mary said with dry eyes, turning momentarily to stare at the man kneeling beside her. "It was my choice, Kyle." Mary stood and walked closer to her fallen partner. "I am so sorry, Marcus," she whispered before leaning down and laying a gentle kiss on his cold brow. "I will see you again."

When she finally rose from Marcus' side, Kyle was already waiting for her at the top of the pyre. She walked towards him and forced herself to meet his eyes. The two champions walked down the scorched marble steps side by side, crossing paths with Lord Louis and Lady Rebecca. When they reached the bottom of the steps, Mary turned back towards the pyre. Large rainbow cloaks were saturated in various oils and laid gently atop the bodies of the fallen men. Two torches were lit, one held by the Golden Defendant, Lady Rebecca, and the other by the highest ranking of the temple masters, Lord Jiro of Koloso.

The high priest, Lord Louis of the Kalian temples, turned to address the crowd of mourners. "We are gathered here to bid farewell to fallen heroes." His voice carried across the silent crowd.

"Prince Eadmund Dektra, former silver student from the Temple of Kale, former Silver Defendant, and Crown Prince of the realm, gave his life in service, protecting the royal line. He is survived by his wife, Princess Annabelle Berhea Dektra, the former golden student of Koloso and a Silver Defendant, and his two daughters, Princess Ameria, golden student of Koloso, and Crown Princess Mariana, golden student of Kale."

Several moments of silence followed before Lord Louis continued. "We also have gathered to honor Lord Marcus, silver student of Kale, heir to the Kingdom of Flos, son of a Red Defendant and nephew to Master Leonardo Desato. In honor of his service to the realm, we bestow upon Lord Marcus the title of defendant, so that he may join others who came before him in the realm of Kalian heroes."

Louis drew a deep breath as though even he were struggling to continue. "We have also gathered to honor Master Leonardo Deasto. Master Leonardo rose from the Temple of Kale, where he served as a golden student, and later as temple master. He served the realm faithfully as the Golden Defendant and also stood as the only defendant in Kalian history to ever win all thirteen Kalian tournaments. He gave his life in protection of the realm and his legacy and teachings will reside in the hearts of all Kalians till the end of time."

"We gather today to honor these heroes. May their names live forever in the hearts of all defendants!" His voice steadily increased in volume. "Honor the fallen Champions and Defendants of Kale!"

As one, defendants, students, temple masters, and all those of the Kalian bloodline drew their swords, and held them high towards the violet sky. "Live to serve, die for honor!" they shouted in a profound unison. "Glory to the Gods! Glory to the Lords of Kale! Glory to Prince Eadmund, the fallen Defendant of Kale! Glory to Lord Marcus, the fallen Defendant of Kale! Glory to Master Leonardo, the fallen Golden Defendant!"

Master Jiro and Lady Rebecca lit the funeral pyre. The flames burst forth with a golden light far different from the blue flames found within the temples. The wind rose with a sudden howl as smoke began to fill the air. Yet all eyes remained on the burning pyre, each man and woman standing completely still, holding their swords towards the Gods.

As Mary's eyes began to burn from the strain of staring into the golden flames, she caught sight of her sister on the far side of the pyre. Dressed in silks of gold, her long blond hair blowing in the wind, Ameria blended with the swirling flames. Only her eyes separated her from the dance, her deep blue eyes, like drops of water among the flames. The two sisters stared at each other across the sea of fire, holding their ancient blades towards the temple Gods.

The Story Continues In...

RISE OF THE TEMPLE GODS:
HEIR TO KOLOSO

NOW AVAILABLE

Acknowledgements & Thanks

I WOULD LIKE TO OFFER a special thanks to a few people who both assisted and supported me throughout the creation of this novel.

First, I would like to thank Scott of the Vancouver Taekwondo Academy for his assistance in my research; both through an extensive interview and allowing me to observe several of his classes. Second, to the instructors and students at East West Martial Arts of West Vancouver for also allowing me to observe their courses and for making themselves available to answer questions. Third, to Andrew J., a martial artist and fellow author who offered a critique of several fight scenes prior to publication.

I would also like to thank my long time writing mentors, Lili, Kate and Mike for instilling within me a passion for writing and reminding me of that passion when it was needed most. Also, to my writing partner, Jonny, for all the hours spent discussing the finer point of writing in that little coffee shop.

Last, I would like to thank my family for their never-ending love and support.

Finally, to my cover designer, Skyla—who takes the jumbled pictures in my head and consistently turns them into the beautiful covers you see upon the books. Your work is nothing short of marvelous.

About the Author

K.L. BONE HAS A MASTERS degree in Modern Literary Cultures. She is American, but is currently living in Ireland working towards her PhD with a focus in vampire and children's literature. She wrote her first short story at the age of 15 and grew up with an equally great love of both classical literature and speculative fiction. She has spent the last few years as a bit of a world traveler, living in California, London, and now Dublin in pursuit of her vampire studies.

Follow her at: www.klbone.com
On Twitter: @kl_bone
Or on Facebook: https://www.facebook.com/k.l.bonebooks

Works by K.L. Bone

Rise of the Temple Gods Series
Rise of the Temple Gods: Heir to Kale
Rise of the Temple Gods: Heir to Koloso
Rise of the Temple Gods: Heir to the Defendants (coming 2015)

The Black Rose Series
Black Rose
Blood Rose (coming 2015)

Other Novels
The Indoctrination

Made in the USA
Middletown, DE
03 July 2015